Scoundrel *in the* Regency Ballroom

Marguerite Kaye

Mills & Boon, an imprint of Harlequin (UK) Limited,
Eton House, 18-24 Paradise Road, Richmond, Surrey TW9 1SR

SCOUNDREL IN THE REGENCY BALLROOM

ISBN: 978 0 263 90680 6

052-0214

Harlequin (UK) policy is to use papers that are natural, renewable and recyclable products and made from wood grown in sustainable forests. The logging and manufacturing processes conform to the legal environmental regulations of the country of origin.

Printed and bound
by CPI Group (UK) Ltd, Croydon, CR0 4YY

Born and educated in Scotland, **Marguerite Kaye** originally qualified as a lawyer but chose not to practise—a decision which was a relief both to her and the Scottish legal establishment. While carving out a successful career in IT, she occupied herself with her twin passions of studying history and reading, picking up a first-class honours and a Master's degree along the way.

The course of her life changed dramatically when she found her soul mate. After an idyllic year out, spent travelling round the Mediterranean, Marguerite decided to take the plunge and pursue her life-long ambition to write for a living—a dream she had cherished ever since winning a national poetry competition at the age of nine.

Just like one of her fictional heroines, Marguerite's fantasy has become reality. She has published history and travel articles, as well as short stories, but romances are her passion. Marguerite describes Georgette Heyer and Doris Day as her biggest early influences, and her partner as her inspiration.

When she is not writing, Marguerite enjoys cooking and hill walking. A confirmed Europhile, who spends much of the year in sunny climes, she returns regularly to the beautiful Highland scenery of her native Argyll, the place she still calls home.

Marguerite would love to hear from you. You can contact her on: Marguerite_Kaye@hotmail.co.uk

In The Regency Ballroom Collection

Scandal in the Regency Ballroom – Louise Allen
April 2013

Innocent in the Regency Ballroom – Christine Merrill
May 2013

Wicked in the Regency Ballroom – Margaret McPhee
June 2013

Cinderella in the Regency Ballroom – Deb Marlowe
July 2013

Rogue in the Regency Ballroom – Helen Dickson
August 2013

Debutante in the Regency Ballroom – Anne Herries
September 2013

Rumours in the Regency Ballroom – Diane Gaston
October 2013

Rake in the Regency Ballroom – Bronwyn Scott
November 2013

Mistress in the Regency Ballroom – Juliet Landon
December 2013

Courtship in the Regency Ballroom – Annie Burrows
January 2014

Scoundrel in the Regency Ballroom – Marguerite Kaye
February 2014

Secrets in the Regency Ballroom – Joanna Fulford
March 2014

The Rake and the Heiress

For A, who makes all things,
especially me, possible. Just love.

Prologue

Paris—August 1815

The doctor closed the bedchamber door gently behind him and turned to the young woman waiting anxiously in the hallway. He noted with sadness that she was showing clear signs of strain following the trauma of the past few days. Her delicate beauty, while still intact, seemed fragile, as if frayed. The sparkle had gone from her cornflower-blue eyes, her creamy complexion was dull and ghostly pale, her blonde hair unkempt, confined carelessly under a bandeau. Despite his stern countenance and insistence on the timely settlement of bills, the doctor was a compassionate man at heart. He sighed deeply. At times like this he cursed his vocation.

The grave expression and resigned shake of his head told Serena all she needed to know. She fought to quell the tidal wave of despair that threatened to overwhelm her.

'You must keep him comfortable, Mademoiselle Cachet, that is all you can do for him now. I will return in the morning, but…' The doctor's shrug was all too eloquent. It was obvious he didn't expect Papa to survive the night.

Valiantly suppressing a sob—for what purpose would tears serve now?—Serena wearily forced herself upright from the support of the door frame she'd been leaning against. She tried to absorb the doctor's instructions, but his clear, calm words barely penetrated the fog enveloping her shocked mind. His voice seemed faint, as if it were coming from a far distant shore. Clean dressings and sleeping draughts would ease Papa's suffering, but not even a magic potion could save him now.

The doctor departed with an admonition to send for him if necessary, giving Serena a final comforting pat on the shoulder. As he opened the strong oak door at the foot of the stairwell which separated their living quarters from the gaming rooms, a sharp burst of drunken laughter pierced the air. With a steady supply of men returning from Waterloo the tables were always busy, but for once Serena cared naught. What use was a full purse without Papa to share its bounty?

Nothing mattered now save making the most of these last precious hours. Papa must see his daughter calm and loving, not tearful and dishevelled. Resolutely tucking a stray golden curl back under her bandeau, carefully straightening the neckline of her dress and taking a deep calming breath, Serena re-entered her father's bedchamber with a heavy heart.

Velvet hangings pulled shut over the leaded windows contained the stifling heat of the room and muffled all noise from the busy street below. A huge mirror above the marble fireplace reflected the rich rugs, the polished wood, the bright gilt and glowing silver fittings of the opulent furnishings. Reflected too, the snowy white pile of linen torn for bandages and the collection of vials and bottles atop the bedside table on which a decanter usually sat. On the floor a mound of bloodied dressings paid testament to Serena's hours of tender nursing. The scent of lavender water and laudanum lay heavy in the air.

Philip Cachet lay on a large tester bed, dwarfed by the mountains of pillows that had been arranged around his tall frame in an attempt to ease the flow of blood from his wound. *Why had he not simply handed over his purse?* For the hundredth time since Papa had staggered through the door clutching his chest, Serena cursed the cowardly footpad who had taken his valuables and now, it seemed, his life too. She was shocked to see how diminished her father looked, his shaven head bare and vulnerable without the wig he still insisted on wearing, despite it being out of fashion. His breath came in irregular, rasping sighs, and in the short time it had taken to confer with the doctor, his skin had assumed a waxen pallor.

Papa had been warned not to move lest the bleeding start again, but his eyes, the same vivid blue as her own, brightened when he saw her. As she closed the door softly, he raised his hand just a little from the silk counterpane in a frail gesture of welcome.

'*Ma belle*, at last. I have something of great import to tell you, and it can wait no longer—I fear my time is almost come.' Ignoring her protestations, he gestured for Serena to come closer. 'No point in denial, *chérie*, I've lost too much blood. I need you to pay attention—you *must* listen.' A cough racked him. A small droplet of blood appeared at the side of his mouth. He wiped it away impatiently with a trembling hand.

Even now, Serena could see faint traces of the handsome man her father had been in his prime. The strong, regular features, the familiar charming smile that had extricated him from many a tricky situation. He was a gambler, and good enough to win—for the most part. For nigh on thirty years, Philip had supported first himself, then she and *Maman* too, by his sharp wits and his skill with the cards. Skills he had practised in countless gaming houses, in countless towns and cities across Europe.

Pulling a chair closer to the bedside, Serena sat down with a rustle of her silk skirts, gently stroking the delicate white hand lying unresponsive on the counterpane. His life was draining away in front of her eyes, yet she had to be strong. 'I'm here, Papa,' she whispered.

'*Mignonne*, I never meant to leave you like this. Your life was to have been very different. I'm sorry.'

'Don't be sorry, I wouldn't have had it any other way. We've had our share of fun, haven't we?' She smiled lovingly at him, the spark of humour in her eyes drawing the shadow of a response from his.

'Yes, but as you know only too well, at the end of any game there is always a reckoning.'

Serena muffled a sob with her handkerchief.

His fingers trembled in her hand. '*Ma fille*, you must be brave. Listen now, and don't interrupt, it's vitally important. Please don't judge me too harshly, for what I am about to tell you will shock you. It will also change your life for ever. *Écoute, petite*, I must go back to the beginning, thirty years ago…'

Chapter One

England—April 1816

Serena paused to catch her breath and admire the beautiful façade of the house. It was much grander and more imposing than she had expected, a classic Elizabethan country manor, the main body of the mellow brick building flanked by two elegant wings, which lent it a graceful symmetry. She had entered the grounds by a side gate, having decided, since it was such a pleasant morning, to walk the short distance from the village rather than take a carriage. It was very clement for the time of year and the spring bulbs were at their best. The grass by the side of the well-kept path was strewn with narcissi, banks of primroses and artfully placed clumps of iris just coming into bloom. The perfume of camellias and forsythia mingled with the fresh, damp smell of new-mown grass.

You must go to England, to Knightswood Hall, the home of my dear friend Nick Lytton. Papa's dying words to her—and amazingly, here she was, in the country of his birth, standing in the very grounds of his friend's home. It had been a wretched few months since her father's death, making ready for the move from Paris, but at least the sheer volume of things that needed to be done were a welcome distraction from the aching pain of his loss. Closing down the gaming salons had realised a surprising amount of money, more than enough to cover the expenses of the next few months and to establish her in comfort if things did not turn out as her father had hoped.

Serena had never been one to plan for the future, having been too much in the habit, of necessity, of living in the present. Of course what she wanted was her own home and her own family, but she wished for this in the vague way of one who had had, until now, little control over her own destiny. She had not met—or been allowed to meet—any man who came close to inhabiting her dreams. And as to a home! She had spent most of the last two years in Paris, and that was the longest she had ever been in one place.

Papa's revelations offered her wealth and position which, he vowed, would change her life completely. Change, she was ready to embrace, but the nature of it—in truth, she was not convinced that Papa's vision for her future was her own. *One step at a time*, she reminded herself. No point in jumping too far ahead. Today was just the beginning.

As she turned her mind to the interview that lay ahead, a cloud of butterflies seemed to take up residence in her stomach. The imposing bulk of the house only served to increase her apprehension. Nick Lytton was obviously a man of some standing. She countered the urge to turn tail and return to her lodgings by making a final check on her appearance. Her dress of lavender calico was cut in the French fashion, high in the waist and belling out towards her feet with rows of tiny ruffles edging the hem and the long sleeves. The shape became her tall figure, as did the three-quarter pelisse with its high collar. Her gold hair was dressed simply on top of her head, also in the latest French style, with small tendrils allowed to frame her cheekbones, the rest confined under a straw bonnet tied with a large lavender ribbon beneath her chin. The kid half-boots she wore were perhaps more suited to a stroll round a city square than the rough terrain of the countryside, but they had survived the walk without becoming too muddied, as had the deep frill on her fine lawn petticoat. She would do.

The path she had taken ran round the side of the house and disappeared towards some outbuildings, presumably the stables. She was about to follow the fork to the right leading to the imposing main entrance of the Hall, when a roar of voices diverted her. Another roar and a gust of laughter followed, too intriguing to be ignored. Lifting her petticoat clear of a small puddle, Serena moved cautiously towards the source of the commotion.

As she had surmised, the path took her to the stable yard, a square of earth surrounded on three sides by horse boxes and outhouses. The arched entrance way in which she stood formed the fourth side. In front of her were not horses, however, but an animated circle of people, men and boys mostly, with a scattering of women standing apart in the shelter of a doorway which presumably led to the kitchens.

In the centre of the circle two men, stripped to the waist, were boxing. The crowd roared encouragement and advice, many people excitedly betting on the outcome. The scent of horse and hay was overlaid by a fresher, richer aroma, of wet wool, sweat and mud. Over the noise of the crowd, Serena could hear the panting breath of the two fighters, the dull thwack of fist on flesh, the soft thud of stocking-clad feet on the hard earth. Though she had witnessed the occasional drink-fuelled scuffle before, she had never seen a mill. Drawn in by a mixture of curiosity and an unfamiliar *frisson* of excitement, she edged cautiously closer.

Both men wore buckskins and woollen stockings, their torsos stripped naked. The larger of the two was a fine specimen of manhood, with a bull-like neck, huge shoulders and hands as large as shovels, but even Serena's novice eye quickly saw that his weight and height hindered him. He was slow, his footwork stolid, and from the look of his left eye, which was closed and weeping, his opponent had already taken advantage of these shortcomings. He looked like a blacksmith, and in fact that is exactly what he was, his bulging biceps the product of long hours at the anvil.

It was the other combatant who captured Serena's attention. Compared to the giant he was slighter, built along sleeker, finer lines, although he was still a tall man and muscular too, without the brawn of the smithy. Most likely he was a coachman, for he exuded a certain air of superiority. His were muscles honed by exercise, not labour. It was, she thought, eyeing his body with unexpected relish, like watching a race horse matched with a shire.

The man held himself well, showing little sign of fatigue. His body, although glistening with sweat, was virtually unmarked. His buckskin-clad legs were long, and as he teased his opponent, dancing forwards and back, landing light punches, then dodging neatly aside, Serena watched entranced. The muscles on his back, his shoulders, his arms, clenched and rippled, tautened and relaxed. Her pulses quickened. She felt the stirring deep within her of a strange, unsettlingly raw emotion.

The sweat that glistened on the man's body accented his honed physique in the dappled sunlight. The control, the energy so economically expended, made her think of a coiled spring. A tiger ready to pounce, assured of dispatching his prey, but content to tease. The lumbering giant in front of him didn't have a prayer.

Around her, the murmuring crowd seemed to agree. 'Looks like Samuel's done for again.' 'Land 'im one for us, Sam, come on, boy!' But the encouragement was in vain. The blacksmith stumbled as a punch landed square and hard on his left shoulder. The crowd prevented him falling, pushing him back into the ring, but he was blown. He made a lunge for the coachman, a wild punch that caught only fresh air and threw him off balance into the bargain. He staggered forwards cursing, righting himself at the last minute.

The other man smiled, a sardonic smile that lit up his dark grey eyes, making Serena catch her breath. He was devilishly handsome, with his glossy black hair in disarray, those wicked grey eyes framed by heavy black brows, his perfectly sculpted mouth curled up in amusement.

The two combatants stood to for one last joust. They circled each other slowly, then Samuel lunged, taking his opponent by surprise for the first time and landing a powerful blow on his chest. The other man reeled, countering with a flurry of punches to Samuel's stomach, the blood from his bare knuckles smearing itself on to the blacksmith's skin, mingling with his sweat. Samuel bellowed in pain and turned to the side to shield himself, trying at the same time to use his hip to push the coachman away. It was a fatal mistake for he mistimed it, leaving his face exposed. A swift hard punch sent his head flying back, and a second under his jaw had him on the ground. It was over.

The crowd roared in approbation. Money changed hands. Samuel staggered to his feet. The victor stood, a triumphant smile adorning his face. His chest, covered in a fine matting of black hair that arrowed down to the top of his buckskin breeches, heaved as he regained his breath. He shook hands with Samuel, and when presented with the winner's purse, to Serena's surprise and the crowd's evident approval, handed it to his opponent.

'You deserve this more than I, Samuel, for you never know when you're beaten.' Laughter greeted this sally—they were obviously old rivals. Now Samuel was saying that in that case the victor deserved a prize too, and the crowd cheered. The coachman stood surveying the scene around him, shaking his head, denying the need for reward as he pulled a cambric shirt over his cooling body. That was when he spotted Serena.

She tried to turn away, but could find no passage through the circle of the crowd. A strong arm caught hers in an iron grip. 'Well, well, what have we here?' His voice was low, surprisingly cultured. His tone was teasing.

Serena coloured deeply, but remained where she was, transfixed by the look in those compelling grey eyes, restrained by his firm grip on her arm. The crowd waited silently, casting speculative looks towards her blushing countenance.

'A kiss from the prettiest woman here will be my prize,' the coachman announced.

He was standing directly in front of her. She could smell him. Fresh sweat, laundered linen, something else deeply masculine she couldn't put a name to. He was tall; she had to look up to meet his eyes. Reluctantly Serena forced herself to hold his gaze, to counter his teasing smile with a haughty look of her own.

His eyebrow quirked. 'Definitely the prettiest woman here. A kiss will be worth all the money in the winner's purse and more.' The words were for her only, whispered in her ear as he pushed back her bonnet, tilting her chin with a firm but gentle finger. As if in a trance Serena complied, her breathing shallow. He hesitated for a tantalising moment, then with a slight shrug pulled her closer, confining the contact to his lips alone.

It was a teasing kiss, like his teasing smile, which lasted no more than a few seconds. His breath was warm and sweet. His lips were soft against her own. The reserve of power she had sensed in the boxing ring was there too in his kiss, daring her to respond.

The crowd cheered lustily, bringing Serena to her senses, reminding her of the reason for her visit. 'Get off me, you ruffian!' she said angrily, pushing him away. *What had she been thinking?*

The coachman who had taken such a liberty in kissing her eyed her quizzically. 'Ruffian or not, you enjoyed that as much as me, I'll wager,' he said, quite unflustered by her temper. 'What are you doing here anyway? This is a private estate—have you lost your way?'

'Are you employed here?' Serena asked curtly.

'You could say I have the honour of serving the estate, yes.'

'Then I'm here to call on your master, Mr Lytton.'

'Well, you're not likely to find him round here, fraternising with tradesmen and servants and ruffians like me, now are you,' he answered with a grin.

Serena gritted her teeth. He was insufferable.

'If you care to call at the front door and present your card, I'm sure he'll be delighted to receive you.' Without a backward glance, the coachman turned on his heel and strode off.

Struggling to regain her rattled composure, Serena found her way back through the yard to the path that led to the main entrance. As she listened to the clang of the doorbell she put the episode firmly to the back of her mind, took a few calming breaths and tried to remember everything Papa had told her. Her heart fluttering with anticipation, she gave her name to the butler, following in his stately wake as he led her through what must have served as the great hall when the house was first built. It was an immense panelled space with a huge stone fireplace on one wall, the staircase leading to the upper floors at the far end. She was given no time to admire it, however, being ushered through a door in the panelling and deposited in a small sunny parlour, which faced on to the gardens at the front of the house. A fire crackled in the grate. A large arrangement of fresh spring flowers scented the room.

'Mr Lytton will join you shortly, madam.' The butler bowed and departed.

Serena pressed her tightly gloved hands together in an effort to stop them from shaking and took stock. It was a cosy room, stylish but comfortable and obviously well used. The warm colours of the soft furnishings, russet-and-gold patterned rugs and deep red upholstery, contrasted with the dark wood panelling that covered the walls, all the way from the wainscoting to a decorative rail just above head height.

How would the owner of this enchanting house receive her? It was bound to be an awkward meeting. Though there had apparently been some letters in the early days, her father and Nick Lytton had not met for nigh on thirty years. Serena was not looking forward to breaking the news that Papa had passed away.

Serena paced the room nervously, noticing the detailing on the wooden panelling for the first time. A frieze of roses was worked into the wood, connected by leaves, briars and little carved animals. *The last rose of summer left blooming alone.* The secret code that Papa had confided in her on that dreadful night when he died of his wounds. The words he had her repeat over and over so that Nick Lytton could be sure of her identity. The phrase had seemed strange, but now she could see it was apt.

What would he be like, this man who held the key to her future? Papa's age, obviously, and, it was clear from her surroundings, a man of wealth and status. A country squire run to fat, as men of that age were wont to do. Like as not he suffered also from the gout.

'Nicholas Lytton at your service, madam.'

Serena jumped. She had not heard him come in.

The tone of the voice was deep. Cultured. Supremely confident. And horribly familiar. The charming smile she had been composing froze upon her face as she turned around.

He had bathed and changed after his exertions in the boxing ring, standing before her elegantly attired in a pair of biscuit-coloured knitted pantaloons and a tailcoat of green superfine cut close across shoulders which had no need of buckram wadding to emphasise their breadth. A clean white shirt and a cravat tied simply, with a striped silk waistcoat and gleaming Hessians, completed the outfit. Raising her head, she saw a strong jaw line, a mouth curved into what could be a smile, glossy black hair combed forwards on to high cheekbones. And those grey eyes.

Nicholas bowed and moved towards Serena, an arm outstretched in greeting. A pink flush tinged her skin, which had little to do with the heat of the fire crackling away at her back. Amusement lurked as he watched her struggling to make sense of the situation, taking advantage of her confusion to usher her compliantly into a wing-backed chair beside the fire while he took the matching seat opposite. 'Coffee will be here any moment. You look as if you could do with some, Miss Cachet.'

He was relishing her embarrassment. Serena sat up straight in her chair, forcing her countenance into a look of cool composure completely at odds with the mixture of humiliation and fury she was feeling. 'Sir, you have already misled me once as to your identity. I beg you not to do so again.'

'I did not mislead you, madam. I said I had the honour of serving the estate and I do. I rather fancy it was you who jumped too quickly to the wrong conclusion. Perhaps your judgement was clouded by your all-too-obvious enjoyment of the base spectacle on offer?'

'There is no need to indulge in more jibes at my expense,' Serena said icily. 'I am here to meet Mr Nicholas Lytton on a matter of some import.'

'*As* I said, I *am* Nicholas Lytton.'

'But—you can't be! No, no, that's ridiculous. The man I have business with is an old friend of my father's.'

'Ah. I expect you refer to *my* father.'

'Yes, that must be it. Of course, your father,' Serena said with enormous relief. 'May I speak with him?'

She leaned forwards eagerly. Her flushed cheeks blushed bright against the creamy smoothness of her skin. With her guinea-gold hair and cornflower-blue eyes framed by startlingly long dark lashes, she looked quite breathtakingly beautiful. Nicholas drank in the vision of loveliness she presented, regretfully shaking his head. 'I'm sorry, I'm afraid that will be quite impossible. He's dead these last ten years.'

'Dead!' Many times in the past few months she had pictured this scene, but this particular twist had never occurred to her. Serena sank back dejectedly in her chair. 'Dead. I did not expect—that is, I'm sorry, but it's rather a shock.'

What on earth was she to do now? Trying desperately to rally her thoughts, she took covert stock of the man opposite. She knew nothing of him save that he could box well and that he took outrageous liberties. Exactly the sort of man Papa would have taken great care to keep well away from his daughter. Perhaps because their life was somewhat unconventional, her father had always been very protective, almost overly so. Naturally, she was banned from the gaming salons. Since their somewhat ambiguous position in society made it impossible for her to socialise in more respectable circles, however, the opportunities to meet men—eligible or otherwise—were few and far between. In fact, Nicholas Lytton was the first man to have kissed her, though she wasn't about to tell him that. He was insufferably arrogant enough as it was. Serena grappled for a solution to what appeared to be an insoluble problem. She was to trust no one save Nick Lytton. Yet Nick Lytton was dead. There seemed to be no way to avoid confiding in his son if she were not to leave empty-handed.

Still, instinct that had nothing at all to do with Papa's urge to secrecy and everything to do with Nicholas Lytton himself made her reticent. That fight. That kiss. The unexpected effect the man himself was having on her. The watchfulness that lurked there, despite the nonchalant way he sat in the chair. Recalling the scene in the stable yard, a heat swept through her, which had naught to do with embarrassment. Shocking though it was to admit it, she had enjoyed the sight of Nicholas Lytton semi-naked, his muscles rippling. When he kissed her, her first instinct had not been to draw back as propriety demanded, but to pull him close, to feel for herself the warm skin, the crisply curling hair, the cord-like muscles and sinew. She had never had such lustful thoughts before. Now was certainly not the time to have them again. Looking up, she became aware of his close scrutiny.

Giving herself a mental shake, Serena sat up straight and licked her lips nervously. A raised brow encouraged her to speak. 'Your father's death makes my errand more problematic, but it does not make it any the less urgent. I believe I must enlist your help.'

'Must? I sense a reluctance to confide, Miss Cachet. Don't you trust me?'

He was toying with her. 'Why? Would I be unwise to do so?'

'That you must decide for yourself, when you are better acquainted with me.'

'Sadly, I do not intend to spend long enough in your company to become so,' Serena replied tartly. 'I am come to reclaim some papers, which my papa entrusted to yours. They are personal documents that he did not want to risk losing on the Continent. You must know that we led a—well, an itinerant life there.'

'You've just recently arrived in England then?'

'Yes, from France. This is my first visit.'

'Allow me to compliment you on your command of our language.'

'I am, in fact, English, Mr Lytton,' Serena said stiffly. 'My father was English, we always spoke that language at home. I can understand your being suspicious—my turning up here unannounced must give a strange appearance—but I assure you I am no fraud. Nor am I a French spy, if that is what you are worried about.'

'*Touché, mademoiselle*. I'm afraid you're doomed to disappointment, though, as I know nothing about your papers. I've been through all my father's effects long since. If they were here, I think they'd have turned up by now.'

'But they must be here! Are you sure he said nothing before he died—could he have perhaps lodged them with his lawyer?'

Nicholas frowned, puzzled by the earnest note in her voice. 'No, I would have been informed if he had.'

'You must remember something. Surely your father mentioned Papa's name at some point?'

Her desperation aroused Nicholas's curiosity. Whatever her tale, she had quite obviously not told him the whole of it. Her lovely face was fixed on him with such a look of entreaty as would melt all but the hardest of hearts. He could not but wonder what effect gratitude would have on her. 'Perhaps if you could tell me a little more, it may prompt my memory.'

'They are private papers, of no value to anyone else. My father's name is on them.'

Her very reluctance to expand was intriguing. 'Cachet?'

Serena bit her lip, more aware than ever of his too-penetrating grey eyes. Though he maintained his relaxed posture, she was under no illusions. Nicholas Lytton distrusted her, and she could not really blame him. 'Not Cachet, Stamppe.'

'Stamppe? Then Cachet is your married name? My apologies, I must have misread your card, *madame*.'

'I'm not married. My name is also Stamppe.'

'Yet your card says Cachet.'

'Yes, because—oh dear, this is most awkward.' Serena risked a fleeting glance up, caught her host's sardonic expression, and looked quickly down again. Nicholas Lytton was smiling sceptically. In her lap, her fingers twined and intertwined, weaving a complex pattern of their own devising, which all too clearly betrayed her discomfort. She clasped them together and forced herself to meet Nicholas's gaze properly. 'Cachet means seal. My real name is Stamppe, though I did not find that out until my father informed me of it on his deathbed. He had a whimsical sense of humour.'

At this, Nicholas gave a twisted smile. 'Amazing what facing mortality will do to a parent.'

'I beg your pardon?'

'I sympathise, *mademoiselle*, that is all, having had a similar experience. It must have come as a surprise.'

'A shock. Papa died very suddenly; he was the victim of a violent robbery. I find it difficult—I still find it hard to accept.' She paused to dab her eyes with a handkerchief plucked from her reticule.

'I'm sorry, I didn't mean to upset you,' Nicholas said more sympathetically. 'Do you have other family?'

'No. No one. At least—no. *Maman* died when I was ten, and since then it has always been just me and Papa. Now it is just me.'

'I find it hard to believe that someone so very lovely as you is wholly unencumbered. Are Frenchmen quite blind?'

'Perhaps it is just that I am quite choosy, Mr Lytton. We seem to have strayed some way from the point.'

'Ah, yes, the point. Your papers, which have lain unclaimed with my father for—how long?'

'Over twenty years.'

'And you have known about them all this time?'

Serena inspected her gloves. 'No. Only since…'

'Don't tell me, Papa told you about them on his deathbed.'

She laughed nervously. 'I know, it sounds like a fairy story.'

'Exactly like one.'

'I see you don't believe me.' *And no wonder*, she thought, rising to leave. She would just have to face the lawyer without her documents. 'I won't waste any more of your time.'

Though he did not doubt that her papers, if they ever existed, were lost, Nicholas was not ready to allow Serena to leave just yet. He was bored beyond measure and she was quite the most beautiful creature he had clapped eyes on in a long time. With her air of assurance and her cultured voice she could pass for quality, but he was not fooled. No gently bred young woman came calling on a single gentleman unaccompanied. Of a certainty, none allowed themselves to be diverted from their call into watching a mill. The more he saw of her, the more certain he became that her gratitude would be worth earning.

'Don't be so hasty, *mademoiselle*, give me a moment to reflect. Your father's name—his real name—does sound familiar. Is there nothing else you can tell me that would help?' He was simply teasing her, drawing out her visit in order to while away the time, so her reply surprised him.

'*The last rose of summer left blooming alone.* I was to say those words so that your father would not doubt my identity.' She smiled in reluctant response to Nicholas's crack of laughter. 'I know, it sounds even more like a fairy tale now.'

'Perhaps it's a clue,' Nicholas said, pointing to the panelling. He meant it as a joke, having no faith at all in his visitor's story, but Serena's reaction gave him pause.

'Of course,' she said excitedly, clapping her hands together. 'A hiding place. How clever of you to think of that.'

A long curl of hair the colour of ripe corn tangled with her lashes and lay charmingly on her cheek. Her vivid blue eyes sparkled like turquoise. She smiled at him quite without guile and he remembered the feel of her soft lips beneath his own. Delicious. She was really quite delicious and he was really very, very bored. 'Of course,' Nicholas agreed lightly, 'a clue. Why not? This house is Tudor, after all, it's absolutely strewn with roses. There are roses on the panelling in almost every room, to say nothing of the ones worked into the stone on the fireplaces, and even hidden away on some of the original furnishings. What's more, when it was built the family were Catholic. We've priest holes, secret passages, concealed doors, the whole kit and caboodle. It could take weeks to search it thoroughly.'

'Weeks!'

Chasing rainbows seasoned with a little light dalliance would pass the time most agreeably, he decided. He had planned to quit the Hall within the week for London or, depending on the news he was awaiting, the Continent. He could not bring himself to care which. Why not indulge the so-charming mademoiselle with some tapping on panels in the meantime? Such enforced intimacy was bound to bear fruit. Delicious, forbidden fruit. 'Perhaps just days, if you have someone to help you—someone who knows where to look,' he said with an innocent look.

'You mean you,' Serena said cautiously.

'Yes, who better? Though you should know that you'd be keeping company with a murderer.'

She could see from the tightening of his mouth and the frown that brought his heavy black brows together that he was no longer teasing her, yet she could not take him seriously. 'I hope you jest, Mr Lytton.'

'No jest, I assure you, although I am not quite a murderer yet. I fought a duel two weeks ago. A stupid thing, but I was in my cups, and my opponent was so very insulting I could not resist the challenge.'

'My papa was given to saying that it is better for gentlemen to fight it out fairly and in cold blood than to resort to what he called fisticuffs in the height of a quarrel.'

'A man of sense. That is exactly what we did. My opponent is a poor swordsman, whereas I am attributed somewhat better than average. I pinked him, a mere warning cut, a perfect lunge that caught his shoulder and disarmed him at the same time. Harry Angelo, my fencing master, would have approved, but my opponent, I am sorry to say, was merely angered. I turned away, assuming all was over. He picked up his sword and lunged at me. I had no option but to fight back, and, in being caught unawares, caused him an injury that may yet prove fatal. So here I am, rusticating and awaiting the outcome, ready to flee to the Continent from the hands of the law should he avenge himself upon me by dying, for duelling is become illegal now, you know. And so you see why I am quite happy to put myself at your disposal.'

The glint in his eye made her uncomfortable, for she could not help wondering what he might want in return. 'That is very kind, but I can't help thinking it would be an imposition. And in any case, it wouldn't be proper for me to spend time here alone with you.'

'Proper! No, indeed, I was very much hoping that it would be quite the opposite.'

Startled by his bluntness, Serena got hastily to her feet, blushing wildly. 'I fear my coming here unaccompanied has misled you as to my character.'

He remained quite annoyingly unflustered. 'That, and the way you kissed me.'

She wrestled with the fastening on her glove, and her flush deepened. 'Well, Mr Lytton, let me put you to rights. Even if I agreed to accept your help—which I have not done—and accepted the risk to my reputation which being here alone with you would engender, I am not the type of female to reward you with kisses.'

'Aren't you? Then I am to assume the kiss after the fight was out of character?' Nicholas took her wrist and dealt expertly with the recalcitrant button.

She tried to pull her hand away, but he held on to it. His fingers were warm through the soft leather of her glove. They were long and slender, the nails trimmed and neat. His knuckles were grazed and bruised from the fight. His touch seemed to flicker from her hand up her arm, raising goose bumps on her skin under the long sleeve of her dress. Nervously, Serena gazed up at him, her hand still lying compliant, knowing she should move, yet caught as before in a trance of awareness. His intentions were unmistakable. He was going to kiss her again. 'No,' Serena said in that curiously breathy voice that did not belong to her. 'I will not pay for your co-operation by allowing you to take liberties. You mistake me.'

'You would kiss a ruffian in a stable yard, but not a

gentleman in a parlour,' he teased. 'I did not take anything from you that wasn't freely given, and I won't now.'

'Then let me go.'

'I will, just as soon as you persuade me you want me to, *mademoiselle*.'

That look of his again—it made her feel as if he could read her thoughts, which meant he would see all too plainly the war between ought and want going on her mind. *It was just a kiss, nothing more.* If he could treat it lightly, so surely could she.

'It's just a kiss, after all,' Nicholas whispered persuasively, echoing her thoughts so precisely she wondered if she had spoken out loud. 'A kiss to seal the beginning of our quest together.'

She opened her mouth to say no, but somehow the words did not come and he took it for an invitation. His lips were cool, exploring, gentle. Questioning. For a breathless moment she hesitated. His mouth stilled. Then she felt her free hand reach up of its own accord to stroke the silken hair at the back of his head. She opened her mouth like a flower to the sun. Softening her lips against his, she melted into his embrace, savouring the taste, the smell, the power. Lost in the newness, the strangeness of it all.

And then it was over. Nicholas took a step back. 'Enough for now, I think; any more would be a liberty. I *am* a gentleman, despite my earlier appearance, and I meant what I said, I will never take anything you do not want to give.'

Serena shook her head, resisting with difficulty the urge to touch her hand to her lips, for they were tingling. 'I have agreed to nothing.'

'Come, come, *mademoiselle*, you cannot possibly be thinking of leaving without these precious papers of yours. What are you afraid of?' Nicholas asked in a perturbingly confident voice. 'Is it perhaps yourself you don't trust?'

No, frankly, she didn't! He was a wolf in wolf's clothing from whom she should run as fast as she could. 'Don't flatter yourself,' Serena replied tartly, 'I have every confidence in my ability to resist your charms.'

'Then you'll allow me to help you?'

It was simple really. Without his help she could not claim her inheritance. She could seek out her father's lawyer, but unless she had the papers—it would be useless. She searched his face for reassurance. 'I have your promise that you will behave properly?'

'I have already given you one promise, *mademoiselle*. I see no need for another.'

They had reached an impasse, and he knew it! Serena fumed inwardly. 'Oh, very well,' she finally conceded rather ungraciously. 'With such a knowledgeable guide as yourself, it can't possibly take too long, after all.'

'Very sensible. Do you wish to start immediately?'

She tried to collect her senses, which by now were utterly scrambled, not least by her own shocking responses to being kissed. And not once but twice!

'Thank you, Mr Lytton, but, no, I have had quite enough excitement for one day,' Serena responded drily. 'I think it best that I return to my lodgings in the village for now. I'll come back in the morning, if that is acceptable to you?'

Nicholas grinned. 'My dear *mademoiselle*, I can think of little regarding you that wouldn't be most acceptable to me. Until morning, then.'

'Until morning, Mr Lytton.'

Chapter Two

Serena arrived at her rooms in the small village of High Knightswood, just over a mile's distance from the Hall, to find Madame LeClerc awaiting her. Madame was a Parisian *modiste* anxious to make her fortune in London. On hearing that Serena was leaving for England, she had offered to accompany her. 'To lend you countenance, *chérie*, as the *bon papa* would have wished. I want to set up my own establishment,' Madame LeClerc had gone on to explain. 'These wars have prevented the English ladies from enjoying the benefits of our French *couture*. Now that we are friends again, it is time for the rich *mesdames* to learn how to dress properly. Like yourself, *mademoiselle*,' she added obsequiously.

Serena had accepted Madame's offer gratefully, being well aware that Papa would not have expected her to travel unaccompanied. Sadly, she soon discovered that the price for Madame's companionship was significantly higher than the generous salary and lodgings the *modiste* had demanded. Madame lent her countenance, but her company was tedious in the extreme.

The journey on the packet steamer made Madame heartily sick. She continued to be sick the entire road to High Knightswood, punctuating bouts of nausea with trembling complaints of everything from the carriage springs to the state of the post roads and the dampness of the sheets at the post houses. She spoke very little English, obliging her employer to intervene when things became difficult. With a shudder, Serena recalled a particular episode involving Madame, the land lady of the Red Lion, and an unemptied chamber pot. Nor could Madame come to terms with the English climate. '*Il pleut à verse.* Rain, rain, rain,' she exclaimed every day, regardless of whether the weather was inclement or not.

As Serena divested herself of her bonnet and pelisse, Madame LeClerc subjected her to a lengthy diatribe on the subject of English food. 'I am sick to my stomach with the *rosbif*. All this meat and no sauces, I am starving.'

Eyeing Madame LeClerc's ample figure, hovering over her like a plump vulture, Serena found this last claim difficult to believe.

'*Look at this!* Just look, Mademoiselle Serena! This *débâcle* is intended to be our dinner. Please to tell me how I, a good Frenchwoman, am meant to eat this?'

With a dramatic gesture, Madame indicated the serving dishes, which were set on the table.

Reluctantly, Serena lifted the covers. She had to acknowledge that their landlady's cooking was somewhat basic, but after the day she'd had, she was in no mood to sympathise. 'It's pigeon, *madame*, with peas, and perfectly edible. Eat it or not, I don't care, but please sit down, I have something to tell you.'

Serena served them both before embarking upon the tricky matter of informing Madame that they would of necessity be delayed in High Knightswood while she resolved a 'personal matter'. Madame, chomping her way steadily through two whole pigeons, distaste writ large on her face, listened in sullen silence. As soon as her plate was cleared, however, she launched into a bitter tirade.

'You promised me we would be headed straight for London. The Season has already started, I need to find my clientele now, before they have all their gowns. This delay will ruin me!' A plump white hand fluttered against her impressive bosom. Serena's companion was for some time loudly inconsolable.

The vague notion she had entertained, of asking Madame to accompany her on her visits to Knightswood Hall, faded from Serena's mind as the *modiste*'s anguish grew. She tried to imagine what Nicholas Lytton would make of her companion. Like as not he would send Madame below stairs if he did not send her packing. Serena would then be responsible for the inevitable fracas between Madame and Nicholas's chef, and no further forward in observing any of the proprieties.

She retired early to bed, but sleep eluded her. In the next chamber she could hear Madame LeClerc's rhythmic snoring all too clearly through the thin walls. Loud enough to rattle the windowpanes, Serena thought grumpily, plumping the bolster in a vain effort to get comfortable. It had been a trying day. The news of Nick Lytton's demise had been a shock, though she supposed it should not have been. She was annoyed at herself for having been so unprepared. His son's promise to help was a mixed blessing. Nicholas Lytton had made it quite clear he did not think her at all respectable.

Nicholas Lytton was a man who gave off danger signals as he entered a room. It would be foolish indeed to ignore them. He carried about him an edge of excitement, as if always on the verge of committing some wild act, about to trespass the safe confines of conduct just for the sport of it. It was this, Serena realised with a start, that drew her too him, rather than the more basic tug of physical attraction. She must be on her guard with him at all times. Despite her unorthodox life, her reputation was spotless. She could not afford to tarnish it now, though it would be a lie to say she was not tempted. A fact of which, unfortunately, Nicholas Lytton was all too well aware.

Perhaps after all she should induce Madame LeClerc to act as her protector. A particularly loud snore came from next door, making Serena giggle. Not even Nicholas Lytton would be tempted to overstep the mark in Madame's presence. But then he would simply get rid of her. Serena closed her eyes. She was going round in circles, far too tired to argue with herself any more. Surely Knightswood Hall was too remote from London for anyone to care what did—or did not—go on there?

As Serena finally dropped into slumber, Nicholas sat in splendid isolation in the small family dining room of Knightswood Hall, musing on the contentious topic of his father's will. The table had been cleared and the covers removed. In front of him lay the latest update on the situation from his man of business. Frances Eldon was not optimistic.

The butler placed a decanter of port and a jar of snuff on the table before feeding another log on to the fire and reassuring himself that the curtains were perfectly drawn. 'Will there be anything else, Mr Nicholas?'

'No, thank you. Tell my man not to wait up, I'll get myself to bed. Goodnight, Hughes.'

'Goodnight, sir.' The butler bowed and withdrew silently from the room.

Nicholas poured himself a small glass of port, idly swirling it around in the delicate crystal glass. His thoughts, like the wine, circled endlessly. He was tired, and no wonder—it had been a closer contest than usual with Samuel. They had been sparring partners since childhood. Ruefully, he examined his raw knuckles in the glow of the firelight. Hardly the hands of a gentleman. It was high time he stopped such foolishness. And yet—he never could resist a challenge.

But he was twenty-nine now, old enough to know better. In less than three months, as Frances Eldon so needlessly reminded him in his letter, Nicholas would be thirty. If they could not find a way to break the will before that date, his fortune would go to his cousin Jasper—unless Nicholas took Frances's advice and married.

He had always been so carelessly certain that his lawyers would find a way to overturn the fateful clause, but as the deadline approached and every legal avenue turned into a dead end the decision loomed over him like a menacing black cloud of doom. He should have instructed them sooner. *Dammit, there must be a way!*

Nicholas rose to stir the fire, carelessly throwing on another log, stepping back hastily as the sparks flew out on to the hearth rug. He was not going to be forced down a path of another's choosing. He would not be blackmailed into the bonds of matrimony, not even by his own dead father.

His parent had remarried late in life. Melissa was a malleable widgeon, a young woman content to play nursemaid to a man in failing health many years her senior. To the astonishment of all who knew him, Nick Lytton, after a lifetime of raking, settled contentedly into domestic bliss and became an advocate for the institution of marriage into the bargain. The present

Nicholas Lytton sighed deeply. He should have seen it coming, after that last uncomfortable interview.

'I hear you've been causing a scandal again, my boy.' The chill which his father had caught while out hunting had taken hold of his lungs. It was obvious he had not long to live. Nicholas remembered each breath his father took as a painfully sharp intake, a long drawn-out rattling exhale. What he couldn't remember now were the exact circumstances of the scandal the old man was so upset about. Some bit of muslin Nicholas had tried to pass off as one of the *ton* at a party, as he recalled. Yes, that was it, a bet, and he had lost when the lady told a rather warm story and had then been recognised by one of her previous protectors.

Before Melissa, his father would have laughed, but with his second marriage the old man had acquired a pompous righteousness. 'You've shamed our name once too often, my boy,' Nick Lytton wheezed.

'For pity's sake, Father,' Nicholas retorted, 'you talk as if I was a libertine. As you very well know, I am scrupulous about confining that sort of thing to the muslin company. As you used to,' he said pointedly. 'I never raise false expectations. I would have thought that was something more to be proud of than ashamed.'

His refusal to repent served only to bring down the full extent of his father's wrath on his head. Nick Lytton had stormed, ranted, cursed and finally, when his son showed no signs of remorse, resorted to threats. 'I'll see to it that you can't carry on this life for ever. You're turning into a damned loose fish, Nicholas, and by God I'll put a stop to it, you mark my words.'

The interview had ended then. Nicholas thought no more of it until after his father's death, when he was informed of the significant change to the terms of his will. He'd laughed and refused to take it too seriously. Until now.

Not even in his salad days had Nicholas come close to being in love, finding that passion faded all too quickly once sated. His dashing looks and flamboyant generosity made him a highly sought-after catch, but not once in all his years on the *ton* had any lady managed to stake a claim. He was far too careful for that, unlike some of his peers. Poor Caroline Lamb's latest attempt to avenge herself upon Byron, so it was rumoured, was a thinly disguised *roman à clef*. Nicholas shuddered at the very idea of encountering the spectre of a rejected lover hovering at a society party, never mind the iniquity of the details of any *affaire* being bandied about in the press.

No, he made a strict point of confining his *amours* to women from a different sphere who understood the rules of the game perfectly well. Over the years he had been fortunate in his mistresses, all of whom combined beauty with experience. When he grew bored it was a simple thing to pay them off. No sulks. No pain. No regrets. Just a few trinkets, a generous sum, a goodbye. It suited him. It was how he had chosen to live his life, and he enjoyed it. He saw no reason to change.

Dammit to hell, he would not *change.* Nicholas consigned Frances Eldon's letter to the fire. When the lawyers had exhausted every possibility, then perhaps he would force himself to contemplate marriage. Right now he had better things to think about. Like the luscious Mademoiselle Serena Stamppe and her preposterous tale of hidden documents and long-lost friendship.

The friendship part could be true—his father had been wild in his youth. The wars with France favoured many a person wishing to hide their dirty laundry in the hustle-bustle of the Continent; no doubt that Serena's dear papa was one such. An adventurer of some sort, of a certainty. She was obviously an adventuress herself—she had given herself away with that remark of hers—what was it—*an itinerant life*.

Stamppe. The name was definitely familiar. He would write to Frances in the morning, tell him to crack the whip over the will, and get him to find out what he could about the lovely Serena and her father. Yawning, Nicholas placed the guard over the fire, snuffed out the candles, and headed wearily for his bed.

In the end, Serena decided not to introduce Madame LeClerc to Nicholas unless it became absolutely necessary—and she refused to allow herself to contemplate just what she meant by that. She made an early start the next morning, leaving her lodgings long before her companion surfaced for breakfast. On the assumption that the search would be dusty work, she wore a simple dress of printed cotton and sturdy half-boots of jean. A short woollen cloak protected her from the early chill of the English spring, and her hair was looped on top of her head, a bandeau of the same material as her dress holding it in place.

Charming was the epithet with which Nicholas Lytton greeted her, himself simply attired in fitted buckskins that clung to his muscular legs, teemed with a dark blue waistcoat and plain dark coat. He clasped Serena's gloved hands between his for a brief moment on greeting, but made no further attempt to touch her. She could not make up her mind whether to be relieved or not.

They sat together in the small morning room over a pot of coffee, discussing how best to tackle the search using the only clue they had. 'I suppose it's safe to assume that the hiding place really is here,' Serena said. 'You don't have any other houses with rose panelling, do you?'

'No. And both the London house and the hunting box post-date the time you said your father gave mine his papers—over twenty years ago, do I have that right?'

Serena nodded. 'He told me he sent them not long after I was born.'

'Where was that?'

'*La Bourgogne*. Burgundy—it is where my mother comes from.'

'So that is where you would call home?'

'No, *Maman*'s family did not approve of the

marriage. My parents would not talk about it. I don't think there's anywhere I'd call home, I've never stayed in one place long enough to put down roots.'

'Why not?'

She thought for a moment, her lips pursed, a small frown drawing her fair brows together. 'It's strange, but I've never really questioned why. Papa said it was expedient for his—his business interests, but I'm not sure that's wholly true. He just liked to travel. I've lived in some beautiful cities, Vienna, Rome, Strasbourg, and Paris of course, but I've always considered myself an outsider. We lived so much, my parents and I, in a little world of their making. I have any number of acquaintances, but I don't really have any friends of my own.'

'May one ask what precisely Papa's business interests were?'

'Oh, he dabbled in lots of things,' Serena said vaguely. 'He preferred me not to become involved in such matters.'

'Whatever your father was involved with, it must have been lucrative. I could not fail to notice the quality, and expense, of that delightful outfit you wore yesterday. Assuming, of course, it was your father who provided the funds.'

He was looking at her with that curling half-smile that made her pulses flutter and raised her hackles at the same time. 'You think I have a rich protector? A fat, elderly gentleman perhaps, on whom I bestow my affections in return for gifts?'

Nicholas felt a sudden and most unexpected pang of jealousy at the thought of anyone being in receipt of Serena's affections. His smile hardened.

'This is a ridiculous conversation,' Serena said, sensing the change in his mood. 'There are no skeletons in my closet, I assure you. Now, can we stop wasting time and start looking for my papers?'

Nicholas shrugged. 'Oh, very well. There are a number of secret panels and a couple of priest holes that I know of, we can start with those. You don't mind getting a little dusty, do you? Some of the places won't have been opened for years. At the very least I suspect we'll find a few spiders. Maybe even some rats.'

'I've encountered much worse, believe me. I'm not fond of them, but they don't scare me. Papa taught me never to be missish; you needn't worry that I'll be fainting into your arms.' Serena looked up to see surprise writ on Nicholas's face, and raised her brows. 'Oh dear, were you *wishing* me to faint into your arms? I do beg your pardon. I suppose I could *pretend* to be afraid if you had your mind absolutely set on it?'

He laughed softly. 'No, thank you. If I wish to have you in my arms, my intrepid Mademoiselle Stamppe, I can think of easier ways of managing it.'

Serena rose from her seat, shaking out her petticoats. 'You take rather too much for granted, Mr Lytton.'

'We shall see,' was all he vouchsafed in return.

* * *

Three hours later they were both smudged with dirt, and Serena had a goodly amount of cobwebs trailing from her frilled petticoats, but of the papers they had found no trace.

In the first priest's hole located beneath a cupboard at the side of a fireplace carved with a number of Tudor roses there had been only some mice droppings.

The second priest's hole was a cunning little trapdoor in the upstairs drawing room operated by turning yet another rose in a nearby panel. When Nicholas lowered himself into it, he found a squashed shallow-crowned hat from a much earlier age. He emerged from the hiding place wearing it. Serena laughed, not so much at the absurd spectacle he presented—for the hat was much too big—but at the ring of dirt it left around his brow when he removed it. With the dusty halo and those gunmetal eyes he looked, she thought fancifully, like a dark angel. Or maybe a devil. She reached up to brush it away, drawing back immediately at his startled look. 'I'm sorry, you have—if you look in the mirror, you have dust on your hair.'

In the large formal dining—once more panelled with a design of roses—a concealed door lifted away to reveal a space built into a hollow column. 'My father was minded to keep his own papers here, until I informed him that the entire household, if not the whole countryside, knew of the place. After that he stuck to the rather more orthodox method of locking them in his desk.' Once more the space was empty.

In the master bedchamber, where Nicholas pulled back one of the window shutters to reveal yet another 'secret' space, a piece of paper fluttered to the ground. He handed it to Serena, smiling at the look of anticipation on her face as she opened it, bursting into infectious laughter when it turned out to be an account for three pairs of evening gloves and six ostrich feathers.

'This was my father's room. I can only assume it was a bill he didn't want my mother to see. Before he married my stepmother, my father was rather free with his favours.'

'Was he? Well, so was my father after my mother died—and before he married her, I presume.'

'Don't you find that shocking?'

'No, why should I? Papa was very much in love with *Maman*, and it was a long time after she died before he took an interest in any other woman. Why should I grudge him pleasant company?'

'What a very enlightened attitude.'

Nicholas's coolly ironic tone irked her. Remembering just in time, however, that it was not in her interests to quarrel with him, Serena took a calming breath before speaking. 'It's not enlightened, it's just—honest. Why pretend the world works one way when it is obvious to anyone who cares to look that it works in quite another?

I don't mean that I approve of such choices, but to deny that they happen would be quite foolish.'

'Foolish, I agree, but it's what most of your sex claim to do none the less. And may I ask if Papa had the same enlightened attitude when it came to his daughter?'

'Of course not. It's different for a woman, as you very well know. I think you're making fun of me.'

'On the contrary, I must commend you for the candour of your outlook.'

Once again she struggled to contain the spark of temper his words ignited, for though he denied it she knew she was being deliberately riled. Biting back the riposte that sprang to her lips, Serena instead executed a mocking curtsy. 'You are too kind, sir. I would that I could commend you for the same.'

'Well done, *mademoiselle*. A hit, I acknowledge it.'

She was forced to laugh. 'Oh, for goodness' sake, please call me Serena. I can't bear to be on formal terms. In any case, it's absurd, to have been grovelling about amongst all this dirt and cobwebs and still to call each other Mr Lytton and Mademoiselle Stamppe, a name I find rather strange, even if it is my own.'

'I'm honoured. Serena is a beautiful name, and I'd be flattered if you'd call me Nicholas.'

'Papa named me for serenity, although I'm not sure he got it quite right. But thank you, Nicholas.'

She pronounced it in the French way, leaving off the last consonant, making awareness curl in the pit of his stomach. There was something inherently sensual about her, made more so because he could not make up his mind whether or not she intended it. *Nicholas.* It was like a caress.

'I take it you don't favour this room yourself,' Serena said, looking around her, oblivious of his stare. 'I'm not surprised, it's quite depressing.'

'I agree,' Nicholas replied, dragging his mind back to their conversation. 'To be honest, I've never been enamoured of the idea of taking over the room of a dead parent. Rather off-putting, I would imagine, especially if one had company. As if one was being watched at a time when one would particularly wish not to be observed.'

Serena gave a startled gasp. 'There was no need to be so blunt! I thought only that the room was oppressive. What you do—or don't do—in your own bedchamber is none of my business.'

'Not yet.' Giving her no time to respond to this challenge, Nicholas grasped Serena by the elbow and headed towards the door. 'That's the last of the hiding places I remember for the present. It has obviously escaped your notice, but it is long past noon, and I am ravenous. I asked Hughes to set out a luncheon for us downstairs, but before you sit down, my lovely Serena, you should know that you have smut on your nose, so I will direct you to a room where you can clean up, and I will see you as soon as you have done so. Don't keep me waiting lest I faint from hunger.'

Turning her by the shoulders, he pointed Serena in

the direction of a doorway down the long corridor and strode effortlessly down the stairs towards the breakfast parlour.

After lunch they engaged in a few more hours of fruitless searching before Nicholas judged it time to call it a day. 'There's always tomorrow,' he said brightly. 'Rest assured I'll rack my brain for more ideas to occupy us then.'

'You don't sound overly disappointed by our lack of progress,' Serena said suspiciously. 'In fact, you sound quite pleased.'

Nicholas flashed her a seductive smile. 'The longer it takes, the more grateful you are liable to be.'

'As I said earlier, Mr Lytton, you take far too much for granted. Right now, what I would be most grateful for is the comfort of my bed. It's been a long and tiring day, I must return to my lodgings.'

'Then I insist you let me send a servant to accompany you. After all, we wouldn't want any aspersions to be cast on your reputation or intentions, now would we?'

'No, Mr Lytton,' Serena conceded with a smile, 'we most certainly would not.'

'If I never see another Tudor rose before I die I'll be happy.' Serena was perched precariously on a window seat in the formal dining room at Knightswood Hall the next day. 'My fingers are aching from tapping and prodding and poking at panelling. I'm beginning to think this is a wild goose chase.'

After hours of searching they were no further forward, but although she knew she should be concerned, she was finding it very hard to fret. Her father had created this situation, giving her no option but to keep company with a man whom she was almost certain was a rake. The world would surely damn her if it ever found out, but she would make sure it didn't, and in the meantime, provided the rake continued to behave, she was enjoying herself.

Nicholas smiled lazily up at Serena from the chair from which he had been watching, with relish, her attempts to reach a rose he had suggested—with no foundation whatsoever—looked particularly suspect. She had had to stretch, giving him a delightful view of her shapely ankles and a tantalising glimpse of her even more shapely rear as her dress was pulled tight. 'Poor Serena, don't give up yet, I'm sure I can think of lots more places to look.'

She turned round to face him, her hands on her hips. 'I'm sure you can. And I expect most of them will involve me clambering up on to something or crawling about on my hands and knees.'

He stood to assist her down from the window. 'It's your own fault for having such a very charming *derrière*.'

'A gentleman wouldn't have looked.'

'No, you're wrong about that. No man, gentleman or other, could have resisted looking, but a gentleman would have pretended he had not.'

'You told me *you* were a gentleman.'

'I lied.'

'You're impossible,' Serena said, trying desperately not to blush, for it only served to encourage him.

And you are adorable, Nicholas thought. A long tendril of hair had escaped its pins and curled down her back over the tender nape of her neck, giving her a charmingly dishevelled air. Not for the first time he found himself imagining what she would look like with all of the pins removed, her hair loosened and allowed to cascade down over her bare shoulders. It would brush teasingly over her breasts, causing the rosy buds of her nipples to stiffen and darken in delicious contrast to the creamy fullness of…

He dragged his eyes away. 'Let's go for a walk. We could both do with some fresh air.' He picked up his coat, which was draped over a chair at the head of the long oak table. Serena was delightful, charming, and fun to be with into the bargain. A very heady and alluring combination. The evidence of that was pressing insistently at the fabric of his breeches. Adjusting the ruffles on his shirt sleeves, he pulled his waistcoat straight. 'Come on, fetch your hat and shawl. It's much too nice a day to stay cooped up in here. A stroll in the gardens is what we need. You'll be relieved to know that it's too early for the roses to be in bloom.' Placing a hand firmly on the small of her back, he guided her from the room.

Outside, Serena raised her face towards the sun,

luxuriating in the gentle caress of its warm rays on her skin. 'You're right…' she sighed contentedly '…this is a lovely idea. Where shall we go?'

'There's a pleasant walk down through the gardens to the trout stream at the bottom,' Nicholas replied. 'It's been dry for almost a week now, so the path shouldn't be too muddy.'

'I wish you'd tell Madame LeClerc so. According to her, it has been raining non-stop since we arrived.'

'The good Madame—and how is her heroic snoring?'

Serena giggled. 'I don't know, thank goodness. I was so tired last night that I barely noticed. I should inform you, though, that her French sense of propriety is extremely offended at my spending so much time alone with you. She is for ever reminding me that my papa would strongly disapprove.'

'And would he?' Nicholas asked curiously.

'That's an impossible question since the only reason I am here with you in the first place is to do as he wishes. He would think our acquaintance—unwise.'

'Perhaps he would be right. Most fathers would think the same way about me, I've a dreadful reputation. After all, I've already kissed you twice—who knows what else I have planned for you?'

Serena stumbled. 'You said you would not take liberties.'

'I said I would not take anything that is not given freely. That's quite a different matter.'

'Oh.' She glanced up at him through her lashes.

'You know, I considered bringing Madame LeClerc here with me to ensure that nothing improper occurred between us.'

'Good God, I'm very glad you didn't. I suspect I'd have resorted to murder.'

'If I have to put up with her for much longer, I'll resort to murder myself. Her dresses may be charming, but her disposition is rather less so. I find her company tedious, and she finds our delay here beyond bearing. I can't wait to be rid of the woman.'

'When will that be?'

'When I get to London. Once I have Papa's papers, I'm to take them to his lawyer there in the city.'

'And then? Do you have plans?'

Serena frowned. 'I thought I did, now I'm not so sure. You'll think me fanciful, but I feel like—oh, I don't know—a ship. All my life I've been safely anchored in a harbour, or becalmed, or tethered to another vessel. And now I've been cut free I can go where I want, do whatever I want to do. I don't really want to make plans just yet. Don't laugh.'

'I'm not—far from it. I find the image of you unfurling your sails most distracting.'

She blushed at the intimacy of his tone, but ventured no reply. They were walking side by side along a small path lined with cherry trees, the blossom just beginning to come into flower. Serena's hand was tucked into Nicholas's arm, their paces matched, so perfectly in tune that neither had noticed.

The atmosphere over the last two days had been relaxed and lightly flirtatious. Until now, Nicholas had shown no sign of wishing to make more serious advances. Which was a good thing, Serena assured herself, and had indeed almost come to believe. Almost. Part of her was tempted to explore the attraction she felt between them, though it was a complication she could well do without. Every time he touched her, no matter how innocuous the circumstances—to hand her a book or her gloves, to seat her at the table or as now, to lend her an arm while they walked—a tiny shiver of awareness flickered inside her. Did he feel it too?

I find the image of you unfurling your sails most distracting. She wished she had not mentioned it, for now she found it distracting too. *Unfurling.* Why was it such a sensual word?

They continued strolling along the path, but their pace slowed. 'There's a seat by the stream and a pretty enough prospect from there over the fields,' Nicholas said, pointing ahead. 'We can rest there for a while in the sun, if you wish.'

There was indeed a charming view from the little wooden bench they made their way towards. 'It's lovely, really lovely,' Serena said delightedly. 'I wonder if my papa and yours spent time fishing here. He told me they knew each other as boys.'

'Did he? Then perhaps they did.' Though Nicholas thought it more likely that Serena's papa poached than fished, he decided not to disillusion her. 'I fish here myself sometimes. There's not much sport, trout and carp merely, and to be honest I haven't the patience for fly fishing. I haven't been here in an age—I'd almost forgotten how pleasant it is.' He wiped the bench with a large handkerchief. Serena sat obediently, but Nicholas continued to stand, gazing off into the distance.

'Don't you spend much time at the Hall?' she enquired.

'No, not really. I have a town house in London—that's where Georgiana, my half-sister, and her mother are at present. Georgie's seventeen now, and Melissa is launching her on to the unsuspecting world. She's a bit of a hoyden, Melissa is quite unable to control her, but she'll be a hit none the less, she's a pretty little thing with a handsome portion. Between my hunting box, visiting friends, and trips to the races at Newmarket, I'm lucky if I spend more than a month or so in a year down here.'

'That seems a shame. It's such a lovely place.'

'Well, the prospect is certainly breathtaking at the moment.'

He was not looking at the view. His meaning was unmistakable. Serena could think of no reply, only of what he would do next. She did not have to wait long.

'Stand up, Serena, I mean to kiss you.'

Somehow she was on her feet. *How did that happen?* He was pulling her close into the warmth of his body. His arm was looped round her waist. She could feel the heat from his fingers through the thin muslin of her dress. Now he was untying the strings of her bonnet with his other hand, tossing it carelessly on to the bench.

'I don't intend to let you,' she finally managed to say.

Nicholas raised a quizzical brow. 'I think you'll find that you do.' He moved closer, watching her all the while, his hold on her still loose, unrestraining, allowing her space and time to retreat. His fingers were on the nape of her neck now, gently exploring, stroking down to her collar bone, up to the shell of her ear. Her body hummed with anticipation, her nerves tingling, her skin, her whole being urging her towards him, as if invisible strings pulled her in, tangled her up, enmeshed the two of them together.

'Serena?' His voice was husky. His eyes, dark and disturbing, searched her face questioningly.

She hesitated as his fingers stilled their caress. His hold on her slackened. She knew she should resist, knew it with certainty.

Chapter Three

His lips were gentle, pulling her bottom lip between his own, moulding his mouth to hers, delicately flicking her mouth open with his tongue. Their bodies nestled, thigh to thigh, chest to chest. The buttons from his coat dug into her through the thin fabric of her dress. Still Nicholas teased, a determinedly slow onslaught on her mouth that licked and sipped and kissed with seemingly no intent but to tantalise.

She was suffused with a warm glow. A hotter flame flickered low in her abdomen, and yet she shivered too, goose bumps rising on her neck, her waist, her arms, everywhere their bodies touched. So different. So lovely. Unfurling.

His breath was warm on her cheek. She wanted to melt into him. To drink deeper of him. To feel more of him. Instinctively she returned his kiss, relishing the myriad of sensations flooding her senses, blocking out all thought, building so slowly from warmth to heat that she hardly registered the change in temperature, the intensifying ache becoming a need for more.

Nicholas's hold on her tightened. The pressure of his mouth increased. His tongue touched hers, or hers touched his, and everything changed. He pulled her so close that even through their clothing there could be no mistaking his arousal. His hand left her waist, trailing lower, gripping the soft flesh of her thigh, cupping and moulding the rounded flesh of her bottom. A throbbing pulse inside her responded to his hardness. Heat sparked.

His mouth became demanding. His tongue penetrated deep, tangling with hers, his lips no longer gentle, no longer sipping, but drinking, driving her towards a place hotter and wilder than any she had been before. She was trembling. Would have fallen were it not for the strength of his grip on her. 'Nicholas,' she said, though what she meant she had no idea. Her voice sounded ragged.

He released her abruptly, breathing heavily, his lids hooded over eyes that were almost black with desire. Serena slumped down on to the bench, her head swirling.

'If I'd known the response I'd get I would have waited until we were indoors,' Nicholas said with a grim attempt at humour, taken aback by the strength of passion that had erupted between them.

'You said you were going to kiss me, not ravish me,' Serena flashed in return, desperately struggling for a modicum of composure. *Just a kiss!* Well, now she knew there was no such thing!

Nicholas turned away, taking his time to adjust his disarrayed neckcloth, allowing himself to be distracted by this small task in order to give them both time to compose themselves. He had intended no more than a teasing kiss, something to test the waters. That they had plunged immediately into the depths was most unsettling.

Serena sat on the damp wood of the seat, wrestling with the tangled strings of her bonnet. Desire and heat warred with shame and guilt as she realised what she had done. *What must he think of her?* What was she to think of herself? For even as she sat here, trying to compose herself, she was distracted by an unfulfilled yearning for more. She barely recognised herself. Perhaps she had become infected by Nicholas's spirit of recklessness.

But it was done now, and she could not regret it. She would put it down to experience—at least, she would at some point, when she was gone from here, somewhere far from this man's disturbing, bewildering presence. In the meantime the best thing she could do was protect her dignity. She was *damned* if she would let Nicholas Lytton see how easily his kisses overwhelmed her. Serena straightened her shawl and smoothed a wrinkle from her glove. 'We should go back.'

Nicholas ran a hand through his hair, smoothing it into something resembling its former stylish disorder and tried to decide what to do. Apologise? No need, surely—he had given her every chance to repulse him. He had done nothing wrong, yet still he felt he had. But then why was she sitting there, looking annoyingly calm, when he was on fire with need, and just moments before he could have sworn she was too. Baffled, he helped her to her feet.

'Thank you, Nicholas.'

Deliberately misunderstanding her meaning in an effort to rouse her out of her irritating self-possession, Nicholas bowed mockingly. 'It's more customary for the gentleman to thank the lady. It was a pleasure, I assure you.'

Serena blushed, and was annoyed at having done so. 'I trust you are suitably refreshed,' she said tartly.

'You're anxious to resume your search, I suppose. You know, Serena, the papers are just as likely to be lost as hidden.'

'I'm perfectly well aware that you don't believe in their existence,' she snapped. 'I am also perfectly well aware that I am simply a distraction for you. You're helping me because you are bored. You kissed me for the same reason. Why the sudden need for honesty—are you feeling guilty? You needn't, it was just a kiss, as you said. You need have no fear that it raised false expectations.'

'If we are to talk of false expectations, I think you have raised a few of your own! Dammit, Serena, you said it yourself, that wasn't a kiss, it was a ravishment.'

The implication made her temper soar, hot words pouring from her like lava from a volcano. 'There is no need to take your frustrations out on me, Nicholas. You had the good grace to comment yesterday on my enlightened attitude. Would that you had the same. Instead you are behaving all too typically of your sex, happy to blame mine for arousing your desires, equally happy to berate us when they are not fulfilled.'

His voice was steely. 'I think I am not the only one to be suffering from frustrated desire.'

They stood glaring at each other on the narrow track. Behind them the weak spring sunshine glittered, casting dappled shadows on the lush green verge. In the brief silence her temper abated as quickly as it had risen. 'You are quite right, I beg your pardon.'

Her simple acknowledgement took the wind from his sails. Nicholas lifted her hand to his lips. 'You are far more gracious than I. I accept your apology unreservedly, and offer my own in turn.'

She snatched her hand back. 'Forget it, there is nothing more to be said. Let us return to the Hall, shall we?'

Nicholas nodded in grudging agreement and, linking Serena's arm through his own, turned back on to the path and led them towards the house.

In London, Mr Mathew Stamppe entered the office in the city of Messrs Acton and Archer, attorneys at law. He was welcomed by the senior partner Mr Tobias Acton, and ushered into a comfortable room at the front of the premises facing out on to the bustle of Lombard Street.

Waving aside the offer of a glass of canary and ignoring Mr Acton's polite enquiries as to the health of Mrs Stamppe and his son Mr Edwin Stamppe, Mathew cleared his throat and got straight to the point. 'What is this urgent matter that requires my presence post-haste? It had better be good.'

Tobias Acton assessed the man sitting opposite him with a lawyer's shrewd gaze. His client was a tall man with a spare frame. Eyes of washed-out blue peered at him testily above the aristocratic Stamppe nose, but overall his features were weak, giving him rather the look of a hunted hare. Mathew favoured the plain dress of the country squire he had been for the best part of the last twenty years, living on his brother's estates in Hampshire. Under his careful stewardship the lands of the Earl of Vespian were in excellent heart. Mathew had looked after them as prudently as he would have done had they been his own. In fact, Tobias Acton thought, he had looked after them for so long that he probably thought of them as exactly that—his own.

And now they were. The lawyer composed his features into those of a man about to deliver ill tidings. 'I'm afraid, Mr Stamppe, we have received the saddest of news. Your brother Philip is, I must regretfully inform you, deceased. He died some months ago from injuries sustained when he was robbed, I believe in

Paris. Please accept my deepest condolences, sir. Or, I should say, Lord Vespian.'

At last! Mathew struggled to contain the smile that tugged at the corners of his thin mouth. Careful not to show his satisfaction, he shook his head sadly. 'My dear brother's passing cannot be said to be a shock, given the way he chose to live, but it is a blow none the less. I shall arrange for the appropriate notices and such, but the main thing is to confirm the legal transfer of the estate to my name. I take it he left his will with you?'

Tobias Acton shuffled uncomfortably in his seat. 'Well, my lord, as to that, I'm sorry to tell you that things are not quite so straightforward. Lord Vespian—your brother, that is—left us none of his personal papers. As trustees we can obviously act with regards to that part of the estate which is entailed, but as to the unentailed property which, as you know, is not insignificant, we have only this.'

He solemnly handed Mathew a sealed packet. 'Our instructions were to give this into your hands in the unfortunate event of his lordship's death.'

Mathew took the packet, his rigid countenance giving no sign of the anger rising in his breast at this caprice of Philip's. Tearing open the seal, he read the contents with impotent fury. Finally, he crumpled the letter into his pocket. 'It seems, Mr Acton, that I have inherited a niece rather than a fortune. My dear brother has posthumously informed me that he was not only married, but that the union produced a daughter who is his rightful heir. The will and testament supporting this was lodged by Philip with a man named Nick Lytton who, to the best of my knowledge, died ten years since. I can only presume my niece—' he broke off to consult the letter '—the Lady Serena, will stake her claim as soon as she has recovered them from his son.'

Tobias Acton's brows rose a notch. 'A most unexpected development, Lord Vespian. May one enquire as to how you intend to handle this somewhat, ahem, delicate situation?'

'That, Acton, is a question I find myself quite unable to answer at this present moment.'

The next morning, Hughes relieved Serena of her hat and pelisse and informed her that Master Nicholas awaited her in the library, which was situated at the far end of the building. Serena opened the door and stepped into a surprisingly modern room with long windows looking out over a paved terrace. The book cases were mahogany, not the oak prevalent in the rest of the house, as was the large desk behind which Nicholas sat. Above the book cases the walls and ceiling were tempered a soft cream. The hangings were dull gold.

'This is quite lovely,' Serena said, 'and so unexpected.'

Nicholas rose from behind the desk to clasp her hand between his in his customary greeting. 'A description I could easily apply to you.'

She felt his intense gaze probe her thoughts, felt the now familiar fluttering that accompanied the touch of his flesh on hers, however slight. They stood thus for what seemed an eternity, the memory of that remarkable, passionate, all-encompassing kiss hanging almost palpably between them.

A polite cough announced the arrival of Hughes bearing a tray of coffee, which he placed on a small table. Serena poured two cups and handed one to Nicholas before sitting down to sip contentedly on her own. 'I've never learned to make good coffee—this is delicious.'

Nicholas raised an eyebrow. 'Not exactly an accomplishment you can have had much call for, surely?'

'On the contrary. There have been times when we were quite down on our luck, Papa and I, unable to afford luxuries such as servants.'

'Not recently, though. No matter how simple the gowns you wear, I'm not deceived—the simpler the design, the costlier the price, is my experience. You're tricked out in the absolute finest of everything—gowns, shawls, hats, even those little boots of yours are kid, if I'm not mistaken.'

'And what, pray, *monsieur*, would you know about the cost of a lady's apparel?'

'As much as you, probably. I've certainly paid for enough fripperies over the years, to say nothing of having to cough up for dressmakers and milliners when the lady concerned is a—let us say intimate—acquaintance.'

'You are referring to your mistresses, I take it.' She was determined not to be shocked, equally determined to ignore the foolish twinge of jealousy. 'However, my clothes are from Paris, *naturellement*, which makes them a little above your touch.'

He remembered her earlier jibe about a protector. What if she had not been joking after all? The idea was distinctly uncomfortable. '*Au contraire, mademoiselle*,' Nicholas said maliciously, 'I am well enough heeled to be able to insist that any lady under my protection wears only the very best. And well enough versed in the latest modes to see that your hard times are behind you, if your wardrobe is aught to go by.'

She gave him a direct look, alerted by the harsh note in his voice. 'You think a man paid for them?'

'Am I right?'

He spoke nonchalantly, but Serena was not fooled. 'Yes.' She waited, but he said nothing, only looked at her in that way of his that made her feel he was privy to her innermost thoughts. 'Oh, for heaven's sake, Nicholas, stop looking so serious. I meant my father.'

He was unaccountably relieved, but managed not to show it. 'Well, he must have made you a generous allowance.' Serena did not deign to reply. 'Do you still miss him?' Nicholas asked her after a few moments, his voice gentler now.

'Of course. We were very close. Don't you miss your parents?'

'The cases are rather different,' he replied wryly. 'I saw more of the servants than my parents when I was growing up. Outside school, there were various tutors, but being without siblings I was largely left to go my own way—exactly as my father did in his youth. I had money enough to indulge in all my whims, and when I grew older to support my gaming and fund my *amours*. My father introduced me to his club and a few of his influential friends when I came of age, and that's about the sum of it.'

'So you are an only child too. Did you wish for a brother or sister? I know I longed for siblings.'

'I *was* an only child,' Nicholas corrected. 'I've got a half-sister now.'

'Yes, but so much younger than you—it's not the same.'

'She's about the age Melissa was when my father married her. There's no fool like an old fool—he was completely infatuated.'

'But Melissa made him happy?'

'He died before he could be disillusioned,' Nicholas said sardonically, 'but not, unfortunately for me, before he became obsessed with a desire to reform me.'

'Poor Nicholas.'

There was just a tinge of mockery in Serena's voice, but Nicholas could forgive her anything when she smiled at him that way, making him feel she understood him very well. He was becoming accustomed to it.

'I would have thought reforming you a well-nigh impossible undertaking,' Serena continued teasingly. 'How on earth did he intend to achieve it?'

'Oh, he had his ways, believe me. He took every opportunity to lecture me about the benefits of marrying a good woman and the wonders of love. All the usual nonsense that a reformed rake is prone to as he grows old and finds mortality staring him in the face.'

'That seems a rather jaundiced way of looking at it. Perhaps he really was in love?'

'Spare me the romantic twaddle, Serena. He was in lust, not in love. And he was a hypocrite, which is something I cannot be accused of. I indulge my passions for gaming, horses and women, but I never play when I can't pay. I never put a horse at a fence it can't take. I never trifle with women who don't know the score. Which is more,' Nicholas concluded bitterly, 'from what I've heard about my father in his younger days, than can be said for him.'

'Perhaps that's part of it—his wanting to prevent you making his mistakes. My father wrapped me in cotton wool for the same sort of reasons, and in some ways—I am only beginning to realise it now—it was suffocating. You, on the other hand, were positively neglected, but that did not prevent your father from wishing to dictate your life.'

'The difference between us is that I will not allow him to. You, on the other hand, are still dancing to Papa's tune.'

Serena bit her lip, for he had hit a nerve. 'For the moment. So,' she continued brightly, 'despite your father's attempts, you have not been converted to the conquering power of love as espoused by Lord Byron.'

'That deluded romantic! The man has almost single-handedly brought love and languishing back into fashion.'

'It seems to me that Lord Byron is more interested in indulging his own rather eclectic tastes and encouraging everyone, poor Lady Lamb included, to worship at the altar of his ego,' Serena said scornfully. 'In any case, real love doesn't come in or go out of fashion, as I have no doubt Lord Byron will. You can't stop it or avoid it. You can't be cured of it and you can't dictate how it happens either. Some people never fall in love because they never meet the right person. My parents were fortunate. It may be that your father was too, with his Melissa. It is possible that his wanting you to change your ways was not hypocritical, but a desire for you to be as happy as he was.' She stopped abruptly, taken aback by the passion of her own response.

'I'm afraid we'll just have to differ on that,' Nicholas said dismissively. 'It's a pretty point of view, and you are a charming advocate, but I remain unconvinced. You know less of the world and its travails than you think if you really mean what you say.'

With difficulty Serena managed to repress the hot retort that rose to her lips. 'I won't quarrel with you, there's no point. *I* won't persuade you, only experience will do that.'

'Indulge me, though, by explaining one thing to me before we drop the subject.'

She raised her brows enquiringly.

'Yesterday by the trout stream you seemed more than happy to encourage me to—for us to—for things between us to take their course. Today you rhapsodise about true love. I'm concerned that we are at cross-purposes.'

'In what way?'

'I can never offer you love, Serena, I won't be such a hypocrite as my father. I can promise you fun, perhaps, pleasure definitely, but it would be a brief idyll, nothing more. I won't pretend to any finer feelings to ease your conscience. If you choose to pick up where we left off from our kiss, you must do so with your eyes wide open.'

Serena paused for a moment before replying. She was not in love, but tossing and turning in her bed last night, she had been forced to acknowledge the depth of her attraction to him. The pang of physical awareness she had felt when first she encountered him, stripped to the waist in the boxing ring, had grown during the hours they spent together. Hidden away from the rest of the world as they were, time slipped by more and more quickly. Whenever she saw him, the urge to give in to temptation became harder to resist, fuelled by the knowledge that once she had her papers their paths were unlikely to cross again. The sensible voice in her head warned her that to give in to her desires was to risk being burned, but this feeling of rightness when she was with him continued to grow regardless.

Nicholas would take whatever she offered, provided she stuck to his terms. His feelings for her were of a fleeting nature. It had been unintentional, but his reaction to her eulogy on true love was a timely warning. 'My eyes are very wide open,' she told him with certainty. 'We are not at cross-purposes, I assure you.'

Did that mean she would grant him more than a kiss? It was on his mind to ask her, but he thought better of it. 'I have some business to attend to for the rest of the morning,' he said instead. 'I'll join you after lunch.'

Mathew Stamppe, lately become Lord Vespian, had had a busy morning, which included a long-overdue visit to the dentist, a fitting with his tailor and various commissions for his good lady wife. The existence of a niece, a chit of a girl heir to the fortune that was rightfully his, vexed him beyond words and continually dogged his thoughts. Tobias Acton had advised him to sit tight and wait on her contacting him, but this, Mathew had decided, was not a course of action to which he could inure himself.

His next piece of business took him to a flash tavern just off the Fleet where he was to meet up with an ex-Runner recommended by his club doorman. Mathew sat uncomfortably in a booth, warily eyeing the unsavoury clientele of the dimly lit room, relieved that he had taken the precaution of leaving all his valuables, save the required purse of money, safe in his lodgings.

A short, compact man in a greasy brown coat approached him. 'You Stamppe?' he enquired loudly.

'For pity's sake, man, keep your voice down,' Mathew hissed.

The man smiled. 'No need to worry on that score, squire. Folk in here have learned the hard way to mind their own business, if you get my meaning. Now, let's see the readies.'

He bit delicately into one of the coins from the bag which Mathew handed him. Satisfied with the quality, he called for a glass of fire water and awaited instruction.

Mathew's orders were vague. When pressed to be more specific, he flapped. 'Just do whatever you see fit, I want no details.'

The ex-Runner smiled knowingly. He had come across the type many times before. Happy enough to pay someone else to do their dirty work, but too squeamish to think about what they had paid for actually entailed. It suited him well enough. He signified his agreement by raising his glass in a toast before tossing it back with a satisfied smack of the lips. Then he was gone.

After a lunch alone, Nicholas still being engaged upon business, Serena flicked through some volumes of Shakespeare in a half-hearted way, searching for the source of the last rose of summer quotation. By the time he joined her she was heartily bored.

'Forget about that for today, let's play cards instead,' he said, lounging in the doorway.

'Cards,' Serena exclaimed in surprise.

'Yes, why not? Can you not play?'

'Very well, actually. Whatever you want.'

'Piquet?'

'If you wish. But just for penny points.'

Nicholas laughed. 'I'm considered to be a very good player.'

'Oh, I'm not worried,' Serena said airily, 'I've played a lot of cards in my time.'

'Another of the skills learned at dear Papa's knee, no doubt,' he quipped.

She chuckled. 'If only you knew.'

'Since you're so confident, we should make the stakes more interesting. A forfeit.'

'It depends what you have in mind.'

'You're expecting me to say a kiss, but I won't be so predictable.'

His smile was irresistible. 'What, then?' Serena asked.

'A lock of your hair. Something with which to remember our time here.' He surprised himself at the fancifulness of his request, was still more surprised when she agreed.

'Deal,' she said, handing him the cards with a glint in her eye that should have worried him.

As the rubbers progressed it became clear that Serena's claim to skill had been no idle boast. Nicholas was losing steadily.

'Well, I make that—let's see…' Serena added up the score and showed him the total.

'Confound it, I never lose by such a margin. Are you sure?'

'Quite sure,' Serena said smugly. 'Now you must pay the forfeit.' She opened her reticule, producing a pair of embroidery scissors, brandishing them before him triumphantly. He ran his fingers through his carefully cropped hair, much alarmed. 'Give me those, I'll do it.'

Serena shook her head. 'To the victor the spoils, Nicholas. What was it you said, *"I never play when I can't pay"*?'

'You're enjoying this.'

She nodded primly, her eyes brimming with laughter.

He made a dive for the scissors, but she quickly put them behind her back. 'Kneel before me, Mr Lytton,' she commanded, 'I would not wish to ruin your coiffure.'

He held her gaze as he knelt, a wicked smile curling the corners of his mouth, his eyes reflecting the laughter in hers. 'You will regret this, *mademoiselle*.'

'I don't think so. Stay still.' She bent over his head. Her dress brushed against his face, which was disconcertingly close to her thighs. Heat rushed through her body.

'I told you you'd regret it,' Nicholas said wickedly, his voice muffled by the material of her skirt. 'I, on the other hand, am finding this position rather delightful.'

Serena froze. *Was that his breath she could feel through her petticoats?* A quick snip and a lock of silky black hair fell into her hand. 'There, you can stand up now,' she managed breathlessly.

He gazed up at her with such a smile that her knees

almost buckled. 'Why don't you come down here and join me? It's very—good God!'

'What is it?'

'The last rose of summer left blooming alone. I've just remembered, it's a song. And there it is. Come here.'

'Very funny. Get up.'

'No, I mean it,' Nicholas said. 'Look.'

She carefully placed his curl in her reticule with her scissors and dropped to her knees beside him. He took her by the shoulders and pointed her at the fireplace. Two panels decorated with delicate plasterwork filled the gap on each side between the mantel and the book cases. On one the figure of a man held a flower stalk in his hand. On the opposite panel was a tomb, around and on top of which the petals of the flower were scattered.

'Oh!' Serena clapped her hands together in excitement.

'*The last rose of summer*. Melissa used to sing it—damned melancholy thing, but it tickled my father. He knew the poet who wrote it, years before it was set to music. I can't think why I didn't remember until now. Go on then, they're your papers, see if you can find the latch.'

The panels were not large, starting from the wainscoting and ending at head height. Carefully, Serena felt her way around the edges of the one on the right, with shaking fingers seeking a gap or a mechanism, but there was nothing. She tried again. Nothing. Disappointed, she sat back on her heels.

'Maybe it's on the other one. Let me try.' Nicholas

joined her, kneeling on the floor beside the panel depicting the young man and the flower stalk. As Serena had, he felt his way around the panel. Then he looked more closely at the stalk, which seemed to be detached from the plaster beneath it. Carefully, he twisted it. It turned. The tombstone with its rose petals slid back to reveal a cavity in the wall. Inside lay a small packet sealed with red wax, a name written in faded ink on the front.

Serena reached in. *Philip Stamppe, his last will and testament.* Her father's name leapt out from the paper in flowing script. She felt herself go faint, and staggered to her feet.

Nicholas poured her a small measure of brandy. 'Sit, drink this.'

Serena drank, spluttering as the cognac seared the back of her throat. Then drank some more, savouring the calming effect of the liquor. 'I'm sorry, it's the shock, seeing his name, that's all. I'm better now.'

He was almost as shocked himself, to find that the papers actually existed. As the implications began to make their way into his brain, Nicholas cursed inwardly, for now his precipitate action had ensured that Serena had no further reason to stay and he was not ready for her to go. Not yet.

She turned over the little packet of documents on her lap, but made no attempt to break the seals.

'Am I permitted to know what they are?'

She was sorely tempted to tell him everything, but to do so would be to call a halt to whatever this thing was between them, and she was not willing to do that. Not yet. 'My father's will,' she conceded, 'and some papers confirming my identity.'

'You don't seem particularly overjoyed to see them.'

She looked up. 'I expect you are, though. It means I won't need to trespass on your time any longer.'

'Must you go straight away?'

'I ought to.'

'That's not what I asked.'

'I know.'

Nicholas stared frowningly out of the window. 'Leave it another couple of days and I'll be able to escort you myself. I should have news of my duelling opponent by then, and in the meantime I can show you a bit of the countryside. Do you ride?'

'Yes, but—'

'Good. We'll go riding tomorrow,' he said decisively.

'I should go to London tomorrow.'

'Stay. Let us have a day's grace, without worrying about papers or panelling or—or anything.'

Serena folded the documents into her reticule along with the lock of Nicholas's hair as she thought through his suggestion. He had not pressed her as to their content. Did that mean he didn't care, or he didn't want to know? And if she stayed another day, what was implied? More than just a gallop across the countryside, or was she reading too much into it? *He would not take what was not freely given.* She believed him, but she did not trust herself. Already, part of her had rushed ahead like a stampeding horse, looking forward to the morrow. She tried to rein it in. 'A day's grace,' she said. 'Yes, I'd like that', though even as she spoke, doubt seized her.

Nicholas took her hand and pulled her to her feet. His smile was warm, drawing from her a response that banished everything save a tingle of anticipation, a rush of pleasure. 'Come on, then,' he said to her, 'I'll walk you back to your lodgings.'

'*Tiens*, I thought you were never coming back, *mademoiselle*, I was about to send someone out in search of you.' Madame LeClerc, arms crossed impatiently, greeted Serena from the doorway. Dressed in her habitual black, her pale eyes peering short-sightedly at her charge, she had the look of a well-fed mole startled from its burrow.

'I'm sorry to have kept you waiting,' Serena said soothingly. 'Let's go in. You'll be wanting your dinner.'

'Pah,' Madame LeClerc said contemptuously, though whether she referred to Nicholas's retreating figure or dinner was not clear. Once inside, she commenced her habitual lament. 'I am tired of waiting, Mademoiselle Serena, when will we be on our way?'

'Not so very long now,' Serena said patiently, 'my business is almost concluded.'

'Business! Is that what you call it. The whole village is talking of you,' Madame LeClerc said spitefully.

Serena turned from the mirror where she had been

tidying her hair. 'You shouldn't listen to idle gossip, Madame LeClerc, I'm sure there must be more productive ways for you to pass your time.'

'What am I to do here, exactly' Madame responded angrily. 'The women dress in sacks and aprons. When I try to advise the cook on how to make a nice French *ragoût*, she orders me from the kitchen. And now there is a strange man pestering me with silly questions.'

'What strange man?'

'A round man with a greasy coat. He knocked on the door and talked at me. I don't know what he said, but I thought he was a person most suspect.'

'He was probably just lost; I shouldn't worry about it.'

'That is all very well for you to say, *mademoiselle*, but you leave me alone all day when you go off to the big house. What if he had ravished me, what then?'

Serena spluttered with the effort of turning her giggle into an unconvincing cough. 'I am relieved he did not.'

'Much you would care if he did!'

Realising that she was genuinely upset, Serena spoke more soothingly. 'I promise you we won't be here for much longer. Now let's forget about strange men, and eat whatever nice English food our landlady has prepared for us before it gets cold.'

They sat down to dinner at the table in the parlour, but Madame was not content to drop the subject of village gossip. 'They say you spend all day in the company of this Monsieur Lytton. They say that you are his mistress,' she informed Serena through a mouthful of rabbit pie. 'They say you must be, given his reputation with the ladies.'

'I'm not interested in gossip,' Serena replied sternly.

'Yes, but, Serena—Mademoiselle Cachet—you should be more discreet; your papa would not be pleased.'

'*C'est mon affaire, madame*, none of your business. Since Mr Lytton's father was one of Papa's oldest friends, I'll thank you to hold your tongue. Eat your dinner; I want to hear no more of this.'

It was only village gossip, but it worried her none the less. She did not doubt that much of the speculation had originated from Madame LeClerc herself, but that was no consolation.

Retiring early to the privacy of her chamber, Serena finally broke the seal on her father's will with shaking fingers. By the time she had worked her way through the lengthy and highly technical content, her candle was guttering, throwing strange shapes onto the walls. The sums of money mentioned staggered her. Until now, she had not quite believed it was true, so outlandish had been Papa's tale, but the facts were there in parchment and ink. She was indeed an heiress, a considerable one.

Getting out of bed, she folded the documents carefully into a drawer of her jewel case before taking out the necklace Papa had given her for her last birthday. It was a simple but beautiful piece of jewellery, a gold locket with a sapphire in the centre, surrounded by a pattern of tiny diamonds. She opened it and carefully placed the lock of Nicholas's hair inside, unable to resist pressing upon it a little kiss. Then she snuffed the candle and climbed wearily into bed.

Lady Serena Stamppe. It sounded so strange to her ears. Not at all like herself, but like someone in a book or in a painting. Someone far more dignified, older, more refined than she. Lady Serena. The Honourable Lady Serena. Nicholas would be amused. No, Nicholas would not be at all amused. She would not think about that. Not yet. Not until after tomorrow.

Next door, Madame's snoring stopped. Taking this as a good omen, Serena fell into a deep sleep.

Chapter Four

Serena woke to a fresh sunny morning. It augured well for the promised outing, which she was looking forward to enormously. She checked her appearance in the mirror one last time before going downstairs. Her riding habit was of deep blue velvet, and the small hat trimmed with feathers of a matching colour sat jauntily atop her golden curls. It was not one of Madame LeClerc's creations, having been fashioned for her by an English tailor in Paris, the mannish cut of the short jacket serving to emphasise the very feminine curves concealed beneath it.

Madame LeClerc was wont to sleep late and had not yet risen, and for this Serena was grateful. She could imagine the fevered speculation that would be aroused by the sight of herself setting off to ride out alone with Nicholas. Madame's expressive Gallic eyebrows would shoot up to new heights, possibly to disappear entirely under the frill of her cap. With a chuckle, Serena gathered the long trail of skirt over her arm and closed the door of her lodgings quietly behind her. She stepped gaily out into the bright April sunshine and set off for the Hall with a sense of anticipation and well being.

The way was damp underfoot. The scent of fresh earth and wet grass carried on the gentle breeze stimulated her senses. Though she missed Paris and greatly looked forward to seeing London, with all the famous sites she'd heard so much of, at this precise moment she was in no rush to get there. In a way, she was starting to think of this lush green land as home. How she envied Nicholas the beauty of Knightswood Hall. How she envied him the casual acceptance and ease of manner with which he took it all for granted. Papa had imbued his daughter with his own excellent address and confidence, but there were nevertheless times when Serena felt overwhelmed by the elegance of Knightswood Hall and its dashing owner. She was not at all convinced of her ability to play the role of a lady for the London Season in which her father had insisted she should take part, once her true position was known. She was even less convinced than ever of her desire to do so.

Overseeing the saddling of the two horses as Serena made the now-familiar short walk from the village, Nicholas was also musing on the subject of his family's ancestral home. During past visits to the Hall the solitude, lack of entertainment and the early country hours had been a trial. In Serena's company he looked on it all with a fresh eye. Seeing the house from her perspective, he could admire its beauty anew, could appreciate its quirks and inconveniences as the product of its evolution, tangible evidence of its history and provenance. For perhaps the first time ever he felt a genuine sense of pride at being the owner and custodian of the Lytton estate.

The fresh green loveliness of the English spring bursting forth in all its glory before him was something else he had missed, since it coincided with the height of the Season and the hustle, bustle and grime of London. He was making up for lost time now. At some point its appeal would begin to pall, he had no doubt. As would Serena's. But not yet.

He knew enough of her to be certain that she would not change her mind about leaving. At best he had only today and tomorrow. He would wait no longer to sample more of her charms. The thought ignited his senses, an unaccustomed sense of anticipation making him jerk on the bridle in his hand. Titus whinnied and flared his nostrils. The dappled grey mare standing next to him pranced skittishly.

'I'll take them round the front myself,' Nicholas said, casually dismissing the groom. Grabbing both sets of reins, he set off on foot through the archway, out of the stable block and towards the house. Rounding the path which led to the front, he met Serena coming from the opposite direction.

Seeing Nicholas stride towards her, leading a horse in each hand, a dazzling smile illuminating his handsome features, she felt her breath catch in her throat. His cravat was snowy white against the strong line of his jaw. A plain dark-brown riding coat buttoned tight across his chest emphasised the width of his shoulders. Looking down, past the cutaway of the coat, the waistcoat of biscuit hue adorned with a single fob, she drank in long muscular legs clad in his favourite buckskins and impeccably polished short boots with long tops. She swallowed. The soft leather of his breeches seemed moulded to his shape so tightly she would swear she could see his muscles ripple underneath as he walked, the square-cut tails of his coat flying out behind him. His hands were clothed in gloves of the same close-fitting soft leather. In one of them he carried a riding whip. He was, Serena thought, not beautiful, that was quite the wrong word, but astonishingly, compellingly attractive.

Trying not to stare like a besotted schoolgirl, she turned her attention to the horses he was leading. The large imperious stallion could only be his. The other horse was smaller, a lovely dappled grey with expressive, intelligent eyes. 'Oh, is this my mare?' She ran the last few steps, going straight to the horse's head, producing some lumps of sugar from a pocket in her habit. 'She's lovely.'

'Yes, she is,' Nicholas said, his eyes on Serena.

He took her hand, pressing a kiss to her knuckles,

smiling into her eyes in a way that left her in no doubt of his thoughts. Serena felt a responsive shiver. Beside her the horse pawed nervously at the ground.

'Her name is Belle,' Nicholas told her, handing over the reins. 'She can be quite lively—do you think you'll be able to handle her?'

'I'm sure we'll get along splendidly. I expect she just needs a gallop. I'm looking forward to it almost as much as she is.'

'Well, just take it easy until we're out in the fields. Come here and I'll help you up.'

She mounted with ease, draping her long skirts gracefully over the pommel. Belle pranced and pawed, held firmly in a light grip. They set off at a brisk trot side by side down the lane and out into the fields. Serena rode well, straight-backed and light handed, the feathers in her hat flying out in the breeze as she urged the mare into a gallop. Beside her, Nicholas and Titus kept pace. The countryside rushed by in a swirl of green and brown accompanied by the thud of the horses' hooves, the whistle of the wind in her ears, an occasional rustle in the undergrowth as some small animal fled from their path. Gradually they slowed to a canter and then to a trot, lazily following the meanderings of a burbling stream.

Flushed from the exercise, her eyes bright with curiosity, Serena asked Nicholas to tell her more about their surroundings, surprised to find that almost all the land belonged to him. Her questions forced him to dig deep into the recesses of his brain for answers. It was gratifying, how quickly it all came flooding back to him.

'I hadn't realised you were such an expert on farming,' she teased.

'I'm not really. My bailiff manages it all; I can't claim any credit for the good heart the land is in.'

'But you clearly understand how the estate works.'

'I spent a lot of time here in my youth, even though I don't come down so often now.'

'It's so beautiful here, I love it. You're very lucky.'

'I suppose I am. Do you plan to stay on in England?' he asked curiously.

'Yes, I think so.'

'In London?'

'I don't know.' In truth she had no idea. 'Maybe I'll find my own place in the country.'

'So your father's will left you well provided for?'

'Yes. But we said…'

'I know, that we wouldn't talk about it today.' He reined in his horse. 'We should go back. If we follow the stream for another mile or so, we can loop round through the West Farm and approach the Hall from the north.'

Serena nodded her agreement. They had passed the main buildings of the farm and were approaching the edge of the grounds of the Hall when she dropped back a little, distracted by a sound from the hedgerow to her left. As she leaned over in the saddle to try to see what creature was making the strange noise, the unmistakable sound of a shot pierced the air. The bullet whizzed over her head, missing her by inches.

Hearing the crack, Nicholas pulled Titus up sharply, turning round in the saddle just in time to see Serena's horse rear up into the air before bolting, with Serena still clinging on. Quickly wheeling Titus round, pressing his heels into the horse's flanks to urge him on, Nicholas galloped after Serena as she hung grimly on to her horse's neck and careered across the field. Coming alongside, Nicholas leaned over precariously to grab the horse's bit. 'Whoah, Belle, whoah, girl,' he said gently. The mare slowly came to a halt.

'Are you all right?' he asked anxiously.

'Yes, I'm fine, I'm fine.' Serena sat up in the saddle. She was as white as a sheet, but had herself firmly in hand. Taking her reins back from Nicholas, she focused her attention on soothing Belle, whispering calming platitudes in her ear. Gradually, the mare ceased her fidgeting. Serena looked up to find Nicholas frowning heavily, staring over her shoulder at the direction from which the shot had been fired. 'What is it?' she asked him. 'Did you see anything?'

'Nothing at all. I felt something whizzing over my head, but I didn't see where it came from.'

'It came from over there.' He pointed to a clump of trees leading into a wood at the boundary of the property. 'I'm going to have a look. There's a barn at the other side of the field, you and Belle can wait there. You've had quite a shock. Are you feeling well enough to ride?'

'I'm fine. But—can't I come with you?'

'No, go and wait for me there. I won't be long. I expect it was a stray shot fired by a poacher, in which case he'll likely be long gone. What he was shooting at this time of year in broad daylight I have no idea though—rabbits, maybe.'

'They would need to be flying rabbits,' Serena said with a weak attempt at humour. 'That bullet would have gone into my head if I hadn't bent down.'

'That thought had not escaped me,' Nicholas replied grimly. 'Go and rest, Serena. I'll join you shortly.'

Giving her no time to protest, Nicholas galloped off in the direction of the wood. Serena headed for the barn, where she dismounted and tied the mare up beside a convenient water trough. The sky was lowering, the morning's brightness giving way to a squally April breeze. Rain threatened.

By the time Nicholas returned half an hour later it had started to pour, and Serena was beginning to fret.

'I thought something had happened to you.'

He grinned at the charming picture she made, framed by the doorway in her blue velvet suit with her bright gold hair dishevelled. 'Don't be silly, did you think the poacher would shoot me? More likely the other way round, as punishment for his recklessness. Go inside, I'll just put Titus beside Belle. We might as well wait out the rain here, it will pass over soon enough'

He had found no trace of a poacher, not that he had

really expected to do so. He had checked with Farmer Jeffries, whom he had spotted working the fields nearby, but he had seen nothing either, although he had heard the shot. The poacher had aimed high, possibly startled into loosing the gun. It was the only explanation that made sense, Nicholas told himself, for the alternative was that someone had shot deliberately at Serena, and that made absolutely no sense at all. He decided not to worry her unnecessarily with this absurd notion. 'It was an unfortunate accident, nothing more, but a most unsettling experience none the less. Are you sure you're all right, Serena?'

She gave him a weak smile by way of reply. She seemed determined to appear little shaken despite the closeness of the bullet. She had real pluck, Nicholas thought with admiration. Every other woman of his acquaintance would have swooned.

'I'm fine,' she reassured him again. 'I got a fright and let my horse bolt, for which I am ashamed. Thank you, Mr Lytton, for being my knight errant. I'm sorry to have put you to the trouble.' She dropped a curtsy.

'It was an honour, *mademoiselle*,' Nicholas replied with a bow.

He closed over the door to block out the rain, which was now falling heavily. 'It's not exactly salubrious, but at least it will keep us dry,' he said, surveying the space. The barn was small, enclosed on all sides. Apart from some bales of hay stacked in one corner and a pitchfork leaning on the wall beside them, it was empty.

Rain pattered on the roof. A gusty wind whistled through the rough wooden walls. Serena shivered, making for the bales of hay, which formed a break against the draughts. 'We can sit over here, it's at least a little more comfortable.'

Nicholas followed her. Serena perched on one of the bales, reaching up to remove her hat. The action stretched the tight-fitting jacket of her habit against the contours of her body, the soft velvet outlining the fullness of her breasts. The long line of her throat showed creamy white above the lace of her collar. Turning, she found Nicholas gazing down at her, desire writ plain across his face.

Her heart picked up a beat. They were alone in an isolated barn. A ramshackle building with only bales of straw for comfort, hardly the setting she would have picked for her first experience in seduction. But the raw need on Nicholas's face was unmistakable. She had only to acquiesce.

Nervously, Serena pushed a stray curl from her eyes. *Did she want this?* Her whole body screamed yes, but still she tried to be certain in her mind. It was an irrevocable step to take. An idyll, that's how Nicholas saw it. She was not so sure she would be able to think of it in quite the same way afterwards.

Afterwards. *Had she then already made up her mind?* The atmosphere between them crackled with tension. Nicholas stood looking down at her, one brow raised. She knew what he was asking. Knew too that he would accept her no, though he wanted her yes. *She* wanted to say yes. Right here, right now, she wanted to say yes more than anything. But would she feel the same way tomorrow, and the next day, and the next? To surrender herself to him could be to cast the dice irrevocably. Was that really what she wanted? But to draw back from the game now would be to regret having done so for ever, wouldn't it?

'Serena?'

Why must he ask? Why must he look at her like that, so she could not think straight? She stood up, reaching to brush a lock of hair from his brow. It was damp from the rain. Black as coal. Soft as silk. She pushed it back, running her fingers along the contour of his skull, trailing them down his neck, fluttering against his skin. *What was he thinking?*

He smelled of rain and horse and man. His skin was cool and damp. She ran her fingers up through the short hair on the back of his neck. *What was she doing?*

Their eyes locked, blue on grey, deepening into dark pools of desire. With a harsh intake of breath, Nicholas pulled her roughly to him, holding her close, gripping her waist, cupping her head through her curls. Angling his mouth on to hers, he kissed her hard, engulfing her in sudden heat and passion and fire. Soft curves melted into hard planes.

He deepened the kiss. She reached her arms around him, under the material of his coat, against the soft linen of his shirt, the silk of his waistcoat, feeling the heat of his skin through the delicate material. Her hands roamed across his back, kneading the rippling muscles, tracing the knotted line of his spine. He was all bone and muscle and sinew. Power and strength coiled tight. Heady. Strange. Frighteningly, dizzyingly exciting.

Nicholas groaned, thrusting his tongue into her mouth, his kisses demanding, hardening, deepening. Long passionate kisses. Tiny licking kisses. Nibbling on the corners of her mouth, sucking on her bottom lip, his tongue tangling with her own, sweeping across the tender skin on the inside of her mouth. Licking and sucking and thrusting.

He pulled her closer, pressing his arousal against her through the soft leather of his buckskins. Shockingly hard. Unimaginable. *Now, now was the time to stop.* To stop before she *did* imagine. What it would feel like. What it would feel like…

She was hot. Her body thrummed, pulsed, pounded, throbbed. She was a hard core of heat, yet she was melting.

Nicholas licked, and she followed. He bit her lip gently, and she nicked his bottom lip between her own teeth. Tentatively touched her tongue to his when he thrust. She wanted to touch him, but did not know how. She knew she should stop, but did not know how. 'Nicholas,' she heard herself say, though surely that was not her voice?

He was still kissing her. Drugging, swollen, swooning kisses, as if he would suck the lifeblood from her. She gave and gave and gave and still he kissed her more. He undid the large buttons of his riding coat and waistcoat, shrugging out of both together. The tiny buttons on her own jacket surrendered to his hands, though she could not have said how. They stood chest to chest. She was breathing as if she had been running. Nicholas, too, his chest heaving, like in the fight. She had no will, no will of her own any more, save to do as he bid.

He tugged the folds of his shirt free from his breeches and took her hands, placing her palms flat on his heated skin. She ran them wonderingly along his ribcage, down the line of his torso to the indent at his waist, relishing the shivering response her touch elicited as she used her hands to draw the map of his body. Her fingers encountered the barrier of his breeches. She pulled her hand back as if she had been burned. She *was* burning.

Nicholas looked down at her anxiously. Her eyelids were heavy over the deep blue of her eyes, the long dark lashes fanned out over her cheeks. Her hair was undone from its pins, rippling down her back in long ringlets, one tress curling provocatively over her flushed cheek. Her lips were swollen from his kisses. She looked every bit as wanton, even more arousing than in all his fevered late-night imaginings.

'Serena?'

She stared up at him. He took her hand again, placed it back on his chest, relishing the feel of her skin on his, while desperately trying to read her thoughts. *Was she frightened?* For a moment he thought so. *Because this was the first time?* For a moment he hoped so. *Because it was not?* No, don't think of that.

Beneath the soft silk of her blouse he could see her breasts rise and fall. He could see the hard peaks of her nipples. Carefully he tugged the lace at her neck, finding the fastenings, slowly undoing them, until her blouse was open to the waist. Her breathing quickened. Her hand curled into the muscle of his chest, but she did not stop him. He pulled the blouse free from the waistband of her skirt. He tugged at her undergarments, expertly freeing her breasts from the wisps of lace and fine lawn cotton that constrained them. At the first touch of his thumbs on her nipples Serena moaned, slumping back against the bales of hay.

She wanted him. Nicholas arranged her gently, supporting her against the straw. She was a picture to rob any man of control, with her golden hair spread out like a fan, her countenance flushed, her eyes heavy with desire. The creamy mounds of her breasts with their rosy-tipped peaks rose and fell alluringly against the white of her undergarments. Just exactly as he'd pictured. The blue velvet of her skirt trailed out beneath her. Nicholas drank his fill of the vision, his breathing heavy, his heart thumping erratically as desire surged painfully through him.

'Nicholas.'

Serena breathed his name in that special way of

hers, watching him through eyes slumberous with desire. She was no vision. She was flesh and blood and heat and luscious, perfect curves. And his, all his. Pushing her legs apart under the voluminous skirt of her riding habit, Nicholas knelt down in front of her. Cupping her full breasts in his hands, he licked the soft undersides, teasing her nipples into hard, swollen fullness between his fingers, pinching them just enough to make her moan with the overwhelming pleasure of it. He leaned in closer, circling her nipples with his tongue, flicking over the hard peaks, sucking gently, then hard, gently, then hard.

She was mindless. She was lost. She was frightened by what was happening to her, but in a way that made her want more. Heat spread out from her belly, a dull glow turning into a burning ember, sparks flying out through her veins, igniting her blood, making her burn. *Was this normal?* Serena writhed restlessly. She didn't want him ever to stop. His mouth on her. His hands on her. He was making her do things. Things she didn't know she knew.

She should stop. She couldn't stop. She arched against him, pushing her body into him, finding the restraining cloth of her skirt, his breeches, an unbearable barrier. 'Nicholas.' She breathed his name again, slanting open her eyes to look at him, hot hands, hot mouth, hot eyes on her. She wanted this, and now she wanted something else too.

Nicholas lifted the hem of her blue velvet skirt,

pushing it up around her waist to reveal the long graceful line of her legs. Little boots laced tight around delicate ankles. Silk stockings clinging to the outline of her calves, their ribbons tied under the lace-trimmed edges of her underwear. *God, so beautiful.*

Serena blushed because he was looking. Blushed because she could see he liked looking. Blushed because she liked him looking. She shifted under his gaze.

The movement caused the gap between her pantaloons to open, giving Nicholas a brief, tantalising view of blonde curls. He inhaled sharply, drinking in her body hungrily, feasting on the full length of her legs, the outline of her thighs under the delicate lawn of her underclothes, breathing in the smell of hay, her flowery perfume, the elusive musky scent of vanilla which seemed to emanate from her skin. With his eyes closed, he ran one hand teasingly from the top of her boot up over her stocking and along the velvet-soft skin on the inside of her thigh, feeling her rippling response. Running his hand over her other leg, he breathed in deeply, relishing the smell of her, the feel of her, the lines and textures of her. A multitude of sensations bubbled through his blood, making him swell with desire, wild with the anticipation of possession.

He reached for the gap in her pantaloons, unerringly finding the source of her heat. Gently, he touched, stroked, pressed. She responded, pushing against his hand. He pushed her legs apart, revealing all the glory of her soft curls, her creamy white thighs, her wet centre.

Serena felt the heat of his mouth, a gentle breath on her thighs. She tightened, her body a bow stretched taut to breaking point. He was licking. The slow sweep of his tongue made her gasp. He licked again, teasing her, circling around the rough edges of desire, homing in, then out again, stroking her with his fingers, pushing her back when she arched against his mouth, his determined control of her frustrating and stimulating at the same time.

Lost, lost, lost. Serena moaned and pushed and twisted against him, wet with need, overcome with wanting. Still the licking teased, brought her to the edge, withdrew, driving her into a frenzy, making her feel as if she teetered on the brink of some huge chasm, wanting Nicholas to push her, wanting to jump, unable to do so without him. She was terrified he would not make her.

Make me, Nicholas, she wanted to say, though she didn't, she couldn't, she wouldn't. *Please.* He heard her. *Did he hear her?* Heat erupted suddenly, ripped through her, and she shattered, her whole body pulsing outwards from the centre of her climax, mindless, falling, whirling, lost. Her hands clenched on the straw at her sides, her heels dug into the bales supporting her, and she moaned over and over in a rhythm of her own, shaking, hot, trembling, wet.

Nicholas raised himself up, bending to kiss her. Serena reached up to pull him close, her mouth hot on his, kissing him back passionately, wild with the need to taste him, to make him feel what she was feeling, to take him to the place where she was.

He breathed hard against her, struggling with the fastenings of his breeches, desperate now to finish what they had begun. The final button on his buckskins gave way, and at last he was free from constraint. He took her hand, placing it on his erection, closing his eyes in pleasure at the feel of her butterfly touch fluttering over him. He was so highly sensitised he could almost feel the ridges and swirls of her fingertips.

Serena looked in awe at the thick jutting length of him. So strange. She could feel the pulse of his blood. She could feel the tension in him etched into every muscle. Here, here was where the centre of all that power was. He took her hand and wrapped it around his hardness. She watched his response with a mounting sense of excitement as she touched him carefully, stroking him, cupping him, watching him, learning from the way he moved, throbbed, moaned under her caresses. Something fierce clutched at her insides. Something powerful and horribly addictive. She ran her thumb over his silky smooth tip. She thought she'd done something wrong. Then she saw from his face that she hadn't.

With a low husky growl Nicholas pushed her back against the hay. As he stood over her, made ready to plunge into her wet, honeyed centre, he became dimly aware of an insistent noise. The door to the barn was being rattled fiercely. He stilled, unable to believe his ears. *Not now. Please God, not now.*

'Who's in there? Is that you, Master Nicholas?'

Nicholas swore furiously. Tearing his eyes from the vision in front of him, he quickly fastened his breeches, carelessly thrusting the ends of his shirt into them. 'Stay here,' he whispered to Serena, making swiftly for the door, slipping outside before Farmer Jeffries could glimpse the scene inside.

'I thought I recognised Titus,' the farmer said. 'Is there anything wrong, Master Nicholas? Only, after the shot, I came out to check things over for myself, and found your horses tied up.'

'The rain,' Nicholas said, running a hand through his dishevelled locks. 'We were sheltering from the rain.'

The farmer looked as if he were about to say something, but to Nicholas's relief he contented himself with a nod. 'Just as you say, Master Nicholas. I'll keep an eye out for that poacher. Good day to you.'

'Good day, Jeffries.'

Nicholas returned to the barn. Serena was huddled on the hay, struggling with the buttons of her jacket. Her skin was flushed, her lips raw and swollen. 'You look quite delectable. Here, let me help you.' He pulled a piece of straw from her hair.

She blushed fiery red, getting to her feet, studiously avoiding his eyes as she brushed out her skirts. 'I should go.'

Nicholas studied her as she adjusted the lace at her

neck and pinned the little hat, its feather still drooping with rain, rather lopsidedly back in place. A few moments ago she had been like molten heat in his arms. Now she was simply embarrassed. The horrible suspicion that he had completely mistaken her could not be ignored. He looked around him at the draughty barn, the forlorn bales of hay, and abandoned any idea of continuing where they had left off. *What had he been thinking!*

He picked up his hat and riding crop. 'You're quite right, you should go home. We'll finish this tomorrow, when we can be sure of no interruptions.'

'Tomorrow.' Serena gave a rather forlorn smile. 'Yes, we'll finish this tomorrow.'

He was perturbed by her tone. 'I'll see you home. We'll ride to your lodgings, I can lead Belle back.'

'There's no need.'

'Come on, before the rain starts again.' He threw her efficiently into the saddle and they cantered back to the village in silence. As she handed him Belle's reins, the rain began again in earnest.

Serena opened the door of her rooms on her return to find an empty grate and a note from Madame LeClerc informing her that the *modiste* had accepted a ride to London with their landlady's son. Crumpling the letter and hurling it into the grate, Serena cursed shockingly fluently in Madame's native language. Her own journey to London would now have to be undertaken alone. Unless Nicholas escorted her. Serena sighed. She doubted very much he'd be inclined to do so after tomorrow.

She lay awake for most of that night, deeply troubled by the day's events. The feelings that Nicholas's love-making had aroused in her were frightening in their intensity. Despite her lack of experience, she knew it was more than mere physical attraction—at least on her part. She was out of her depth, in danger of drowning in the heady potion of desire, attraction and affinity that made up their relationship. In her heart of hearts she knew what she felt for Nicholas was not the fleeting fancy of a spring idyll. If the farmer had not interrupted them, she would have lost more than her innocence. She would have lost her heart.

As a grey dawn crept through the folds of the heavy curtains, Serena forced herself to acknowledge the inevitable. The time had come for her to fold her cards. Any notion she had of returning to Knightswood Hall and finishing what they had started yesterday was foolish beyond belief. Casting all chances of future happiness with someone else to the winds for the sake of a few hours' idle pleasure would be madness. No matter how much she might yearn for it. No matter how right it felt. Madness.

She tried very hard to picture that someone else of her future, but he stubbornly refused to resemble anyone other than Nicholas. Her country house always turned into Knightswood Hall. Her children all had dark hair and slate-grey eyes. It was useless.

Perhaps she would have more success when this was over. Perhaps, after all, immersing herself in the balls and parties of the London Season would be a wise next step. Not towards matrimony, but away from danger. At least it would give her something to occupy her mind other than what might have been. What now would never be, she thought morosely. For Nicholas would not, in any case, be interested in her once she told him the truth. She had come close today to making him break his own rules, though he did not yet know it. Nicholas Lytton was not a man who would take kindly to that sort of betrayal. A lonely tear tracked down her cheek. Whichever way she looked at it, she dreaded the coming interview. However she tried to imagine it, right now, at this moment, her future seemed bleak.

Nicholas did not sleep much either. Tossing and turning in his tangled sheets, he cursed his over-vigilant tenant. The image of Serena spread out on the hay occupied his mind with tortuous clarity. He had never felt so desirous of a union of the flesh in his life. He had never felt so frustrated in his life. He groaned, turning over again in a vain attempt to find a cool spot in the rumpled bed. Tomorrow. If he did not have her tomorrow, he would go insane.

* * *

He was rudely awoken in the morning by a brisk rap on his bedroom door, which most certainly did not emanate from his considerate valet.

'Nick, you dog, get up.' Standing in the doorway was Charles, Lord Avesbury, a notable Corinthian and Nicholas's best friend. Closing the door behind him, he strode over to pull back the window hangings before sitting himself on a chair by the dressing table.

Nicholas sat up in bed. 'Lord, you must have made an early start. What the devil brings you here? Not, you understand, that I'm not delighted to see you, but your timing is appalling.'

'I was staying with the Cheadles,' Charles replied. 'It's not more than fifteen miles away. There was talk of a picnic or some such nonsense today, so I thought I'd make my escape for a few hours.'

'I see. Lady Cheadle still hopeful, is she?'

'It's my mother's fault. She and Lady Cheadle are bosom buddies. She will have it that it's the dearest wish of her heart to see me leg-shackled to her friend's eldest daughter.'

'And you, Charles? Is it the dearest wish of your heart, to wed Penelope Cheadle?'

'Steady on, Nick, I wouldn't put it that strongly. I'm getting on though, about time I was setting up my nursery. I'm turned thirty.'

Nicholas stretched up to tug the bell for his valet. 'I hope you know what you're doing, Charles. Rather you than me. I'm going to get dressed. Go down to the breakfast parlour, Hughes will bring you some coffee. I'll join you shortly, then you can tell me all the news.'

'Not much to tell. Truth is Nick, you're mostly the news at the moment.'

'Don't tell me my duelling opponent has inconveniently died?'

'No need to worry on that score, he's making an excellent recovery. You may come back to London whenever you're ready. No, it's not the duel. Get dressed, we can talk over breakfast. I'll be dammed if I'll sit here with you when you're not even wearing a nightshirt.' Refusing to be drawn any further, Charles retired downstairs.

Chapter Five

Nicholas did not tarry over his *toilette*, joining his friend in the breakfast parlour some twenty minutes later. Charles was gazing out of the window where a long line of men were scything the lawn. He was a good-looking man, famed for the perfect cut of his coats, which he had always from Weston, and the intricacy of his cravats, which he always tied himself. He was neither as tall nor as well built as Nicholas, but he had a leg shapely enough to look well in the tight pantaloons and tasselled Hessians he wore—from Holby, naturally—and his amiable countenance showed surprisingly few signs of wear despite his solid membership of the hard-drinking, hard-playing Corinthian set.

As Nicholas entered the room, Charles raised his quizzing glass. 'I'm not sure I like the way you've tied your cravat. These country ways are making you lax. Time you were back in town.'

Nicholas laughed, sitting at the table to carve some ham. 'I was never so fastidious as you, Charles. Tell me, for I'm on tenterhooks, what on earth can have made me the talk of the *ton*.'

'Hear you gave Diana Masterton her *congé*.'

'Yes, she was becoming tedious in her demands, I told Frances Eldon to pay her off. Don't tell me that's it?'

'No, of course not. At least…' Charles took a sip of coffee. 'Bumped into your cousin Jasper at White's the other day. Asked me if I knew aught about the Cyprian who's keeping you company here. Wondered if she was the reason you'd rid yourself of the fair Diana. Needless to say I couldn't tell him anything, except that I doubted the truth of the rumour, since you're always so careful to keep your fancy pieces at a safe distance.'

Nicholas paused in the act of cutting into the slice of ham on his plate, frowning at his friend. 'She's not a fancy piece.'

'What!' Charles exclaimed, startled into spilling his coffee. 'You mean to tell me it's true, there's a woman here? Come on, Nick, that's not your style. What are you thinking of?'

'She lodges in the village, not here. And I'd like to know how Jasper found out about her.'

'I never thought to ask. Wouldn't surprise me if he bribes your servants though, sort of thing he would do. Seemed mighty put out about it in any case, on account of your birthday being so close.'

Nicholas gave a sharp crack of laughter. 'So that's

what he's worried about. He's well off the mark—I have no intentions of marrying Mademoiselle Stamppe.'

'Oh, so she's French,' Charles said dismissively, as if that explained everything.

'No, English actually, although she's lived on the Continent all her life.'

'What's she doing here with you, then, if she's not your mistress?'

'It's a long story, Charles.'

'You can't fob me off so easily, Nick.' Lord Avesbury took an enamelled box from his waistcoat pocket and flicked it open expertly with the tip of his thumb. 'Tell me the whole tale.' Taking a delicate pinch of snuff, he sat back in his chair with a grin. 'Anything's preferable to Lady Cheadle's picnic party. Go on, I've got all day.'

Cautiously skirting over the more personal aspects of their relationship, Nicholas recounted the events of the past few days.

Charles listened, running the full gamut of emotions from incredulous to sceptical. 'So what's in those papers of hers, then?'

'Her father's will and proof of her identity.'

'Why would she need proof of her identity? Sounds a bit shady to me. And now I come to think about it, her name sounds familiar too. Can't put my finger on it just at the moment, but it'll come to me. What's in the will?'

'I don't know. She promised she'd tell me, but events yesterday got in the way somewhat.'

'Events?' Charles laughed. 'I see. That's what you meant by my bad timing. Take it she's a looker, then, your *mademoiselle*?'

A bell clanged in the distance. Nicholas stood up, looking towards the door. 'You'll see for yourself in a few moments. I fancy that's her now.'

Serena entered the parlour a few minutes later. 'Oh, I beg your pardon, Hughes didn't mention that you had company.' She had been so busy rehearsing over and over in her mind the speech she intended to deliver to Nicholas that it quite overset her composure to find he was not alone.

Nicholas came over to take her hand in his familiar clasp. 'Serena, this is Charles, Lord Avesbury, my dearest and oldest friend. Charles, may I present Mademoiselle Serena Stamppe.'

Charles produced his quizzing glass to inspect the goddess who had appeared before him, his brows rising as he took in the perfection of Serena's beauty. She was dressed in a printed cotton dress of Turkey red, the small puffed sleeves intricately pleated and tapering tightly down almost to her knuckles. The neckline was trimmed with freshly laundered white ruffles, matching the frilled hem of her petticoat, beneath which her feet were clad in her favourite half-boots of kid. She had discarded her pelisse and hat when she arrived, and the full glory of her golden curls, piled high on her head, competed with the morning sunshine gleaming through the window panes.

Tucking the eyeglass into the pocket of his waistcoat, Charles trod over to take Serena's hand, bowing with great elegance. 'Your servant, ma'am. Forgive me, Nicholas did not warn me I was about to encounter such a vision of loveliness. Your presence alone has made my journey worthwhile.'

Serena smiled politely, rather nonplussed to find herself in such obviously elevated company. 'How do you do,' she said, remembering her manners just in time, and dropping an elegant curtsy. She turned to Nicholas. 'Forgive me, if I had known you had a guest I wouldn't have intruded.'

He smiled reassuringly. 'Charles is a very good friend, there's no need to worry. Stay for coffee at least.'

She agreed because it would seem rude not to, sitting down in her usual chair by the fire. In the presence of Nicholas's friend all the impropriety of their situation hit home with a vengeance. She was embarrassed and disconcerted. Frustrated, too, for she had hoped to get the difficult conversation she had resolved to have with Nicholas out of the way as soon as possible.

Charles chatted amicably about the house party he had temporarily abandoned, the latest *on dits*, and a wager made on a race between a frog and a chicken. By the time Nicholas recounted the story of his first meeting with Serena, she had relaxed enough to be able to laugh about it.

'I thought he was a groom. It never occurred to me

that I was watching the master of the house stripped to the waist and fighting the local blacksmith.' She looked up teasingly at Nicholas, who was standing with his back to the fireplace. He returned the look with a smile of such warmth that she raised a hand towards him, remembered that they were not alone, and dropped it. Remembered, too, her resolve to put an end to things between them.

Charles observed the by-play with interest. Now he had met her, it didn't surprise him that Nick had kept such a beauty hidden away. She was almost flawless, the mysterious Mademoiselle Stamppe, it would take a strong man indeed to resist her charms. It wasn't like Nick to be so reticent about his lady loves. He had carefully refrained from discussing Serena, though it was obvious they were intimate. Their bodies gave them away, constantly moving towards one another. The way they looked at each other, too. And that smile—they might as well have kissed. Nick was in deep with his adventuress. Charles wondered if he realised just how deep.

'I hope you won, Nick. The fight, I mean.'

'Of course I did. Samuel landed a couple of good punches, but he's slow.'

'You're getting too old for that sort of thing.'

'I know, I know.' Nicholas looked down at his hands, the faint scars the only reminder of the recent mill. 'I tell myself that I won't do it any more, but you know how it is. I can't resist a challenge.'

'Yes, but the next time you might lose. Give it up, Nick, you're almost thirty. Time you settled down.'

'I'll be the judge of that,' Nicholas said curtly. He didn't want to think about his father's damned will.

'You've got less than three months left,' Charles continued blithely.

'Not now, Charles.'

Watching him, Serena was confused by the less-than-subtle change of subject. The awkwardness of her situation returned to her. She rose to go. 'I'll leave you two to catch up. It was a pleasure to meet you, Lord Avesbury.' She curtsied, then turned to Nicholas. 'May I speak with you tomorrow? There is a matter I am most anxious to resolve with you.'

'You are not the only one who is anxious for resolution,' Nicholas whispered in her ear.

Serena blushed furiously, then looked stricken. 'I will see myself out.' She left, resolutely closing the door before he could demand to know what was wrong.

Nicholas and Charles passed a pleasant day tooling Charles's phaeton round the countryside, before partaking of a rustic meal at an inn some miles from High Knightswood.

'I bumped into your sister and your stepmama at Almack's the other day,' Charles said, touching his whip to his horses. 'Georgie was queening it over a pack of young pups.'

'Brat. Did you speak to them?'

'Of course I did, for I had already determined to come and see you. Georgie wanted to know when you were coming back to town, and said to be sure and tell you that she's a blazing success. Melissa was—well, you know what Melissa's like.'

Charles concentrated on overtaking a lumbering cart. 'Dashed attractive woman, that Serena of yours,' he continued when the manoeuvre had been stylishly executed.

'Very,' Nicholas agreed drily. 'What are you implying?'

'Ain't implying anything. I'm happy to tell you straight to your face, Nick, it's obvious how things are between you two. The way you were looking at each other put me to the blush. Don't tell me it's finally happened,' he said with a sudden guffaw of laughter. 'Has the lovely *mademoiselle* given you a *coup de foudre*?'

'You're being ridiculous Charles, I'm not in love with her.'

'Whatever you say. It's just occurred to me, though—maybe Jasper wasn't too far off the mark after all.'

'What's my cousin got to do with this?'

'Fretting himself to death at the thought of you getting hitched.'

'But I've no intention of getting married. Leastways, not until it's absolutely necessary.'

'Lawyers still claiming they're making progress? Depend upon it, they'll be saying that on the day of your birthday, it's what you pay 'em for. Don't believe a word of it. You need to get hitched, no two ways about it, and the perfect candidate's fallen like a ripe peach into your hands. Beautiful, obviously more than willing—in fact, I'd say the chit's besotted with you, although you don't notice, of course—and, what's more, not someone who will give you any trouble.'

'You're serious,' Nicholas said incredulously, staring at his friend as if he had just escaped from Bedlam.

'Of course I am. Think about it for a moment. I don't think you've quite grasped the severity of your plight. If you don't marry, you'll lose everything.'

'Not everything, I'll still have the Hall and estate.'

'Much good they'll do you without funds. You'll have to give up your gaming, your expensive women, your hunters. You'll have to rusticate here for ever, in penury.'

'It won't come to that.'

'It's coming mighty close,' Charles said exasperatedly. 'You can't let Jasper inherit, Nick. What isn't swallowed up by his debts will be tossed away on the hazard table. He's playing very deep these days, he'd be back under the hatches in less than a year.'

'I am aware of that. But it doesn't alter the fact that I have no desire at all to be married.'

'What makes you so much against it?'

'An inherent dislike of being coerced into doing something I have no desire to do, for a start.'

'Bloodymindedness, in other words.'

'If you like.' Nicholas sighed deeply. 'Of course I don't want Jasper to inherit.'

'Then marry your Serena,' Charles said stubbornly. 'Devil take it, Nick, it's not like you to be so dense. She's perfect. My guess is she's the by-blow of some gentleman, you don't get a nose like that from common stock. She's well mannered, well turned out—need I go on?'

'So you're suggesting a marriage of convenience.'

'Convenient enough for both of you, certainly. You keep your fortune. She gets your name. You can pension her off after a respectable time—say a year.'

'You underestimate my dear parent. There is a clause in his will that no one else, not even Jasper, has knowledge of. If my marriage is terminated by anything other than death, Jasper inherits.' Nicholas smiled at the shocked expression on his friend's face. 'My father constructed a matrimonial prison for me, with a life sentence as punishment. I will find a way to break it—I must. Now let us drop the subject, once and for all.'

Charles pulled the phaeton up at the front door of the Hall, refusing the offer of a bed for the night. 'Didn't mean to offend you, Nick.'

'It's all right, Charles. I simply won't be told how to run my life. Not by my father, not by Jasper or even, my dear fellow, by you.'

Charles grinned. 'Truth be told, Nick, I'm pretty set on doing the deed myself. Don't want to offend the future mother-in-law, best be on my way before they send out a search party.'

'Give my regards to Lady Cheadle, and accept my felicitations, if I'm not being premature.'

'Well, it's fairly certain. I'm to have an audience with Lord Cheadle in the morning—settlements, you know. She's a compliant little thing, Penelope, she'll do well enough. Take a leaf from my book, Nick, before it's too late.' Charles pulled his caped driving coat more securely around him and tightened the reins. With a crack of the whip he set his horses trotting briskly down the path, only to pull them up almost immediately. 'Stamppe,' he called back, 'knew it would come to me. It's the family name of the Vespians. Saw the announcement in the *Morning Post* the other day, the fifth earl died in Paris last year. Your Serena must be some distant relative.' With a twirl of his whip, he set off again.

Nicholas headed for the library, demanding the last few days' copies of the *Morning Post*. While Hughes retrieved the newspapers from the butler's pantry and hastily ironed them flat, Nicholas poured himself a glass of Madeira and thought about Serena.

Inevitably his mind returned to the image of her yesterday lying wanton in the hay, her hair fanned out, brighter gold than the supporting bales, her creamy flesh flushed. He couldn't wait to plunge into the hot wet core of her, to feel her tight around him, to… Damnation! He was fantasising like a school boy. If he continued in this vein he was in for another night like the last one, tortured by adolescent fantasies and frustrated with longing.

Looking at the clock on the mantel, he realised that it was almost dinner time. Tomorrow he would make sure their love-making was not interrupted. Tonight he would have to content himself with trying not to think about what that would entail.

Hughes arrived with the stack of newspapers and the day's post. There was a letter from Frances Eldon at last. Nicholas opened it with a smile of anticipation. As he quickly scanned the neatly crossed pages his smile faded. By the time he had finished, his face was a mask of fury.

He was waiting for her on the front steps of the Hall the next morning. The day was dry but cold, making Serena glad of the warm woollen cloak she wore over her dress of pale blue muslin. At the sight of Nicholas's tall figure her heart did a little flip of excitement. It was all very well to tell herself that they must never share so much as another kiss. Faced with the man himself, her will power weakened.

You are not the only one anxious for a resolution. His parting words to her yesterday. Excitement turned to anxiety, which dissolved into dread when she saw his face. No sign of his usual careless smile, his mouth was drawn into a tight line and he was frowning, his eyes a cold slate grey that seemed to glitter like polished granite. 'Is there something wrong, Nicholas?'

She faltered to a halt on the step below him. He looked down, his eyes travelling slowly over her, from her face, sweeping down her neck, the length of her body, with contempt. An icy coldness clutched at her heart. 'Nicholas?'

'Come in. There's coffee waiting,' he said curtly, preceding her into the house, giving her no choice but to follow him, hastily abandoning her bonnet and cloak to Hughes's care.

They sat opposite each other in front of the fire as was their custom. The clock ticked on the mantel. Outside, the sun danced in and out of scudding clouds, slanting shadows of light and dark onto the polished wooden floors. Everything familiar, in its usual place, yet somehow nothing felt the same.

Nicholas's brows met, giving him the look of a brooding devil. The long fingers of his right hand drummed a slow beat on the arm of his chair. He sat with careless grace, his long legs, clad today in tightly fitting pantaloons and polished Hessians, sprawled out in front of him, but there was no mistaking the tension in him. He was coiled. Ready to spring. And Serena felt horribly like his prey.

His mood alarmed her, all the more because he had himself so tightly under control. She carefully replaced her half-full coffee cup on the tray lest her shaking hands betray her. Nicholas had not touched his. The clock ticked.

'Alone at last, Serena,' Nicholas said, looking positively predatory.

She managed an uncertain smile.

'I've given Hughes instructions to deny me to any callers. What with Farmer Jeffries and then Charles, I think we've had too many interruptions lately, don't you?'

Her mouth was dry. She licked her lips. 'Nicholas, I…'

He raised an eyebrow. 'Nervous, Serena? There's no need to be. Surely our experience in the barn was sufficient to prove that the conclusion to our little idyll here will be pleasurable—on your part, at least. We have yet to determine how I will like it.'

Colour flooded her face and drained just as quickly, leaving her ashen. 'Why are you being so beastly?'

'You're tense. We should do something to help you relax. A game of piquet, perhaps? Or what about dice? I'm sure Papa taught you how to load the bones as well as how to fix the cards.'

'I don't cheat.'

'Oh, but you do, Serena. You have been cheating me since the day you turned up on my doorstep.' He stood, the tension in him blatantly obvious now, in the way he clenched his fists by his side, the way he held his shoulders rigid. He reached into his coat pocket and pulled out a letter. 'I had this from Frances Eldon, my man of business, yesterday. Combined with your uncle's announcement in the *Morning Post* and your own revelations, it has helped to make a lot of things much clearer.'

She realised at once that it was too late. If he knew

from someone else what she should have told him from the first, he would never forgive her. 'You had your man of business investigate me,' she said flatly.

Nicholas coloured. 'Since you were so sparing with the truth I had no option.'

She stood up shakily. 'Don't say you had no option, it's not true. You could have waited. I came today to tell you, but I see there is no need, your Mr Eldon has saved me the trouble of a confession.'

'You lied to me.'

'You did not trust me,' she flung at him, her temper flaring. 'And I did not lie to you, Nicholas. I may have misled you, but you were perfectly happy for me to do so.'

'What do you mean by that?'

'You claim you were suspicious of me from the start. Suspicious enough to have someone investigate me. But you never asked me. You never said, *Serena, I'm not sure about this story of yours*.'

'Would you have told me?'

'Yes! No! Probably. It doesn't matter, you didn't ask because you didn't want to know. And then when I found my papers, the same thing. I would have told you straight away, even before I had read them, if you had pressed me. But you did not. Instead you suggested a day's grace.'

'Which you were more than happy to agree to.'

She nodded and took a calming breath. 'Yes. Yes, I was. It was wrong, I knew it was wrong, but I agreed because I wanted…' She blushed, but forced herself to continue. 'Because I wanted what happened in the barn. Now I know it was a terrible mistake.'

Her admission threw him. He reached for her, but she stepped back. 'No, Nicholas. It's too late now. I must go. I should have gone two days ago.'

'Sit down, Serena,' Nicholas said coldly, 'you don't get off so lightly. I want to hear it for myself. All of it.'

She would rather do almost anything, but she owed it to him, and he was mostly in the right, so she sat down, stiff-backed, hands clutched tight together in a bitter parody of their first meeting. Nicholas sat down too, his gaze unwavering. That look of his that made her feel he could read her mind.

'Well, as you have obviously surmised, Papa made his money from gambling. Gaming salons, but I assure you he was neither a cheat nor a sharp.' As she sketched a picture of their life, she watched Nicholas watching her, but his face gave away nothing. 'We followed the wars, for where there are wars there are officers and hangers-on and plenty of money,' she continued. 'Most recently we settled in Paris.'

'And you, did you preside over the tables?'

Despite the circumstances, the very idea forced a smile from her. 'Hardly. I've told you several times, Papa was extremely protective. He forbade me from entering the salons when they were open. I was his hostess at private parties—when he played for pleasure with his particular friends, all older men, respectable men. I played too, sometimes. And of course, I practised with him.'

'A fine education for you!' He was unaccountably angry on her behalf. 'What about the dangers you must have been exposed to, the sights you must have seen, the type of men you must have met?'

'It wasn't like that. You don't understand.'

'No, I don't. What did he intend for you, your sainted papa? You're—what, twenty-two, twenty-three? Did he not wish to see you settled?'

'I'm almost five and twenty. Of course he wanted to see me settled, that's why I am here. He would have brought me himself if it was not for the war.'

'That is complete nonsense, he could have returned any time if he'd really wanted to. Your father sounds to me like a selfish bastard.'

Serena was silent. Papa had explained, but even then, through the grief of knowing he had only a few hours left to live, his excuses had sounded weak to her ears. It had been more than thirty years, after all. 'You're right, he was a little set in his ways. I suppose the truth was that he had grown used to his life and did not wish to be constrained by his responsibilities in England.'

'His life as the Earl of Vespian.'

'Yes, my father was Lord Vespian.'

'Which makes you the Lady Serena—assuming, of course, that a marriage actually took place between your parents. Was there one?'

She cast him a wounded look. 'Of course there was.'

He was unrepentant. 'I'm only saying what everyone else will ask. Charles did say it was curious, your need to prove your identity.'

'You told Charles all this? You had no right.'

'Charles won't say anything. He liked you.'

'Well, I'm relieved to know that someone does.' Serena reached for her reticule and pulled out a small leather pouch, which she handed to him. 'I thought my father was being excessively cautious, but he insisted I should have this as well as the legal documents.'

Nicholas undid the ties. Inside was a ring, intricately worked in gold, a strange antique setting wrought around a large black pearl. Frowning, he traced a long finger over the pattern. 'An heirloom, I presume,' he said, returning the ring to its pouch and handing it back to Serena.

'Another of his deathbed bequests,' she said with intentional irony. 'I've to give it to my uncle. It seems it is always worn by the heir to the earldom.'

Nicholas strode over to the window. In the brief time they had spent together the narcissi had started to fade, the cherry blossom to fall. In the distance he could see a horse and plough readying a field for planting. He had been beguiled, even Charles had spotted it. Locked away from the world, he had been careless of everything save the overwhelming attraction between them, the shared laughter, the gravitation of their bodies towards each other. He had been happy. And no matter what she claimed, he had also been duped.

A gust of rage seized him. 'Tell me, Lady Serena,' he said, turning back from the window to the beautiful deceiver sitting in front of the fire, 'just why you felt it so necessary to keep your real identity a secret.'

'You know why.'

'I'd like to hear it from you.'

Her knuckles where white, so tightly was she gripping them. 'Very well, if I must. I did not tell you because I knew that while you would be happy enough to dally with Mademoiselle Cachet of no particular place and no particular family, you would run a mile from Lady Serena Stamppe. I needed to find my father's papers. You only helped because you were bored and you thought I was fair game. You would not have thought Lady Serena fair game, would you, Nicholas? And I would not then have found my father's will. I don't know why you're making me say this—no doubt you wish to humiliate me. No doubt I deserve it—but do not paint yourself as whiter than white in this tawdry episode.'

'I did not think you *fair game*, as you call it. How dare you!'

'You hardly treated me as you would a respectable female.'

'You hardly gave me grounds to do so. The first time I set eyes on you, you kissed me while I was half-naked in front of a crowd of spectators.'

'*You* kissed *me*!' She flung herself to her feet. 'And then you kissed me again, here in this very room.'

'You didn't put up much of a fight.'

'Oh, how dare you. *How dare you!* You turn everything to your own account. I came alone here because I *am* alone. What relatives I have don't even know I exist yet. I thought I was calling on a man my father's age. You made it perfectly clear from the start that you didn't think my papers existed, or if they did that they had long been lost. I've told you, time and again I've told you, that I led a sheltered life, yet you chose not to believe that either. You talked about the rules of the game, and not playing if you couldn't pay, and no commitment, at every opportunity so that I knew—*how could I not*—that you would consign me to the ends of the earth if you found out that I was the type of female who could be *compromised*.'

'That explains why you lied, it does not explain why you let me make love to you. The other day—in the barn—I gave you every opportunity to say no. *Dammit*, Serena, you know I did.'

'Yes, you did,' she whispered. 'And I didn't. I should have, but I didn't. I don't know what came over me. I was not thinking straight. I thought I could play to your rules, that I could indulge in what you call a spring idyll, but I realise that I am not, after all, the type to treat such *affaires* lightly. It meant nothing to you, but I discovered it *should* mean something to me.'

'You left it rather late in the day to discover something so fundamental. There is a name for that type of behaviour, but I will not sully your ears with it.'

Serena recoiled as if he had hit her, but met his gaze resolutely. 'I deserved that. I know how it must look, but it was not my intention to—I mean, it *was* my intention to—what I mean is, at the time I meant it. But afterwards, I realised that I risked throwing away my chances of future happiness with someone else. Throwing it away on someone who did not—would never—offer me what I want.'

'Marriage, of course,' Nicholas said disgustedly. 'I should have known you weren't really that different from the rest of your sex. Well, you'll be able to take your unsullied pick now, Lady Serena.'

'Yes, I will,' she said, finally driven by hurt to goad him. 'I'm not only titled, I'm vastly wealthy too, you know. An heiress and a lady—you're right, I *will* be able to take my pick.'

Charles had been right. The perfect candidate, he'd called Serena, and that was before he knew all. That Frances Eldon had also urged matrimony on his employer in his latest epistle added fuel to the flames. 'I hope you will be more honest with the poor clunch, whoever he turns out to be, than you were with me. Will you tell him that he's taking a lying, scheming, card-sharping temptress to his bed? Will you tell him that he's not the first to touch you? To kiss you? To make you cry out with pleasure? Or will you play the innocent virgin with him? I warn you, you will have to polish up your act a bit if you do. Respond to him as you did to me, and he will not believe you any more than I do.'

Serena flinched. 'You don't mean that, Nicholas. You know I wasn't acting.'

'I know that I am the one left aching with frustration, while you at least were satisfied,' Nicholas responded crudely. 'All I've been thinking about, day and night, is you, you, you. The vision of you lying there with your hair undone haunts me. And now it will always haunt me. I will never be rid of you,' he said heatedly, grabbing Serena by the shoulders. 'Don't you see what you've done? Because I will never have you I will always be imagining what might have been.'

He pulled her towards him and kissed her roughly. His lips were hard on hers, his tongue thrusting into her mouth. She could smell the scent of his soap, feel his breath warm on her skin, sense the barely controlled anger in the tension of his fingers bruising the soft flesh at the top of her arms.

It was a punishing kiss, a possessive kiss, the hungry kiss of desire too long pent up. It was the kiss of a man intent on slaking his thirst. Then suddenly it was a passionate kiss. Unable to stop herself, Serena responded, kissing him back urgently, meeting fire with fire. Nicholas groaned, releasing his grip to slide his arms around her, pulling her close into the hard length of his body. Then abruptly she was free. 'It would have been better for us both if your father had left his papers with a lawyer.'

'You wish we had never met?'

'With a passion.'

'Don't be like this, Nicholas, don't let us part on such terms.'

'For God's sake, what other terms can there be?'

'We are both overwrought. You think I have deceived you, but I have not. I'm the same person I was when first we met. A title does not change who I am. I admit, I did not tell you the whole truth, but I did not lie to you. And as to what has happened between us—you have not broken your rules. Your conscience is clear, you did not take anything I was not willing to give, and thanks to the arrival of your tenant, I did not give you enough to be truly compromised.' She managed a watery smile.

Her willingness to absolve him from the blame he suspected he deserved melted Nicholas's anger, leaving him feeling strangely empty. He saw she was making a valiant attempt not to cry, and felt guilt perch like a brooding raven on his shoulder. 'Go and pack,' he said gruffly, struggling to resist the desire to pull her back into his arms. 'I'll pick you up at noon tomorrow.'

'Don't be foolish, Nicholas. I'll hire a chaise. I won't be more than a night on the road.'

'It is you who are being foolish. It's too dangerous for you to travel alone with only your snoring Madame for company, and Charles told me yesterday that I'm no longer *persona non grata* in London, since my duelling opponent is well on the road to recovery.'

Serena coloured. 'Madame LeClerc is gone ahead of me.'

'Then that settles it. There have been a spate of robberies on the London road. A highwayman, Hughes says. It's not safe.'

'I'll hire some outriders,' Serena said stubbornly.

'Serena, I insist. If you don't agree, I'll simply make sure you can't hire your own chaise in the village. One of the advantages of being the local landowner.'

'That's not fair. Nicholas, it's better if you don't, really…'

He took hold of her hand between his own. 'I could not be happy with you travelling alone. Indulge me in this. We both need time to order our thoughts, and I to cool my temper. You are right, we should not part on such terms. We deserve better.'

Her conscience warred with her desires, and her desires won. She could not resist the temptation of a few more days of his company. 'Very well.' Refusing his escort on the grounds that he too must attend to his packing, Serena departed Knightswood Hall.

It was only when she had gone that he realised she had still offered him no explanation for her willingness to make love to him.

Chapter Six

The air in the public room of the King's Arms, the tavern owned by the legendary heavyweight Thomas Cribb, was stifling. Acrid wood smoke from the roaring fire hung heavy, despite the grimy windows flung open wide to the street. The pungent aroma of unwashed human bodies mingled with the smell of spilt ale and cheap spirits.

Jasper Lytton paused on the threshold, wearing the habitual sneer that marred the handsome lines of his countenance. Of late the place had become overrun with the *hoi polloi*, so much so that even the distinction of being invited to partake of daffy within the sanctity of Cribb's own private parlour was become a dubious pleasure. He raised his quizzing glass to survey the room. From the window embrasure a thin man beckoned with a long white finger. Jasper joined him reluctantly.

'I th-thought you weren't going to turn up, Jasper. I've been here an age.' The man spoke with a slight stammer. He was young and elegantly dressed, but dissipation was already taking a heavy toll, thinning his hair, etching a deep groove on either side of his mouth. The pale eyes were bloodshot. His hand shook as he reached for the decanter to top up his glass, filling Jasper's at the same time.

'God, Langton, you look like hell.' Jasper lolled on the hard wooden seat, watching his friend's hand tremble with malicious pleasure. Though Langton could give him at least five years, and he himself drank harder and gamed deeper, no one would take Jasper for the senior man.

'S-so would you, in my position. Well, do you have it?'

Jasper shifted uncomfortably, unwilling to meet the other man's gaze. 'No, not yet.'

'*You promised!* I need it back immediately. If I d-don't have it—God, you know what these people are like.'

'Only too well, I introduced you to them myself, remember?' Watching his friend gulp down the fiery liquid, Jasper felt a minute twinge of guilt. It wasn't as if the five thousand he owed Langton was such a great sum, but it *was* a debt of honour. Introducing Hugo Langton to his own moneylender of choice had been intended as a stalling tactic, nothing more. Carefully reaching into his jacket pocket, Jasper withdrew a small roll of notes. 'There's two hundred here on account. I'll get the rest soon. I just need a run of luck.'

'Or your cousin to bail you out,' Langton muttered, snatching at the money.

Jasper's smile hardened. 'That's unlikely. Nicholas made it perfectly clear that he wouldn't be towing me out of the River Tick again.' The bitter memory of that last uncomfortable interview with his cousin still rankled. Why couldn't Nicholas see that paying off Jasper's debts for him was simply advancing money that would be rightfully his in the very near future anyway?

'How long is it now until the great day?'

'Less than three months.' He'd be lucky to hold his creditors at bay that long. There were bailiffs at his lodgings. Duns at his club. Damn Nicholas, why was he making him wait?

Across the table Langton emptied the dregs of the decanter into his glass. His hand no longer shook. The rough liquor gave him courage. When he spoke his voice was free from its stammer. 'Three months, and you'll be a rich man—provided your cousin doesn't get leg-shackled in the meantime.'

Jasper's thin lips tightened. Waving an imperious hand at the beleaguered landlord for more brandy, he quelled the panic that threatened to overwhelm him every time he thought of the consequences were his cousin suddenly to announce his nuptials. 'He wouldn't do that,' he said grimly.

The fierce look that he drew forced Langton to

cower back in his seat, all thoughts of teasing banished. 'If you s-say so. I merely thought…'

'What have you heard?' Jasper asked sharply.

'Just a rumour. Came from Charles Avesbury, if you must know.'

'Avesbury,' Jasper exclaimed. 'He said Nicholas was to be married?'

'Well, not as such. But he did see the lady in question. Said the two of them were smelling of April and May.'

Jasper scowled. 'We'll see about that.'

'What d'you mean?'

'Never you mind.' Jasper pushed back his chair. 'I have business to attend to.' Swatting the landlord's arm from his shoulder, Jasper indicated, with a careless nod of the head, that the new decanter was Langton's responsibility. Without a backward glance he strode for the door of the inn, casually kicking a flea-bitten terrier from under his feet.

'Business,' Langton mused, pouring himself another glass of brandy. 'Dirty business, if I'm any judge.'

At mid-morning the next day Nicholas's travelling chaise and four arrived outside Serena's lodgings. After a curt greeting, he stood by the chaise, watching as she supervised the loading of her luggage, admiring the graceful figure she cut in her woollen travelling cloak, the gold of her hair glinting under a poke bonnet.

Yet another sleepless night had taken its toll on Serena's mood. She had expected Nicholas to be angry, but had not anticipated he would feel quite so betrayed. Castigating herself for not having been truthful with him from the start only served to make her feel worse, however, for she could not ignore the fact that only by doing so had she come to know him so intimately.

As her dressing case and jewellery box were stowed inside the chaise, Serena wearily acknowledged the truth of the matter. She had fallen in love with Nicolas Lytton, plain and simple. No wonder his touch set off such extreme sensations. No wonder she felt a fizz of excitement every time she looked upon his handsome figure. No wonder she felt as if the sky was falling down when she thought of a future without him. She loved him. She wished with all her heart it had been possible, just once, to make love with him. Now her only consolation was that he had no idea of how she felt. And that was how it must remain, for if ever he had an inkling of her feelings—knowing Nicholas—he'd probably see it as another form of entrapment.

He helped her into the coach, his expression unreadable. Serena disposed herself beside her boxes as he took the seat opposite. The coachman pushed shut the door and they were away. She leaned back against the squabs and closed her eyes. She was exhausted, but sleep would be impossible with Nicholas sitting so close that his knees brushed hers. He was angry still. She knew better than to try to coax him out of it, could only hope that at some point on the long journey ahead his mood would mellow. Today should be a time for looking forward to whatever her new life would bring. She had an uncle, an aunt, perhaps even cousins. She was rich. She was in the fortunate position of being able to suit herself, neither beholden to an employer nor dependent upon a husband. The future was hers to define. Yet she could not bring herself to think about anything other than the brooding man sitting impassively opposite her. As they left High Knightswood behind, Serena fell into a troubled doze, her head resting awkwardly on her shoulder.

Nicholas watched, torn between frustrated desire and guilt. A surfeit of brandy last night had failed to prevent their last conversation replaying over and over in his mind. Serena was right, she had not really deceived him. He had asked Frances Eldon to investigate her because he knew her story was not the whole truth. And she was, unfortunately, right about his willingness to be deceived. He wanted her so much that he had deluded himself. Had failed to examine closely the inconsistencies in her story, the apparent contradictions in her character. It was a bitter pill to swallow, that she had also ultimately saved him from breaking his own damned rules. He had not compromised her, but he could not stop imagining what it would have been like if he had.

This morning he had an aching head and an unusually active conscience. Time would cure the former. The latter, having little experience of, he was less sure how to tackle. He owed her an apology at the very least. She had every right to reproach him for the things he had said yesterday, but she had not. He still couldn't understand why, if her claims to innocence were the truth, she had allowed him such liberties. It didn't make sense. He wished to hell she hadn't. He wished to hell she'd allowed him more. He wished—he didn't know what he wished any more. The only thing of which he was certain was that he was not ready for Serena to quit his life.

As the horses slowed to turn into the yard of the posting inn for the first change, Serena was startled into wakefulness. Reaching up to straighten her bonnet, she smiled at Nicholas, an unaffected smile, forgetting for a moment all that had gone between them.

'We should take some refreshment while they put the horses to the traces,' he suggested.

She nodded her agreement. 'Coffee would be most welcome.'

Nicholas helped her down the step, calling imperiously to the landlord to see to her request. It was late afternoon, the day dull and damp, not actually raining, but the smell of rain was in the air. Serena stretched her aching limbs, removing her gloves and reaching up to rub the stiff muscles on the back of her neck. She looked over to find Nicholas watching her, and smiled tentatively.

'I must apologise for my overreaction yesterday,' he said stiffly.

She put a hand on his arm. 'Don't say any more. We both spoke in haste. Let us cry friends and forget about it.'

'Friends with a woman,' Nicholas said with a rueful smile. 'That will be a first, but for you, *mademoiselle*—Lady Serena—I'll try.'

The ostlers made the final adjustments to the tackle holding the four new horses to the chaise, then they were back in the carriage and on their way. The atmosphere was restored—almost—to the easy camaraderie of Knightswood Hall.

Lulled by the motion of the coach, Nicholas slept fitfully. Dusk approached and darkness began to fall. Serena was cold despite the rug she had tucked round her knees and the swansdown muff enveloping her hands. Outside she could hear the pounding of horses' hooves, the occasional snatch of conversation between the two coachmen. Once, she heard the hooting of an owl.

Opposite her, Nicholas stirred restlessly against the squabs, one leg stretched forward, resting against her knees. She longed to sit beside him, to pull his head on to her shoulder, to smooth his silky black hair away from his brow, to feel the warm, reassuring heat of his body against hers.

In an effort to distract herself, she stared out at the night sky, where a waning moon could just be seen through the scudding light cloud. Surely it could not be much longer before they stopped for the night? She was stiff and sore from the journey. Nicholas mumbled, shifted in his seat, and quieted again. The sharp crack of a shot startled her from her reverie.

The coach jolted forwards as the horses reared at the noise, throwing Serena from her seat. Strong arms clasped her, preventing her from falling. A solid wall of warm muscle supported her. A reassuring voice asked her if she was hurt.

'No, no, I'm fine. Nicholas, I think I heard a shot.'

He pulled her up on to the seat beside him and held her close as the coach slowed to a stop, feeling in his pocket for his pistol. 'I didn't hear anything—are you sure?'

'Yes, it was quite unmistakable. Nicholas, do you think…?'

The words died on her lips as the door was wrenched open. A man stood framed in the doorway, his body muffled from head to toe in a black frieze coat, a large handkerchief wound up over his face so that only his eyes showed. The muzzle of his pistol pointed directly at Serena's head.

'Don't move, lady, or I'll use this, make no mistake.' The man turned to Nicholas. 'You, cully, do as you're told and no harm'll come to you.'

Realising that the highwayman would search him, finding not only the large purse of money he carried, but the silver-mounted pistol too, Nicholas carefully slipped the gun into Serena's hand, which was hidden in her swansdown muff.

A warning squeeze of her fingers and the faintest

shake of his head were enough to make her understand. Serena grasped the pistol carefully, her eyes on the highwayman. Nicholas prayed she knew how to shoot.

'All's safe, Jake.' The guttural voice came from outside, obviously an accomplice.

The highwayman jerked his head, indicating that Nicholas and Serena descend from the chaise. 'Any false moves and the mort gets it,' he warned.

Nicholas nodded coolly. Outside, the coachman was calming the team of horses, the second highwayman's gun trained on him. The other coachman was neatly trussed up at the side of the road, where two saddled horses were tethered to an old gate post.

'Keep yer ogles on him, Ned.' The highwayman named Jake nodded in the direction of the man holding the horses, then turned his attention once more to Nicholas, although his gun remained pointed at Serena. 'You, empty yer pockets. Let's see the rhino.' His voice was harsh, his small eyes hard, the hand holding his pistol unwavering. With a curse, Nicholas handed his purse over.

'Now the watch,' Jake said, emitting a soft whistle as he felt the weight of the purse.

Serena stood rooted to the spot, the long muzzle of the horse pistol pointing at her stomach. She was not frightened. Knowing that highwaymen did not risk killing unless they had to, her overriding emotion was anger. Desperate as she was to put Nicholas's pistol to use, however, she was not foolish enough to risk her life. She prepared herself for the loss of her jewels, an obvious target in their distinctive box, and was grateful that her precious papers, along with the black pearl ring, were sewn carefully into the lining of her muff. She was wearing her locket under her travelling dress.

The horses whinnied, pawing the ground nervously. The tackle jangled against the poles as they moved a couple of paces forwards in an effort to bolt again. 'Keep them prancers still,' Ned, the more nervous of the two men, growled threateningly at the coachman trying to hold them.

Jake pocketed the valuables he had retrieved from Nicholas. 'Right now, cully, I'm afraid Ned here's going to have to tie you up, just to keep you out of harm's way,' he said, nodding to his accomplice.

Ned left his position by the coachman, threatening the man with instant death if he so much as moved from the horses. Producing a length of rope, he moved towards Nicholas.

'There's no need for that,' Nicholas said angrily. 'You've got what you wanted. If any harm comes to us, you'll hang for this.'

Jake cackled as if heartily amused by Nicholas's wit. 'Lord love you, we'll be dancing the Newgate hornpipe if we're caught on the bridle way whether we kills you or no. You've no need to fret, we don't mean you any harm, sir. And just to prove that to you, I'll leave off this here gag if you promise to keep your mouth shut.'

As Ned started to bind Nicholas by the wrists, juggling pistol and rope, Jake turned his attention back to Serena. 'Move.' His voice changed to a snarl that made her skin crawl. For the first time since the chaise had ground to a halt, she felt fear. Making no attempt to search her for valuables, Jake indicated that she walk to the other side of the coach, out of sight of Ned and Nicholas.

'What are you doing with her?' Nicholas demanded sharply.

'Shut your mouth.' All traces of humour were gone from Jake's voice. 'Might as well say goodbye to the mort, she's as good as dead.'

It all happened so quickly. 'No,' Nicholas shouted, bringing his half-tied wrists up under Ned's chin, sending him flying back.

'Now you've done it,' Jake snarled, turning his gun from Serena to Nicholas.

'Nicholas,' screamed Serena, withdrawing the silver-mounted pistol from her muff and firing in one fluid movement.

The sharp report of the bullet leaving the gun startled the horses again. They plunged forwards. It startled Ned, too, still reeling from the blow Nicholas had given him, watching in comical disbelief as Jake crumpled to the ground, a bright red stain blossoming on the back of his coat.

But it didn't startle Nicholas. Almost before the bullet entered Jake's shoulder, he kicked the pistol from Ned's hand with one booted foot. Ned swore and lunged, wrapping one filthy hand around Nicholas's throat, but he was no match for a man who had sparred with Gentleman Jackson, and severely hampered by his highwayman's cloak into the bargain. Nicholas landed a doubler clean in the middle of Ned's abdomen, winding him so that he dropped his hand from Nicholas's throat. Showing a singular lack of sportsmanship, Nicholas followed up with a swift kick to his adversary's knees. Grabbing the rope which had been destined for his own wrists, he quickly deployed it on Ned, neatly trussing him hand and foot.

Serena stood rooted to the spot with shock, hypnotised by the dark stain of blood spreading slowly over the wounded highwayman's coat. Jake moaned and stirred, his hand creeping towards his horse pistol, lying on the ground where he had dropped it. As his fingers closed on the muzzle, the polished toe of a Hessian boot kicked it from his grasp. Jake swore long and hard. Nicholas picked up the pistol.

Serena blinked, as if waking from a trance, moving like a sleepwalker towards him.

'Nicholas.'

He caught her with his left arm as she tottered, holding her upright, all the while pointing the pistol at Jake, prostrate and groaning on the ground. 'Serena, don't faint on me now. *Serena*,' Nicholas said urgently.

She blinked again, focusing on his face. Though she

leaned heavily against him, he could sense her struggling to regain control over herself.

'Go and sit in the coach. I'll join you shortly, I promise. Go on.' He pushed her towards the chaise, watching to see that she climbed inside, before turning his attentions to the highwayman at his feet.

Unbuttoning Jake's frieze coat, Nicholas retrieved his purse and watch. Then he inspected the bullet wound. It was high in the right shoulder, not likely to be fatal. A perfect disabling hit. Grinning, he wondered if Serena had managed such a shot by luck or design. Whatever it was, her courage was impressive. Where other women would have swooned and screamed, Serena kept a cool head. Perhaps the *bon papa*'s upbringing had been to some purpose after all.

A groan reminded him that he had unfinished business. Nicholas hauled Jake into a sitting position, the rough movement causing blood to flow anew from the man's wound. Paying no attention to the stream of expletives that ensued, he pulled the muffler from Jake's face, revealing a weasel-like countenance made distinctive by the long scar running from the his left ear to the corner of his mouth.

'Shut up,' Nicholas said harshly, as the man continued to curse. 'You're lucky not to be dead. I want some answers or you *will* be dead. I'll have no compunction in shooting you, and no doubt either that the law will be on my side.'

Jake groaned. 'Ain't nothing to tell. We meant you no harm.'

'No, but you had other intentions for the lady.'

'Aye,' the highwayman agreed with a leer.

With a snarl, Nicholas positioned the muzzle of the pistol close against the man's temple. His other hand tightened around Jake's throat until he choked.

'Stop! Stop, guvnor, I…'

The grip relaxed enough to allow Jake to take a few breaths. 'The truth then.'

'We was to kill her. That's what we was paid for—and mortal good pay it was. No harm then, I thought, since she was such a fine-looking wench, in having a bit of fun before we put a bullet in her. No harm…'

But Jake's sentence was destined never to be completed. Strong fingers clenched round his throat and Nicholas's face, a grim mask of white teeth and black brows and slate-grey eyes, closed in on him. *Like the very devil himself*, thought Jake as he lost consciousness.

He came to trussed and bound beside his comrade. The coachman had been freed, and was readying the chaise for the road.

'Who paid you?' Nicholas demanded icily.

'I can't tell you that,' Jake replied groggily, clutching at his throat and coughing.

'Can't or won't? I'll find out either way, you know, but it would be far better for you if you co-operated.'

Jake shook his head. 'It won't make any difference. We're bound to dangle for this night's work.'

'Perhaps. But I am a gentleman of some influence. If you co-operate, I can put in a word for you. You may get away with deportation.'

'Truth is, I couldn't tell you either way, guvnor. He was a flash cull, that's all I know. Found Ned and me at the Queen's Head tavern on the Fleet. We was to come down here and watch you, report back if we saw you with the mort—the lady. Which we did. So he sends word, the flash cull, that we've to bide our time and kill her. Not to harm you, just her. When we heard yesterday you was heading for London, it seemed too good to be true—a hold up on the King's highway being what comes natural to me and Ned, you understand.'

'And this *flash cull* who paid you—if you did not know who he was, how then did you keep in touch with him?'

'We'd to write to a Jimmy Ketch, care of the Queen's Head. But Jimmy Ketch ain't his name, as anyone there'll tell you.'

'How do you know?'

Jake gave a wheezy laugh. 'And here was me thinking you was a wise one. Jimmy Ketch is flash cant for the hangman.'

There was obviously no more to be had from the man. The two coachmen were mounted on the seat and the chaise positioned on the road. Leaning over to check the ropes that bound the captive highwaymen, Nicholas gave a satisfied nod.

'You can't be leaving us here,' Jake shouted. 'If I don't get this bullet out I'll die.'

'Yes, possibly.' Nicholas's saturnine smile made Jake cringe in genuine fear. 'And if you don't die of the wound, I have no doubt you'll face your Maker on the gallows soon enough. However, you won't be alone for long, don't fret. I shall be sending the local magistrate to attend to your needs as soon as we reach the next posting inn.'

Nicholas turned his back on the highwaymen and rejoined Serena in the chaise.

'Nicholas, thank God,' Serena cried with relief, throwing her arms around him. 'Are you all right? Did they hurt you,' she asked anxiously, scanning his face in the pale glow of the moonlight.

He hugged her tight against him. 'I'm fine. And you? You're chilled to the marrow. Come here.' He pulled the door closed and sat down on the seat, taking Serena with him. As the chaise started off, he wrapped his arms protectively around her. 'You'll be better directly. It's not far to the posting house.'

Serena laughed shakily. 'I've never shot anyone before.

'I should think not. I could only hope when I gave you my gun that you knew what to do with it.'

'Papa taught me.'

'The *bon papa*. I guessed as much. I never thought I would say this, but I am grateful to him. You were very brave Serena.'

'Oh, no, I'm so ashamed, I went to pieces after I fired the shot.'

'Don't be silly. The important thing is that you didn't go to pieces beforehand. You kept your head, which is more than any other female—and probably most men—of my acquaintance would have done.' Nicholas reached for her hand, holding it in his own reassuring clasp. Serena nestled against his shoulder. He could smell the flowery scent she wore, feel her hair tickling his chin.

Now he had her safe, cold fear gave way to overwhelming relief. When it dawned on him just exactly what the highwaymen intended, he had been overtaken by a terrifying mixture of rage and horror. It had taken all his will power *not* to kill Jake with his bare hands. He dared not think what would have happened had he not given Serena the gun. His hold on her tightened. She was safe, he reminded himself, which was the most important thing.

Serena sat up, reluctantly disentangling herself from Nicholas's grasp. 'What did that man—Jake—what did he mean to do with me?'

'It's best not to think about it.'

She stared at him, trying to discern his expression in the gloom. 'Was he going to kill me?'

'Yes,' Nicholas admitted curtly.

'But I heard him tell you that you wouldn't be harmed, when he was tying you up,' she said in a puzzled voice. 'That doesn't make sense. And why did he take me out of sight behind the coach? Was he going to—oh!' Serena turned chalk white.

The horses turned into a brightly lit courtyard. The door swung open and the steps were let down. Calling for a parlour and brandy—at once—Nicholas scooped Serena up and carried her into the welcoming warmth of the posting inn, laying her down on a settle beside the fire in the private room to which the landlord directed him.

Brandy arrived. Serena took a sip from the glass Nicholas held to her lips, choking as the alcohol burned its way down her throat. She sipped some more and sat up, reaching with relief to untie the strings of her hat, casting it on to the floor at her feet. Recklessly, she downed the remainder of the drink, feeling a warm glow working its way up from her empty stomach to her face.

'Do you want another?'

'Thank you.' This time she sipped cautiously, placing the glass on a side table to stand and remove her cloak and gloves, sighing with satisfaction as the heat from the fire warmed her numbed fingers. 'Have you ordered dinner?'

'Yes, in half an hour. Your room is ready too, I asked one of the maids to unpack your portmanteau.'

'That was thoughtful. I think I'll go and tidy myself before we eat, I must look a fright.' She got unsteadily to her feet, waving Nicholas away. 'I'm fine, I promise. I won't be long.'

While she was gone, Nicholas occupied himself by

writing a note summoning the local magistrate to the scene of the crime. Then he stared anxiously at the door until Serena reappeared, telling himself he was being ridiculous, only just resisting the urge to check on her.

She returned to the parlour with her hair tidied and a fresh fichu round the neck of her gown, just as dinner arrived. She was pale but calm. Her smile lit up the room. Her presence had the usual immediate effect upon his body. Nicholas grimaced inwardly. It seemed it would take more than a couple of highwaymen and a near-death experience to quell his desire for her.

They ate the rustic meal of roasted capons and game pie followed by a ewes'-milk cheese in companionable silence, but, knowing Serena only too well, Nicholas was not surprised to be faced with an enquiring and very determined countenance as soon as the covers were removed and the servants gone from the room.

'Nicholas, you're keeping something from me—what is it?'

He did not answer immediately, pouring himself a glass of port to buy some time, swirling it around in the glass thoughtfully. He was immensely reluctant to tell her, but she should know, especially since he could claim no right to protect her in the future. 'Those two men were hired with specific orders to kill you, Serena. Who would stand to benefit if you did not claim your inheritance?'

Her mouth went dry at this bald statement of fact, though it was no more than she had already surmised herself. 'I'm not sure. I suppose my fortune would go to my Uncle Mathew, who is now Lord Vespian.'

'Is it a lot of money?'

'An immense amount. I can't quite believe how much.'

'So you really are an heiress. And your uncle would inherit it all?'

'Yes, I don't have anyone else. But although he may well have learned of Papa's death by now, he knows nothing of my existence,' Serena replied confidently, blissfully unaware of the letter from her father, recently come into her uncle's possession, which informed him of precisely that.

'Are you sure? If he knows your father is dead, then surely…'

'No. The circumstances are such that Papa did not tell Mathew of either his marriage or my birth, I don't know why. Your father was the only one who knew, and even then, I think just the bare bones of his marriage to my mother and my birth—they did not keep in touch after that. Papa wrote once a year to his lawyer, just to let him know that he was safe. I presume that if he has not had a letter this year he will have made enquiries, which is why my Uncle Mathew may know that he is now Lord Vespian. But as to me—no, he knows nothing about me.'

'Why was your father so secretive?' Nicholas asked exasperatedly.

'I don't know, and I didn't get the chance to ask him.

All I do know is that when he was dying he told me most particularly to go to your father and retrieve my papers before seeking out my uncle. Those were his instructions, so that's what I did.'

'Well, it seems to me that your papa has put you in a damned awkward situation.'

'You're thinking that if he had left everything in my uncle's hands we wouldn't be in this mess together. I'm sorry.'

'I didn't mean that at all,' Nicholas said with a twisted smile. 'I tell myself it would be better if we had not met, but I cannot bring myself to regret it.'

'Nor can I,' Serena said softly.

In the silence that followed a dog barked outside in the courtyard. A gust of male laughter came from the tap room. Serena had never felt so alone. Nicholas would leave her in London. If he was right in his surmise, her family, whom she had been relying on to introduce her into society, were trying to kill her! She remembered the shot from the poacher's gun at Knightswood Hall, and wondered if that too had been an attempt on her life. She realised it was what Nicholas thought, but had not said.

Her life really was in danger. Then Nicholas's life was in danger too, as long as he was near her. If things had turned out differently along the post road… She shuddered. They could both have been killed, their existence cruelly snuffed out; denying them for ever the chance to experience what might have passed between them. It was an unbearable thought. 'Nicholas, do you realise that we might have…?'

'Don't think about it,' he said roughly, taking her in his arms. 'We are alive. You are safe now.'

'Alive,' she repeated. She recalled that first day they met, and the sense of recklessness that had infected her ever since. She felt it again now, a gust of desire so strong it was as if she was being squeezed breathless. 'Make love to me Nicholas,' she whispered, reaching up to touch his face, tracing the high planes of his cheek bones, the strong line of his jaw, the sculpted line of his bottom lip. She loved him so much, her heart ached with it.

He removed her hand. 'Don't, Serena. You're upset, you don't mean it.'

She reached for his hand, spreading open his fingers, measuring her own against it palm to palm, marvelling at the contrast in size, her own white skin against his tan, her veined wrists narrow beside his more sinewy, masculine width. She remembered him stripped to the waist in the boxing ring. She recalled the scent of battle, his lust for victory. The thought of his strength, the sheer male power of him, so different from her own fragile femininity, made her shiver. She kissed his wrist, a butterfly touch, tracing the line down to his thumb with her tongue.

'Serena, stop it.'

His voice sounded harsh. He did not pull his hand away. She remembered how he had guided her most intimate touch on him. Remembered how it had felt, touching, watching, feeling. Pleasure and pleasuring. She glanced up at him. Pressed another butterfly kiss on to the tip of his thumb. He exhaled. Daringly, her heart pounding, she pulled his thumb into her mouth, caressing the length of it with her tongue, releasing it to taste the skin between his thumb and his index finger.

'Serena. Oh God, Serena, you don't know what you're doing. It would be a mistake. You'll regret it.'

More butterfly kisses along the next finger, then the length drawn into her mouth a little more confidently. Something—fear, excitement, anticipation—twisted inside her. She reached the next finger, sucked a little harder, held it there a little longer.

She looked up through eyes hooded with burgeoning passion to find Nicholas's face a mask of untrammelled desire. He swept her into his arms and carried her from the room, striding effortlessly up the stairs, along the corridor and into her bedchamber. Closing the door firmly behind him, he gazed searchingly into her eyes, shaking his head before laying her gently down on the bed.

'This is insane,' he said, as if to himself.

Chapter Seven

Serena could feel the soft feather mattress moulding itself to her contours, the solid weight of Nicholas lying next to her. He was staring at her, his eyes glittering, watching her. She could feel his breath, his mouth as he pressed urgent kisses on to her eyelids, her cheeks, her ears, her neck. She could smell him, male heat and the elusive scent that was just Nicholas, distinctively Nicholas, only Nicholas. And she could hear him. 'Serena, Serena, Serena', his voice so weighted with need that she could not be mistaken and she could not resist, not now.

He kissed her. No butterfly kisses this time, no teasing, just unleashed, untamed passion. Lips and tongues and teeth clashing, biting, licking, kissing. Hot kisses, hard kisses, deep kisses. Kisses which sought to know. And now hands too, seeking, searching, learning.

There were too many clothes between them. Nicholas released Serena's mouth, pulling her upright. 'I need to see you.' He shrugged his own coat off, dropping it carelessly to the ground before turning her round to untie her dress, loosening it, easing it off, kissing her neck, licking into the hollow of her throat, trailing a line of kisses across her shoulders. He pulled the long sleeves down her arms, helping her step out of the dress, leaving it pooled on the floor on top of his coat.

He made short work of the intricate lacings of her corset. A tiny part of her mind noted jealously how expert he was with buttons and ribbons and fastenings, then she forgot all about it. Her long petticoat was next, carefully pulled over her head, his hands running over the curve of her waist, her ribcage, the outline of her breasts as he removed it, touching each indentation, learning her body as if memorising it. Standing before him in her chemise, Serena shivered under his scrutiny, a wild excitement taking hold of her in the heat of his gaze, relishing the feeling that he was devouring her with his eyes. No fear this time. Not even embarrassment. His urgency made her shameless. Her nipples hardened, clearly outlined against the thin cotton.

His eyes on her were like polished slate as she reached up to remove the pins that held her hair in place. Long tresses uncoiled from her coiffure. Nicholas groaned, kissing her, twisting the molten gold in his hands, fanning it out over her shoulders, crushing her hard against his body.

Still too many clothes. Impatiently he tugged off his neckcloth. Equally impatiently tugged his shirt free from his breeches and over his head, sighing as Serena pressed herself against his muscled chest, her hands roaming over his torso, across his back, his shoulders, his ribs, her mouth trailing kisses.

And still too many clothes. Nicholas rapidly divested himself of his top boots, buckskins and undergarments, to stand before her naked. Watching him from the bed, Serena shyly drank in the long legs, the line of his buttocks, the indentation of his waist, the breadth of his chest and shoulders. Beautiful, she thought. 'Beautiful,' she whispered, sitting up on the bed, reaching out to touch as he stood before her, allowing him to part her legs so that he could stand between them. She stroked his chest, flattening her palms over his nipples, feeling him shiver beneath her touch as she stroked downwards, spreading her hands over his muscled buttocks, round to the soft skin on the inside of his thigh, experimentally running her fingertips along the silken length of his erection.

Nicholas closed his eyes, his expression strained, almost grim with pleasure as she stroked and touched, learning this part of him in the same way as she was learning the rest of his body. *He wanted her. He ached for her.* It made her head spin. It made her heart contract. It made her into a wild creature she barely recognised.

Leaning forwards she cradled his heavy length

between her breasts, rubbing the hard peaks of her nipples against his stomach, relishing the hot surge of pleasure the movement gave her, reaching round to pull him closer, moaning with the heat and roughness and satin smoothness of him.

Nicholas muttered something incoherent. He disposed of her chemise, her pantaloons. He pushed her back on the bed. She was completely naked save for her silk stockings, their ribbons fluttering at her knees, and her little laced boots. A vision. He drank it in, breathing heavily. Exactly as he remembered, golden hair, alabaster skin, luscious pink mouth, cornflower blue eyes. Downwards his gaze went, to the dark pink of her nipples, the curls between her legs. She was a dream, like the painting of a courtesan kept discreetly locked away in the back room of a certain type of club. Like a wanton. Ripe, lush, and ready.

Mine, Nicholas thought possessively, *mine*, his last coherent thought before he lowered himself on to the bed beside her, skin on skin, muscle, bone, soft curves and hard planes melding into one as they kissed, pushing, arching, rubbing urgently closer.

Serena was on fire, driven by the insistent beating pulse deep within her that made her writhe against him, moaning his name, demanding something, anything, to satisfy this burning quivering knot of pleasure inside her. 'Don't stop, don't stop, don't stop,' she said to herself, or whispered aloud, feverishly reaching, anxiously searching for the place she wanted to be, was almost afraid to find, the place Nicholas knew, where he would take her.

He kissed her again, a deeply possessive kiss, a thirsty kiss. He licked his way down her throat, the valley between her breasts. She heard herself moan. He turned his attention to her nipples, biting gently, sucking hard, each movement sending out a current of feeling which connected up to the pulse further down. She felt his erection press hard against her stomach. She dug her nails into the muscles of his back, bracing her heels in their laced boots into the mattress the better to push against him.

Nicholas rolled away, moved down her body, his fingers stroking the inside of her thighs, touching her curls, parting the folds of the skin underneath, uncovering the source of all her heat. He touched her delicately. Serena tensed. He touched her again, sliding his finger over the heat, down, back, around, rubbing, delicately increasing the pressure until she felt as if she would break with the exquisite tension. He stopped. She clutched at his shoulder, then moaned as she felt his mouth, his tongue on her, even more knowing than his fingers, a long sweeping movement just exactly where it needed to be, and she couldn't stop it, she was lost, flying, soaring, plunging towards pleasure.

Nicholas pushed carefully into her as her climax pulsed around him, breathing hard as he entered her, cupping the rounded flesh of her bottom to tilt her up towards him. Gently he pushed, discovering she had not lied, meeting resistance, overwhelmed with the knowledge, pausing, trying to stop, thinking he should stop—or trying to think he should stop. Then she tightened her muscles around him and arched up and he was there, where there was no going back, engulfed in hot wet desire, and it felt so right. He pushed, withdrew, pushed deeper. Serena urged him on with tiny gasps of encouragement, gripping him tight with new-found muscles until they found a rhythm, and he was lost to everything save the need to drive towards his own climax, pouring himself into her, taking her with him over the edge, released, lost as he never was before, in the terrible beauty of shared passion.

They breathed, entwined together, limbs tangled, bodies joined, hearts thumping, savouring the warm glow of their lovemaking. She could no longer tell which was Nicholas and which was Serena. Floating in the euphoric aftermath of sated desire, Serena wanted to stay this way for ever. This was lovemaking. It felt so right. Surely he felt it too. For a moment she allowed herself to dream.

The dream did not last. Nicholas opened his eyes, staring at her as if seeing a stranger. *What had he done?* He rolled away abruptly, ignoring the empty feeling the movement created.

He had never felt this way before, wild elation and crushing guilt clashing so strongly it was as if he were being ripped in two. He was angry. With himself for succumbing, with Serena for being irresistible. As he looked at her, the little voice in his head whispered *mine, mine, mine*, and he exalted in the knowledge that that part, at least, was true. She *was* his, she had given him what she had given no one else. Which fed his fury *and* his desire. Nicholas wasn't used to feeling remorse. Or possessiveness. Or out of control. He had never been so swamped by emotions when making love. *What had he done?*

'What's wrong?' The bleakness of his expression made Serena's stomach churn.

'What's wrong?' Nicholas sat up, his muscles rippling. His torso glistened with sweat. He stared past her, his brows drawn together in a fierce frown, trying to garner his thoughts. 'We shouldn't have let ourselves get carried away. A not-unnatural release from the emotion of our ordeal perhaps, but unwise all the same,' he said, spouting the first thing that came into his head.

He might as well have slapped her. One thing to be told not to expect anything from him, another to be dismissed so degradingly quickly. Her first time, and he knew it. He should have been holding her, soothing her, telling her how wonderful it was. Except it obviously hadn't been wonderful, for him. Serena felt a flare of temper. *He could at least have pretended!* Her whole body yearned towards him, seeking comfort, reassurance, tenderness, and there he was no doubt already wondering how soon he could be rid of her when they reached London. She deserved better.

She sat up, wrapping the sheet around her body. With

her hair streaming down over her naked shoulders and her lips swollen from kissing, she looked both unbearably lovely and unbearably vulnerable. 'Serena.'

She brushed his hand away dismissively. 'How can you talk so, calling it a *release*! And an unwise one, at that.'

'It was unwise. If anyone ever hears of this night's doings, you'll be ruined.'

'So that's what this is about! You're feeling guilty. What is it you're worried about, Nicholas, that I'll tell?'

'Of course not.'

'No, it's not that, is it? It's your precious rules. You've broken them and now you're worried about the consequences. Well, you needn't worry about that either, I have no desire at all to drag you up the altar and spend the rest of my life shackled to someone who doesn't give a damn about me.' She bit her lip. 'You have forgotten that it was I, and not you, who *initiated* this—this episode. You did not take. I gave. Obviously *what* I gave didn't live up to your expectations. I must apologise for my lack of experience, perhaps my next lover will be more appreciative.'

Next lover! 'Don't talk like that, as if you are some lightskirt,' Nicholas growled, gripping Serena by the shoulders. The sheet slipped, revealing a tantalising glimpse of pink nipple before she grabbed it again and pushed him away.

She glared at him, angry flags of colour flying in her cheeks. As suddenly as it came her temper fled, leaving her deflated and fighting back the tears. 'Look, Nicholas, it's been a very traumatic day,' she said shakily. 'Highwaymen, attempted murder, now this.' She blinked, managing a weak smile. 'Let us put it down to shock, write it off as an emotional release, call it what you will. Call it the end of an idyll, even, but let us put it from our minds. Don't let us quarrel any more, Nicholas, because I can't bear it.'

'Serena, I didn't mean…'

'It doesn't matter, it is done, let us forget it. Go to your room and rest, for we have an early start. In the morning we will wipe the slate clean, there will be no need to mention it again.'

'Serena, I…'

'Please, Nicholas, do as I ask,' she said with a catch in her voice.

Her very refusal to reproach him made his guilt swell to unbearable proportions. What she said made such perfect sense he could almost have said it himself, but it felt wrong to leave her like this. He battled with the urge to take her back into his arms and tell the world and the consequences to go hang, but his instincts told him this would be to heap madness upon folly. 'Very well,' he agreed finally. He took her hand, pressed a warm kiss on her palm. 'It shall be as you wish. But you are completely wrong about one thing. You lived up to and beyond all my expectations.' He kissed her swiftly. Before she could muster a reply, he had pulled on his breeches, picked up the remainder of his clothing, and hurriedly left her room.

Even without the conflicting voices of his conscience, temper and libido, Nicholas would have spent a sleepless night, since his chamber faced the front yard of the busy posting house, which seemed, to his rattled senses, to tend to customers constantly throughout the long hours of darkness. As a grey dawn rose and his exhausted brain was on the brink of succumbing to sleep, the horns of the Bristol Mail jolted him rudely into full wakefulness. The Mail was followed by the stage, and then any number of vehicles and deliveries, for the inn was on the main road to London. By the time he joined Serena in the parlour for breakfast he was pale, exhausted, short-tempered and no nearer to understanding how he really felt than when he had left her in the early hours of the morning.

Though she too had lain awake for most of the night, Serena presented Nicholas with a determinedly collected countenance. Lying alone in the bed rumpled by their frenzied caresses, wrapped in the sheet that bore traces of Nicholas, she had finally given way to tears. The perfection of their lovemaking served only to confirm beyond doubt the perfect nature of her love for Nicholas. She would always love him, but it changed nothing. She must take her own advice and start the day with a clean slate. She would not flatter his ego by wearing the willow for him. He would never know how she felt. She would not waste her life wishing for the impossible.

Clad in her travelling dress and showing, to Nicholas's exhausted eyes, infuriatingly little signs of yesterday's traumas, Serena responded to his abrupt good morning with a polite smile. He sat down at the table, watching gratefully as she carved him some ham and placed it, with a large chunk of fresh bread and a foaming tankard of ale, in front of him. Reluctant to meet her eye while confusion still reigned between the opposing voices in his head, Nicholas took a reviving draught of the excellent ale, and addressed himself to his plate. Serena sat opposite nibbling a slice of bread and sipping on her coffee. Her papa had been right after all, thought Nicholas, when he named her. *Serenity.* She was the easiest company he had ever kept. A calming presence when he wanted quiet. Lively and witty at other times, making him laugh with her teasing, filling him with a zest for life he usually only felt when boxing or fencing. She was brave, unfaltering in a crisis, and a truly passionate lover. He had never before encountered anyone who could so perfectly match their needs with his. Never before met anyone to arouse such needs in him in the first place, he acknowledged ruefully.

Nicholas sighed. It was all true, but it added up to—nothing. He had no idea what today would bring, save their parting. The one thing he didn't want to have to contemplate.

'Would you like another slice of ham?'

'No.' He rose from the table. 'I'll go and pay the shot. Be ready to leave in ten minutes,' he said brusquely. Try as he might, he could not rid himself of the ill temper brought on by this most unsatisfactory state of affairs.

The mood between them did not improve within the confines of the long coach journey. Each of her careful conversational gambits was greeted with a monosyllabic response. Eventually, Serena surrendered herself to sleep.

By the time the mud-spattered chaise, horses steaming, finally pulled up at the Pulteney Hotel, Nicholas had come to no decisions, save the certainty that he could not simply abandon Serena to her fate. He was almost certain her uncle had arranged at least one, if not two attempts on her life. She had been vague about her plans and he had not pressed her, but his conscience demanded he do something. He needed time to think. 'I'll call for you tomorrow,' he said curtly, cutting short Serena's stumbling, awkward attempt at a farewell. 'I'm coming with you to the lawyer's office. The sooner your identity is established, the safer you will be. In any event, you will need me as a witness to authenticate the papers.'

'Nicholas, there is really no need. I am perfectly capable of looking after myself, I have been doing so since Papa died.'

He shook his head, unwilling to attempt to explain

what he could not himself wholly understand. 'I'll call for you at eleven tomorrow.' Leaning towards her, he kissed her swiftly on the lips, then pushed her towards the open door of the carriage, giving her no time to object.

Serena stood alone on the street, watching as her bandboxes and portmanteaux were unloaded efficiently and taken through the doors of the hotel. Through the thick glass of the chaise she could see Nicholas rubbing his forehead with his hand. Then he leaned back on the squabs, closing his eyes. He did not wave farewell. With her shoulders back and her head high she entered the hotel and demanded their very best suite of rooms.

When Nicholas stepped through the front door of his town house in Cavendish Square not long after, his butler informed him that both his stepmother and half-sister were at home, taking tea. Resigning himself to an hour of tedium, he discarded his driving cape and hat and adjusted his necktie in the large mirror in the hallway before mounting the stairs to join them.

The drawing room on the first floor was pleasantly proportioned, the plainly plastered walls tempered a pale yellow. The curtains at the long sash windows, which looked out on to the square, were of dull gold damask, matching the coverings of the assorted chairs, sofas and *chaises-longues* set out in conversational groups around the room.

'Nicholas!' Georgie jumped from her seat by the

fire, rushing to greet her elder brother. She was a pretty girl, obligingly free of any tendency towards either puppy fat or spots despite her tender years. Aside from her striking grey eyes, Georgie was unlike her handsome brother in almost every way. Her hair was dark brown, her little mouth a perfect rosebud, and her skin as correct a blend of white and pink as any English rose could desire. A crooked front tooth, a schoolgirl giggle and a slight clumsiness of manner, which in some young women might have been a drawback, were deemed in a girl with such an excellent portion to be merely part of her charm.

Decked out in sprig muslin trimmed with ribbons, she presented a pretty enough picture as she reached up to plant an affectionate kiss on her brother's cheek. Nicholas responded with a hug, telling her she looked bang up to the mark.

Georgie grinned and dropped him a curtsy, spoiling the effect somewhat by treading on one of his toes. 'Dearest Nicholas, I'm so pleased to see you, I've got much to tell you. Why did you not send word of your arrival, we had no idea you were coming today? I met Charles at Almack's last night and he was so kind as to compliment me on my *toilette*. Coming from such a notable Corinthian, that is high praise indeed. Did you get my letter? And did you—?'

'Georgiana, hush now. Ring the bell for fresh water, your brother will be wanting some tea. Nicholas, how do you do?'

The voice from the fading beauty on the sofa gave the impression of suffering stoically borne. Like her daughter, Melissa Lytton was petite, her sylph-like frame giving her the appearance of a wraith on the verge of fading for ever into eternity. She was impeccably attired in a grey silk dress with long sleeves, her raven locks dressed in an intricate knot on the back of her head, the tiny little cap she wore the only indication of her widowed status. Not yet forty, in temperament and appearance she was nearer fifty. Melissa did not rise to greet her son-in-law, merely extending a long thin hand from her semi-prone position.

Nicholas grazed the hand with a kiss, and sat down beside her. 'Well, Melissa, I can see you are in your usual health.'

'Alas, I was never strong, Nicholas, and though I am determined to make sure your sister has a good Season, it is already taking its toll.' She raised her vinaigrette to her nose and took a delicate sniff. 'I try my best, and as you know, dear Nicholas, I never complain,' she said with a sad smile.

'Oh, Mama,' Georgie said impatiently, 'the Season's barely started. I hope you're not going to sell me short, we've got engagements every day for weeks and weeks still.'

Melissa sighed. 'Pour your brother some tea, he will be glad of it after his journey, then no doubt he will want his bed. Have you the tic, Nicholas? I know that if *I* had made such a journey, I would be prostrate.

I shall have them put a hot brick in your bed. You should rest before dinner.'

'Don't fuss, Melissa, I'm perfectly well.' Nicholas sipped distastefully on the dish of Bohea his sister handed him. He abhorred tea. 'Tell me all about your latest conquests, Georgie. Did you know Charles is betrothed? He's giving a party.'

'Yes, we already have the card, though Mama thinks it may be too much for her.'

Judging by his stepmother's few words and pained demeanour, it wouldn't be long before Melissa took to bed to indulge in one of her regular—and lengthy—recuperations. Poor Georgie, she deserved better than to be left to her own devices while Melissa quacked herself.

His sister was not the only one in need of a companion. Serena and Georgie would be perfect for each other. Of course Serena had not exactly said that she wished to launch herself into society, but what else was she going to do here in London? She could certainly not rely upon her murderous uncle to help her. Life above a gaming salon did not prepare one for *ton* parties. Nicholas knew only too well how cruel and vicious genteel society could be, what sport could be had with the naïve outsider. He doubted Serena was prepared for this. It mattered a great deal to him that she be well received. It would go a long way to ease his guilty conscience if she were established.

Established. The word gave him pause, for he was not prepared to think too specifically about its implications. He decided not to, and instead set about putting his idea in train. 'I brought a new acquaintance into town with me,' he said, interrupting his sister's account of a visit to Vauxhall Gardens. 'The only daughter of an old friend of our father's. She's older than you, Georgie, but she's new to London; it might be a good idea if she accompanied you to a few parties, give your mother some much-needed time to rest and regain her strength.'

'Oh, *no*, Nicholas, not if she's old.' Georgie pouted.

'I said older than you, not old, silly. She's four and twenty. Very beautiful, but luckily she's blonde; she'll be the perfect foil for you. What do you say, Melissa? That way you won't be so knocked up by having to escort Georgie everywhere.'

'Is she a respectable female, Nicholas?' Melissa asked dubiously.

'Very,' he said emphatically. 'She's the daughter of Lord Vespian. The previous, recently deceased Lord Vespian, that is, who was Father's friend many years ago. Her name is Lady Serena Stamppe.'

'You may bring her to meet me,' Melissa consented, 'then we'll see.'

It did not seem to occur to his mother-in-law to ask Nicholas how he became acquainted with Serena. Melissa was a caring enough mother, but vacuous, and consequently rather poor company for a vivacious girl like Georgie. In comparison, Nicholas had no doubt that Serena would be an instant hit with his sister.

Satisfied with his afternoon's work, Nicholas placed his half-full dish of tea back on the tray. 'I'll present Serena to you tomorrow. I'm off to my club now. I'll see you at dinner—if you're not dining out?' Receiving a graceful assent, Nicholas went upstairs to change into clothes more suitable for the stroll down Bond Street to St James's.

He was greeted warmly at White's and with some surprise, his erstwhile duelling opponent having only just been given a clean prognosis. The club was thin of company, but Nicholas found Charles at the window table along with some of his cronies discussing a race that was to be held the next day. Nicholas listened with little interest, waiting until the odds were settled and entered into the book, before requesting a private word with his friend.

'I am to congratulate you, Charles. I take it your discussions with Lord Cheadle went well the morning after you left me?'

Charles smiled thinly. 'Yes. I hadn't appreciated just how tedious settlements could be. Not content with dowries and dowagers, the man actually wanted to talk about his grandchildren. We're not even married yet, and he wants to dictate which school my sons will attend.' Charles shuddered. 'I tell you, Nicholas, it's one thing to bring yourself up to the mark and tie the knot, but it's quite another having to discuss your future offspring with your future father-in-law when you're future wife hasn't even allowed you to kiss her!'

Nicholas laughed at the pained expression on his friend's face. 'Well, you can't say I didn't warn you. I trust you have kissed her now? After all, you *are* officially engaged.'

'Oh, you know how it is,' Charles said with an embarrassed laugh, 'we're never permitted to be alone. On the odd occasion we've been left together, Penelope is the soul of propriety. When I asked her for her hand I was granted a peck on the cheek. I can only pray that her mama has informed her she'll be expected to give rather more of herself on her wedding night, otherwise Lord Cheadle is going to be deprived of those damned grandsons he's counting on.'

'Charles, you can't go to the altar without at least being sure she'll be compliant. What are you thinking of, man?'

'Lord, Nick, there's nothing unusual in the case. She's an amenable little thing and she's not repulsive, I'm sure we'll get on well enough once we're married, provided she can breed. What strange notions you have about marriage. I don't look to a wife for that sort of pleasure, I get that elsewhere, as you do—as most men we know do.'

Nicholas stared at his friend, struck by the casual callousness of his words, though he could not argue with the truth of them. More strongly than ever he felt that marriage on such terms as those would never be for him.

'I'm glad you're back, Nick,' Charles said. 'Never mind my wedding, did you think any more about your own? You didn't by any chance take my advice and ask Serena?'

'I believe I've already told you not to be ridiculous on that subject, Charles,' Nicholas said sharply. 'She's here in town, as a matter of fact.'

Charles raised both eyebrows, for him a sign of extreme surprise. 'Is Jasper aware of this?'

'What's it got to do with him?'

Charles smiled. 'I told you, Jasper knows that you had a female in tow at the Hall. He was worried enough about it to ask me what I knew. He's up to his neck, you know, and from what I hear he's playing deeper than ever. Some hell down in Piccadilly, you know the sort of place. I don't say the dice are loaded, but…'

'Does he know her name?' Nicholas interrupted sharply.

'Well, if he does, it didn't come from me. What does it matter?'

'Because you were right about her aristocratic nose,' Nicholas responded with a wry grin. 'Turns out my Serena, as you call her, is the Lady Serena Stamppe, daughter of the late Lord Vespian, and a considerable heiress.'

'Good Lord.' Charles paused in the act of taking snuff, a comical expression of disbelief on his face. 'And you haven't asked her to marry you? Are you mad? Devil take you, Nick, what's stopping you?'

Nicholas paused. What was stopping him, exactly? Serena could be his, and only his. She would be safe with him. He would with a single act secure her presence in his bed and his father's fortune. He would be set up for the rest of his life. But that was just it of course—*for the rest of his life*. 'You're becoming a bore on the subject, Charles. Just because you're getting leg-shackled doesn't mean you have to wish it on everyone else.'

'Thing is, Nick, don't you think you *ought* to marry her now? If word gets out that she was at the Hall—practically living there—to say nothing of what I presume has been going on between the two of you—well, I don't need to say any more.'

'Fortunately there is no one to tell, save yourself, and I know that I can trust you implicitly. Serena assures me she does not consider herself compromised,' Nicholas said, choosing his words carefully.

'Does not consider? What does that mean?'

'I have nothing more to say on the matter,' Nicholas responded angrily. 'Now oblige me by changing the subject, if you please.'

Charles grimaced. 'God, you're like a stag being baited by the hounds. I know something that will cheer you up. The divine Eleanor is on the market for a new protector. Since you paid off the Masterton, the odds have shortened in your favour. She's a choice piece.'

Nicholas shrugged. A few weeks ago the news would have intrigued him. Eleanor Golding was reputed to be even more talented than Diana Masterton. Now, the only emotion he could summon up was indifference. It was all Serena's fault. He cursed her roundly. He had to get her out of his system.

Watching his friend frown, Charles decided not to waste his own blunt by betting in Nicholas's favour, and diplomatically turned the conversation to less controversial affairs. Soon they were joined by a group of friends intent on a hand or two of whist before dinner.

Nicholas played, but his mind was on other things, and he lost badly. He returned to Cavendish Square for dinner but ate sparingly, listening with detachment to the chatter of his sister and the gentle remonstrations of his stepmother before retiring unusually early to bed.

The next day at eleven o'clock precisely Serena was waiting for him in the foyer of the hotel. She was turned out extremely modishly in a silk walking dress of her favourite blue with a pleated hem. A pelisse in matching blue velvet and a poke bonnet trimmed with three ostrich feathers made her the most elegant and most admired woman in the hotel. Nicholas, who had until now seen her only in simpler clothes more befitting the country, bowed formally over her hand and complimented her on her outfit.

She smiled, trying to ignore the beating of her heart, which seemed to leap into her throat at the sight of his familiar tall, handsome figure. 'Thank you. Coming from such a self-confessed arbiter of ladies' costume, that is a high compliment indeed.'

'Are you comfortable here? Did you sleep well?'

She nodded, hoping that the large rim of her bonnet hid the dark shadows under her eyes. Nicholas climbed into the very high-perched phaeton which he had left in the care of his groom, and leaned over to help Serena up.

At the offices of Messrs Acton and Archer, Mr Acton received the woman claiming to be the Lady Serena, daughter of the late Lord Vespian, with undisguised interest. 'I take it that you have proof of your status,' he asked, his natural cautiousness quickly reasserting itself.

From her reticule, Serna took the packet of documents. 'I think you will find all the proof you need here. My papa lodged everything that you have in front of you with an old friend, a Mr Nicholas Lytton, for safekeeping. The gentleman here with me is his son, Mr Lytton having died some ten years ago. He can vouch for their authenticity.'

Tobias Acton inspected Nicholas carefully. 'Indeed,' he said. 'Perhaps if you will be so good as to give me a moment to peruse these papers?'

They waited as the lawyer read his way painstakingly through the will with frequent reference to the other documents. Finally, he looked up. 'Well, this seems to be in order. I don't like to ask this, but I'm afraid I must. How can I be sure that you came about these papers legitimately, Lady Serena?'

'Papa gave me this.' Serena withdrew the antique ring from its leather pouch and placed it on the blotting pad of the desk in front of Mr Acton.

'Ah! I know this well. The black pearl. Yes, the last time I saw your papa—I was just a clerk—he wore this. I have to say, now that I see you, you do bear a strong resemblance to you dear departed father. Well, this settles things. Welcome, Lady Serena. I am most—indeed extremely—pleased to make your acquaintance.' The lawyer made Serena a low bow. 'You are aware, I take it, that you have an uncle, Mathew, now Lord Vespian? With your permission I will send him an express informing him of your arrival.'

'He is aware of my existence then,' Serena asked.

'Indeed, yes. Your father left him a letter informing him of his marriage and your birth. I gave it to Lord Vespian myself, here in this very office a few days ago.'

'Is her uncle aware of the extent of Lady Serena's inheritance?' Nicholas asked.

'I did not read the letter myself, you understand, but I believe that is the case,' Tobias Acton said cautiously.

Nicholas looked at Serena. 'How did he react?' she asked.

Mr Acton pursed his mouth. 'I'm afraid your uncle was rather shocked at first. "It seems, Mr Acton, that I have inherited a niece rather than a fortune." Those were his very words. As I said, it was a shock. I expect he has now become reconciled to the idea and is looking forward to welcoming you into the family.'

'I doubt it,' Nicholas said. 'In fact, he—'

Serena placed a restraining hand on his arm, and shook her head. 'Not here.'

The meeting came to an end shortly afterwards, with Serena agreeing to return the next day once the lawyer had time to assimilate the full implications of the will. Nicholas helped her back into his phaeton and took the reins from his groom, who had been walking the horses. 'We'll go for a drive in the park, it should be quiet at this time and there's something I need to discuss with you.'

Chapter Eight

Sitting in the carriage, Serena felt curiously numb. Now that the long-awaited meeting with Mr Acton was over, her future was a blank canvas she had neither the energy nor inclination to paint. Beside her, Nicholas's expression gave her no clue as to his feelings. She admired his skill as she sat beside him, making their way through the crowded streets of the city, and resigned herself to waiting. Hawkers called their wares from every corner, everything from pints of ink to quarts of milk. Clerks carrying thick bundles of papers tied with ribbons wove fearlessly through the traffic. Two men selling rival newspapers competed with each other to see who could ring their bell the loudest. In comparison, the park was an oasis of peace, occupied mostly by children and nannies, the fashionable hour for the *ton* and the *demi-monde* alike not having arrived.

Nicholas allowed his horses to slow to a sedate trot. 'You're very quiet.'

'Are you surprised? I no sooner discover I have a family only to have it confirmed that they wish me dead. Do you really believe my uncle hired those highwaymen to kill me?'

'I'm really sorry, but it does seem likely.'

'Papa's only brother.' She opened her reticule to search for a handkerchief. 'I'm sorry, I'm just so—it's just so incredible.'

'At least he is not likely to make another attempt, now that Acton has met you.'

'The way I'm feeling right now, he's quite welcome to make another attempt.'

'Don't say things like that, Serena. If I didn't know you better, I'd think you were about to indulge in a fit of the vapours.'

She managed a watery chuckle. 'I don't think I know how to.'

'That's better.'

'I have an aunt and a cousin as well as an uncle. Do you think they wish me dead too?'

'No, of course not. No one who's met you could wish you other than well.'

She blushed. 'Compliments now?'

'The truth.'

'Do *you* wish me well?'

'You shouldn't have to ask that. I wish you more than well. I wish you to be happy. Have you thought about what you're going to do next?'

'Not really. Everything seems to be happening so quickly. It's only a few days since I first visited Knightswood Hall, but it seems like weeks. I must see my uncle, I suppose, though what I am to say to him I have no idea.'

'Shall I deal with him?'

'No, I am perfectly capable of looking after myself, you know, and he is hardly likely to pull a gun on me over a glass of sherry. What is it you wished to say to me, Nicholas? If it's about the other night, I don't want to—'

'No, it's not. What you said made perfect sense.'

'Oh.' She did not know what to make of this and could see no possible good in asking him to clarify, so she inspected her gloves and waited.

'I've told you about my sister Georgiana, haven't I? She's here in town with Melissa, her mother, my father's second wife.'

'Yes, I remember you said,' Serena replied, now completely at a loss.

'Georgie needs someone to take her about—to parties and balls and such. It struck me that you and she could bear each other company. You'll like her.'

'I'm sure I will, but I haven't decided—'

'It's a perfect solution,' Nicholas interrupted ruthlessly. 'She's pretty much up to snuff is Georgie, even though she is young; she'll see that you meet all the right people, do all the right things. Melissa will get you vouchers for Almack's and I'll hire a caper merchant for you, too, so that you'll know all the latest steps.'

'With what purpose in mind, might I ask?' Her voice was decidedly cool.

Nicholas kept his eye on his horses. 'Your father wanted you established, that was surely his purpose in sending you here.'

'Yes. But as you've pointed out, had he been absolutely set on it he would have brought me himself. In any case, I am not so sure it is what I want.'

'Of course it is—what else will you do?'

'You have it all thought out.'

Nicholas glanced over, but her face was set, she looked firmly ahead. 'I'm trying to help you, Serena.'

'Yes, I'm sure you are.'

'So you'll come to tea in Cavendish Square?'

'I'll think about it.'

He was tempted to ask her what was wrong, but was not at all convinced he would like the answer and opted, in what he assured himself was a sensible manner and not at all cowardly, to revert to the earlier subject. 'I was thinking, perhaps your father was more prescient than you realise.'

'How so?'

'I thought it strange before, his insistence that you find your papers and take them with that ring to the lawyer, rather than seek out your uncle. Strange, too, that he did not trust his brother with the knowledge of your birth.'

'You mean he suspected that Uncle Mathew would—surely not?'

'What we've taken for whimsy on his part has probably saved your life. I've been meaning to ask you, why did he leave England in the first place. Was it a duel?'

Serena hesitated.

'I sense another secret.'

'He left under something of a cloud. He was accused of murder.'

The horses, used to the lightest of hands on their sensitive mouths, veered off the path as Nicholas jerked the reins. He swore under his breath and quickly got them back under control. 'I should have known. Mitigating circumstances, no less—now I understand why he didn't come back sooner. Nothing involving your papa is straightforward, is it?'

Serena gave the ghost of a smile. 'He was no more a murderer than you are. He took the blame for a friend.'

Nicholas looked sceptical.

'I know what you're thinking,' Serena said, 'but it's true.'

'Go on then, reveal all.'

She closed her eyes, forcing her mind to drift back to that night. The sickroom, the sense of impending gloom as she watched her father fade in front of her eyes. 'He and some close friends had been playing cards most of the night,' she said, doing her best to recall his exact words. 'Dawn was breaking when one of them took it into his head to visit his *chère-amie* and Papa decided to accompany him.' She smiled ruefully.

'I asked him why he would do such a thing, and he was very embarrassed. He said she had a sister.'

'Charming. His determination to keep you wrapped in cotton wool did not prevent him from sullying your ears with some sordid tales.'

'I'm sure you could come up with something equally sordid if you set your mind to it,' she said acerbically.

'I don't tell tales, sordid or otherwise.'

She was silent.

'I'm sorry. Please carry on.'

'They arrived at the village where the two women lived, but their brother answered the door. He was drunk, and refused them entry to the house. Papa's friend had a temper. They started brawling, he and the brother, right there on the doorstep. The fight was vicious. The brother was a brute. Papa's friend was distracted by his light o' love, standing on the doorstep wailing like a banshee, apparently.'

Nicholas gave a crack of laughter. 'I can imagine.'

'Papa's friend succumbed to a—a sweet uppercut, Papa said. Have I that correct?'

'Quite correct. If you recall my fight with Samuel, I delivered just such a punch myself.'

'And just as successfully too. Papa's friend went down, just as Samuel did. Papa thought it was all over there and then. He went to help his friend up, laughing at his muddied clothes.' Serena stopped to assemble her thoughts, finishing the story in a rush as it came back to her. 'His friend suddenly pulled a dagger from his coat and plunged the blade straight into his opponent's heart. For an instant Papa thought it some cruel jest, but the man crumpled to the ground, lay completely still in the mud, blood pooling around him. Papa's friend begged him to help him. He was engaged to be married at the time, you see, whereas Papa had no ties, so he agreed to take the blame. He always expected to hear word from his friend that he had made things right. He always intended to return, but…'

'But he never did,' Nicholas finished for her. 'And who was he, the real murderer?'

'I don't know. Papa wouldn't tell me. He wanted me to know he was not guilty, but right to the end he insisted on protecting his friend's identity.'

Nicholas shook his head slowly. 'Serena, I swear your life is like a Gothic novel come to life. No wonder you find Byron's poetry insipid! If you tell me your papa left you no clue, I will be horribly disappointed.'

Serena bit her lip guiltily in an attempt to suppress a slightly hysterical laugh. 'No.'

'It bothers you, doesn't it?'

'I don't like to think of Papa branded a murderer if he is innocent.'

Nicholas looked thoughtful. 'It may be possible to trace the woman involved by finding out the name of the murdered man. Through news sheets or court records. I could set Frances on to it.'

'I think you've asked Mr Eldon to do enough investigating of my family.'

'I suppose I deserved that.' They had arrived back at the gates to the park. A few moments later he pulled his carriage up in front of Serena's hotel. 'You'll come to Cavendish Square this afternoon, won't you?'

'I'm not sure.'

'Please. Come to tea, that's all I ask.'

It would be churlish to refuse. She nodded. Without waiting on his help, she leapt nimbly down from the carriage and entered the hotel.

Jasper Lytton awoke to the sound of persistent pounding on the front door of the Albany lodgings where he rented rooms. Clasping a hand to his head in a vain effort to suppress the sensation that his brain was being pierced by a selection of steely knives, he opened one bloodshot eye and felt with the other hand for his watch, lying discarded on the table by his bed. Two o'clock. Cautiously, he peered over at the window. Daylight. Afternoon, then.

The pounding stopped. His man must have answered it. No doubt it would be duns. A scratching at the door of his chamber preceded his valet. 'There is a gentleman demanding to see you.'

'I am not at home,' Jasper said curtly, wincing as

he sat up. The knives in his brain were joined by a red hot poker.

'I said a gentleman, not a creditor,' his valet responded impatiently. An employer such as Jasper, who owed him the last two quarters' wages, did not merit politeness.

'R-r-rather a gentleman *and* a creditor,' Hugo Langton said, pushing past the valet and closing the door in his face.

'What do you want,' Jasper asked wearily.

'I w-want my money,' his one-time friend said angrily. 'I have it on excellent authority that your cousin is about to get hitched, and I want what you owe me before you land in the Fleet prison.'

'Been listening to Charles Avesbury, have you?' Jasper sneered. 'He's talking nonsense.'

'Not Avesbury, my sister,' Langton responded. 'She had it from some new dressmaker who's all the rage. A Frenchie, just come from High Knightswood, if you must know.'

'What?' Jasper got out of bed, clutching his head.

'Thought that would make you pay attention,' Langton said, his stammer disappearing as his confidence grew. 'The woman told my sister that she came over from France with a young lady who subsequently spent the duration of their stay closeted with your cousin at Knightswood Hall.'

'One of his bits of muslin,' Jasper said dismissively, though he knew it was a lie.

'No, thought about that,' Langton said vehemently, 'but can't be. Your cousin's not a loose fish, wouldn't keep a mistress in his own house. Must be something more to it than that. Face it, Lytton, you're done for.'

'Don't be so sure,' Jasper said with a nasty smile. 'Now get out, I need to dress.' Ignoring Langton's protests, Jasper pushed him bodily out of the room, calling for his man to bring him his shaving water. Stepping out into the late afternoon an hour later, his rage was cold, his intentions calculated and his step decisive.

Serena presented herself at Nicholas's house in Cavendish Square with mixed emotions. Though she had once looked forward to entering society, she was not at all convinced that she wished to do so now, so alien would it be from the milieu in which she had been raised. She was annoyed with Nicholas for his too-obvious attempt at easing his conscience by fobbing her off on his sister. She was annoyed, too, at the arrogant way he was choosing to assume control over her life, and the mixed signals he continued to give her, first pushing her away, then pulling her back into his orbit. But more than anything, she was angry with herself for granting him the power to do so. Knowing full well she was nurturing foolish hopes, she nevertheless continued to nurture them.

In the end, common sense and a rather shameful curiosity had got the better of her. Foolish she might be in falling in love with him, but in every other sense, Serena was determinedly practical. It would be stupid to dismiss, in a fit of pique, the opportunity that his promised introductions offered. And if she were honest, sharing Nicholas's company for a few more weeks, days, hours, whatever he would give, while immensely difficult, would not be half as painful as not sharing his company at all.

The tea party went well. Melissa was happily uninterested in the circumstances surrounding Serena's arrival in England and her relationship with Nicholas. Pleased to find a sympathetic ear, she passed a pleasant half-hour regaling Serena with the merits of country over town air, debating the possible healthful effect of Lord Byron's reputed diet of vinegar and potatoes, and recommending the services of a Dr Leland whom she had found to be most sympathetic should Serena ever suffer, as Melissa herself did, from sick headaches.

Serena nodded and smiled with good grace, contriving—most of the time—not to catch Nicholas's eye for fear of giggling. Only once, when Melissa offered her an old family receipt for the relief of gout, did she resort to muffling her laughter behind a handkerchief, refusing steadfastly to respond to Nicholas's question into the condition of her own mercifully gout-free joints.

Georgiana's sharp eyes missed nothing. Lady Serena was quite beautiful, even if she was almost past marriageable age. It was so very unlike her brother to take an interest in any female of the *ton* that Georgie had, from the outset, been sure of an intrigue between Nicholas and Serena, and it did not take her long to find evidence of the intimacy between them to confirm her suspicions.

As Serena appeared to listen attentively to a list of Melissa's latest symptoms, Georgie caught a look—a glance, no more—between their visitor and her brother. They were laughing together at some shared joke. When Nicholas turned his attentions to Georgie, his sister had every opportunity to see how Serena's eyes were drawn every few minutes to look at him wistfully. She was convinced that here was a case of star-crossed love for her to help resolve.

Serena did not stay long, but she was enough of a hit with Melissa to be asked to accompany them to a rout party the next day. 'Just a small affair, with some intimate friends. You know the kind of thing, my dear Serena—you will not mind my using your name, since your papa and my husband were such friends?' Melissa dabbed at her eye with a tiny flutter of linen and lace. 'No dancing, you understand. Just cards and pleasant company.' With a sigh, Melissa collapsed back on to the sofa, requesting Nicholas see their visitor out.

He stood to give Serena his arm. 'I would recommend that you stay away from the card tables,' he said, his eyes alight with amusement, 'I don't want to be hearing that you've fleeced all of Melissa's friends.'

'If Melissa's friends are anything like herself they won't have the energy to play cards, so there's no need to worry.'

They spoke softly, but Georgie's ears were sharp. 'Why must Serena not play cards? Does she cheat?'

'Georgie, you let your tongue run away with you overmuch,' Nicholas said sharply. 'What's more, you are being excessively rude to our guest.'

'Oh, I do beg your pardon.' Georgie curtsied, tripping on the edge of a rug. 'But I don't think you're at all offended, are you, Lady Serena? I saw you laughing at Mama with Nicholas when you thought no one was looking.'

'Oh dear, then it is I who should apologise to you, Miss Lytton.'

'Don't be silly. And do call me Georgie, I hope we're going to be friends.'

'Very well then, I will. Thank you for the tea, I look forward to seeing you at the party.'

Leaving the room on Nicholas's arm, Serena turned to him questioningly. 'Can I look forward to seeing you at the party also?'

He shook his head. 'Come in here, I need to talk to you,' he said, pulling her into a small parlour on the ground floor.

'What is it now, Nicholas?' Serena asked, instantly becoming defensive as she wondered what new social solecism he thought she had committed.

'We can't be seen in each other's company.'

'Why not?'

'Whether we like it or not, there is an unmistakable air, an aura between us, which we cannot hide. We may both offer silence on the subject of our lovemaking, but our actions betray us all too eloquently. You saw my sister—she realised straight away that we are not mere acquaintances. Other people would see that too. There would be gossip.'

'And as you have pointed out to me several times, Nicholas, you steer well clear of any friendship with a lady that may be construed as flirtation. I understand,' she said coldly.

'I'm not talking about mere flirtation,' Nicholas said exasperatedly.

'Then what are you talking about?'

'I am talking about your reputation. If people ever found out what has passed between us you would be ostracised. And if they see us together they would know instantly. Georgie noticed. Charles saw it.'

She was angry, the more so because she knew he spoke the truth. 'You wish to ease your conscience by staying clear of me and having your sister put me in the way of eligible men, in other words.'

'Yes. No, that is not what I meant.' Putting her in the way of other men was the last thing on his mind. 'I just want to see you established.'

'No, that is not what you want, Nicholas,' she contradicted him coldly. 'You wish to wash your hands of me.'

'You are deliberately misunderstanding me, Serena.'

She glared at him. 'Enlighten me, if you please, then. How exactly do you wish me to feel, because frankly I have no idea.'

Nicholas ran a hand through his hair in exasperation. 'What I want is for you to be happy without me. Serena, you must realise that the nature of our acquaintance forced us into an unusual intimacy. What we felt, thought, did during our time at High Knightswood, it was not real. Everything—our seclusion, your circumstances—all served to fuel, to intensify a physical attraction that in any other situation would not have flourished. Had it not been for our near-death experience, I doubt we would have consummated our passion. But we did.'

'Yes, we did. A mistake, we both agreed. But not one for you to feel guilty about. You did not coerce me.'

'It makes no difference,' Nicholas responded hotly. 'Can't you see that?'

'I still don't understand what it is you want of me.'

'What I want of you!' He tugged at his neckcloth as if it were too tight. 'I want nothing more on earth than to make love to you until we are both totally sated.'

'No,' she said flatly, 'I will not be your mistress. I told you that I would not play the game on such terms. I have no wish for an *affaire* that will end with a few trinkets when you have had enough of me. I have no desire to be the latest in the infamous Nicholas Lytton's long line of conquests.'

She stood facing him, her arms crossed challengingly, a martial glint in her eyes, looking so beautiful, so angry, so infuriatingly, completely desirable, that Nicholas lost his head and shook her.

'You're hurting me.'

He released her immediately, breathing heavily, frightened by his own fury. 'I never, not for one moment, think of you in the same light as any other woman.' The words were clipped, his lips narrow, his eyes almost black, glinting at her beneath a frown so deep that his brows met. 'You asked me what I want of you, I spoke the unvarnished truth. I also know that I cannot have what I crave. But what I can do is ease your entrance into society. I can do that much for you—or at least Georgie and Melissa can. And in this way our relationship will become what it should always have been, that of common acquaintances.'

'In other words, you hope familiarity will breed contempt.' Tiredness washed over her. It had been a very long day. 'Very well, Nicholas. We shall nod and smile at one another from a distance until you become bored. You will sate your passions in your usual way, and perhaps I will sate mine by taking a husband,' she said maliciously, conscious of the need to inflict on him just a little of the hurt she felt.

'With your new-found fortune, I do not foresee any difficulties on that score,' he agreed sarcastically. 'You can replace me in your bed soon enough.'

But I will find you impossible to replace in my heart, Serena thought wretchedly. Determined not to let him see how much he had hurt her, she curtsied quickly. 'I must thank you for your kind offices. I am not so foolish or so rude as to turn down your sister's offer of friendship. We have both said enough to understand each other perfectly. Goodbye, Nicholas.' Without waiting for a response, she swept from the room.

'Serena!'

She heard him call, but ignored it. Nodding to the butler, who opened the large front door, she left the house in Cavendish Square with straight shoulders and head held high, determinedly ignoring the anguish tearing at her heart.

Serena spent the night telling herself she was well rid of such a heartless beast as Nicholas and torturing herself with imagining in vivid detail just exactly what she would be missing out on in the lonely years to come. As a consequence she was not in the best of humours when she was informed the next morning that two gentlemen wished to see her. Uncle Mathew had travelled post-haste to reach town upon receipt of an express sent by Mr Acton. His son Edwin accompanied him.

She was unprepared. Having assumed that a man who could arrange her murder would not hasten to pay a morning call, she had not yet decided how to handle the situation. Schooling her expression into one of polite surprise, she executed an elegant curtsy and decided that discretion would serve her best for the present.

'My dear niece. I cannot tell you how good it is to meet you at last,' Mathew said effusively. 'As you see, I came up to town as soon as I had word you were here. How do you do?' He bent his sparse frame stiffly over her hand.

'Uncle Mathew.' He had not her father's looks, but the family resemblance was plain. A bluff man, a country squire with little town polish, if his clothes were anything to go by. Serena granted him a cool smile.

'And here is your cousin Edwin come to meet you—my son, you know. Edwin, make your bow lad.'

Like his father, Edwin was tall and spare of frame, with the piercing blue eyes of the Stamppes. Youth lent his hollow features an attraction lacking in his father's countenance. Had he the sense to dress simply, as became his physique, he would have passed as a well-enough looking young man. Sadly, Edwin had no such sense, having ambitions to join the dandy set. In the mistaken belief that he was bang up to the mark, he wore his coats pinched tightly into the waist, the shoulders exaggerated and peaked with the assistance of immense amounts of stiff buckram wadding. As if this was not enough, the enormous brass buttons on the coat served to emphasise the meagreness of his sparrow-like chest, and the tightness of his knitted pantaloons the stick-like quality of his spindly shanks. To this *toilette* he added shirt points starched so high that he could not turn his head, a waistcoat embroidered with pink roses, and so many fobs, rings, quizzing glasses and the like that he positively clanked when he minced down Bond Street each morning.

He had dressed with special care for the meeting

with this new cousin. The hat he swept from his pomaded locks was so tall that street urchins competed to knock it off with stones as he passed. His coat required the combined efforts of his valet and the butler to squeeze him into it, so tight was it cut, and his cravat, tied in the intricate *mail coach*, had taken over an hour to perfect. He bowed with a flourish over Serena's hand, bestowing upon it a rather clammy kiss. 'Cousin. *Enchanté.*'

Such a pink of the *ton* would of a certainty have nothing to do with anything so sordid as murder. Serena suppressed the urge to laugh. 'I'm overwhelmed, Cousin Edwin. You'll both take some refreshment, I hope?'

'A glass of Madeira would be most welcome, my child,' Mathew said obsequiously. 'We must sit down and get acquainted, but first it behoves me to offer my commiserations, belated as they are, for the death of your father, my dear brother.' Under her cool gaze, Mathew coloured.

'I believe I should congratulate you on your newly acquired title, Uncle. My loss is your gain.'

'Well, as to that…'

'Though you have been managing the estates for so long now, you must almost have thought them your own.'

This was rather too close to the bone. 'I have certainly kept the land in excellent heart. I only hope I can continue to do so on the somewhat reduced income I will have once your inheritance has been paid.'

Serena gave him a direct look. Having met him, she could not believe that he posed any further threat to her safety. He was clearly a foolish opportunist, a rather grasping man who acted without thinking. The sort of man who would always bet on the outside odds and blame everyone but himself when, predictably, he lost. Enough had been said—or not said—to make him aware of her suspicions. After all, apart from her ridiculous cousin, he was her only blood relative. There could be no benefit in pursuing the matter.

An awkward silence reigned. Edwin shifted uncomfortably in his seat, aware that his beautiful and rather intimidating cousin was in some way angry with his father, but unable to imagine why, since they had never met.

Finally, Mathew spoke. 'Well, well, there is no point in dwelling in the past. We should be rejoicing to be reunited as a family,' he said bracingly. 'Now that you are acquainted with your cousin Edwin here, I expect you will see a good deal of one another, what with going to the same balls and—and such.'

Mathew rubbed his hands together as a brilliant idea formed in his head. The marriage of his niece to his son was the perfect solution, well worth the expense of a dispensation, if that proved necessary. He wished it had occurred to him earlier, he could have saved himself the gold he had expended on that incompetent ex-Runner. The man had diddled him, that's what he had done, with his claims that it was too dangerous to try again. Poppycock!

Looking at his son, forced into a rigid sitting position on the small gilt chair by the combination of starched cravat, over-tight lacing at his waist, and pantaloons that threatened to unknit if he moved too suddenly, Mathew experienced a twinge of doubt. Serena was a fine-looking filly, and quite a catch, with all that Vespian gold on her back. She'd be bound to go off well despite the fact that she was near five and twenty. Nevertheless, he owed it to the estate to make a push on his son's behalf. 'Aye, you can rely on Edwin to take care of you, Serena dear. He's quite a ladies' man,' Mathew said, looking encouragingly at his son.

Serena looked somewhat sceptical. Edwin blushed furiously.

Mathew smiled suggestively. 'I'm thinking it best for now if I leave you two young 'uns to it, and I'll take a look in at my club,' he said with a knowing wink.

His meaning was unmistakable. Serena bit her lip. If only Nicholas were here, how he would have enjoyed it. She couldn't wait to tell him. Then she remembered. She bit her lip again, though she no longer felt like laughing.

'No, no, I'll come with you, Father.' With one eye on Mathew's retreating figure, Edwin looked like a startled fawn yearning for its mother's protection.

'Don't go yet,' Serena called to Mathew. 'I have something for Edwin. Wait here.' She left the room, hastening back bearing a small leather pouch, which she handed to her cousin. 'Papa said it's always worn by the heir to the earldom. I'm not sure it will be to your taste, it's very old-fashioned, but none the less it's yours by right.'

Edwin opened the pouch and took out the ring. Mathew, looking over his shoulder, gave a gasp of surprise. 'The black pearl. Acton said you had it, I knew there was no question of your identity if you had.'

'Papa said it would be thus. It's Edwin's now.'

Edwin regarded the intricate gold that encased the huge pearl with something akin to horror. 'There's not any sort of curse or anything on this? Because if there isn't, there ought to be.' Seeing Serena's face, he remembered that the ring had been her father's. 'What I mean is, thank you for passing it on and everything, but I'm not actually required to wear it, am I?'

'Not wear the black pearl!' Mathew was shocked.

Edwin handed the ring to his father. 'If you're so fond of it, you wear it. Grotesque thing like that, I'd be a laughing stock.'

Mathew was a weak rather than a cruel man. He refrained from pointing out that his son was already such a laughing stock that the addition of an antique pearl ring was unlikely to make much difference, and instead put it on his own finger.

Edwin creaked to his feet. 'Very nice to meet you, Cousin Serena,' he said with a bow. 'Coming, Father?'

Reluctantly, Mathew followed.

Even without the revelation of her true identity and the added benefit of her fortune, Serena's entrance on to the London scene would have caused a stir. The Season was not yet halfway through, but already the *ton* were bored to distraction with meeting the same company, day in and day out, at the various balls, outings, parties and concerts. A new face was always welcome. Such a very pretty face as the Lady Serena's, doubly so. The tale of her lineage and her inheritance ensured that she was besieged with invitations almost as soon as she was introduced.

Nicholas was, as expected, not present at the rout party that first night. Serena, a vision in a half-dress of sea-green gauze with a petticoat of silver muslin, noted his absence with a sinking heart as she nervously entered the coach containing Georgiana and Melissa. She should be thankful, she told herself, but she could not help wondering if he was already pursuing his next conquest.

Becoming an instant success was, however, a pleasant balm to her bruised ego and a boost to her confidence, as were the flood of envelopes, flowers and trinkets which greeted her over the following days. She was little inclined to vanity, and thought the tributes more likely to be a consequence of her fortune than her face, but she could not remain wholly untouched at finding herself so sought after when she had so lately felt utterly alone in the world.

Of Nicholas she saw precious little. As he had promised, they were on nodding terms only. They were not once alone. Only in the dark of night did Serena allow herself to think of him, longing for him with such an ache that her future unravelled before her like a long black tunnel. In the cold light of day she remembered how useless it all was and resolved anew to forget him.

Tobias Acton managed to secure her a pretty little furnished house in Upper Brook Street, into which she moved with astonishing ease. The days passed in a flurry of parties, dances, tea-taking and shopping. Serena did her best to enjoy herself in this new social whirl, but she found it strangely unsatisfying, not to say occasionally tedious. There was no one to share her sense of the ridiculous. No one with whom to laugh. No one in whom to confide. Too often, her quips fell on deaf ears. Too often the phrase *what can you mean*, or, worse, a blank look, were the responses she received to a witty remark. At times she had to stamp down hard on the absurd urge to shock the company with a lurid story from the gaming salons. In the crush of a ball, with her dance card full and her partners fawning, she felt more lonely than she would have thought possible.

She had already decided that this would be her only Season. Her brief stay in Knightswood Hall had made her certain of more than one thing. She had endured enough of city life. Since marriage to anyone other than Nicholas was out of the question, she must turn her mind to a different kind of future. In the summer she would start looking for a property of her own. One with a home farm, and a kitchen garden, where she would churn her own butter and dry her own herbs. She might even start up a village school. Being an only child, she had always planned to have a large family. A nursery full of brats, as Nicholas would say. *Damn!* Resolutely consigning the endearing image to the back of her mind, she turned her attention to her *toilette*.

Chapter Nine

The following Wednesday, Serena accompanied Georgiana and Melissa to Almack's. Dressed in a simple gown of her favourite pale blue satin, with matching dancing slippers and a pair of long kid gloves a deeper shade of blue, which fitted so perfectly that they roused the envy of several other young ladies present, she fastened her evening cloak and tripped lightly downstairs to await the carriage.

Almack's was an old-fashioned club that demanded that all gentleman wear knee breeches and stockings. This fact alone was sufficient to keep Nicholas from ever darkening its portals. Despite being perfectly well aware of this, Serena could not help but look wistfully at the empty place in the town coach, wishing he would make an exception just this once. She had never danced with him. She longed to share the story of her uncle's visit, knowing just how amused he would be at the idea of a match between herself and her ridiculous cousin. She thought of how he would laugh when she mimicked the look on Edwin's face as he saw the black pearl ring. And she would tell him how easy it had been to put what he would call *the frighteners* on Uncle Mathew.

Serena danced, talked and smiled, all the while nursing a growing—and, she was perfectly well aware, irrational—resentment at Nicholas's treatment of her. Without a doubt he was slaking his thirst for her in some other bed. She was well rid of such a fickle, rude, ill-tempered, infuriatingly attractive man. She checked the time on the wall clock. It wanted but fifteen minutes to eleven, the hour at which the doors of the club were closed to newcomers. The evening stretched uninvitingly out in front of her. She longed for the comfort of her bed.

Shutting her fan with a snap, she looked around for Melissa and Georgie. A tall man clad elegantly in knee breeches and a dark, well-fitting coat stood in the doorway, imperiously surveying the room. Her heart lurched. She felt his eyes bore into her. She looked away, opening her fan again, frantically waving it in front of her overheated face. Her emotions see-sawed annoyingly from resentment to a fizzing sense of anticipation.

'Lady Serena,' the familiar voice said, as he bowed deep in front of her. 'I trust I am not too late to claim a dance with you.'

'Mr Lytton,' Serena responded breathlessly, 'what a surprise.'

'Another first for you to rack up,' Nicholas said drily.

Serena looked up, trying to gauge his mood, raising her brows questioningly.

He indicated his attire. 'I am not in the habit of tricking myself out in this way, but I found I could no longer resist the allure of dancing with you.'

'Wanting to see if the money you invested in the dancing master was well spent, you mean. I am honoured,' Serena said, taking his arm, feeling the familiar *frisson* of awareness, powerless as ever to resist him.

The orchestra struck up a waltz. Fortunately she had been granted permission by one of the patronesses to take part in the dance. She stepped into Nicholas's cool clasp, smiling up at him, looking so breathtakingly beautiful that his hands tightened on her waist. 'I've missed you,' he said. The words were out before he could stop them.

Such a simple admission, but it was more than she could have hoped. She had forgotten that feeling, as if her blood was filled with champagne bubbles. It was so lonely, this new world, with no one to share it. Serena responded recklessly, moving closer into his embrace. If he did not care for the gossip-mongers tonight, she would not.

They waltzed effortlessly, gracefully, their steps perfectly in time. Oblivious of the curious glances from the other dancers, they talked, smiled, touched, looked, caught in their own little bubble on the busy dance floor. He laughed wholeheartedly as she knew he would when she recounted her meeting with Mathew and Edwin. When the music stopped, they left the floor still entwined, engrossed in Nicholas's description of his first encounter with his former duelling opponent—taking fencing lessons!

They went down to supper still talking, oblivious of Nicholas's sister staring at them blatantly from a nearby table. Charles Avesbury joined Georgie to watch, his fiancée Penelope, pale and silent, at his side. Nicholas and Serena sat close, their heads bent together, their arms resting on the table, fingers almost touching. Serena said something, smiling with those big blue eyes of hers, the curve of her full mouth tender, making Nicholas laugh. He leaned closer to whisper in her ear, twisting a long strand of her golden hair round his finger. She blushed, picked up her glass, sipped, put it down, never once taking her eyes from his. Charles looked away, embarrassed and envious.

'Nicholas, it's lovely to see you,' said Serena, 'truly it is, but why have you turned up out of the blue like this? I don't understand, I thought we were to remain—'

'I've got a surprise for you,' Nicholas interrupted, smiling at her in a way that made her light-headed. 'Frances Eldon has managed to track down the name of the man your father is supposed to have murdered.'

'What?'

'And his sister. The—er—lady in the case. You look surprised.'

'I'm astonished. I didn't think for a moment that you meant it when you said you would instruct him to look into the matter.'

'Well he has done so, and as usual he has been successful.'

'Is she still alive, the sister?'

'I don't know, I'm afraid. It happened in a village called Mile End, not too far east of here. If she hasn't departed this life, she's probably still there. Aren't you pleased?'

'I hardly know what to think. Do you think you could—no, it's too much to ask, never mind.'

'Ask me. I find it almost impossible to say no to you.'

She looked at him, aware that it was the truth, equally aware that it was only half the story. He would have no difficulty at all in refusing her the dearest wish of her heart. But she would not think such thoughts tonight. 'Would you escort me there?'

'If you're sure.'

'I'm not at all sure. I had quite decided to let sleeping dogs lie, but now that you've found her…'

'If she's still alive.'

'I can't not go now.'

He laughed at that. 'I think I understand.'

'I'm glad you came tonight. I was angry with you, and hurt when you so patently avoided my company. But the truth is,' she said with a nervous smile, 'that I've missed you too.'

Nicholas thought back over the last two weeks and

all his efforts to resume his old way of life. He had watched Charles race his precious greys against an old enemy and win by a gratifyingly large margin. The evening that followed was spent in a dubious tavern in the Haymarket favoured by the opera company. Some of the dancers joined them. Vast quantities of daffy, gin and water were consumed. The alcohol made Nicholas feel curiously detached from the proceedings. Charles disappeared upstairs with one of the dancers. Nicholas brushed one away. He drank more. The result was a deep melancholy and a blinding headache the next day, which did nothing to improve his humour.

Georgie had obligingly kept him informed of Serena's successes, ensuring that Nicholas was aware of every time Serena danced more than once in an evening with a favoured beau. Nicholas granted his disappointed sister no sign of the insane jealousy her revelations should have given rise to. Of course Serena was a hit, he had predicted it himself, had he not, he told Georgie curtly, setting off to spar viciously at Jackson's. It did not help. He had donned his knee breeches tonight with a mixture of resentment and expectation.

'I think you have cast a spell on me,' he admitted with a self-conscious laugh. 'I can't get you out of my head.'

Serena swallowed. The air between them crackled with tension. She could feel the heat of Nicholas's hand beside her own. A shiver of awareness twisted low in her stomach. Her mouth was dry. She stared at his hand. Beneath the white ruffle of his shirt sleeve she saw that his knuckles had healed. No trace now of that fight with Samuel. No trace in the immaculate ballroom costume of the wild, reckless boxer she had first encountered. But it was there all the same, lurking in his eyes. She felt the response deep in herself, a wakening urge to throw in her lot with him and flee, no matter what the consequences.

'Nicholas,' she whispered, telling herself that it would be madness, knowing already that she had made up her mind.

'Serena,' he said huskily, tracing the plane of her cheek-bone with a long finger.

He didn't love her, he would never love her, she knew that. But he missed her. He had sought her out. Another first, he said. Surely it could do no harm.

It could, and she knew it. Deeper and deeper she would fall. But right now, at this moment, she was ready to hurtle herself into whatever depths Nicholas chose for her, regardless of the consequences. She reached up to touch his hair.

'Really!' The exclamation came from a dowager at the next table, her scandalised countenance reminding them both of their surroundings for the first time since Nicholas had entered the club.

'Serena,' Nicholas said urgently, 'let's get out of here.'

'Are you sure?'

He smiled wryly. 'I should be asking you that, but I don't think I could bear it if you said no. I've never been more sure of anything in my life. Tell me you feel the same.'

'Take me home, Nicholas.'

He needed no further invitation. Across the supper room, Hugo Langton, alerted by the dowager's exclamation, stared at the scandalous couple. With surprise, he noted that one of them was Jasper Lytton's cousin. 'W-what was the name of the female your dressmaker mentioned?' he asked his sister. 'The F-frenchie.'

Lettice Langton wrinkled her brow. 'Serena, I think it was. I remember thinking it was a pretty name. Why?'

Langton nodded over at Nicholas and Serena, now preparing to leave. 'Know who that is?'

'The latest heiress,' Miss Langton replied. 'She's very beautiful, but quite old.'

'And her name is Lady Serena,' her brother told her with a grin and no trace of a stammer.

Lettice Langton's little mouth dropped. 'Well,' she tittered gleefully, 'I wonder what Mama will make of that little bit of news.'

'Never mind Mama,' Langton said, 'I know someone who will be even more interested.'

The short drive to Upper Brook Street seemed to take an age. Serena was acutely conscious of Nicholas's leg brushing against hers through the thin satin of her gown. Each time the carriage jolted on the cobblestones they touched. Nicholas gripped her long-gloved hand in his own, so tight she thought her fingers would break. She could hear his breathing. She could feel the heavy thump, thump, thump of her heart. She felt weak with anticipation.

He was out of the carriage and pulling her down after him almost before it stopped at her front door. Dragging her up the shallow flight of steps, he summarily dismissed her footman with a curt nod, telling the astonished servant that he would let himself out. Thrusting Serena through the first door he came to—which fortunately was a comfortable parlour—he turned the key in the lock. 'I don't want a repeat of last time.'

'Most considerate of you,' she responded with a shy smile.

'Come here, Serena,' Nicholas said softly.

She walked into his arms. It was like coming home. Loneliness, anger, hurt evaporated with his touch. She rubbed her cheek against his chest, relishing the scent and feel of him, caught up in the magic that was Nicholas, lost in the wonder of the love she felt welling up inside her.

He held her tight, his face in her hair, remembering the scent and feel of her, the combination of skin and curves and light and laughter that was Serena. *His* Serena. The tension of the last few days dispersed into nothing, replaced with tension of a different sort. The pervading sensation that something was terribly wrong took flight, giving way to a heady certainty that everything was right.

Serena stirred against him. She looked up at him, her

eyes clouded with desire. 'Nicholas.' She said his name in that way no one else said it, and he was lost in the grip of a crushing, crashing, overwhelming passion.

His hands roamed along her shoulders, pushing aside her heavy evening cloak. Down the line of her back, feeling her curves through the sheer satin of her dress, he remembered every inch of her. 'Serena. Oh God, Serena, I want you so much.' The words were torn from him painfully. He rained kisses on to her neck, tangled long fingers through the spun gold of her hair, kissed her eyelids, the tip of her nose, returning always to her lips to drink deep, thrusting his tongue urgently into her mouth, desperate to cover every inch of her with kisses.

Serena matched passion with passion, kissing, licking, tugging, scratching. The clasp that held her cloak gave way. It fell to the ground, spilling around her feet. The tiny puffed sleeves of her gown were pushed down her arms to free the neckline of her dress and release her breasts. Cupping them in his hands, Nicholas dropped his face to scatter kisses over the yielding flesh, into the valley between, on to her nipples, lighting little paths of fire everywhere he touched, stoking the flames of the furnace burning lower down.

Serena moaned, fierce with desire, urging him onwards with hands and tongue and lips and body. Nicholas scooped her up to lay her down on a sofa, kneeling down beside her. He ran his hand up the inside of her leg under her gown. She felt her skin tingling beneath the material of her underwear. Her pulses thrummed. The focus of her world narrowed. She was aflame with pinpoints of desire.

Writhing on the sofa, she parted her legs, wanton in her need for him to touch her, reaching to caress his erection through the silk of his knee breeches. Nicholas moaned, his fingers curled into the heat between her thighs. He struggled to undo his buttons. 'Touch me, I need you to touch me.'

Serena ran a gloved hand over the throbbing length of him, closing her fingers around his girth, caressing him with aching familiarity, knowing just exactly where to touch, to stroke, to rub, relishing the feeling of power it gave her to make him shiver and close his eyes with the pleasure of it.

His fingers plunged deep inside her, sliding slickly out, up, rubbing harder on her wetness, plunging in deeper again. Serena gasped, tightened her hand around him. That heady, dizzy, terrifying exhilarating need to jump possessed her. She breathed hard in anticipation. Nicholas kissed her roughly on the mouth. Pulled his hand away. Removed hers.

Serena opened her eyes. He pulled them both to their feet before she could protest, and in one fluid movement bent her over the sofa, hoisted her skirts around her waist and plunged into her from behind.

'Oh!' She clutched at the back of the sofa for support, momentarily overcome by the hardness and suddenness of his possession. Cautiously, she wriggled her bottom against him, drawing a satisfying groan from him in response. He withdrew almost to the tip of his hard length, then plunged again, at the same time reaching under her dress at the front to touch her with his fingers, rubbing and circling as he thrust hard into her, harder, and harder, filling her, until she climaxed around him, and he lost control, pounding into her, clutching at her, pulling her close as he exploded inside her, saying her name over and over.

When he finally withdrew, Serena closed her eyes, bracing herself for the inevitable rejection, but it did not come. He pulled her close, cradling her in his arms, collapsing on to the sofa with her on his lap, stroking her hair, pressing kisses onto her face, hugging her as if trying to mould her to his shape. A sense of euphoria swept over him, so unlike the usual depression that he was afraid to move lest he lose it.

Serena would gladly have climbed inside Nicholas's skin and stayed there if she could have. She felt spent, sated, and blindingly happy. 'We've still got our clothes on.' Her satin evening gown was creased beyond recovery. Nicholas's neckcloth was half-undone, his shirt ripped open, his coat hanging off his shoulders.

Self-consciously, he shifted to adjust his breeches. 'I had not this in mind when I put these dammed things on to go to Almack's tonight.'

'And was it worth the effort?' she teased, made confident as much by the contented look on his face as his earlier admission of his need.

'I don't know. We haven't finished yet,' Nicholas said with an endearing grin.

'Mr Lytton, so soon,' Serena exclaimed in mock astonishment, astounded to feel a stirring of excitement between her own thighs.

'Lady Serena, I do believe so,' he answered. 'Perhaps you would like to investigate for yourself.'

Serena rolled from his embrace to kneel before him. 'I think perhaps I should,' she murmured wickedly, taking him delicately into her mouth.

Later, they made more leisurely love on the floor in front of the unlit grate, falling asleep, finally naked, in one another's arms.

Nicholas left Upper Brook Street just before dawn, kissing Serena tenderly. At peace for the first time in days, he failed to notice the man lurking in the shadow of an opposing doorway, keeping an eye on Serena's house. He made his contented way north to Cavendish Square under the light of the new-fangled gas lamps. At home, he slept dreamlessly, well into the late morning.

He awoke to a new-found resolution. Charles Avesbury was right. He would never find a better match than Serena. What he felt for her would probably fade in time, it was the way of things, but she was like her name, serene, and would remain an amenable companion for life. She would be his for always, exactly as she should be, for as long as he wanted her. Reconciled as Nicholas was to the fading of his own passion, he could not bear the idea of Serena giving herself to anyone else. The news, broken tentatively by Frances Eldon after breakfast, that his lawyers had failed in the final attempt to break his father's will, only confirmed him in his resolution. The gods had spoken. Nicholas could find no fault with his decision to make Serena his wife.

It was as if a weight had rolled from his shoulders.

He was in excellent spirits as he strolled down Bond Street towards St James's. Until he encountered Mathew, Lord Vespian, coming the other way.

'Ah, glad to have bumped into you, Mr Lytton,' Mathew said. 'I believe I have you to thank for taking care of my niece's papers.'

'It was a pleasure.' Nicholas eyed Mathew appraisingly. 'I wonder, Lord Vespian, if you would care to join me for a drink in my club. It's just here, and I have something of a private nature to impart to you.'

Mathew looked surprised and not particularly keen, seeing the saturnine look in Nicholas's eye. 'Well, I have an engagement, you know.'

'It will take but a few moments.' Nicholas placed a firm grip on the older man's elbow.

Mathew had no choice but to follow him the short distance along the street, through the entrance vestibule of White's, and into a back room, which, at this time of day, was empty of other members. Smoothing the sleeve of his coat, he sat down huffily, demanding that Nicholas be brief. 'I can't think what can be so important, but there was no need at all to compel me, you know. Your father was another such one, impetuous, always in trouble, just like my brother Philip. You are very alike, in character as well as features, if your behaviour towards me is anything to go by.'

'Yes, yes, let us agree that my behaviour in coercing you was abominable,' Nicholas said dismissively. Despite the early hour, he called for brandy. If Serena's uncle did not want it now, he was like to be in need of it once Nicholas had spoken.

'I will be blunt and to the point, Lord Vespian. Lady Serena is a rich woman, and I believe that the price for her wealth comes at a cost to your estates. Am I correct?'

'Not that it's any of your business, but, yes, it's true enough.'

'And may I ask if I'm correct in assuming that the money reverts to you if anything happens to your niece?'

'Yes, naturally. What has that to do with anything?'

'There have been two attempts on Lady Serena's life. In order to deduce who made them, it is necessary to understand who would benefit from her death.'

'*Two* attempts?' Mathew exclaimed in astonishment.

Nicholas frowned. Perhaps the first bullet had been fired by a poacher after all. 'A near-miss not long after she arrived in England. Then a rather more serious attempt by two highwaymen who held up the carriage she was travelling in. Both times, luck was on her side. I would not like her to rely on chance a third time.'

'Highwaymen!' Mathew poured himself a brandy with a shaking hand. 'Are you sure my niece was not just unfortunate? To assume that a hold up was an attempted murder is surely rather over-imaginative.'

'Not at all. It was quite obvious that the whole point was to murder Serena.'

'How can you be so certain, Mr Lytton?'

'Because I escorted her to London from Knightswood Hall, which is where my father kept her papers. Her French companion had unfortunately left her quite alone.'

'You spent two days on the road in my niece's company without an escort?' Mathew exclaimed, outrage written large on his face.

'I can assure you, sir, that all the proprieties were observed,' Nicholas said angrily. 'Let us put things in perspective here, my lord. *I* only had Serena's—Lady Serena's—best interests at heart. *I* was trying to protect her. Whereas you, Lord Vespian, have now tried twice to kill her.'

Mathew's face crumpled and his shoulders sagged dispiritedly. 'No, no, not twice. Not twice, I assure you. And the first time was only—oh, I have been so foolish.' He rested his head dejectedly in his hands. It was one thing to hand over a sum of money to arrange for some vague harm to come to a complete stranger.

Quite another to have the deed named cold-blooded murder, especially now that he had met his niece, found her quite charming and intended her for his daughter-in-law.

Nicholas waited impatiently for Serena's uncle to regain his self-control.

Mathew wiped his face with a large handkerchief and took a swallow of brandy. 'What must you think of me? It was a foolish thing, done in the heat of the moment. You must understand, my brother's death, the will, the existence of my niece—I found this all out in the contents of one letter. It was a shock, and I admit I behaved very badly. I paid a man to arrange for my niece to meet with a—an unspecified accident. He bungled it, and refused to try again for fear of discovery, for which I am profoundly thankful.'

'Had he not, rest assured you would be having this conversation with a magistrate, not with myself,' Nicholas said acerbically. 'What was he like, this bungler you paid?'

'I can barely remember. He was an ex-Runner. Small, fat, he wore a greasy coat. I don't know any more.'

'And you had nothing to do with the highwaymen?'

'No! No, on my oath. Nothing. I swear, I thought the better of it, and now that I have met Serena, I could not wish her any harm. You must believe me, Mr Lytton. I'm an honest man. You cannot make me feel any worse than I already do.'

'I'm not concerned with your repentance, only

with your promise to take no further action. If any harm should come to Lady Serena, I will know where to look.'

'She will take no hurt from me, you have my word.' Mathew took another reviving tot of brandy, relaxing as the spirit took effect on his empty stomach. He mopped his face once more, and smiled knowingly at Nicholas. 'My niece is a very attractive young woman, I am not surprised that you take such an interest in her. But she has her family to look after her now, Mr Lytton. And—I'm sure you will forgive my blunt speaking—a man of your reputation would be rather a liability to a young woman seeking to make a respectable match. You understand me, I'm sure.'

Mathew made to rise, but a strong hand on his shoulder and a snarling face breathing hard into his own forced him back on to the seat. He sprawled there gasping like a fish out of water, his terrified gaze staring into the face of the very devil.

'Your definition of *looking after* your niece entailed doing away with her, let me remind you, Lord Vespian. I shall not forget that. What's more, Lady Serena is of age, and if she chooses to spend time in my company, that is for her to say—as it is for her—and only her—to choose not to! Your concern for your niece's reputation will, I am certain, ensure that you keep your base suspicions about my own behaviour to yourself. I bid you good day, sir. I can see no need for our paths to cross again unless I find that Serena is in danger. I trust that there will never be such an occasion. If there is, then I can promise you will regret it.'

Nicholas brushed Mathew aside and stormed out of the club, ignoring the offer, from a friend just arrived, of a game of whist.

Mathew lay gasping in his chair, sweat, which had broken out on his forehead, dripping into his eyes. After a few moments he recovered his breath, and with the aid of yet another snifter of brandy, his composure also. Nicholas Lytton had given him much food for thought. Why, if it ever got out that he and Serena were—close?—she would be ruined. There would be no offers for her hand, for who would take Lytton's leavings? No one. Except perhaps Edwin.

Despite the stress of the interview, things might yet work out to his advantage. With something approaching nonchalance, he left White's and sauntered off to meet with his tailor, so content with the morning's findings that he ordered not one, but two new coats.

Though he was deeply perturbed by the possibility that a second person might have designs on Serena's life, Nicholas put it to the back of his mind as he made his way back to visit her in Upper Brook Street for the second time that day. As her legal protector, he would be able to make sure she came to no further harm.

The door was opened by the same footman he had so summarily dismissed the night before. The man boggled at him, and Nicholas grinned good-humouredly. 'Is your mistress at home?'

He was shown up to a sunny drawing room on the first floor with three long windows overlooking the street. He did not have long to wait. Serena came in, a vision in sprig muslin and green ribbons.

He clasped her hands between his, smiling down at her. Serena returned the smile shyly. 'I didn't expect to see you again until tomorrow,' she said, the day they had fixed upon for the journey to the village of Mile End.

'There is something I wish to discuss with you. Come and sit down.'

She took a seat by the fireplace, looking at him expectantly.

Nicholas sat opposite her, stood, looked out of the window, then sat down again. 'I think we should get married,' he said abruptly.

Silence. Serena stared, trying to muster her thoughts, her heart fluttering in her chest like a songbird in a cage. 'Do you?' was all she could manage, desperately waiting for the words, those three precious words, which must surely follow such a proposal.

'It makes sense,' Nicholas said, staring at his boots.

Not those three words. Hope withered in her breast. 'Why?' she asked neutrally.

Nicholas looked up. Discomfited, he realised he had assumed Serena would say yes and throw herself into his arms. He should have known better. His smile was twisted. 'There are many reasons, but there is one that I have not disclosed to you.'

Serena's expression brightened, a tiny flicker of hope rekindled. 'What is it?'

'I think I mentioned when we first met that your father was not the only one with a quirky sense of humour.' Bluntly, he explained the terms of his father's will and his lawyer's failed attempts to break it.

As she listened, Serena felt her blood turn to ice. 'I thought there were to be no more secrets between us.' Her voice faded as she valiantly swallowed a sob. *She would not cry!* 'So you think we should marry in order for you to protect your inheritance,' she managed after a few seconds.

'No, that's just a part of it. Last night—'

'I wondered when we would get to that.'

He stared at her, trying to suppress the panic that threatened to engulf him. The possibility of his first-ever proposal of marriage being turned down had not occurred to him. 'Last night confirmed, if confirmation were needed, that we are extremely compatible. I have said it before, Serena, what we have is special.'

'Since I have no previous experience, I will have to take your word for that.'

'Serena, what I'm trying to say is that I think we could make a good marriage,' Nicholas said exasperatedly. 'We enjoy one another's company. We give each other immense pleasure. Even when passion has been spent, I do not think we will make one another unhappy. We understand each other in that way too. I will always be discreet. You will be comfortably established. And on top of all that, our marriage will prevent my cousin from throwing away my inheritance on cards and horses.'

'And when passion, as you say, is spent, what must I do?'

'What do you mean?'

'Am I to live the life of a nun when you are done with me? Perhaps I will occupy myself with the nursery full of brats you want nothing to do with? Or do you simply wish me to be as discreet as you plan to be?'

'Don't be ridiculous, Serena, you will be my wife. I would not tolerate your infidelity.' He spoke without thinking, reacting only to the idea of her in anyone else's arms but his own. It was a mistake—he knew it as soon as the words were out.

'You are a hypocrite, Nicholas, I thought better of you,' Serena said angrily. 'How dare you propose marriage to me on such terms!'

'I didn't mean it that way. You once told me that for you marriage meant fidelity. I was assuming you had not changed your mind.'

'I have not. But fidelity applies to both partners in my book, not just one. And I was actually referring to love, if you remember. Which in your case,' she added pointedly, 'is not an issue.'

'You're being preposterous! I offer you marriage, something I have never in my life offered before. But

I am not the hypocrite you accuse me of being. I know passion will fade, it always does. I won't make you false promises.'

'You don't love me, in other words,' Serena said flatly.

'What has that to do with anything?' Nicholas demanded. He stood, paced over to the window, returned to face her from behind a sofa, leaning his hands on the back of it, reminding her of the use they had put a similar sofa to only a few hours earlier.

The urge to take what he was offering was strong. It was not everything, but it was so much more than she had. But she knew in her heart she could not. 'I can't marry you, Nicholas,' Serena said firmly.

Abruptly, he changed tack. 'If you don't, you will be compromised. Last night, our behaviour in Almack's, leaving together in the way we did, can have left no one present in any doubt of our relationship.'

Serena shrugged. 'I don't care. I've decided to leave London.'

'I thought you planned to settle here.'

'I've changed my mind.' Better a clean break than a long agonising death. She saw that clearly now. 'No,' she said with resolution. 'I can't stay here.'

'Can't?'

'Won't. I have no reason to stay. My only relative wants me dead or married to his son. I have no other ties. Perhaps I will return to Paris and open a gaming salon,' she said defiantly. 'Since my reputation is in tatters anyway, it cannot do me further harm.'

Nicholas sat down beside her and took her hand in his familiar grasp. 'Won't you reconsider?'

She knew a marriage based on one-sided love could never succeed, no matter how unshakeable that love might be. He would discover the truth, and he would resent her for it. The more he resented her, the more she would feel guilty. It was impossible. She shook her head sadly. 'No, Nicholas, it wouldn't work. You would not be happy with me. I could not bear that. I'm afraid you will have to resign your inheritance to Jasper.'

'Damn Jasper and my inheritance,' Nicholas said vehemently, 'I simply don't want to lose you. Not yet.'

Not yet. Serena disentangled her hand. 'It's for the best. Last night was perfect. Let us leave it at that and say no more.'

He hurled himself to his feet. 'I will not demean either of us by begging. I will see you tomorrow.' Thwarted, deflated and frustrated beyond measure, Nicholas stormed out.

Alone in the drawing room, Serena tore her handkerchief to shreds in an effort to hold back her tears. It served no purpose. Every flicker of hope had been extinguished from her heart, leaving it as cold and hard as a block of ice. A block of ice that was fissured and cracking, breaking into myriad splintered pieces. Hot tears dripped and burned like acid on to the tattered lace she clenched between her trembling fingers.

Chapter Ten

The next day dawned bright and sunny in stark contrast to Serena's mood. She gazed out of the window on to the street. She knew Nicholas would turn up, for he had promised, but she dreaded his arrival. Her resolution to leave as soon as possible had hardened overnight. She had been fooling herself for too long now. To continue to be in Nicholas's company would be senseless torture. The time had come for her to face the truth. But she was not at all convinced of her ability to cope with seeing him again so soon.

Nicholas pulled up in his high-perch phaeton drawn by a pair of showy chestnuts. Knowing how much he hated to keep his horses standing, Serena hurried down to meet him. She wore an emerald-green walking dress and warm pelisse, and a fetching straw poke bonnet trimmed with ribbons of the same colour.

Nicholas helped her up, tucking a rug around her

knees, carefully moving along the narrow seat to avoid touching her. With a sinking heart, Serena met his saturnine smile.

'You look as charming as ever,' he said, flicking his leader's ear with the whip. 'We have quite a way to go and my horses are fresh—you'll forgive me if I refrain from making polite conversation.'

The journey was completed in silence. They travelled out through the city and headed eastwards. Cobbled streets gave way to country lanes as they followed the direction of the River Thames towards the village of Mile End, reaching it around midday.

As they drew nearer to their destination, Serena forgot about the tension between them and thought only of Papa. His deathbed description of the scene that morning almost thirty years ago came back to her with the clarity of a painting. For thirty years he had borne the blame for a crime he did not commit. For thirty years, his unknown friend had avoided justice. Now she was on the verge of discovering his identity. Nervously, Serena smoothed an imaginary wrinkle from her York tan gloves. Anxiously, she gazed at the little village ahead of them.

Nicholas pulled up at the only inn, shouting for someone to stable the horses. Startled to be called upon to deal with such a fine equipage, a toothless ostler tugged at his cap and led the phaeton into the yard.

'Wait here,' Nicholas barked, disappearing into the dark interior of the inn.

Serena sat in the sunshine on a convenient bench, watching the antics of a small kitten playing with a lazy spaniel. The ostler re-appeared from the stable yard accompanied by a scrawny boy. They stared. Serena fidgeted with her reticule.

Five minutes later Nicholas returned. He looked down at her drawn face. 'Are you all right?'

'Fine. A bit nervous.'

'I enquired inside. Eliza Cooper is alive and well and still living in the village, amazingly. She's Eliza Baker now, a widow.'

'Oh.' Serena swallowed. 'I'm terribly sorry, but I feel a little faint.'

'Come on, Serena, this is not like you.'

She smiled wanly. 'It's been a—an eventful few days.'

He laughed derisively. 'Eventful is certainly one word for it.'

'Nicholas, I know it's foolish, but I have a horrible premonition about this Eliza woman. I'm not sure I want to know what she's got to say.'

He looked at her in surprise. 'It's not like you to be faint-hearted. We can leave now if you would rather, but I think you would regret it later.'

'The thing is, what if it was Papa after all,' she said agitatedly.

Surprised to see her so distraught, Nicholas chose his words with care. 'Do you think that is a possibility?'

'I don't honestly know.' She stared down at her reticule, whose strings were now hopelessly knotted.

'Papa believed he was not guilty. The problem is, I have come to realise that he could be less than honest with himself.'

'That may be so, but you are a very different creature. I think you would rather know the truth, no matter how painful.'

His perception drew a smile from her. 'You are quite right, Nicholas. I would always be wondering.' She rose from the bench wearily.

'Serena.'

Blue eyes under fair brows looked up at him. A day resolutely trying not to think of her and a night pacing the floor of his bedchamber had left him no clearer. She could not be his mistress. She would not be his wife. Yet he simply could not let her go. He sighed in exasperation as he looked at her troubled countenance. Now was not the time for whatever discussion his quandary required. Perhaps if he could help her clear her father's name, she would feel differently about—about everything.

'What is it, Nicholas?'

He shook his head. 'Nothing. Let us find the infamous Mrs Baker. I wonder if we will be able to discern any traces at all of her charms?'

Serena giggled. 'I think that's highly unlikely.'

She was proved correct. The woman who answered the door to which the innkeeper had directed Nicholas was enormously fat and rankly odorous.

'Mrs Baker,' Serena asked doubtfully. 'Eliza Cooper that was?'

The woman smiled, revealing several unsightly

black stumps that had once been teeth, adding the smell of stale food to the general stench that surrounded her. 'Been a long time since I heard that name,' she said, eyeing Serena curiously. 'Who wants to know?'

'My name is Stamppe. You may have been acquainted with my papa, Philip Stamppe.'

Eliza Baker looked startled. 'Acquainted with him? He killed my brother.'

'That's not true,' Serena asserted, 'and you know it. The man who killed your brother was your protector, and I want to know who he was.'

Eliza narrowed her eyes. 'Why?'

'My papa is dead. I want to clear his name.'

'And who might you be?' Eliza said, turning her attention towards Nicholas for the first time. 'Not a magistrate, I 'ope. I've done nothing wrong.' She gave a gasp, raising a hand to her face. 'Gawd help us. I thought it were him for a minute.'

Nicholas surveyed her disdainfully.

Eliza staggered back against the doorway of her cottage. 'I never told. I kept my promise, I never told,' she gabbled. 'Never, never, never.'

Nicholas looked at her in astonishment.

'I never said a word. Tell your father, I kept my promise,' Eliza continued, backing into the cottage.

'What has *my* father got to do with this?' Nicholas demanded.

Eliza stared at him. 'It was him 'as done it. Your father killed my poor brother.'

'No, no,' Serena said, appalled. 'That can't possibly be right.'

'Are you calling me a liar?' Eliza snapped, recovering quickly from the shock of seeing a ghost from her past. 'I know who was keeping me warm at night and paying for the privilege.'

Nicholas shuddered with distaste at the ghastly image the vile crone's words had conjured up.

'And I know who killed my brother, God rest him. Saw it with me own eyes. I know who paid me to keep my trap shut too. Nick Lytton, that's who. And you,' she said, pointing a filthy finger at Nicholas, 'are his living spit.'

'Nicholas, surely there must be a mistake,' Serena said, looking with anguish at his darkening countenance.

He pushed Eliza's grimy hand away. 'When did you last see him?' he demanded.

Eliza shrugged. 'Not long after it happened. He gave me a handsome sum, helped me turn respectable, become a lady of leisure, so to speak.' Her laugh dissolved into a violent coughing fit, which she relieved with a hawking spit. 'Haven't seen hide nor hair of him since.'

'Nor will you again. He's dead these past ten years.'

'What business have you coming round here stirring up trouble for, then? You'd do well to leave it alone, missy,' Eliza said, looking accusingly at Serena. 'What's done is done.'

'How can we be sure you are telling the truth, that

this is not just some kind of sick joke?' Nicholas interjected.

'Want proof, do you?' Eliza cackled. 'Well, proof you shall have. Wait here.' She disappeared into the gloomy recess of her cottage, emerging a few moments later clutching something wrapped in a filthy rag, which she handed to Nicholas.

As he looked at the object within, Serena saw his expression shift from disbelief to horror. 'Nicholas, what is it?'

'A miniature. A likeness of my father. I fear there is no doubting the truth now.'

'Gave it to me as a token of 'is affection, he said,' Eliza informed them. 'Not valuable enough to sell, so I held on to it as a keepsake.'

'As an insurance policy, more like,' Nicholas said disdainfully. He flicked a coin to the ground in front of Eliza. 'For your trouble. You'll get nothing more from me, you've already been paid in full.'

Serena shrank back against him, white and shaking. 'I didn't know. I wouldn't have—oh, what have I done?'

'Let's get out of this abominable place,' Nicholas said bitterly, 'our very presence here offends me.' He took Serena's arm and led her away.

Eliza shrugged, pocketed the coin and slammed shut the door of her cottage.

Serena trembled so much she could barely walk the short distance to the inn. 'I'm so sorry, Nicholas, you must believe I had no idea, not the slightest inkling,' she said desperately, unable to bear the bleak look on his face. 'His best friend! No wonder Papa would not tell me. I should have left well alone. Oh God, I could almost wish it had been Papa who was guilty after all. I am *sorry*.'

'Now you are being ridiculous. You have nothing to apologise for. It is I who am sorry, deeply sorry, and ashamed. That it should have been my father who kept you in exile on the Continent. My father who exposed you to the life you led. My father who deprived you of your rightful inheritance until now. It only adds to the irony that it was I who insisted on uncovering it all.' He laughed bitterly. 'You could say I have been the architect of my own downfall.'

'*Nicholas!* You mustn't think like that. Those were Papa's choices. None of this is your fault.'

He looked at her bleakly. 'What are you going to do now?'

'Do?' She looked confused.

'Surely you wish to clear your father's name?'

She turned even paler. 'I'm not going to do anything, Nicholas,' she said. 'It was thirty years ago. As if anyone even cares any more. If a scandal is more than a week old, it is forgotten about.'

'You don't have to say that just to make me feel better.'

Serena stamped her foot angrily. 'I make my own choices, and bear the consequences of them myself. Stop trying to appropriate all the blame, it's insulting.'

'As ever, Serena, your unusual take on life astonishes me. You are an extraordinary woman.'

'I wish I could believe that. I don't feel at all extraordinary right now. I feel tired and confused. Will you take me home now?'

'Yes, I think that would be best. We will talk of this tomorrow, when we have both had a good night's sleep and a chance to assimilate the implications.'

'There's nothing to talk about. Now we know the truth it need go no further. Papa would not have wanted it to. Like me, he made his own choices. Papa did not seek justice. He would not have wanted you to make reparation on your father's behalf either, especially not knowing that we are—are friends.'

Nicholas took her hand, pressing a warm kiss on to the palm. 'Friends. At least you grant me that. Thank you.'

Serena was due to attend a farce with Edwin that evening. Her cousin had been as dutiful an escort as her Uncle Mathew could wish, though for very different reasons than the dreams his father nurtured. Georgiana, whose youthful exuberance was much more to Edwin's taste than his intimidatingly beautiful cousin, was the real reason for Edwin's faithful attendance. They had arranged to meet Georgie and Melissa at the theatre. Edwin found Serena alone in front of the unlit grate of the small downstairs parlour. To his horror, she was crying.

'Cousin Serena, I did not mean to intrude. I beg your pardon,' Edwin said, retreating back towards the doorway.

Serena jumped up, brushing away her tears with the back of her hand. 'It's all right, I won't weep all over you. I had forgotten our engagement. I'm afraid you must go without me, I'm in no fit state for company.'

'What on earth has happened to upset you? Is it to do with Georgiana's brother?'

She was taken aback. 'No, why should it be?'

Edwin blushed. 'Nothing. Georgie said—only I'm sure she was mistaken.'

'Georgie said what?' Serena asked in a voice that made Edwin quake.

'Only that she thought it was a case between you,' he stuttered.

'Well, you can tell Georgie she's very much mistaken,' Serena said tartly. 'I'm upset about my papa, if you must know.'

'The murderer,' Edwin said sagely.

'He was not a murderer!'

'Apologies. Only going by what my father says.'

'That is a fine thing, coming from him,' Serena said feelingly, thinking of the bullet her uncle had arranged for her.

Edwin looked puzzled. 'Has my father been plaguing you about it? Thought it was ancient history by now, don't understand what you're so upset about.'

'I know Papa was innocent, but I am not in a position to prove it, that is all.' Serena sat up and mopped her eyes with a handkerchief. 'You are quite right, it is ancient history. Do go on to the theatre and make my apologies. Don't tell them I was upset, I beg of you.'

She retired early to bed, hoping that a night's rest would restore her equilibrium. Instead, the cloak of night brought darker thoughts to the front of her mind. She lay awake for long hours, thinking of the pain today's revelations had caused Nicholas. If only she had not sought that awful woman out. Nicholas, poor Nicholas—she could not bear to see him unhappy. Only two nights ago they had lain together in the room downstairs. Foolishly, she allowed herself the indulgence of reliving their lovemaking. The memories heated her blood, filling her with longing. The thrum of frustrated desire made her toss and turn between the tangled sheets.

She lay, hot and miserable, listening to the muffled sounds of the London night through the heavy window hangings. The watch called the hour. A party of merrymakers passed with a gust of laughter. Eventually the street fell silent, but still sleep eluded her. With an exasperated sigh, Serena pushed away the bed covers and got up, pulling back one of the curtains to open the window, breathing in the cool night air as she looked out on to the quiet street. The lamps cast shadows on to the cobblestones. There was silence save for her own breathing, and a sharp tinkling in the background.

A tinkling? Serena stepped back from the window to listen. It was the sound of breaking glass, and it seemed to be coming from downstairs. Carefully, she opened the door to her bedroom and listened. Nothing. Perhaps she was mistaken? Some sixth sense kept her standing there until the creak of a board informed her that someone was climbing the stairs.

A housebreaker. But why did they not first look in the dining room, the kitchen, even, where the silverware was kept? Perhaps they were after her jewellery. Pulling the bell to summon aid was a waste of time, since it rang in the basement, and the live-in servants slept in the attics. If she was to act, she would have to act alone.

Serena looked round the room in search of a weapon; her eyes alighted on the tall pewter candlesticks that sat beside the mirror on her dressing table. She picked one up, holding it tightly in her hand, and crept stealthily to stand behind the bedroom door, hoping that the small element of surprise this gave her would provide sufficient advantage to overcome the intruder. She prayed there was only one of them.

Her heart pounded like a hammer striking the anvil, so fast and loud she was sure that the man outside must hear it. Her bedchamber faced the top of the stairs at the centre of the house, next to the drawing room. The footfalls paused. The man must have removed his boots, he made so little sound. She could hear his shallow breathing through the wooden door. She heard the door of the drawing room open. A pause, then it closed again. He had not gone in, for she heard the tiny creak of the floorboard as he resumed his inexorable journey towards her.

Everything happened as if in slow motion. The door opened stealthily. The figure paused on the threshold to look in, saw that the room was unoccupied, made to turn away. Noticed that the bed was unmade and stopped. Came into the room. Looked around. Checked behind the thick curtains at the window, leaning out of the open sash to look down into the street. In the dim light she could see that he was a small man, wiry, no more than twenty or so, with a wizened face much older than his years. He turned from the window, paused again. Made to head for the large cupboard standing in the corner. Checked. And then he saw her standing behind the door.

They moved towards each other. Serena screamed at the top of her voice and pushed the door away, holding the heavy candlestick high over her head. She barely had time to notice the lethal flash of his dagger, hardly registered the cold kiss of steel deflected from her heart to her arm as she brought her own weapon down on the man's head with all her might. He crumpled, an astonished look on his face, his body toppling to the floor as if all the bones had been removed from it. Serena dropped the candlestick from trembling fingers. With surprise, she noticed that the drip, drip, drip she could hear was the blood from her arm falling on to the boards. At the sound of footsteps outside in the hallway, she felt a dizzy, whirling rush through her brain, and dropped in a dead faint beside the prostrate housebreaker.

* * *

It was Georgiana who broke the news to Nicholas. She had called on Serena the next morning with the intention of suggesting a trip to the Royal Exchange, and was astonished to find her still abed looking pale and wan, an intriguing sling supporting her arm. Serena's bravery, and the casual way she dismissed the entire incident, raised her to heroic status in Georgie's eyes, casting all thoughts of silk stockings and ribbons with which to trim a new bonnet from her mind.

Georgiana excitedly told her driver to return her to Cavendish Square. Her brother must be told immediately that his Serena—for in her mind, Georgie always thought of her friend in this way—had only narrowly escaped death.

Nicholas was in the library. *The Times* lay on a table by his side, but, judging from the freshly ironed lines, had not yet been opened. As Georgiana stormed into the room, he was engaged in the frustratingly addictive task of trying to decide which made him feel worse—his father's perfidy or Serena's refusal to entertain his proposal of marriage.

'Nicholas, the most awful thing has happened. Serena has been attacked in her own house.'

Her brother turned a most satisfactory shade of grey in front of her very eyes. 'What! Georgiana, don't fun with me. Is this true?'

'Oh, indeed, yes, I have just this minute come from Upper Brook Street. Poor Serena has been wounded.'

'Is she badly hurt?' Nicholas asked, a catch in his voice.

'The doctor came last night to attend her, and will return today to cup her—though she said she would not let him. She looks dreadful.'

Georgiana stood in front of the mirror that hung over the mantel to remove her bonnet, noting her brother's anxious reflection carefully. 'The attacker found her in her bedroom. She was undressed. Alone. In her bedchamber.' She checked Nicholas's expression in the mirror again, and shivered at the fierceness of his frown. 'She says he was a housebreaker, but I could not help wondering if the man was intent on *ravishment*.'

She said the word with such obvious relish that Nicholas laughed in spite of himself. 'I hardly think so. It's much more likely he was intent on her jewellery case.'

'Oh, that is just what Serena said.' Georgie cast her bonnet aside and turned to face her brother, placing her hands on her hips in a challenging attitude. 'Serena has been attacked in her home and is injured. Aren't you in the least bit concerned?'

'Of course I am concerned—don't be so stupid, Georgie. Do I look as if I am unconcerned?'

Looking at him carefully, she thought he looked more tired than anything else, and said so.

'A few late nights, that's all.'

'With Serena?'

'Don't push your luck, Georgie, and don't interfere.

You're far too young to know anything about it. Both Serena and I are perfectly capable of managing our own affairs.' He only wished that were true.

Georgie looked sceptical, managing a fair imitation of her brother's expression. 'You don't seem to be doing very well as far as I can see. Edwin says she was crying last night when he went to collect her. She did not come to the theatre with us after all.'

'I expect she was tired,' Nicholas said curtly. He did not like to think of Serena upset. More importantly, he did not like to think of her in danger. 'Tell me—without any more of your deliberate exaggerations—exactly what happened.'

Cowed, Georgiana recounted what Serena had told her of the housebreaker, who had been handed into the care of the Watch by Serena's footman. The wound he had received from the candlestick had been sufficient to knock him cold, but caused no more permanent injury than a nasty cut and a large bruise. Serena's own injury had bled copiously because it had been to the fleshy part of her arm, but already it was healing, and the sling, she had informed Georgiana, was more to appease the doctor than to ease her pain. The housebreaker was well known to the Watch—Georgie pronounced the name 'Fingers' Harry with relish—and was acting alone. No, he had not taken anything. It was fortunate that Serena had disturbed him. In fact, Georgie reminded her brother, Serena had been a *heroine*, for she hid behind a door in order to trap 'Fingers' into thinking the room was empty.

'Do you not think that she was very clever?'

'Very.' His response was disappointingly matter of fact. 'She is a very resourceful young woman.'

Georgie sniffed and pouted. 'And she's perfect for you, if only you could see it,' she said defiantly, leaving the room with a flounce, knocking *The Times* to the floor as she passed.

Nicholas was left with much to think about. Housebreakers rarely worked alone and to his knowledge did not normally carry knives. With a houseful of unoccupied rooms, to choose the master bedroom as his starting place was an unlikely tale. It was too much of a coincidence. Yet if not Mathew, who could be at the bottom of it? He had to find out, and at present there was only one person who could tell him. He pulled the bell rope and sent for his man of business.

Frances Eldon was the eldest son of the local schoolmaster at High Knightswood. A plainly dressed young man with a reserved air and a studious countenance, he had received many strange requests from his employer over the years. He listened impassively as Nicholas issued him with very precise instructions. He was to go to Bow Street where a certain 'Fingers' Harry was being held. With the use of a bribe—here Nicholas handed over a purse—he was to induce 'Fingers' to divulge who had paid him to break into a particular house in Upper Brook Street.

Satisfied that he would soon have an answer, for Frances had never yet let him down, Nicholas set off in haste to call upon Serena.

He found her, looking pale and tired, dressed neatly in lemon yellow muslin, with no signs of a sling. She had known he would come. Despite herself, she was delighted to see his reassuring, handsome face. She had so few hours left to engrave him in her memory. She could almost hear the sand dripping through the hourglass, marking them off.

'Georgie told me what happened. How are you?' He took her hand, leading her over to a sofa, where he joined her, sitting so close his thigh pressed against hers.

She shifted, struggling as usual to contain the shiver of awareness his touch set off. 'I'm fine. I think I frightened the poor man—he wasn't more than a boy, really—more than he did I.'

'As usual, you are too modest. No doubt you will tell me that you dealt with worse in those gaming houses on the Continent.'

It was meant as a joke, but served to remind them both of the revelation precipitated by their visit to Mile End. There was an uncomfortable silence.

'Serena, I am so sorry. You cannot imagine how bad I feel to have discovered—'

'Nicholas, please,' she interrupted, 'let us not discuss it. Your father and mine were friends. Papa never sought retribution, and let us not forget that it was his choice to remain on the Continent for all those years. I doubt very much if he would ever have come to England again, whatever the circumstances. He would have seen the responsibilities that the earldom entailed as chains—I realise that now. No, it is another closed chapter in my life. I must move on,' she added bleakly.

'And what of us, are we still a closed chapter?' he could not resist asking.

'Nicholas, we are a closed book. Nothing has changed. You do not love me. I cannot marry you.' She strove for a smile, but could only summon a thin grimace. 'I will attend the Cheadles' ball tonight, I promised Georgie I would go with her. Then tomorrow I will make arrangements to leave London.'

He felt a sinking feeling in the pit of his stomach. 'I can't let you leave.'

'You can't stop me, I'm afraid. It is for the best.'

'Goddammit, Serena, why must you be so obstinate!'

'Not obstinate, clear sighted. The point about idylls is that they are just that, a perfect moment in time cut short. I have no desire to witness the destruction of ours. I most certainly don't want to be around on the day you wake up and find you are bored with me.'

'I think you are being muddle-headed Serena, not clear sighted.'

Everything that had happened in the past weeks—the discovery of Serena's identity, the highwaymen, the disgust and shame at his father's cowardice, this new attack on her, the utter turmoil his mind and life had been thrown into since he met her—all suddenly overwhelmed him. Nicholas flung himself from the seat to pace around the room like a caged tiger. 'You walk into my life, you turn it upside down, and now you are planning on walking casually out of it again without so much as one regret, leaving me weighted down with guilt and no means of easing it. Well, I should be glad to see you go. I should be happy to be able to return to my old ways. I was content enough without you.'

Content, but not happy, he knew that now. 'I have not known whether I have been on my head or my heels since the minute you walked through my door. You have lit a fire inside me that only you can put out and yet you deny me even that satisfaction.' Nicholas raked a hand through his hair, staring down at the beautiful cause of all his ire. 'Leave, then, if you must.'

'I must.'

He pulled her to her feet, wrapped her in his arms so close it hurt, his hands moulding the curve of her spine, as if he would make one person out of two. He kissed her hard on the mouth. Then he flung her from him and was gone.

Serena stayed where she was, listening to Nicholas's footsteps receding down the stairs. The front door slammed with an air of finality. Resolved to shed no more tears, with a dejected sigh and a heart that felt too heavy for her breast, she mounted the stairs to select her outfit for the ball. If this was to be her last appearance in London society, she thought determinedly, then she was going to make sure she made a spectacular exit.

For the first time in his life, with absolutely no idea what he should do next, Nicholas stood on the front steps for some minutes, trying fruitlessly to find a way out of this ridiculous situation, fighting the impulse to turn around and force Serena into submission. No, kiss her into submission, he thought savagely, that made far more sense. Hunching his shoulders, he headed off in the direction of the Haymarket in search of someone to spar with at Jackson's.

Two hours later, emerging tired but if anything even more despondent, he met Charles as he turned into Bond Street.

'Nick. Been meaning to have a word with you before tonight.'

Nicholas groaned. He had forgotten all about the Cheadles' ball.

'You ain't thinking of ratting on me, are you?' Charles asked anxiously. 'You remember that you are engaged to dine with us beforehand? Could do with a friendly face.'

'No, I won't rat, though I could see it far enough.'

'Not as far as I could,' Charles said feelingly. 'Come with me to Brooks's. I've got something I need to tell you.'

They traversed the short distance to the club in silence, settling in a quiet back room.

'Hope you don't mind my saying so, but you look like hell, Nick.'

'Thank you. That is exactly how I feel.'

Charles shifted uncomfortably in his chair. 'Sorry to have to bring this up, bit of a delicate matter.'

'Go on.'

'It's about that Serena of yours. Gossip all over the *ton* is that she's your mistress.'

'I see.'

'People are saying she was living with you down at the Hall.'

'And how would people have found out that particular piece of information?' Nicholas asked threateningly.

'Don't vent your spleen on me, Nick, nothing to do with me.'

'I should have known better. I beg your pardon, Charles.'

'No need.' Charles took snuff. 'Bothered me, too, that question, so I've taken the liberty of asking about a bit. Appears your Serena's French chaperone is behind it. She's set up shop in Bond Street, you know, been dropping hints to everyone she sells a dress to, it seems.'

'Madame LeClerc.'

'Eh?'

'That's her name. The dressmaker.'

'Don't matter a jot what her name is, Nick. What matters is that your Serena is on the verge of being ostracised. Lady Cheadle took quite a bit of persuading not to withdraw the invite tonight. Not surprising, after the way the two of you behaved at Almack's the other day. I saw you myself. Might as well have undressed one another in public.'

'Oh, yes, how could I forget,' Nicholas said bitterly. 'One can behave as one likes in private—' this with a meaningful look at Charles '—but one must stick to the rules in public.'

'You've never had any problem playing to the rules before.'

'I have never met anyone like Serena before.'

'Don't understand you at all, Nick. If you'd set out to ruin the girl, you couldn't have made a better fist of it. Question is, what are you going to do now?'

'I don't know. You don't know the half of it, Charles.' Briefly he recounted the visit to Mile End.

'Good God!' Charles eyed his friend sadly. 'You've made a complete mull of it, Nick, no mistake. Very attractive young woman, Lady Serena. Dare say there's any number of men will still take her on with a fortune like that.'

Nicholas had been thinking he could not feel worse, but he was wrong. Charles was managing to rub salt into his wounds without even trying. 'I've already asked her to marry me. She won't have me.'

Charles seemed unsurprised. 'Expect you put it badly.' He sighed. Discussing such delicate matters seemed to him frightfully bad form, but someone had to set Nick right. 'Did you tell her you love her?'

Nicholas stared at him. 'No, of course I didn't.'

'Why not?'

'She's never actually said she loves me.'

'Have you ever asked her?' Charles waited for an answer. 'No, thought not. It's obvious she's in love with you, anyone with eyes can see that.' Charles shook his head again. 'Not thinking straight, that's your problem.'

He was right. A host of other things flitted through Nicholas's mind. The seeming contradiction of Serena's admission that she could no longer play the game on his terms, followed by her surrender to him. Her views on love. Even her refusal to marry him—*because you do not love me*, she'd said. *Serena was in love with him!* He had been blind not to see it. Had he been similarly blind to his own feelings?

'What about you?' Charles said, echoing his thoughts.

'What?'

'Do you love her, you dolt?'

'How can I tell, Charles?'

Charles looked embarrassed. 'Afraid I can't help you there, never having experienced that sort of thing myself. But I suspect it's something you feel rather than know, if that makes any sense.'

It was as if a light had come on. He couldn't know how things would work out. But he felt, *knew* at some fundamental level beyond thinking, that his life no longer worked without Serena. Really, it was suddenly painfully simple. Nicholas sat up in his chair and smiled ruefully at his friend, the smile reaching his eyes for the first time in days. 'You know, Charles, for someone who goes to such lengths to affect indifference, you can be a most a perceptive fellow.'

Charles looked pained. 'Don't go broadcasting that about, I beg you. It would ruin my carefully assembled reputation.'

With this comforting *non sequitur* Charles called for a bottle of brandy to fortify him prior to the evening's celebrations.

Returning home in much improved spirits to change his clothes, Nicholas found his man of business waiting for him. Frances Eldon had not let him down. Nicholas had not thought he could feel more guilty in terms of the misfortune he and his family had visited on Serena. Now he discovered he had been mistaken.

Chapter Eleven

Serena was due to dine at the Lytton household in Cavendish Square prior to the ball. She made her *toilette* in a defiant mood. A final check in the looking glass satisfied her. Her gown was of gold satin, the low neckline exposing more of her creamy flesh than she had hitherto dared. The tiny puffed sleeves were trimmed with seed pearls and conveniently hid the discreet bandage that covered her wound, but otherwise the dress was completely plain, relying upon the figure of the wearer to show it off. This Serena did to perfection, enhancing the effect with a long scarf of sarsenet around her shoulders. She had piled her hair on top of her head with just a few stray, artfully positioned curls left trailing across her cheeks.

The knocker announcing the arrival of the Lytton carriage sounded downstairs as she turned from the glass, allowing her maid to fasten the buttons on her tight evening gloves and drape the long cloak around her shoulders. She was ready. The world would see whether the Lady Serena Stamppe gave a fig for their gossip. Nicholas Lytton would see just what exactly he was going to miss for the rest of his life. At least, until he found someone to replace her.

'Serena, you look stunning. Doesn't she, Mama?' Georgie's sharp eyes looked at her searchingly. 'Nicholas dines with Charles, so we are a gentleman short.'

'Oh, he did not mention it when I saw him earlier.' He was no doubt avoiding her. Serena told herself it was for the best, but the disappointment threatened to overset her.

'So he did call. I knew he would,' Georgie said with a gratified smile. 'I told him about your housebreaker. He was most concerned.'

'Well, as you can see there was no need to be. I am perfectly recovered,' Serena said with a bright smile. 'Now tell me, who are you going to favour with the first dance? Will it be my cousin?'

By the time the carriage arrived to take them to the ball, Serena's face was aching from forced smiling, and her head buzzed from rather too much wine and far too little food.

She saw Nicholas immediately, standing just behind Charles at the top of the stairs, looking so absolutely perfect, as she knew he would, that for a moment she forgot to breathe. He saw her and smiled. Without thinking she smiled back. Then she remembered the terms on which they had parted, and her smile hardened.

Nicholas drank in the vision before him. She was breathtaking, a goddess in gold, the bright satin gown emphasising the perfection of her natural colouring, the white of her skin, the deep blue of her eyes, the spun-sunshine colour of her hair, which put the dress to shame. His eyes followed the delicate line of her throat down to the alluring valley revealed by the low décolleté. He could see her breasts rising and falling as she breathed. He remembered the softness, the fullness of them in his hands. He remembered the scent of her, that elusive mixture of floral perfume and vanilla that seemed to rise from her skin, the heat of her as she wrapped herself around him. He remembered…

'Nicholas.' Georgiana waved at her brother. 'Nicholas. You are staring at Serena.'

He started. Georgie, her glance flicking from her brother's flushed face to that of her friend, became all at once perfectly aware of the train of his thoughts, and blushed.

'You must learn, child,' Serena whispered, 'that there are times when it is politic for young ladies to pretend they have not noticed they are being stared at. Men, even your brother, have thoughts it is best to know nothing of.'

Georgie giggled nervously. Nicholas looked as if he would say something, then thought the better of it. Serena curtsied, just enough to allow him a tantalising glimpse of her cleavage, and the three of them joined the line waiting to greet their hosts.

Charles stood in the place of honour beside his intended. His appearance was as immaculate as ever, but his expression was harried, and he gripped Nicholas's hand with all the appearance of a man reaching out to a piece of driftwood to save himself from drowning.

'Penelope, here is Nicholas's sister, Georgiana, and Lady Serena too.'

The future Lady Avesbury was, as her intended described her, a compliant little thing, neither plain nor ugly, neither blonde nor brunette. She smiled nervously, but did not speak.

Nicholas observed Serena's reception carefully. Penelope looked embarrassed. Lady Cheadle barely acknowledged her. Proceeding through to the ballroom, Georgiana was immediately surrounded by swains, but it appeared to him that the claims for Serena's hand were less in number than usual. Charles was right, the rumour mill was turning.

Upon leaving Charles this afternoon, he had been filled with an optimism that he had come, as the evening progressed, to believe was entirely misplaced. Events were conspiring against him. His father's heinous crime, and now Frances Eldon's revelations added significantly to his burden of guilt. Then, too, there had been time—too much time—to reflect on his hasty words to Serena this afternoon. He had been cruel, there was no getting away from it.

He could see she had not forgiven him. She was brittle tonight, all sharp edges and glittering surface. Whatever she might have felt before, he could see no trace of it now. The certainty that a declaration would put all right had faded as the hours ticked by. The knowledge that he was in love had taken firm root. What Serena felt now, he was almost afraid of finding out. It seemed, to his exhausted brain that there were simply too many things for her to forgive. She had a generous nature, she might forgive him. Then again, she might simply pity him, and he could not bear to be pitied.

To cap it all there was this damned ball. They could not be alone here. He had a whole evening to endure with the sword of Damocles suspended over him hanging by a thread, a thread that Serena could cut or reel in with one word. And with her own reputation in tatters—his doing again—he couldn't in all conscience even dance with her. The sense of gloom that had been threatening him all evening descended like a black cloud. Would that he were anywhere but here.

Serena, smiling tensely and marking up her dances, watched Nicholas turn towards the card room without so much as asking her for a dance. It was her last ball. She would not let him off so lightly. 'Mr Lytton,' she called after him.

Nicholas turned, frowning. She seemed hellbent on her course to ruin.

'Nicholas—Mr Lytton. I have but one dance left. I saved it for you.'

Devil take it, all eyes were upon them. Serena, perfectly aware of this, looked at him challengingly. If he let her down, she would be crushed. Though all his instincts warned him against accepting, he could not betray her so publicly. They would dance together and devil take the consequences. If she did not care, why should he? He was growing very tired of the hypocrisy that surrounded him. 'Make it the final dance and I will be honoured, Lady Serena.' He bowed low over her hand for effect before turning away. He would wait it out in the card room. He would not torture himself by watching her with anyone else.

The evening passed in a whirl. Georgiana granted her first dance to Edwin. Serena, working her way up the same set, watched in amusement the progression of this flirtation, which would have her uncle tearing his eyes out.

Supper time came. As Serena entered the room, a group of ladies stopped talking to stare at her, one of them quite deliberately turning her back. She shrugged indifferently, but her temper simmered. Unable to face any of the delicate pasties and jellies her swain selected for her, she partook rather more than usual of the iced champagne cup. It made her light-headed enough to flirt vivaciously, showing just how little the Lady Serena Stamppe cared for the opinion of the world.

She surveyed the room under cover of her fan, but Nicholas was not present to be impressed by her popularity with the other gentlemen. Their conversation this afternoon had obviously put an end to all between them. Knowing him so well, she knew he would already be regretting having been so persistent. Another champagne cup did nothing to ease the pain of this thought.

Finally the orchestra struck up for the last waltz of the evening. Seeing Serena standing un-partnered, a small group of men gathered around her, calling for her to take pity on one of them and grant them the honour. Despairing of the stubborn man named on her dance card, she was about to place her arm on the nearest supplicant when it was taken rather forcibly by a tall devil in an elegant black coat.

'Mine, I think.' Nicholas pulled her towards the crowded floor, glaring fiercely at anyone foolish enough to stand in his path.

Serena barely had time to catch up her reticule before he turned towards her, and then she was clasped in his arms and swept gracefully out on to the floor in a firm hold, much closer than propriety dictated, but not close enough for either of the participants.

They danced one turn around the room in silence. Nicholas guided her effortlessly clear of the other dancers, steering her with the lightest of touches. For a few moments Serena noticed nothing save the hand on her waist, the warm clasp of his other hand in hers, the beating of her heart against his chest, the feeling of his breath on her cheek. Gradually, she became aware that every pair of eyes on the floor—and off—were focused on them.

'We seem to be providing all of the other guests with a spectacle,' she said with a bitter smile.

'And you do not care a jot,' Nicholas said, looking down at her with an unreadable expression. 'In fact, it was your intention to provoke just such a reaction.'

Filled with a wild rashness from too much champagne, too many emotions, too much Nicholas, too much everything, Serena decided she didn't care any more. 'Whatever these people are thinking about us, it's more or less the truth. I've been in your bed. Well, in point of fact we haven't actually made it to bed yet, have we? Let us put it more crudely. We have experienced carnal pleasures together. I am no longer a virgin. Unfit for marriage. No better than a courtesan, in fact, were it not for my fortune. Being an heiress, I can always be sure of finding some man whose need of cash makes the idea of soiled goods palatable.'

'Serena, for God's sake, shut up.' He gave her a little shake. 'You don't know what you're saying. I fear you have had a little too much wine.' The words were growled in her ear lest any of the other dancers, already straining with interest towards them, should overhear.

Serena glared at a couple passing so close that Nicholas had to whisk her round in a turn that would have made his dancing master clap his hand with glee. Following him effortlessly, Serena was unimpressed at his prowess. 'On the contrary, I have not had nearly enough. I am perfectly well aware of what I'm saying,' she said coldly.

'I should never have agreed to dance with you tonight.'

Her cheeks were flushed. By now most of the dancers and many of the onlookers were watching their progression round the floor with open interest, but Serena cared for nothing save the urgent need to provoke a reaction from her infuriatingly heart-stopping and stupidly stubborn partner. 'Yet you were keen enough to dance when I was Mademoiselle Cachet,' she said, deliberately misunderstanding him.

'As I recall, you were every bit as desirous of taking part in that particular dance as I was.'

'That is true, I was. But now I am the Honourable Lady Serena I must pay the consequences by providing these good people with something to talk about over their morning chocolate,' she said, bestowing a dazzling smile on a passing couple.

His grip on her waist was so tight she was sure there would be fingermarks on her skin. The expression on his face was so devilish that most people would have quailed beneath it.

Not Serena, though. 'My only regret is that you did not enjoy yourself more. Foolishly I thought my somewhat unsophisticated steps would be a pleasant change for you. Since you have repeatedly assured me that the charms of my presence in your bed will inevitably wane, I can only assume I was wrong. I was merely a convenient stopgap until you found someone more accustomed to pleasing such a demanding gentleman as yourself.'

To her astonishment, this sally was greeted with a burst of laughter. 'You know perfectly well that is not true. I have made my feelings on the subject of your presence in my bed, as you call it, perfectly plain.'

She was silent.

'We can put an end to this scandal quite easily you know,' Nicholas said, speaking close to her ear, 'by legitimising it.'

She came back down to earth with a jolt. 'Not here, Nicholas, please don't ask me again.'

'What better place,' Nicholas countered, suddenly unwilling to wait any longer. 'It is an engagement party after all.'

Serena blinked away a tear. 'Another loveless marriage in the making. No, thank you, Nicholas.'

'You think I want to marry you to redeem your reputation.'

'That, and your inheritance. And because you feel guilty on account of your father. Oh, yes, and because of our *compatibility*.'

'You know, Charles pointed something out to me today that changes everything.'

'It seems to me that you pay far too much attention to what Charles has to say, and very little attention to anyone else,' Serena said sarcastically. 'What was it this time?'

'He said you are in love with me. He said I should ask you if it's true.'

Serena stumbled. Nicholas pulled her closer, leaning into her ear. 'Well?'

'Well, what?' she whispered shakily.

'Is it true? Are you in love with me?' he asked, his breath warm on her ear.

He was mocking her. Serena shivered, cold with mortification. 'What difference would it make, Nicholas? Do you not feel guilty enough, is that it? Do you wish to add unrequited love to the burden you insist on assuming? Well, I won't let you.' As she tore herself from his hold, the music stopped.

'Serena,' Nicholas called after her, cursing his own ineptitude. 'Serena,' he called more urgently, pushing his way through the staring crowds.

A hand on his arm stayed him. 'Congratulations, cousin, for this very public display of dissent, thanks to which I will now have no problems in staving off my creditors.'

Jasper's sneer was not long lived. With a low frightening growl, Nicholas grabbed his cousin by the throat and trapped him against a pillar. *'You!'*

'Remember where you are, for God's sake,' Jasper croaked.

'It is surely rather too late for you to worry about the conventions,' Nicholas hissed.

'Let him go, Nick, now is neither the time nor the place.'

Nicholas looked up. Charles stood by his side with Lord Cheadle. A circle of people watched with eyes agog. In the minstrel's gallery he could see the orchestra leaning over the better to obtain a view. Reluctantly he released his grip. 'My apologies—you are right, of course. Let us repair to somewhere more appropriate, Jasper.' There was no mistaking the glint in his eye.

'No, no, Nicholas, you can't call your cousin out,' Charles protested.

'Can't I? Not even when he insulted my future wife?'

'Your future wife,' Jasper croaked nastily, 'that piece of soiled goods. Even if you still wanted her, it's perfectly obvious that she don't want you.'

Nicholas lunged at his cousin again. Jasper cringed away. Charles and Lord Cheadle grabbed one of Nicholas's arms each. 'Through here,' Lord Cheadle said, puffing with the effort of restraining his guest. 'For God's sake, man, away from the ladies.'

All four repaired to the card room. Lord Cheadle ushered the bemused whist players out and shut the door. Jasper tugged nervously at his neckcloth.

'You shall answer for this,' Nicholas said through gritted teeth, his hands clenched by his sides. 'Name your friends.'

Jasper paled. 'You can't call me out.'

'Think he can, given the circumstances,' Charles said diffidently. 'Perfectly good reason, as he said. You insulted his future wife.' He turned to Nicholas, the proprieties having been observed. 'Take it you'll want me to act for you?'

Nicholas nodded.

'If you require my services, too, I will be only to happy,' Lord Cheadle offered, to the astonishment of his future son-in-law. 'Pretty little thing, that Lady Serena,' he explained with a roguish smile. 'Happy to defend her honour, provided you do intend to make an honest woman of her, young man,' he said, turning to Nicholas.

'As soon as she'll have me, my lord,' Nicholas replied.

'Name your friends, then, Lytton,' Charles said coldly to Jasper.

Truth be told, he struggled to think of any. 'I will have them call on you,' he replied haughtily.

'Immediately,' Nicholas interjected.

'Eh?'

He smiled grimly at the three startled countenances. 'We fight tomorrow morning. That way it's less likely that someone will inform on us. I don't want to be arrested before I've had a chance to run my cousin through.'

'Come now, Nick, you know it's actually for your cousin to name the time and place,' Charles intervened conscientiously.

'No, if we must fight, then why not let it be immediately?' Jasper agreed. 'Either I will kill my cousin, in which case I will inherit the funds I am in rather urgent need of, or he will kill me. Whichever is the case, my creditors will be satisfied, and my somewhat precarious financial situation resolved. Really, I cannot think why the solution did not occur to me before. Let it be swords at dawn tomorrow in the Tothill Fields.'

'Nick?' Charles looked enquiringly at his friend. Receiving his nod, he announced himself satisfied and handed his card to Jasper. 'I will hear from your friends in due course, I presume.'

With a curt nod, Jasper took himself off.

'I must go too. I have unfinished business.' Nicholas turned towards the door.

'Don't, Nick, not a good idea. Leave her to calm down. Besides,' Charles said practically, 'much better to get your fight out of the way first. If someone does inform on you, you could be deported. If you kill Jasper, you'll have to flee the country, and if he kills you—well, you see how it is.'

'I have no intention of killing my cousin, as you very well know. Serena has lived all her life in exile, I would not wish that on her again. As to Jasper killing me—believe me, it will not come to that,' Nicholas said grimly.

'All the same, much better to wait.'

'But…'

'Nick, think about it. If you go there tonight, Serena's bound to find out that you called Jasper out. Any other female would swoon and feel flattered, but Serena—there's no knowing what she would do.'

'She would probably offer to take my place,' Nicholas said with a smile. 'You're right. At the very least she would try to stop me. She is unaccountably keen not to allow me to fight her battles for her.'

'Well, then. Best thing you can do is go home and

rest. See Serena in the morning, after you've seen to Jasper. That way it will all be over before she's even had breakfast.'

'After I've seen to Jasper,' Nicholas repeated thoughtfully. 'You are quite right, I must get Jasper out of the way first.'

He found Georgie waiting with Edwin outside the door of the card room.

'Did you call him out?' she asked excitedly.

'Mind your own business,' Nicholas replied shortly. 'Did Serena take the carriage?'

'I procured a chair for her, she insisted,' Edwin said stiffly. 'She said she wouldn't use your carriage.'

'I see.'

'I feel obliged to tell you, sir, that you have treated my cousin abominably,' Edwin continued nervously. 'She was most upset. Were it not for the fact that I understand you now have a prior engagement, I would feel it incumbent upon myself to call you out on her behalf.'

Nicholas looked startled. 'There is no need, I assure you. Despite appearances, I have your cousin's honour very much at heart.'

'Oh, Nicholas, I knew it,' Georgie said, jumping up and squealing excitedly. 'You're in love with her.'

'Be quiet, Georgiana,' her brother replied repressively. 'I am taking you home now. And if you know what's good for you, you won't breathe a word of tonight's events to your mother.'

'Oh, no, I would not. I promise you.'

'May we offer you a ride home?' Nicholas asked Edwin.

'No, I thank you. I must see my cousin. I have something of a personal nature to impart to her.'

'You never mentioned it to me,' Georgie said, looking miffed.

'That is because it is personal,' Edwin said pompously. 'Family business.'

'Fine, keep your stuffy secrets,' Georgie replied, turning her back on Edwin and marching off on her brother's arm in high dudgeon without saying goodnight.

'Edwin, please don't mention my meeting,' Nicholas called.

But Edwin, in discussion with Lord Avesbury, did not hear him. He took a chair the short distance to Upper Brook Street, unwilling to risk the possibility of mud, horse manure or worse marring the perfection of his evening attire.

Serena answered the door herself, having dismissed her footman. Fully expecting Nicholas intent on continuing their argument, she was as astonished to see her cousin as he was to see her opening the door clad in such a revealing gown.

'Edwin!'

'Cousin Serena!'

She ushered him into the ground-floor parlour. 'What on earth brings you here at this time of night?'

'Are you all right?'

'I'm fine, Edwin. If you are referring to my disagreement with Mr Lytton…'

'Mr Lytton has another dispute to settle now,' Edwin blurted out.

'What do you mean?'

'I should not have said, I mean…'

But Edwin was no match for Serena. Pretty soon she was in full possession of the story. 'They are to fight a duel tomorrow morning,' Edwin said.

Serena was outraged. 'How dare they!'

'But, Cousin Serena, it is only right that he defend your honour if you are to be married,' Edwin protested.

Serena stamped her foot. 'We are not to be married.'

Edwin was shocked. 'But, Cousin, they say you are—that is, they say—I mean, if you are not to be married…'

'Edwin, it is none of your business. What is it you want?'

He handed her a letter. 'From my father—he said to give it to you and you would understand.'

She took the missive curiously and broke open the seal. Inside was a brief note from her uncle enclosing another letter written in a faded, spidery hand.

'The other night, when you were so upset about your papa being a murderer, I realised I didn't actually know the whole story,' Edwin explained. 'I asked my father about it. Told him what you said, *that's a fine thing coming from him*. Didn't know what you meant—still don't know—but he got very upset. Said he was sorry. Said to tell you he never meant any harm.'

'He said nothing else?' Serena asked, anxious to hear that Edwin remained in ignorance of Mathew's murderous intentions.

'No. Just gave me this letter, told me it was important you received it as soon as possible. Said to tell you he hoped it would make things right between you.'

Serena stared at the letter, a strange excitement rising in her breast. 'Thank you, Edwin. I think I'd like to be alone to read this now, if you don't mind.'

Her cousin was only too relieved to be on his way. He was halfway to the door when Serena called him back.

'Where is the duel going to be fought?'

'Tothill Fields, so Avesbury said.' He shuddered. 'Why? You're not thinking of calling the magistrates, are you? Affair of honour, you know, cousin.'

'I promise I won't call the magistrates, you may set your mind at rest on that score. Goodnight, Edwin. Thank you again.'

Serena closed the door on her cousin. She lit a branch of candles on the mantel and sat down to read. The covering note from her uncle was brief and to the point.

I surmise from something my son let slip that you are aware of my foolish behaviour with regards to yourself. I am deeply sorry for behaving so very badly and can only hope that in time you will forgive me. I feel that I owe it to you to atone with something more meaningful than my apologies, however, and hope that the enclosed *missive will serve that purpose. It was sent to me almost twenty years ago, but I did not act upon it. At the time your father was settled on the Continent and I was settled in managing his estates. I saw no reason to disturb that equilibrium, and informed the author of the enclosed letter that your father was dead. Do not judge me too harshly, my motives were for the best. You may decide for yourself whether or not to use the letter to obtain justice for your father. In the light of the rumours I have heard regarding your personal preferences for a certain gentleman, I expect it is more likely that you will not. I leave the matter entirely in your hands. With all respect, I hope to continue your loving uncle.*

With a shaking hand, Serena turned to the second letter. *Dear Mathew*, it began. *What I have to disclose is of a shocking nature, but I find myself, on the eve of my second marriage, unable to continue to live a lie.* She read to the end, a smile slowly suffusing her face.

Nicholas must see this. It would be a fitting note on which to say goodbye. She would take it with her to Tothill Fields, for she was determined to prevent him fighting his cousin. No one had the right to fight her battles, especially not if by doing so he took on responsibility for her ruin, which she was determined he would not bear. She would be gone from London soon enough, but it was his home. She would not have people think ill of him.

Looking at the clock on the mantel, Serena cudgelled her brain in an effort to recall what Papa had told her about the conducting of affairs of honour. Daybreak, that is when they were held. Daybreak at Tothill Fields. About four hours away. Time enough to snatch some sleep.

Nicholas was denied the luxury of any such respite. His nerves were strung tight as a bow as he lay wide awake in bed. While the clock moved painfully slowly towards the appointed hour, a cold rage possessed him. He would not kill his cousin—he had no wish to grant Jasper the pleasure of condemning him to a life of exile from beyond the grave—but he determined to make it so close a thing as to strike the fear of death into him.

In any case, darker forces already had Jasper in their grip. If he was in the hands of a cent-per-cent, as Charles had hinted, he was in deep trouble. Moneylenders, especially the type who lent funds to desperate men, had no compunction in murdering defaulting clients. With any luck, Nicholas consoled himself, one of them would rid the world of Jasper, saving him the bother. He could not find it in him to pity Jasper such a fate. As far as he was concerned, his cousin was beyond the pale.

Dressing himself carefully in a plain dark waistcoat and coat in the early dawn light, Nicholas tried to quell the rising panic that arose every time he thought about Serena. After last night's débâcle, and the terrible, terrible mess he had made of his declaration, there was a strong chance she would have nothing more to do with him.

He must not think such thoughts. That way madness lay. For too long now he had been buffeted, first this way, then that, by fate and the whims of others. His father. His cousin. Even Serena's papa. It was a feeling he neither liked nor was familiar with. Now he was determined to wrest control back, to dominate rather than be dominated, beginning in the most elemental, brutal way possible. Winning the duel would make reparation, and assuage some of the guilt consuming him.

Then he could turn his attention with a clearer conscience to Serena. By noon his fate would be decided one way or another. If she wouldn't have him… No! He halted the thought in its track. He would make her, even if it took him the rest of his life. With grim determination, Nicholas made his way down the dark staircase and unbolted the front door.

Charles and Lord Cheadle arrived promptly with the apothecary in Lord Cheadle's town coach. 'Lovely morning for it,' Lord Cheadle said bracingly. 'Haven't acted for anyone in a long time, duelling seems to have gone somewhat out of fashion. Glad to see someone keeping the tradition going,' he added with a nod in Nicholas's direction.

They made their way through the empty streets, the

clatter of the horses' hooves on the cobblestones the only sound to break the early morning silence.

Arriving at the duelling ground, they found Jasper already present. The two sets of seconds conferred, selected a suitable flat piece of ground and carefully tested the length of the pair of wicked-looking foils that Jasper had provided.

Nicholas stripped off his coat and waistcoat, rolling up the ruffled sleeves of his shirt. His boots were next, leaving him in his stockinged feet on the early morning dew. Jasper did not strip to advantage beside his cousin. Though of similar build, what had been muscle in his salad days was now running to fat. Dissipation showed in the deep grooves that ran from his nose to his mouth. Though he had exercised some caution in the amount he had drunk the previous night, his grey eyes were dull and red-rimmed from lack of sleep.

None the less, Nicholas knew he would be foolish to underestimate the effect of desperation on his cousin's fighting prowess. Jasper was no novice. He looked his cousin over with contempt, his eyes glinting steel grey, colder and more dangerous than the foils with which they were now arming themselves. Even such a hardened one as Jasper quailed before such a look.

The seconds called time. The opponents stood face to face. They shook hands curtly. Sunlight winked on the lethal steel as they assumed the *en garde* position. The seconds stood to on either side of the duellists. To

Lord Cheadle fell the honour of calling a start. *'Allez'*, he enunciated clearly, and the duel began with a hiss of tempered steel in the crisp morning air.

Chapter Twelve

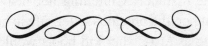

She had overslept. Too much champagne cup had given her an aching head. Too much champagne cup had made her act stupidly beyond measure. In the grey light of dawn, Serena was mortified. She had behaved appallingly. One thing for she and Nicholas to be the subject of gossip following that night at Almack's. That had been both their doing, and she still could not bring herself to regret it. But for last night there was no excuse. She had been angry and intent on revenge. Nicholas did not deserve such treatment. His only crime had been a failure to love her, and she had degraded him in front of his friends. Worse. He had tried to stop her folly, but she had merely made it worse. True, he had been angry, but she had made him so. She deserved every harsh word he threw at her. She could only be thankful to have hung on to the tiny scrap of dignity left to her, in refusing to admit her love for him. But he must not be allowed to fight another of her battles. He must not come to any harm.

Because of the difficulty of first locating a hackney carriage, then persuading the driver to take her to so remote a location as the Tothill Fields at such an early hour, Serena arrived late on the scene. As she paid off the cab, she could see the two swordsmen facing each other in the distance. Clutching her heavy woollen cloak about her, the precious letter safe in her reticule, and running as fast as her kid boots would carry her through the long grass heavy with dew, she reached the scene just as Lord Cheadle gave the command to start.

She heard the clash of steel on steel, and had the presence of mind to come to a halt on the periphery of the ground marked for the duel. It was too late to intervene. All she could do was try to avoid distracting Nicholas. With her heart in her mouth, she watched as the contest raged.

They were almost equal in height and reach, but it was immediately obvious to Serena that Nicholas had the lead. His finely muscled body was in perfect shape, and he carried himself with the balance and control of an athlete. But it was his keen eye, his steady hand and total focus that gave him the real advantage over Jasper, whose late nights, compounded with the imminent threat of debtors' prison, made his eye bleary, his hand shaky and his concentration patchy.

Bare knuckles and not foils were Nicholas's preferred sport, but he had been schooled well enough.

Jasper, who fenced regularly, had the better skill, though not sufficient to compensate for his body's shortcomings. A few years ago they would have been very evenly matched.

Serena watched with bated breath, aware of the tense silence surrounding them, save for the hiss of the blades, the pad of feet on soft ground, the harsh breathing of the duellists as they thrust, parried, and thrust again. The seconds watched with almost as much concentration as the fighters, unconsciously swaying back and forth, their actions mimicking that of the combatants. Their own swords pointed downwards, ready to intervene in the event of foul play. Stockinged feet shuffled lightly across the grass as Jasper and Nicholas danced forwards, then back, with each lunge and retreat.

Jasper breathed heavily, his skin a waxen pallor, his cheeks stained with the red flush of exertion. Nicholas was coping better with the fast pace of the fight, his shirt clinging with sweat to his muscled torso, but his face still grimly focused, his breathing even, his piercing eyes never wavering from his opponent. Relentlessly he fought, patiently waiting for the mistake that would allow him to breach Jasper's defence.

Jasper's wrist began to ache. The attacking moves had all been his, but now he was blown, all his energy focused on avoiding a hit. Nicholas was toying with him. Several times he could have inflicted a fatal wound, but on each occasion he feinted back at the last minute. On the sidelines, caught up in the visceral thrill of the battle, certain of Nicholas's victory, Serena had to repress the urge to shout encouragement.

Jasper, becoming desperate, thrust wildly at Nicholas's shoulder. The counter-riposte was lightning quick, the foil touching Jasper's chest, pulling back at the last minute. 'What is this truly about? What is it you want, Cousin?' he gasped.

'The truth,' Nicholas replied, easily deflecting the next thrust with another counter-riposte, touching Jasper's shoulder with the point of his foil, withdrawing. 'I know all about your evil plot.'

'I don't know what you're talking about. I—' Jasper broke off as Nicholas's foil sliced into his left arm with a surface cut.

'Tie it up,' Nicholas commanded.

'But surely honour is satisfied,' Charles intervened.

'Tie it up,' Nicholas repeated harshly, 'my honour is very far from satisfied.' Roughly, he pushed away Charles's restraining arm. 'Damn it, leave me alone. I have not finished with him yet.'

'Nicholas! Nicholas, stop this.'

'Serena!'

She threw herself at him. 'Enough, you must stop. I'm sorry. I'm so sorry for last night. Whatever he said, your cousin, I probably deserved it. I won't have you risk your life for me.'

'You have nothing to be sorry for, you had provocation enough. And in any case you are mistaken,

Serena,' Nicholas said, looking contemptuously at his cousin, 'this does not concern last night.'

Jasper sneered. 'Would you have me dead, Nick, is that it? Why not, for I'm as good as, anyway.' With a careless shrug and a strange smile Jasper resumed the *en garde* position.

Nicholas pushed Serena to the sidelines. 'Wait there. Trust me,' he said.

She had no option. The seconds stood back. The swordplay resumed.

Jasper fought with a new wildness, sweat pouring down his face. Nicholas parried, broke through his guard, touched his chest, retreated again. Like a cat playing with a mouse, Serena thought, caught up anew in the exhilaration of the fight.

'Let us cut to the chase,' Nicholas said, his own breathing annoyingly even as he shortened his sword arm, lunged, touched, retreated. 'My man of business spoke to your latest employee yesterday. One "Fingers" Harry, currently awaiting trial in Newgate.'

Jasper struggled for breath. His mouth thinned in an evil smile. 'So that's what this is all about.'

'It was you,' Serena gasped from the sidelines

For a split second, Nicholas shifted his attention from his opponent. Jasper capitalised, breaking through his guard, his near-fatal lunge deflected only at the last moment. Serena watched in terror, her hand covering her mouth, but Nicholas was safe. 'Well,' he demanded, 'do you admit it?'

'Yes, damn you to hell, and damn that bitch over there with you.' Sweat clouded Jasper's eyes. He blinked, shook his head in an effort to clear his vision, thought he saw an opening, and thrust. He felt rather than saw the lightning *redoublement* thrust that Nicholas made into his right shoulder. The foil clattered from his twitching fingers. Blood spurted from the wound.

For a few long moments no one moved. Jasper stood looking uncomprehendingly at his foil, the wicked blade glinting on the ground, the first bright red drops of his own blood spattering the grass beside it. Then the seconds rushed forwards. The doctor hurried from the carriage.

'One moment.' Nicholas pushed the apothecary away. 'I want to know the whole,' he said, staring down at Jasper, whose wound was now bleeding copiously. 'Were the highwaymen your doing too?'

Jasper silently nodded his assent.

'Once could be construed the impulsive act of a desperate man,' Nicholas said contemptuously, 'but to plot twice to kill an innocent girl is the act of a cold-blooded evil one.'

'In that case, I wish you had finished him off.' Serena said, surveying Jasper distastefully. 'In fact, if you give me your sword, I will run him through myself.' She reached imperiously for the foil.

Jasper recoiled. 'Keep her away from me.'

'Did the *bon papa* teach you swordsmanship as well as how to handle a gun, then? Really, Serena, much as I wish to oblige you in all things, I cannot agree to your murdering my cousin, especially in front of witnesses,' Nicholas said with a sardonic grin, handing his sword to Charles.

She stilled, caught in his gaze, momentarily forgetting everything save his presence and her overwhelming love for him.

'Lady Serena, you should not be here. Nick, I take it honour is satisfied now?' Charles waited for his friend's nod before pushing the doctor forwards. 'Let this man through before the blighter bleeds to death.'

'One last thing.' Nicholas leaned over his cousin's prone body. Jasper's face had assumed a waxen pallor. His wound bled sluggishly, bright blood spilling crimson on the dewy green grass. 'You sought twice to secure my inheritance for yourself by having my potential bride killed. Why Serena? Why not me?'

Jasper snorted. 'I wish I had. She has more lives than a cat, that one, you would have been easier prey. You think me beyond redemption, but I found the idea strangely repugnant. Much as I despise you, you are, after all, the only family I have.'

'Preferred to murder a defenceless female instead,' Charles said contemptuously.

'Not so defenceless,' Jasper wheezed.

'Man deserves to be hanged,' Charles exclaimed.

'If his creditors get hold of him, he will wish he had been,' Nicholas replied.

Beside them on the grass, Jasper fainted. The doctor

ripped open his shirt and exposed the wound. Charles turned green. Nicholas tugged Serena over to the shelter of a copse of trees, out of earshot of the rest of the duelling party.

'When did you find out about Jasper?' she asked.

'Yesterday.'

'So you weren't defending my honour after all,' she said with a wry smile.

'I was trying to atone. Between my father and my cousin, we've treated you abominably,' Nicholas explained.

Serena returned his gaze, a frown marring the perfect alabaster of her brow. 'Let us not forget my own family's rôle in this. Edwin did not come to visit me last night in order to inform me of your duel. He came to deliver this.'

She handed Nicholas Uncle Mathew's note and the letter that he had enclosed, watching with bated breath as Nicholas read his father's confession.

'Secrets and deceit at every turn,' she said when he had finished.

'Yet I cannot feel sorry for it now—without those secrets, we would not have met.' Nicholas handed her back the letter. 'So this is why you came. I had supposed you wanted to stop the fight.'

'Yes. No. I came for both those reasons. And one other.' She smiled bravely, blinking away the tears that welled up as she looked at his beloved countenance. 'I came to say goodbye. Our acquaintance started with a fight. I thought it only fitting,' she said with an attempt to smile, 'that it should be ended by one.'

Nicholas took her hand, pulling her close. 'Not goodbye, Serena,' he said urgently. 'Never that.'

She laid her cheek on his chest. In his shirt sleeves and stockings, with the sweat from the fight cooling on his heated body, he was just as he had been that first day. For a moment she allowed herself to be held. To experience for one last time all the coiled power and recklessness and overwhelming maleness of him. To breathe in the essence of him. Then she pushed herself away. 'Nicholas, I—'

'I'm sorry for last night,' he interrupted tersely. 'I was inept.'

'*Inept!* It is I who was inept.'

'No, you were merely overwrought and rather intoxicated. Much as it pains me to admit it, I was the inept one. My only excuse is that I've never actually said the words before. I found myself apprehensive, unsure of your reaction. That is why I tried to make you say it first. A mistake, I realised straight away, but by then it was too late.'

Serena felt as if her heart had suddenly decided to take up residence in her throat, and it was severely impairing her breathing. 'I'm not altogether sure I understand you. What words?'

Nicholas smiled down at her, a strange, tender look in his eye she had never seen before. 'Dearest Serena, I love you. I'm in love with you. I think I have been in love with you from the very start, but was too blind to see it. I finally realised yesterday that it was the only explanation for this unshakeable feeling I've had from the very first day we met. That you were mine and only mine.'

She heard the words through a haze, a shimmering, mesmerising haze of pure joy and unbridled happiness. 'Oh,' was all she managed to say.

A clearing of the throat startled them both. 'Your servant, Lady Serena,' Charles said diffidently. 'Sorry to interrupt, but we're ready to leave.' He nodded at one of the departing coaches. 'Doctor's gone off with your cousin. You'll be relieved to know he thinks he'll make a very slow and painful, but full, recovery. We're off in the other coach for breakfast.'

'I think we'll pass on that, thank you, Charles. Serena and I have some rather important things to discuss.'

'Oh, right. Arrangements.' Charles nodded knowingly. 'Take my advice, make it a special licence, Nick. Happy to stand beside you if you need support.' With this, he left them to rejoin Lord Cheadle.

'We are not getting married,' Serena said rather uncertainly.

Nicholas smiled. 'You may not think so, but we are.' The slam of a door made him look in the direction of the departing carriage. 'I would very much like to discuss it with you—in fact, I'm looking forward immensely to persuading you—but right now we seem to have a transportation problem.'

'I noticed there was an inn not far from where the hackney dropped me,' Serena suggested helpfully.

Nicholas raised an eyebrow. 'It is hardly likely to be respectable.'

She giggled. 'Nor are we. As you have informed me many times, I am a ruined woman, and you, Mr Lytton, are a rake. I think it will suit us very well.'

Nicholas drew her a long look. That strange smile again. The new light in his eyes that made her quite light-headed. 'Why not? We have business to finish, Lady Serena, and I have no desire to finish it in the open.'

Serena eyed him blatantly as he donned his jacket and boots. 'That is the second time I have watched you fight,' she said, tucking her arm into his as they walked across the fields towards the smoking chimney of the thatched inn. 'I must confess, I enjoyed it even more than the first. Once I knew you were going to win, that is.'

'Most women would have had hysterics, fainted at the very least.'

'I considered that, of course, but I realised it would have been a distraction. And I do so very much want you to stay alive.'

They continued in silence until they reached the inn. A startled landlady showed them to the taproom, looking at them dubiously, but promising they would not be disturbed, telling them to ring the bell if they wished to partake of breakfast.

'She thinks we are up to no good,' Serena said.

'I hope to prove her right.'

She felt the familiar tingle in response.

'Come here, Serena.'

She walked into his arms. She belonged there, it was obvious. Nicholas shook his head at his own stupidity. 'Before Charles interrupted us, I told you I love you. Just in case you think you may have misheard me, I think I should tell you again. I love you, Serena, I love you with all my heart.'

'Oh, Nicholas,' Serena said, bursting into tears.

'I don't like to be too dictatorial at this early stage in our relationship, but I'd really rather you didn't cry whenever I tell you I love you. Especially since I aim to tell you every day for the rest of our lives.' Giving her no time to answer, however, Nicholas kissed her.

His mouth was warm, his lips gentle. It was a new kind of kiss. Serena felt her heart soar as if it had grown wings. Tenderly, Nicholas licked away the tears that glittered on her cheeks, touched her brow, her neck, kissed the lobe of her ear, her eyelids, murmuring her name over and over, holding her as if she was the most precious thing in all the world.

Somehow, she could not have said how, Serena was on his lap on the settle, her arm around his neck, her head resting on his shoulder, her bonnet discarded. 'Are you sure?' she whispered tremulously.

'I've told you before, I don't make false promises. I love you. I think I've loved you from the moment I set eyes on your beautiful face in the stable yard at Knightswood Hall, but I was too foolish to understand.

I blamed it on your irresistible body. I blamed it on our isolation. I blamed it on—oh, everything I could think of. When Charles suggested I marry you to protect my inheritance I leapt at the idea, because it gave me an excuse to call you my own without admitting what I felt. When you turned me down, I realised my life had lost its meaning. That's when I finally admitted to myself that I wanted you for no other reason than that I couldn't live without you. I can't be sure, but I'm willing to take the chance if you are.'

'Oh, Nicholas, I love you so very much,' Serena said, wrapping her arms around his neck. 'I'm afraid I'll wake up to find this is all a dream.'

His arm snaked round her waist to pull her closer against the heat of his body. He smiled, that smile of his that always made her wish to throw caution to the winds. 'If it's a dream, it's a wonderful one,' he murmured, kissing the corners of her mouth. 'Quite the most wonderful one I have ever had,' he continued, licking along her full bottom lip, pulling her astride his lap.

Serena wriggled deliberately. She felt him harden against her. Shivering with pleasure, she wriggled again. 'Why, Mr Lytton, I do believe this morning's duel has left you a trifle overexcited,' she said wickedly.

Nicholas shifted to lift her up, slipping his hand up her thigh under her dress, closing into the heat between her legs. 'Lady Serena,' he said, his breathing becoming ragged, 'I regret to inform you that it has had the same effect on you.'

His touch lit the torchpaper of passion, setting them both aflame in an instant. Blue eyes met grey for one long slumberous moment, then they were kissing wildly, devouring each other with their mouths, their tongues, their hands, clothing pushed frantically aside, buttons torn, ruffles ripped in their haste to be one.

'Oh God, Serena, I've missed you so much,' Nicholas said, tugging at her dress and touching her with a stunning certainty, just exactly where she needed to be touched.

Serena moaned, fumbling with the fastenings of his breeches, shuddering with need as she wrapped her hand round his length. Digging her hands into his shoulders, she braced herself, pulling him deep inside her with one long luxurious thrust, relishing the feel of him hard against her muscles. Gripped in the vice of a passion almost painful in its need for release she thrust again, then again, slow and hard, pressing her weight on to him and against him, clenching her muscles to feel every inch of him as she moved, her arms entwined around his neck, kissing him feverishly.

His hands were on her waist, steadying her, pulling her to him. Her name was whispered over and over again in her ear, against her mouth, in a voice hoarse with passion, becoming inarticulate as he thrust with her, into her, higher, deeper, harder, faster until the world exploded, a million pieces shattered and reformed as one. For long moments afterwards they lay spent in one another's arms. One body. One mind. Utterly and completely content.

'I don't know how you do that,' Nicholas said huskily some time later, stroking Serena's hair tenderly back from her brow. 'One minute I'm a perfectly sane and rational person, the next I'm a seething cauldron of need and cannot think of aught save you, and this.' He laughed softly. 'You know, if the landlady chooses to come in at the moment, she's going to get the shock of her life.'

She gave a muffled giggle. 'My reputation will be in tatters.'

He kissed her gently before lifting her from his lap and standing up to tidy himself. 'Your reputation is almost beyond recovery.'

Serene straightened out her skirts as best she could. 'Almost!' Catching a glimpse of herself in the spotted glass above the fire, she laughed. 'My hair. Oh dear, I see what you mean. I look—'

'You look absolutely beautiful,' he interrupted, turning her away from the mirror and pressing a kiss into the warm centre of her palm.

'Despite my ruined reputation,' Serena reminded him.

'About that.'

She caught her breath as she met his gaze, such a blazing look of love as was writ there.

'Actually,' Nicholas said with a smile, 'it's not about that at all. I don't want you to marry me to retrieve your reputation. I don't want you to marry me in order to secure my inheritance. I don't want you to marry me to ease my guilt. I don't even want to marry you because it means I have the right to do as I will with this delicious body of yours—though that is, of course, an added attraction. I want you to marry me because I love you, and because I can't live without you, and because now that I've found you I realise I've been waiting for you all my life.' He pulled her close, gazing deep into her eyes. 'So I most humbly beg you, Lady Serena, to be my wife, because you want me as I want you, and for no other reason.'

'I wouldn't have it any other way,' Serena replied, her face flushed with love. She curtsied. 'And therefore, Mr Nicholas Lytton, I thank you most kindly for your very beautiful proposal and I say yes, yes, yes, with all my heart.'

The kiss that sealed their pledge was tender and would have become passionate were it not for the sharp *'ahem'* that announced the land lady's presence.

'Begging your pardon, I'm sure,' she said with a reproving look. 'But would you be requiring breakfast? Only this *is* the taproom, and we have other customers who was wishful to share it.'

'Breakfast is an excellent idea' Nicholas said. 'I don't know about you,' he continued, grinning at Serena, 'but I find I am unaccountably famished.'

She giggled. 'I find I am also rather hungry,' she agreed. 'The fresh air, you know.'

'And the exercise,' he concurred, causing his affianced bride to blush wildly.

'So is that a yes?' the landlady asked impatiently.

'It is a yes,' Nicholas said.

'It is a very, very definite yes,' Serena said.

'About time,' the landlady snorted, slamming the door.

'Indeed,' Nicholas said, 'I think that will be the opinion of most of our acquaintance.'

'Do we have to face them?' Serena blushed charmingly. 'It's just—I would prefer to be alone with you. We have a nursery of brats to make, in case you had forgot.'

He laughed. 'I never thought I'd say this, but a nursery of brats is now very high on my list of wishes. In fact, I think it is so important we should give it top priority. What do you say to a special licence and an extended stay at Knightswood Hall? It is where we met, and it holds a special place in both our hearts I think.'

'That, Nicholas would be perfect.'

And so it was that the marriage of Mr Nicholas Lytton and Lady Serena Stamppe took place in private at the country home of the groom not many days later. Not long after the groom placed the ring on his bride's finger, they lay entwined in one another's arms, pressed close, heart to heart, under the vast canopy of a four-poster bed. It was a position with which they would become very familiar, so all-consuming and long-lived was their passion. And in tribute to the quest that first brought them together, the ring that Serena wore on her left hand had embellished upon it a tiny Tudor rose.

* * * * *

Innocent in the Sheikh's Harem

For Joan (Johanna), who taught me to read,
inspired me to read lots, and who was there that day
on the beach in Cyprus when Kit and Clarissa
first popped into my head. Thank you, and love.

Chapter One

Summer, 1818

'Oh, George, do come and see!' In her excitement, Lady Celia Cleveden leaned precariously over the side of the dhow in which they had just completed the last leg of their journey down the northern part of the Red Sea. The crew lowered the lateen sail which towered high above their heads and steered the little craft skilfully through the mass of other dhows, feluccas and caiques, all jostling for space in the busy harbour. Celia clung to the low wooden side of the boat with one gloved hand, the other holding her hat firmly in place, watching with wide-eyed wonder as they approached the shore.

She was dressed with her usual elegance in a gown of pale green sprigged muslin, one of several which she had had made especially for the trip, with long sleeves and a high neckline which in London would have been quite out of place but which here, in the East, she had been reliably informed, was absolutely essential. A straw hat with a long veil, also essential, covered her distinctive copper hair, but her tall, slender figure and youthful creamy complexion still attracted much attention from the fishermen, boatmen and passengers of the other craft currently vying for space in the busy port.

'George, come and see,' Celia called over her shoulder to the man sheltering under the scant cover provided by a tattered tented roof over the stern. 'There's a donkey on that boat with a positively outraged expression. He looks exactly like my uncle when a parliamentary vote has gone against him in the House,' she said with amusement.

George Cleveden, her husband of some three months, made no move to join her, and clearly was in no mood to be amused. He too was dressed with his usual elegance, in a cutaway coat of dark blue superfine teamed with a striped waistcoat from which a selection of elegant fobs dangled, and buckskin breeches worn with top boots. Sadly, though his outfit would indeed have been perfect for a coach journey from his mother's house in Bath to his own lodgings in London, or even for the ride from his London lodgings to his small country estate in Richmond, it was very far from ideal for a trip down the Red Sea in the blazing heat of summer. The starched points of his neck cloth had wilted many hours ago. His head ached from the heat of the sun, and there was a very distinctive rim of sweat marking the band of his beaver hat.

George eyed his young bride, looking confoundedly

cool as a cucumber, with something akin to resentment. 'Blast this infernal heat! Do come away from there, Celia, you're making a show of yourself. Remember you are a British diplomat's wife.'

As if she needed reminding! Celia, however, continued to marvel at the spectacle unfolding before her eyes, choosing to ignore her husband. It was something at which she had become surprisingly adept during the short period of their marriage. The wedding had taken place on the very day upon which they had set out for the long journey to Cairo, and George's new diplomatic posting. George, the collected, organised undersecretary who worked for Celia's father, Lord Armstrong, at the Foreign Office, had proved to be a rather less than intrepid traveller. This left Celia, who was no more experienced than he when it came to traversing the globe, to manage as best she could the challenging task of getting them—along with their mountain of baggage—from London to Egypt via Gibraltar, Malta, Athens, and an unplanned stop in Rhodes, when their scheduled ship had failed to arrive, and much of their luggage had disappeared. For this, and for a plethora of other minor mishaps which were the result of Celia's naïve but plucky determination to get them in one piece to their destination, George blamed his wife. Damp sheets or no sheets at all, poor wine and much poorer food, insect bites and insect stings, nausea-inducing pitching seas and seas that were becalmed—George had borne none of these with the equanimity Celia had so much admired in the man she had married.

She put much of it down to the tribulations of travel,

and maintained an optimistic outlook which she had intended to be reassuring, but which seemed to have rather a contrary effect. 'How can you be so damned jaunty?' George had demanded during one particularly uncomfortable crossing, memorable for its weevil-infested ship's biscuits and brandy-infested ship's captain. But what was the point in lying abed and bemoaning one's fate? Far better to be up on deck, watching hopefully for land and admiring a school of porpoises with comically smiling faces swimming alongside them.

But George could not be so easily distracted, and eventually Celia had learned to keep her fascination for all things strange and colourful to herself. Foreign climes, or at least Eastern foreign climes, clearly did not agree with George's constitution. This was rather a pity, since fate had brought them here, to a clime so foreign Celia had never even heard of it and had been forced to ask one of the consuls in Cairo to point it out on a rather large and complicated map kept under lock and key in his office.

'A'Qadiz.' Celia said the word experimentally under her breath. Impossibly exotic, it conjured up visions of closed courtyards and colourful silks, of spices and perfumes, the heat of the desert and something darker and more exciting she could not put into words. She and her next sister, Cassandra, had read the Arabian tales, *One Thousand and One Nights*, in French, sharing an edited version with their three younger sisters, for some of the stories hinted at distinctly decadent pleasures. Now here she was in Arabia, and it looked even more fantastic than she had imagined. Watching from the dhow as the dots on the harbour became people and donkeys and horses and camels, as the distant buzz became a babble of voices, Celia wondered how on earth she would be able to convey to Cassie even a tenth part of what it actually felt like.

If only Cassie were here with her, how much more fun it would be. As quickly as the very unwifely thought flashed through her mind, Celia tried hard to suppress it—an act rather more difficult than it should be, for though she had been married for exactly three months, one week and two days, she did not feel at all like a wife. Or at least not at all as she had expected to feel as a wife.

The match was of her father's making, but at four-and-twenty, and the eldest of five motherless girls—two of whom were already of marriageable age—Celia had seen the sense in his proposal. George Cleveden was Lord Armstrong's protégé. He was well thought of, and great things were expected of him.

'With a hostess like you at his side, he can't fail,' Papa had said bracingly when he'd first put forward the idea. 'You've cut your teeth in diplomatic circles as my hostess, and a damned fine fist you've made of it. You can hold your own with the best of them, my girl, and let's face it, Celia, it's not as if you've your sister's looks. You take after my side rather than your mother's, I'm afraid. You're passable enough, but you'll never be a toast, and it's not as if you're getting any younger.'

Celia bore her father's casual assassination of her appearance with equanimity. She neither resented nor envied Cassie her beauty, and was content to be known as the clever one of the five Armstrong girls. Elegance, wit and charm were her accomplishments—assets which stood her in excellent stead as her father's hostess and which would stand George in equally excellent stead as he rose through the diplomatic ranks, as surely he would if only he managed to shine in this posting. Which of course he would—if only he could accustom himself to being away from England.

George, it seemed, was the type of man who needed the reassurance of the familiar in order to function properly. It had been his idea to postpone the consummation of their vows. 'Until we are settled in Cairo,' he had said on their wedding night. 'There will be enough for us to endure on our journey without having to contend with that as well.'

Even at the time his words had struck her as somewhat ambiguous. Though lacking a mother's guidance, Celia was not entirely unprepared for her marital duties. 'As with so many things in life,' her stately Aunt Sophia had informed her, 'it is an act from which the gentleman derives satisfaction and the lady endures the consequences.' Pressed for practical details, Aunt Sophia had resorted to obscure biblical references, leaving Celia with the vague impression that she was to undergo some sort of stamina test, during which it was vital that she neither move nor complain.

Slightly relieved, though somewhat surprised, given Aunt Sophia's certainty that gentlemen were unfailingly eager to indulge in this one-sided game, Celia had agreed to her husband's proposed abstinence, spending her first night as a married woman alone. However, as the nights passed and George showed no inclination to change his mind, she could not help wondering if she had been wrong—for surely the more one postponed something, the more difficult it became to succeed? And she wanted to succeed as a wife, eventually as a mother too. She liked and admired George. In time she expected to love him, and to be loved in return. But love was built on sharing a life together, and surely sharing a bed must play a part in that? Lying alone in the various bunks, pallets and hammocks which had marked their progress across the globe, Celia had swung between fretting that she should do something about the situation, and convincing herself that George knew best and it would all come right in the end.

But after a week in Cairo, with George restored almost to his pleasant and agreeable self, he had still shown no interest in joining his new wife in her bed. Plucking up all her courage, Celia had tried, extremely reluctantly, with much stumbling, blushing and almost as many vague biblical references as Aunt Sophia, to broach the subject—a particularly difficult task, given her lack of any certain knowledge of what the subject actually entailed.

George had been mortally offended.

He was trying to be considerate, to give her time to adjust to married life.

They barely knew each other.

It was highly unnatural of Celia to show such a morbid interest in these things which all the world knew only women of a certain class enjoyed.

And finally, he was doing her a favour by restraining

himself from imposing what he knew she would find unpleasant upon her, and she had thrown that favour in his face!

Celia had retired, confused, mortified, hurt and a little resentful. Was she so unattractive? Was there something wrong with her? Certainly George had implied that there was.

Or was there something wrong with George? Not her first unwifely thought, but the most shocking. She banished it. Or tried to. In the absence of any other woman to consult—for she could not quite bring herself to confide such intimate matters to the forbidding Lady Wincester, the wife of the Consul General of Cairo—she had resolved to write to Aunt Sophia. But it was such an awesome task, and putting her fears into words seemed to make them more real, and perhaps George was right—it was just a matter of time. So she had instead written colourful descriptions of all she had seen and all she had done, and made no reference at all to the fact that her husband continued to spurn her company after dark.

When this special assignment on which they were now engaged had come up, it had been with immense relief that Celia had turned her attentions to preparations for the trip. She had accompanied George against the express wishes of the Consul General. A'Qadiz was no place for a gently bred woman, apparently, but on this matter George had stood firm, and refused to go without her. Impressed by what he took to be a newlywed husband's devotion to his wife, Lord Wincester had most reluctantly agreed. Under no such illusion, Celia had prepared to resume her role as chief nurse, comforter and courier with an air of sanguinity she'd been very far from feeling.

The scenery through which they had sailed was enchanting. The deep waters were clear enough for her to watch the shoals of rainbow-coloured fish just by hanging over the back of the boat. Reefs with coral all the shades of sunset and sunrise could be seen just below the surface, shimmering like tiny mystical cities teeming with life. Along the shoreline were palm, orange, lemon and fig trees, olive groves and a myriad of plants with scents so heady that it was, as she had said to George at dusk one night, like being inside a huge vat of perfume.

'It's playing havoc with my hay fever,' he'd sniffed, putting paid to the eulogy she had been about to deliver.

The port of A'Qadiz in which they had now arrived looked impossibly crowded, swarming with people swathed in long robes. The women were all veiled, some with light gauze such as Celia's own veil, others draped in heavier material, with only slits for their eyes. A stack of enormous terracotta urns stood on the quayside, waiting to be loaded for transport north. Through the open doors of the warehouses could be glimpsed bales of silks in a rainbow of colours, and hundreds more of the large urns.

As the dhow pulled alongside, it was the noise which struck Celia next. The strange, ululating sound of the Arabic language, with everyone talking and gesturing all at once. The high-pitched braying of donkeys, the rumbling of carts on the rough stony ground, the low-pitched bleating of the camels which reminded Celia of the rumbling noise her father made when he was working up to an important announcement. Picking up her skirts and leaping lightly to the shore, careful to make sure her veil remained in place, she couldn't help thinking that the camels themselves, with their thick lips and flaring nostrils, looked rather like Aunt Sophia.

She turned to share this mischievous thought with George, but he was clambering awkwardly to the shore with the assistance of two of the crew, cursing under his breath and frowning heavily in a way that did not bode well for his temper. She made a mental note to share it instead with Cassie, in her next letter.

Rummaging in her reticule for a little bottle of lavender water, Celia tipped a few drops onto her handkerchief and handed it to her husband. 'If you wipe it on your brow it will cool your skin.'

'For God's sake, not now! Are you determined to show me up, Celia?' George batted the scrap of lace away.

It fluttered to the ground, where four semi-naked children contested for the honour of retrieving it and handing it back. Laughing at their antics, Celia thanked them all solemnly in turn. By the time she looked up George was disappearing into the crowd, following the trail of their baggage, which was being carried on the heads of the crew of the dhow, ushered on its way by a man dressed in flowing black robes.

Struggling through the small forest of children's hands clutching at her dress, her gloved hands, her long veil, Celia made slow progress. The colours dazzled her.

In the relentlessly glaring light of the sun, everything seemed brighter, more starkly outlined. Then there were the smells. Sweet perfumes and incense, spices that tickled her nose, the dusty dryness of the heat, the strong musty smell of the camels and donkeys all combined to emphasise the incredible foreignness of the place, the far-awayness, the overwhelmingly exotic feel of it.

Except, she realised, stopping amid her small entourage of children to try and locate the train of her luggage with her husband in its wake, it was really she who was the foreigner here. She could no longer see George. *Had he forgotten all about her?* Panic and a spurt of temper made Celia instinctively push back her veil in order to obtain a better view.

A startled hiss came from the people in her immediate vicinity. The children all turned their heads away, covering their eyes. Fumbling for her veil with shaky fingers, she managed to catch the gauzy material in a hat pin and grew flustered. *Where was George?*

Anxious now for a glimpse of her husband, she cast a frantic look around the crowds. The docks were set into the shade of a low outcrop, and many of the storehouses and animal pens were built into the rock itself. Celia's eyes were drawn to the top of the hill, where a lone figure sat astride a magnificent white horse. A man dressed in traditional robes, and if anything even more magnificent than the beast which bore him.

Outlined against the blazing blue of the azure sky, dazzling in his white robes, he looked like a deity surveying his subjects from the heavens. There was something about him—an aura of authority, a touch-me-not glaze—which dazzled and at the same time made her want to reach out, just to see if he was real. He both compelled and intimidated, like the golden images of the pharaohs she had seen in Cairo. And, like the slaves in the murals she had seen on the walls of the temple the day she had finally persuaded George into taking a sightseeing trip, Celia had an absurd desire to throw herself to her knees at this stranger's feet. He seemed to command adoration.

Where on earth had that come from? Celia gave herself a little mental shake. He was just a man. An extremely striking man, but a mere mortal all the same.

He was dressed entirely in white, save for the gold which edged his *bisht*, the lightweight cloak he wore over the long, loose tunic which all the men here favoured. There was gold too, in the *igal* which held his head-dress in place. The pure white of his *ghutra* fluttered like a summons in the light breeze. It fell in soft folds, and must be made of silk rather than cotton, she noted abstractedly. Underneath it, the man's face showed in stark relief. His skin seemed to gleam, as if the sun had burnished it. It was a strong face, the clean lines of his cheeks, his nose, his jaw, contrasting sharply with the soft, sensual curve of his mouth.

His eyes were heavy-lidded—a little like hers. She could not see their colour, but Celia was suddenly acutely aware that his piercing gaze was trained directly on her. She was not properly veiled. He should not be looking at her thus. Yet he showed no sign of looking away. Heat began to seep through her, starting from somewhere in her stomach. *It was the hot sun!* It must be, for it was most unlike her to feel so unsettled.

'My lady?' Celia turned to find the man who had taken charge of their bags standing before her, his hands pressed respectfully together as if he was praying.

Reminded by his averted eyes to pull her veil back into place, Celia dragged her gaze away from the god on the hilltop and returned the gesture with a slight bow.

'I am Bakri. I have been sent by my master, His Highness the Prince of A'Qadiz, to escort you to his palace. I must apologise. We were not expecting a woman.'

'My husband does not travel well. He needs me to take care of him.'

Bakri raised a brow, but swallowed whatever words he was about to say. 'You must come,' he said instead. 'We must leave soon—before night falls.'

Sheikh Ramiz al-Muhana, Prince of A'Qadiz, watched her go, a frown drawing his dark brows together. The man with the weak face could only be the English diplomat, but what in the name of the gods did he think he was doing, bringing a woman companion? His wife? His mistress? Surely he would not dare?

Ramiz watched as the woman followed Bakri to where the Englishman waited impatiently by the camels and mules which would form their small caravan. She was tall and willowy. In the East, where curves were seen as the apex of womanly beauty, she would be deemed unattractive, but Ramiz, who had spent much of his adult life in the great cities of the West, completing his education and later acting as his father's emissary, was not so biased. She moved with the grace of a dancer. In her pale green dress, with her veil covering her face, she made him think of Guinevere, the queen from Arthurian legend. Regal, ethereal, temptingly untouchable. Definitely not a mistress, he decided, yet she had not the demeanour of a wife either.

Ramiz watched in disgust as her husband chastised her. The Englishman was a fool—the type of man who blamed everyone but himself for his faults. He should not have let her out of his sight. The woman was not responding, but Ramiz could see the tension in her from the way she stood a little straighter. Her cool exterior was belied by that flame of hair which he had glimpsed when she had thrown back her veil. She would be magnificent when angry. Or roused. Despite her married state, Ramiz was certain her passions slumbered still. He wondered what it would take to awaken them.

Her husband was not just a fool, but obviously inept. It was one of the things which Ramiz found incomprehensible—this reticence the English had regarding the arts of love. No wonder so many of their women looked uptight. Like buds frozen into permanent furls by frost, or simply withered through lack of the sun, he thought, as he watched the Englishman struggle to mount one of the camels. The woman was organising the loading of their baggage onto the mules. She made short work of seating herself on the high platform which formed the camel's saddle, arranging her full skirts with elegant modesty, for all the world as if she rode one every day. Unlike her husband, who was clutching nervously at the pommel, making the animal dance playfully, the woman sat with her back straight, holding the reins at precisely the correct angle, swaying in tune to the undulating movement of the beast.

Ramiz cursed under his breath. *What did he think he was doing, looking upon another man's woman in such a way?* Even if the man appeared to be an incompetent fool, honour forbade it. The Englishman was his guest, after all, and here at his invitation.

Ramiz was under no illusions. The English, like the French, were waiting in Cairo like vultures, ready to prey upon any sign of weakness as the Sultan of the once-great Ottoman empire struggled to retain his control over the trade routes. Already the ruthless Mehmet Ali had taken Egypt. A'Qadiz, with its port on the Red Sea, could prove a valuable link to the riches of India. Ramiz was in no doubt about the benefits to his country that playing such a role might bring, but nor was he blind to the disadvantages. Westerners were desperate to plunder the artefacts of the old world, and A'Qadiz was a treasure trove of antiquities. Ramiz had no intention of allowing them to be hauled off and displayed in private museums by greedy aristocrats with no understanding of their provenance or their cultural value, any more than he intended handing control of his country over to some conquering imperialist. As Prince al-Muhana he could trace his lineage back far beyond anything English or French dukes and lords could dream of.

Examine what is said, not he who speaks. His father's words, and wise as ever. The Englishman deserved a fair hearing. Ramiz smiled to himself as he turned his horse away from the harbour. Three days it took to travel across the desert to his palace in the ancient capital city of Balyrma. Three days—in which time he could observe, study and plan.

Six camels and four mules formed their caravan as they wound their way up the hill from the port of A'Qadiz into the desert, for Prince Ramiz had assigned them three guards in addition to Bakri, their guide. The guards were surly men, armed with alarming curved swords at their waists and long slim daggers strapped to their chests, who eyed Celia with something akin to disgust and muttered darkly amongst themselves. Their presence was alarming, rather than reassuring to her. George, too, seemed uncomfortable with them, and stuck close to Bakri at the head of the train.

This part of the desert was much rougher underfoot than Celia had anticipated—not really sand at all, more like hard dried mud covered with rock and dust—and it wasn't flat either. After the first steep climb from the sea, the land continued to rise. In the distance she could see mountains, sharp and craggy, ochre against the startling blue of the sky, which was deepening to a velvety hue as the sun sank. The sense of space, of the desert unfolding for miles, beyond anything she could ever have imagined, was slightly intimidating. Compared to such vastness, she could not but be aware of her own insignificance. She was awestruck, and for a moment completely overwhelmed by the journey they had travelled and the task ahead of them in this land as shrouded in mystery as the people were shrouded in their robes.

However, as the caravan made its way east over the desert plain and she became more accustomed to the terrain as well as to the undulating movement of the camel, Celia's mood slowly lifted. She amused herself by picturing Cassie's face when she read of her account of her ride on the ship of the desert, and revived her flagging optimism by reminding herself of the very high esteem in which George, as a diplomat, was held. This mission would be a success, and when it was, George would stop fretting about his career and turn his mind to making an equal success of his marriage. She was sure of it!

They came to a halt in the shelter of an escarpment, the terracotta-coloured stone glittering with agates, as if it were chipped with diamonds. Above them, the sky was littered with a carpet of stars, not star-shaped at all, but huge round bursts of light. 'You feel as if you could just reach out and touch them,' Celia said to George, as they watched the men put up the tent.

'I'd like to reach out and touch my four-poster just at the minute,' George said sarcastically. 'Doesn't look like very luxurious accommodation, does it?'

In truth, the tent did look more like a lean-to, for it had only three sides, with a curtain placed down the middle to form two rooms. The walls were woven from some sort of wool, Celia thought, feeling the rough texture between her fingers. 'It must be goat's hair, for I don't think they have many sheep here. I'm pretty sure that was goat we had for dinner, too,' she said. 'You should have tried some, George, it was delicious.'

'Barbaric manners—eating with their hands like that. I was surprised at you.'

'It is their custom,' she replied patiently. 'You're supposed to use the bread like a spoon. I simply copied what they did, as *you* must do if you are not to starve. Now, where shall I put this carpet for you?'

'I'll never sleep like this, with the guards snoring their heads off next door,' George grumbled, but he allowed Celia to clear the rocks from a space large enough to accommodate him and very soon, despite his protestations, he was soundly asleep.

Celia sat outside the tent, looking up at the stars for a long time. She was not in the least sleepy. Such a vast space this desert was. Such beauty even in its apparent barrenness. When it rained, Bakri said, it was a carpet of colour. She thought of all the little seeds sleeping just below the surface, ready to burst into life. *Promise is a cloud; fulfilment is rain,* Bakri had said.

She was obviously expected to share the same room as George, but she couldn't bear the idea of their first night together to be *this* night, even if her husband was fully dressed and already sleeping. Celia took her carpet and found herself a quiet spot a short distance away, tucked up behind a large boulder. 'Promise is a cloud; fulfilment is rain,' she murmured to herself. Perhaps that was how she should think of her marriage. Not barren, just waiting for the rain. She fell asleep wondering what form such a rain would take if it were to be powerful enough to fix what she was beginning to think might be unfixable.

Above her, still and silent, Ramiz watched for a long

time over the dark shape of the sleeping Englishwoman who could not bring herself to stay in the tent beside her husband. Then, as the cold of the true night began to descend, he made his way back to his own small camp some short distance away, wrapped himself in his carpet, and settled down to sleep next to his camel.

Chapter Two

They came just before dawn. Celia was awoken by the sound of camel hooves. She sat up, cramped from her sleeping position, and peered out over the rock at the cloud of dust moving frighteningly fast towards the tent. A glint of wicked steel drew her attention. Whoever these men were, they were not friends.

There was still time. A few moments, no more, but enough. She must warn the guard. She must save George. It did not occur to Celia that it should be the other way round. She scrambled to her feet, and had taken one step from behind the rock when a large hand covered her mouth and a strong arm circled her waist. She struggled, but the hold on her tightened.

'Keep still and don't scream.'

His voice was low, but the note of command in it was perfectly apparent. Celia obeyed unhesitatingly, too frightened even to register that he spoke English.

The hand was removed from her mouth. She was twisted around to face him, though still held tight in his embrace. 'You!' she exclaimed in astonishment, for it was the man she had seen yesterday on the hill.

'Get back behind the rock. Don't move. No matter what happens, do not come out until I tell you. Do you understand?'

'But my husband...'

'What they will do to him is nothing to what you will suffer if they find you. Now, do as I bid you.'

He was already dragging her back towards her sleeping place. Behind her she could hear shouts. 'Please. Help him—save my husband.'

Ramiz nodded grimly and, wresting a glittering scimitar from its sheath at his waist and a small curved dagger from a silver holder in the same belt, he gave a terrifying cry as he leapt, sure-footed as a lion, over the short distance to the tent, calling out to the three hired guards to come to his aid.

But the guards were nowhere to be seen. Only Bakri stood between the English diplomat, cowering in the far corner of the tent, and his fate. Ramiz cursed furiously and turned his attention to the first of the four men, shouting to Bakri to see if the Englishman had a gun.

Whether he had or not, it was destined never to be used. Ramiz fought viciously, utilising all his skills with the scimitar, slicing it in bold arcs through the air while defending himself with his *khanjar* dagger. It was four to his one. Trapped in the circle of the men, he fought like a dervish, managing a disabling cut in the shoulder to one man before swirling around, his scimitar clanging against that of his enemy with a last-minute defensive move, the strength of which vibrated painfully up his arm.

Two down. Two to go. As Ramiz fought on, sweat and dust obscuring his vision, he became dimly aware of a cry coming from the corner of the tent. Turning towards it, he saw one of his own hired guards raising his dagger over Bakri. 'Help him! In the name of the gods, help him,' he cried out to the Englishman.

It all happened so fast after that. The Englishman moved, but instead of attempting to lend his assistance he pushed past Bakri and his attacker, making for the entrance of the tent. Bakri fell, clutching the dagger which had been plunged deep into his heart. Ramiz abandoned his attempts to slay the other two men and lunged forward. The Englishman was running away. Disgust slowed Ramiz's steps. Even as he reminded himself that the foreign coward was nevertheless his honoured guest, it was too late. One of the invaders raised his scimitar and sliced deep into the Englishman's belly.

A piercing scream rent the air. The woman abandoned her hiding place and, running full tilt towards them, distracted everyone. They would kill her as they had killed her husband. He realised it was what they had come for, these men of Malik, the ruler of the neighbouring principality, for it could only be he who would have contemplated such a dastardly plot. Fuelled by fury, Ramiz launched himself at the two men. They had already reached the woman, yanking her hair back and pressing a lethal dagger to her throat. A well-aimed kick sent the first one flying, unconscious, his dagger soaring through the air in the opposite direction. The sight of Ramiz, his face taut with rage, his scimitar arching down towards his head, sent the other man prostrate to the ground in the time-old attitude of abasement.

'Please, Lord. Please, Your Highness, I beg of you to spare me,' the man muttered, over and over.

Ramiz yanked him up by the hair. 'You have a message for me from your prince?'

'Please, do not. I beg of you. I…'

Ramiz twisted his hold, making the man scream. 'What does Malik have to say?'

'To invite strangers into our house is to risk disaster.'

Ramiz dropped his hold and turned the man onto his back with the toe of his boot. 'Tell Malik that I invite who I choose into my house. Tell Malik he will live to regret this day's work. Now, go—while you still have your life—and take your sleeping friend with you.'

Needing no further encouragement, the man scurried over to his unconscious comrade and roughly bundled him onto a camel, before mounting one himself and galloping off in a cloud of dust.

Ramiz knelt over the body of the fallen diplomat, but there was nothing he could do. As he got slowly to his feet, the Englishwoman staggered towards him. Instinctively Ramiz stood in front of the body, shielding it from her gaze.

'George?' Her voice was no more than a whisper.

Ramiz shook his head. 'It is best you don't look.'

'The guards?'

'Traitors.'

'And Bakri?'

Ramiz shook his head again. Bakri, who had been his servant since he was a boy, was dead. He swallowed hard.

'You saved my life. I'm sorry I didn't listen to you. But I heard George, you see. My husband. I thought—I thought…' Celia began to shake. Her knees seemed to be turning to jelly. The ground was moving. 'I'm a widow,' she said, a touch of hysteria in her voice. 'I'm a widow, and I've never really been a wife.' As she began to fall, Ramiz caught her in his arms. The feel of them, securing her to the solid, reassuring bulk of his body, was the last thing Celia remembered.

She was climbing through a tunnel. Slowly up through the thick darkness she went, fighting the urge to curl up and stay where she was, safe, unnoticed. A slit of light lay ahead. She was afraid to reach it. Something horrible waited for her there.

'George!' She sat up with a start. 'George!' Celia struggled to her feet, clutching her head as the ground rolled and tipped like the deck of a ship in a storm. She was in the tent. *How had she got there?* It didn't matter. She staggered out into the open air.

The blaze of the sun dazzled her eyes, temporarily blinding her. When her vision cleared, she clutched at the tent rope for support. The blood had dried dark on the ground, and she remembered, in a rush, what had happened. The men arriving in a cloud of dust like something from the Bible. The man from yesterday. *Who was he? And what was he doing here?* Then the fighting. The cries. And George running. Running away. Even though he had a gun. Even though he used to practice shooting at Manson's every week. He had been running away. He hadn't even looked for her.

No! She mustn't think that way. He had just panicked, he would have come back for her.

A clunking sound coming from the back of the tent distracted her. Celia made her way cautiously, already knowing in her heart what she would find. Sure enough, the stranger was there, his gold-edged cloak discarded on a rock. His headdress was tied back from his face, which glistened with sweat from his exertions. He was smoothing sand over a distinctive mound of desert earth. He must have found a shovel with the supplies their traitorous guards had left when they'd fled.

He was facing away from her. The thin white of his tunic clung to his back with sweat, outlining the breadth of his shoulders. He looked strong. A capable man. Capable of saving her life. A man who knew how to take care of things. Who didn't run away. *Stop!*

He put down the shovel and wiped the sweat from his brow. She must have moved, or made a noise, or maybe he just sensed her, for he turned around. 'You should stay in the tent, out of the sun.'

He spoke English with an accent, his voice curling round the words like a husky caress. His eyes were a strange colour, like bronze tinged with gold, the irises dark. He walked with a fluid grace. Celia could not imagine that such a man was regularly employed in manual labour. It struck her then that she was quite alone with him, and she shivered. *Fear?* Yes, but not as much as there should be. She was too shocked, too numb to feel anything much at the moment.

He stopped just in front of her, was watching her with concern. She didn't like the way he looked at her. It made her feel weak. She didn't like feeling weak. She was normally the one who took care of things. Celia straightened her back, tilting her head up to meet the stranger's eyes, forgetting all about protocol and hats and veils.

'Who are you?' Her voice came out with only the tiniest of wobbles.

'Sheikh Ramiz al-Muhana,' he said, bowing before her with a hint of a smile, lending a fleeting softness to the hard, rocky planes of his face. It lightened his eyes to amber, as if the sun shone from them. Everything about him gleamed. She remembered thinking yesterday of the ancient pharaohs. He had that air about him. Of command.

'Sheikh Ramiz…' Celia repeated stupidly, then realisation dawned. 'You mean Prince Ramiz of A'Qadiz?'

He nodded.

'We were on our way to visit you in Balyrma. George is—was…' She drew a shaky breath, determined not to lose control. 'I don't understand. What are you doing here? What happened this morning? Who were those men? Why did they attack us?'

Her voice rose with each question. Her face was pale. Her eyes, with their heavy lids which gave her that sensual, sleepy look, were dark with a fear she was determined not to show. She had courage, this Englishwoman, unlike her coward of a husband. 'Later. First you must say your farewells, then we will leave this place.'

'Farewells?'

Her lip was beginning to tremble, but she clenched it firmly between her teeth. Big eyes—the green of moss or unpolished jade, he thought—turned pleadingly towards him. Ramiz took Celia's arm and gently led her towards the graves.

Two graves, Celia noticed. And another two at a distance. Prince Ramiz had obviously laboured long and hard as she lay unconscious. Such labour had spared her much. She could not but be grateful.

They stood together, she and the Prince of A'Qadiz, in silent contemplation. Sadness welled up inside Celia. Poor George. A tear splashed down her cheek, then another. 'I'm so sorry,' she whispered. 'I'm so sorry.'

They should never have married. George hadn't really wanted a wife, and she—she'd wanted more from her husband than he'd been prepared to give. It was as well he had not, for were she standing here a real wife, with three months of real marriage behind her, the pain would be unendurable.

Overcome with remorse, Celia clenched her eyes tight shut and prayed hard for the husband she knew now she could never have loved, no matter how hard she'd tried. 'I'm sorry,' she whispered again.

'He is at peace now. He walks with his god.' Ramiz broke the silence. 'As does Bakri, who was my servant, and my brother's, and my father's before that.'

Celia roused herself from the stupor which threatened to envelop her. 'I'm sorry—I didn't realise. It must be a great blow for you to lose him.'

'He died an honourable death.' Ramiz closed his eyes and spoke a prayer in his native language. His voice was low, and the strange words had a simple beauty in their cadence that soothed. 'Now, go back to the tent. I will finish here.'

An honourable death. The unspoken criticism hung like a weight from Celia's heart as she made her way slowly back to the tent. Though common sense told her she could not have saved George, that to have disobeyed Ramiz when he'd told her to hide would almost certainly have resulted in her own death, it did not prevent her from being racked with guilt for having survived.

George was dead. She was a widow. George was dead—and in such a horrible way that it was as if she had dreamt it, or imagined it as a tale from *One Thousand and One Nights.* If only it had been. If only she could wake up.

But she could not. All she could do was behave with what dignity she could muster. With the dignity her father and Aunt Sophia would expect of her. With the dignity which others would expect of George's wife, a representative of His Majesty's government, she reminded herself strictly.

Thus, when Ramiz joined her half an hour later, though she longed to sink onto the carpeted floor, to curl up under the comfort of a blanket and cry, Celia forced herself to her feet. 'I must beg your pardon, Your Highness, if I have offended you by appearing rude,' she said, turning towards Ramiz, remembering belatedly to avert her eyes from his face. 'I must thank you for saving my life, and for the trouble you took with—with my husband.' She swept him a deep curtsy. 'I realise I haven't even introduced myself. I am Lady Celia Cleveden.'

'I think we are long past the need for such formalities,' Ramiz replied. 'Come, we must leave this place if we are to find another shelter before dark. I don't want to risk spending the night here.'

'But what about—? We can't just...'

'There is nothing more we can do. I have already formed the animals into a caravan,' Ramiz said impatiently.

She had not the will to argue. Questions tussled for prominence in her mind, but she had not the strength to form them. And she had absolutely no desire at all to remain here, in the presence of the dead, at the scene of such horror, so she followed the Prince obediently to where her camel was tethered, and when it dropped to its knees at Ramiz's barked command Celia climbed wearily onto the high wooden platform which served as a saddle. Vaguely she noticed that the beast Prince Ramiz mounted was as white as his horse yesterday had been. That its saddle cloth was silk, intricately embroidered with gold, and that the tack was similarly intricately tasselled and trimmed with threads of gold.

He mounted with the ease of long practice, and took up the halters of the leading camel in the caravan, as well as a halter attached to Celia's own camel. Under any other circumstances she would have been furious to have her mount's control taken from her. Now she was simply relieved. It was one less thing to worry about.

They rode for about two hours. When the sun began its spectacularly fast slide down towards the horizon, striping the sky with gold and crimson, they stopped and made camp. Unbelievably, Celia had dozed for part of the way. Distance and rest had already started the healing process. As she fulfilled each of Ramiz's curt instructions her mind sorted and sieved through the events, forming questions which she was determined he would answer.

They sat by a small fire, eating a simple meal which Celia prepared from their supplies. A new moon was rising. *Hilal.* The crescent moon. The sign of new beginnings.

'Do you know what happened this morning? Why it happened, Your Highness?' Celia asked when they had finished their food. 'How did you come to be there?'

'Ramiz. You may call me Ramiz while we are in private. I was following you. I wanted to see what kind of man your government had sent to talk to me. I wanted to run the rule over him before our official meeting. I had not anticipated him bringing his wife. If I had known you were coming I would certainly have made alternative arrangements for your journey to my citadel.'

'Just because I am a woman it does not mean I need to be wrapped in cotton wool. I am perfectly capable of dealing with the hardships of a trip across the desert.'

'From what I saw, you are far more capable than your husband was,' Ramiz said dryly, 'but that is beside the point. In my country we take care of our women. We cherish them, and we put their comfort before our own. Their lives before our own. Unlike your husband.'

Celia shifted uncomfortably on the carpet. The narrow skirts of her robe made kneeling difficult. 'George was just—George was not—he was…'

'Running away,' Ramiz said contemptuously. 'Was he armed?'

'He had a gun,' Celia admitted reluctantly.

'He could have saved himself and the life of my honoured servant.'

'Your Highness—Ramiz—my husband was a good man. It is just that this was all—and the attack—it was terrifying. He acted on—on instinct.'

'A man whose instincts are to abandon his wife in order to save his own skin is not worth saving. Nature has bestowed upon women their beauty for man to appreciate. To man has been granted the strength to provide and protect them. To break such rules is to go against the natural way of things, the formula civilisations such as mine have been following very successfully for many thousands of years. Your husband was a coward and therefore not, in my eyes, worthy to be called a man. I am sorry to be so harsh, but I speak only the truth.'

Though all her instincts told her to defend George, Celia found she could not. To a man like Ramiz, what George had done was indefensible. And in a small corner of her own mind she agreed. She turned her attention to obtaining answers to the rest of the questions she knew would be asked of her when she returned to Cairo. Nothing could bring George back, but she could brief the Consul General, provide at least some information about this principality of which they knew next to nothing. In a tiny way it would mean that George had not died in vain. 'You knew the men who attacked us today, didn't you?' she asked. 'Who were they?'

Ramiz threw his head back to look up at the stars, suspended like lanterns so close above them. 'Until two years ago my elder brother Asad was the ruler of A'Qadiz. This kingdom and those surrounding it are lands of many tribes, many factions, and my brother embroiled us in many battles. He believed that the sword was mightier than the tongue. It was to cost him his life.'

'What happened to him?'

Ramiz shook his head slowly. 'He was killed in a pointless, ultimately futile skirmish. I don't share his philosophy. I believe most men are reasonable, and reasonable men want peace. Peace is what I have been working tirelessly to achieve, but not all my neighbours agree with me. Nor do all accept my strategy of negotiating with foreign powers such as the British. Today was a warning, and I must act swiftly or everything I have begun to achieve will crumble into dust. It is unfortunate that you have been caught up in this, but there is nothing I can do about it for now. It is another two days' journey to Balyrma. We must start at first light.'

'Balyrma!' Celia exclaimed. 'But surely—I mean, I had assumed you would take me back to Cairo.'

'There can be no question of that. I must return home urgently.'

'Can you not provide me with another escort?'

Ramiz indicated with two spread arms the vast empty expanse of the desert night. 'You think I have magic powers? You think I can summon an escort for you by sheer force of will?'

'I'm afraid I was not briefed, and my husband chose not to share the details of this mission with me. I can be of little use to you in that regard.'

'It is of no matter. It would not be appropriate to hold such discussions with a woman in any event,' Ramiz said dismissively.

She already knew that. George had said as much, and it wasn't really so very different from the way things were back home in England. 'If that is the case, surely it would make more sense for me to go back to Egypt. It is but a day's travel to the port and…'

'I have spoken. You would do well to remember that in this country my word is law.'

Celia was taken aback by the abrupt change of tone. Ramiz had removed his headdress. His hair was black, surprisingly close cut, emphasising the shape of his head, the strength in his neck and shoulders. Now he ran his fingers through it, making a small lick stand up endearingly on his forehead, and Celia realised he was younger than she had thought, perhaps only two or three and thirty. But his looks belied his maturity. He spoke with the voice of authority, the voice of a man used to being obeyed without question. A man, she reminded herself, who held the power of life and death over her.

Celia, however, was not a woman to whom unquestioning obedience came naturally. 'Is it because of the attack this morning?' she asked carefully. 'Are you worried they may return?' She had not thought of this until now—how vulnerable they were, only the two of them. Nervously, she peered out into the inky black of the desert, but she could see nothing beyond the vague contours of the hills.

She was immensely relieved when Ramiz shook his head decidedly. 'They would not dare return now they know of my presence here.' His mouth thinned. 'It is a stain on my honour, and on that of A'Qadiz, that they came at all.'

'You saved my life.' Without thinking, Celia laid her hand over his. 'You could not have known that your own men would turn traitor.'

Her hand was cool. Her fingers were long, that same lovely creamy colour as her face. Women with such colouring so often turned an ugly red in the sun, or freckled, yet she looked to be flawless. Ramiz wondered how flawless. Then he reminded himself that he should not be wondering. He removed her hand deliberately. 'You will come to Balyrma with me, and that is an end to it.'

'For how long?'

Ramiz shrugged. 'Until I decide what is to be done with you.'

Celia frowned. It seemed she had no option. Would it not be best to accept her fate rather than estrange her host by arguing? Though she did not know the details of George's mission, she knew much depended upon it. In any case, even if she was granted her wish to return to Cairo immediately, as George's widow she would not be permitted to stay. She would be sent home. Was that what she really wanted? The answer to that question was obvious.

'Where will I stay in Balyrma?'

'In the palace, as my guest.'

'I don't think that would be good idea,' Celia said uncertainly. 'As an unaccompanied woman it would not be appropriate for me to stay in your palace, especially as you are clearly going to be occupied by urgent matters of state.'

Ramiz laughed harshly. 'You may talk like a man, but you are a woman, are you not, Lady Celia? You need not worry about your virtue. You will be housed in the women's quarters, to which no man but me is permitted entry.' He turned towards her. In the firelight, his eyes seemed to glow like amber.

'Do you mean I am to stay in a harem?' Celia's eyes widened in shock. Images from *One Thousand and One Nights*, of scantily clad concubines oiling themselves and lolling about on velvet cushions sprang to her mind. 'You expect me to form part of your harem? You're not serious. You can't be serious.' Her voice had a panicky edge to it. 'I am not—you expect me to…'

It was that word—*harem*. Ramiz saw immediately what she was thinking. He had encountered the same misunderstanding time and again during his travels as his father's emissary. Europeans imagined a harem to be some sort of exclusive bordello. It angered him to have such inaccurate assumptions made, so he no longer tried to explain. If their fevered imaginations wanted to conjure up scores of nubile women in a perpetual state of arousal waiting for their lord and master to take them to his bed, let them!

'The harem is the place for women in the palace, so that is where you will stay.'

'Your Highness—Ramiz—I am flattered that you should consider adding me to your collection of wives, but…'

'My wife! You over-estimate your value. A sheikh may only marry an Arab princess of royal blood. It is the custom. A Western woman, even a titled one, could not aspire to such an exalted position. At best perhaps she could serve as a concubine.'

Celia gave an outraged gasp. 'You expect me to be your concubine? I absolutely will not! How dare you? How dare you suggest such an outrageous, indecent…?'

He moved so suddenly she had no chance of escape. He seemed to uncoil, to pounce, so that one minute she was sitting next to him, the next she was being dragged helplessly to her feet, held in arms so strong it would be pointless to struggle. Tall as she was, Ramiz topped her by several inches. She was pressed against him, thigh to thigh, chest to chest. His breath was on her face. She could smell him, warm and overpoweringly male. She had never been held thus. She had never been so close to a man before. Not like this, held in such a way as to make her unbearably conscious of her own powerlessness. She should be afraid, and she was, but she was also—something else.

'What do you think you're doing?' Her voice was annoyingly breathless. 'Let me go.'

'You think me a savage, don't you, Lady Celia?' Ramiz said, his voice low and tight with anger.

'I do not! You are obviously educated, your English is flawless, and…'

His grip on her tightened. 'You think the ability to speak a simple language like yours is a measure of being civilised? I also speak French, Greek, German, Italian and at least four variations of my own language. Does that make me more civilised than you—or less? I have travelled widely too, Lady Celia,' Ramiz said with a vicious look. 'Far more widely than you or your pathetic husband. But still all of that means nothing to you, does it? Because I respect the traditions of my own country, and those traditions include keeping a harem. So I can never be anything other than a savage in your eyes, can I?'

Her temper, rarely roused, saved Celia from fear. 'I don't for one moment think of you as a savage! Your country is older by far than mine. I would not be so arrogant. I think it is you who are the one making assumptions about me.'

He had thought her slender, but even through the ridiculous constraints of her English corsetry he could feel her curves. The swell of her breasts pressed against his chest. The dip of her waist made the gentle undulation of her bottom even sweeter. She smelled of lavender and soap, and faintly of that enticing tang of female. The idea of her as his concubine, thrown at her out of anger, was shockingly appealing. Such a vision it commanded, of her creamy skin spread delectably before him, of her delightful mouth at his command, of her long fingers touching him, doing his bidding. Of her submission. He wanted her. Badly. Blood rushed to his groin, making him hard.

Celia struggled to free herself. 'I won't be your—your love-slave, no matter what you do to me. Anyway, they're bound to come looking for me when they hear nothing from George, and if they find me in your harem—'

'Enough!' Ramiz pushed Celia contemptuously away from him. 'I am a sheikh and a man of honour. I would never take a woman against her will. It is an insult that you think me capable of such an act.'

Realising just how foolishly she had leapt to all the wrong conclusions, Celia felt her cheeks burn. 'I'm—I'm sorry,' she stuttered. 'I'm not thinking straight. It's just, with everything that's happened…' A sudden wave of exhaustion hit her with such violence that she staggered. The horror of the day's events came back to her. George was dead, and she was alone in the desert with a man who seemed to think the world should do his bidding. This world was his world; he had good reason for making such an assumption.

Noticing how pale she had become, Ramiz eased Celia back down onto the carpet by the fire. 'You must rest now. We have a long day's travel ahead of us tomorrow. The camels are an excellent early warning of danger, and I will be here by the fire. You need have no fears.'

In the light of the stars her skin looked translucent and pale as the new moon. Her eyes were glazed, vulnerable, and no wonder. She had been through much today, and endured it with a stoicism and bravery that was impressive. His anger fled like a falcon released from its fetters. Ramiz covered her gently with a blanket, then placed himself at a short distance, laying his scimitar within easy reach, and prepared himself for a long night's vigil. He didn't think the assassins would strike again, but he was taking no chances.

Chapter Three

Celia slept heavily, waking the next morning just before dawn with a thumping headache and a brain which felt as if it was made of cotton rags. Ramiz was already up and about, readying their caravan, and a pot of sweet black coffee was bubbling appetisingly on the embers of the fire.

Ramiz seemed distracted, a heavy frown drawing his dark brows together under his *ghutra*, making him seem both more intimidating and older. As they wended their way inexorably east across the huge stretch of desert, following a trail which to Celia's untutored eyes made only fleeting appearances, she had ample time to observe him. Despite the fierce heat of the sun, which made the horizon flicker hazily and seared relentlessly through her thin dress and the veil which she kept in place to protect her from the dust, Ramiz sat bolt-upright in the saddle, on full alert. One hand sought the constant reassurance of the curved sabre in its silver sheath. His eyes—the only part of his face she could see, for he had pulled his headdress over the rest of his face—were slits of bronze, casting their keen gaze in front, to each side, to the rear of the caravan. On one occasion he stopped, pulling his white camel up so suddenly that the beast seemed to freeze in mid-trot. It would have been comical had it not been frightening. Celia pulled up beside him, peering anxiously where he pointed.

'Something moved,' he whispered, though she could see nothing, and could still see nothing when he relaxed. 'Just a rabbit,' he said, pointing at a tiny dot a few hundred yards away. 'If I had my falcon we could have had it for dinner.'

'Your falcon?'

'The wings for my heart,' Ramiz said. 'And a good provider too, out here.'

'You have an affinity with animals, I think. What happened to your beautiful horse? The one I saw you with the day we landed?'

'Stabled near the port. I think, from the way you hold your seat on a camel, that you like to ride?'

'Very much, and to hunt too. My father owns a string of racehorses and my sisters and I were thrown into the saddle almost before we could walk.'

'You have many sisters?'

'Four. I'm the oldest.'

'And your father? What does he do apart from race horses?'

'He is a statesman. Lord Armstrong—he is quite well-known in diplomatic circles.'

Ramiz's eyebrow lifted. 'You are Lord Armstrong's daughter?'

'You know him?'

'I met him once, in Madrid. He is a very influential man. Your marriage was of his making, then?'

'Why should you think so?' Celia asked, riled by his cool and annoyingly accurate assumption.

'It's obvious, having such a strategist as a father, and with such excellent family contacts—your uncle also serves in the British government, does he not?'

Celia nodded.

'Despite my own poor opinion of your husband, he must have been well thought of, and also very ambitious to have been given and accepted this mission. A most welcome addition to your father's sphere of influence, in other words. He would have been foolish not to recommend the match. Am I correct?'

Put like that, her marriage seemed a very cold affair indeed. But Papa had not put it like that. She could have said no—couldn't she? And George—he'd thought of her as more than some sort of useful social appendage, hadn't he? Celia found herself rather unwilling to answer this question.

'It is true my marriage had my father's approval, but the choice was mine. Just because such things are arranged in your country, you should not assume that we do things the same way.'

She could tell by the way Ramiz's eyes narrowed that she had made a mistake. It was not like her to speak so rashly. In fact she was known for her tact—one of the few virtues which George had openly admired in his wife. But there was something about Sheik Ramiz al-Muhana that put her constantly on the back foot. He was so sure of himself. And unfortunately so often right!

'I think it is you who are making assumptions, Lady Celia,' he said.

He was right. She was wrong. Yet she could not bring herself to apologise. 'Tell me, then, did your own wives have a say in the matter?'

'My wives? How many do you think I have?'

'I don't know, but I do know it is the custom here to have more than one.'

'Another lazy assumption. It may be the custom, but the reality is very much the choice of the individual. Some men have only one wife, others nine or ten—though that is very rare. Men provide their wives with the protection of their own household, they give them children and shelter, an established role. Women have a better life married than single. What is wrong with that?'

'What is *wrong* with it?' Celia bit her lip. She should not comment on things she did not understand, even things that just felt—wrong. Slanting a look at Ramiz from under her lashes, she wondered just for a moment how much of what he was saying he actually meant. The thought came to her that he was teasing, punishing her for her naïvety and a little for her English prejudice—which perhaps she deserved. 'I would not have liked to share my husband with another woman,' she said cautiously.

'I doubt your husband would have had either the capacity or the inclination.'

Once again, although Ramiz's words were shocking, he had merely voiced what Celia herself had begun to question. Entrenched loyalty and guilt, rather than faith in what she was saying, made her leap to George's defence. 'You are quite right, he wouldn't,' Celia said shortly. 'Because unlike you he believed in constancy.'

'He was so constant to you that he left you to die. If you were my wife…'

'I am very glad I am not.'

'If you were, at least you would know what it meant to be a wife.'

Celia bit her lip, torn between the desire to ask Ramiz what he meant and the knowledge that she would not like the answer.

'One of the differences between our cultures,' Ramiz continued, sparing her the indignity of asking him to elaborate, 'is that in mine we appreciate that women as well as men have needs. If you were my wife, they would have been generously satisfied. As George Cleveden's wife…' He shrugged.

She was extremely glad of her veil. Heat flushed Celia's skin, prickling uncomfortably on the back of her neck. *What did he know? How did he know?* Though her curiosity was certainly roused, embarrassment got the better of her. 'In my country, such things are not mentioned.'

'Which is why, in your country, so many women are unhappy,' Ramiz countered.

Were such things discussed in the harem? If that was where she was destined to go—not that she would for a minute actually allow Ramiz to… But if it was where she was going, would she be able to find out from the other women? Another wave of heat spread its fingers over Celia. 'We should not be discussing this,' she said primly.

'Between a man and a woman there is nothing more important to discuss.' Ramiz could see she was mortified, but somehow he couldn't stop himself. There was something about the too-cool Lady Celia that made him want to test her limits. And, though he should definitely not be thinking such thoughts, now that he had, in his imagination, placed her within his harem, he could not stop picturing her there. 'To take pleasure, one has also to give. In order to give, one must have knowledge. If you were to be my concubine,' Ramiz said outrageously, 'then I would first need to understand what gives you pleasure. And you would need to do the same for me.'

'But I am not going to be your concubine,' Celia said, the tension in her voice evident. 'You said so yourself.'

'True. But I wonder, Lady Celia, what bothers you more? The idea of being my concubine or the knowledge that, if you were, you would enjoy it?'

She was nonplussed by this question, as it had never occurred to her to think that this imperious sheikh, who could have any woman he wanted, might actually find her desirable. No one else ever had. Until George had asked her to marry him she had never been kissed. In fact, rather shamefully, no one had ever even tried to kiss her, whereas they seemed never to stop trying to kiss Cassie.

Men wanted to make love to Cassie. They wanted to make conversation with Celia. She was obviously lacking something. She was witty, she could be charming, she was educated and she was good company, but she wasn't desirable. It was not something which had bothered her until recently. Not until George had—or had not! Now, it was a curiously deflating feeling.

Was Ramiz toying with her? Celia peered through her dusty veil, trying to read his face, but with only his eyes visible, and those carefully hooded by his heavy lids, it was impossible. 'I think,' she finally said, after a long silence, 'that I have enough to cope with in real life without indulging in hypothetical and frankly ridiculous speculation.' She couldn't know for sure, but she sensed that he was smiling beneath his headdress. 'Can we change the subject, please? Tell me about Balyrma. There is so little written about your country, I don't know very much about it at all beyond the name.'

They had been in the saddle for most of the day, riding through the heat of noon which, under less pressing circumstances, Ramiz would have avoided. Celia had made no complaint, sitting straight in the saddle, drinking water from the canteen only when it was offered, maintaining by some miracle a cool, collected appearance in clothes more fitted to a stroll in an English garden than a long trek across the merciless heat of the desert. Looking at her now, Ramiz felt a faint twinge of guilt. She might not have loved her husband, and in his view she was well rid of him, but she had endured a hugely traumatic time with remarkable courage, and deserved to be indulged a little.

So he told her of Balyrma, and became so engrossed and passionate when talking of his beloved city and its people, of their ancient traditions and its sometimes violent history, that he barely noticed the miles being eaten up. He discovered in Celia an attentive and intelligent listener, with a wide frame of reference, who surprised him with some of the astute observations she made. She was enthusiastic too, and eager to find links between A'Qadiz and the ancient Egypt of the pharaohs whose tombs she had explored. Her enthusiasm was infectious. In his anxiety to defend a point she disputed, enjoying the cut and thrust of their debate, Ramiz almost forgot she was a woman.

'You may be right about the true purpose of the Sphinx,' Celia said triumphantly, 'but the fact is you will never be able to prove it, for nothing like that was written down.' The sun was sinking. Ahead, she could see what looked like a small copse of trees. Thinking she must be mistaken, Celia pushed back her veil and shaded her eyes with her hand. It certainly looked like greenery.

'It is an oasis,' Ramiz explained, 'where water comes up from the ground and provides succour for plants, animals and weary travellers alike. We will stop here for the night. You will be able to bathe, if you wish.'

'Bathe!' Celia breathed the word ecstatically.

It was the first time Ramiz had seen her smile. It changed her completely, warming her complexion, softening the clean lines of her face with the curve of her full bottom lip, highlighting the slanting shape of her eyes, giving him the most tantalising glimpse of the sensual woman hidden beneath her cool exterior. There was something incredibly alluring about her. Unawakened. He remembered now that it was how she had first struck him. Perhaps it was the implied challenge in that which aroused him. Yet again he reminded himself that he should not be thinking such things.

They had reached the oasis. It was small—a watering place, no more—not big enough to encourage permanent settlement. But it was a well-known stop and Ramiz was surprised to find they were the only ones there. His camel dropped obediently to its knees and he dismounted, going immediately to assist Celia, who clambered stiffly down. Ramiz put his hands around her waist and lifted her clear of the pommel. She was light as a feather. He set her to her feet and reluctantly let her go.

'I will see to the animals. The bathing pool is over there, away from the well.'

Ramiz lifted her portmanteau down from the mule and handed it to her. Needing no further encouragement, Celia headed in the direction he had indicated. Underfoot, the sand of the oasis was much softer than the rough track they had followed, much more like the gently undulating desert she had imagined. The trees she had seen were palms, growing high in clusters by the drinking well, around which also grew little patches of green scrub. The bathing pool was an ellipse of vibrant blue set into the sand, no more than ten feet across, backing into a high wall of rock. Water trickled out from a fissure a couple of feet above the level of the pool. Over the years it had worn a track, so that now it formed a tiny waterfall.

Celia longed to stand beneath it. A quick check assured her that she was screened by the palm trees. In minutes, she had discarded her dusty layers of dress, petticoats, stays and stockings, and stood, for the first time in her adult life, shockingly naked, outdoors. It was a fantastically liberating experience. She stretched her arms above her head, tilting her face to look up at the first twinkle of the stars. A scatter of pins and her hair fell in a heavy sweep down her back.

She stepped into the warm pool. The sand sloped gently down, soft and firm underfoot. The water caressed her skin like velvet. At the deepest point, in the middle, it came up to her waist. She sank down to her knees, sighing with contentment as it worked its balmy magic on her aching limbs and dusty skin, before lying flat on her back, floating, her hair trailing out behind her. She soaped herself thoroughly, then washed her hair, rinsing it under the crystal-clear waterfall, relishing the contrasting icy cold of the water trickling over her shoulders before it merged with the warmer water of the pool. The crescent moon was reflected on the surface. In its pale light her skin seemed milky, other-worldly, as if she were a statue come to life.

She had never really looked at her body before—had taken for granted her unblemished skin, her slim figure, well-suited to the fashion for high-wasted narrow dresses, but otherwise unexceptional. Now, released from the fetters of her corsets and the bounds of polite society, she explored her shape. Standing under the waterfall, she watched the paths each drop made, down her arms to nestle in the crook of her elbow, between the valley of her breasts, along the curve of her ribcage to the dip and swell of her stomach. So familiar, and yet so new. She lay on her back again, floating weightlessly, gazing up at the stars. How would her body look to someone else. Too skinny? Too tall? Too pale? Her breasts were not small, but they were hardly voluptuous. Was this good or bad? What would a man think? Ramiz, for example…

'I was beginning to fear you had drowned.'

Celia started up out of the water, then sank quickly to her knees under it. 'How long have you been there?'

'You looked like Ophelia, with your hair trailing out behind you like that. Only unmistakably alive, I'm relieved to say.'

The look on his face was also unmistakable. He liked what he saw. The knowledge was shocking, but it gave her a little rush of pleasure all the same. Ramiz was barefooted, and without his headdress or his cloak. Even as she noticed this he began to unbuckle the belt around his waist, which held his knife and scimitar. Then he tugged at the little pearl buttons at the neck of his robe, giving her a glimpse of smooth skin, lightly tanned. It was only as he made to pull the *thoub* over his head that Celia realised he intended to join her. 'You can't come in,' she yelped. 'Not while I'm still here.'

'Then come out,' Ramiz said.

'I can't. I haven't anything on.'

'I couldn't help but be aware of that,' he said with a crooked smile. 'I'll look away, I promise.'

Still crouched below the water, Celia considered her options. She didn't even have a towel. The idea of boldly standing up and walking past him naked was horrifying, even if he did keep his eyes closed, but not nearly as alarming as the idea of waiting for him to take off his clothes and join her before she made her escape.

'Celia?'

Ramiz sounded impatient. Bored, even. He had probably seen hundreds of women without their clothes. And she was getting cold. And feeling a little foolish.

'Close your eyes,' she instructed, and as soon as he did so Celia took a deep breath and stood up. Wrapping her arms protectively round herself, she splashed her way out of the pool with as much grace as she could muster, trying to persuade herself that she was fully clothed and not dripping wet and stark naked.

Her clothes were in the shade of the palms to Ramiz's right. She just had to walk past him as quickly as she could. The sand was hot under her feet. She caught her toe on a stone and stumbled, only just retaining her balance. Glancing up she saw that Ramiz had kept his word. His lashes fanned dark on his cheeks. It was the strangest experience, standing there without her clothes, knowing all he had to do was to open his eyes. She felt exposed, and just the tiniest bit excited. Celia paused. What if…? Then she panicked, and headed quickly for the shelter of the palm trees.

He felt rather than heard her hesitate, so intensely conscious was he of her tantalising presence. He didn't need to look. He could imagine her all too clearly as he heard the soft sigh of the water yielding her up, the shiver of the sand as it cradled her feet. Her retreating form, so tall and slender, would glimmer in the moonlight, her hips swaying like a call to pleasure. Her hair, dripping down over her shoulders, would be clinging lovingly to the pouting tips of her breasts. As her footsteps retreated quickly over the sand, he imagined her disappearing into the fringe of palms like a nymph into a forest.

The urge to follow her there, to enter the forbidden garden of such delights, was so strong that Ramiz took a step forward before he managed to stop himself. He opened his eyes. She was safely out of sight. She should be safely out of mind. As the widow of a British diplomat sent to discuss a treaty, and the daughter of an eminent statesman with influence across Europe, she was definitely not for him. Never before had it been so difficult to make his body do his mind's bidding, but he managed it. Honour. His god. He managed it, but only just.

A few yards away Celia dressed hurriedly in a clean nightdress. It was cotton, with long sleeves and a high neck, and in combination with her pantaloons and a shawl was, she decided, perfectly decent for a night in the open—for Ramiz had, to her relief, left the tent behind. She could not bear the thought of sleeping in her stays again, and banished the image of Aunt Sophia's shocked face by reminding herself that Ramiz had already seen her almost nude anyway.

Don't think about that! But she couldn't help it. He found her attractive. There had been no mistaking that look on his face. It was dangerous, not something she had taken into account at all, but it was also exciting.

It was not until she was making her way back across the sand to the fire, carrying her portmanteau, and saw Ramiz standing under the waterfall that she realised something quite astonishing. The attraction was mutual. At least she thought it must be attraction she was feeling—this sort of fizzing in her blood at the sight of him, this little kick of something in her stomach. The way her eyes were drawn to him. She hadn't felt it before. Ever. But she wanted to look. No, more than look—to devour him with her eyes.

He had his back to her, was leaning his hands against the rock and allowing the spray to trickle over his head, to find a path down his shoulders, his spine, to where she could just see the curve of his buttocks emerging from the pool. His skin gleamed, smooth and biscuit-coloured in the moonlight, stretched tight over the bunched muscles of his shoulders. She wondered how it would feel to touch. Then she realised she was spying on him, and decided that she didn't want him to catch her in the act, so she forced herself to walk back to their camp without once looking back.

By the time Ramiz joined her, dressed once more in a *thoub*—a clean one, she noticed—his hair damp, smoothed like a cap sleekly to his skull, Celia had the makings of a meal ready, and a composed expression on her face.

She fell asleep almost as soon as she had eaten, curled up in a blanket by the fire. She slept deeply at first, but then the dreams came. Strange dreams, in which she chased George through labyrinthine buildings, up stairs with no end, through rooms whose walls suddenly closed in on her, across endless passageways with too many doors. And always he was behind the one she couldn't open, or had only just closed. It was George, she knew it was George, but in the way of dreams he took many forms. All of them aloof from her. All of them despising her. In her dream she grew smaller. Frailer. More frantic with every attempt to find him, until finally she opened a door which proved to be in the outside wall of a high tower and she fell, fell, fell, waking with a startled cry just before she landed.

Strong arms held her when she was about to sit up in fright. A hand smoothed the tangle of her hair back from her face. 'A dream. It was just a dream.' A voice, soothing as the softest of cashmere in her ear. 'Go back to sleep, Celia. You're safe now.'

'I tried,' she mumbled. 'I really tried.' Her cheek rested on something hard and warm and infinitely comforting. Vaguely, she registered a slow, regular bump. Like a heart beating. 'Safe,' she mumbled.

A kiss on her brow. A fluttering kiss, cool lips. 'Safe,' the voice said, pulling her closer.

The nightmare faded into the distance, like a black beast retreating with its tail between its legs. She knew it wouldn't dare come back. Celia slept the rest of the night dreamlessly.

She woke feeling much refreshed. Curled up under her blanket by the fire, she could see by the sky that it was not yet morning. The air was cool on her face. She had been dreaming of George. It came back to her now—the running, the never quite catching. She tried to picture her husband, but his image was blurry, like an old painting covered with the patina of age. The months of her marriage felt unreal, like a spell from which she had been freed, a play she had not meant to attend. Just as she had never quite seen herself as a wife, now she could not believe in herself as a widow. She was just Celia, neither Armstrong nor Cleveden, for none of these names meant anything here. Here she was alone in this desert wilderness, her fate in the hands of the man who lay sleeping on the other side of the fire. She was free to be whoever it was she chose to be, and no one in the real world would ever know. It was an intoxicating feeling.

As she crept carefully past Ramiz, heading for the washing pool with her clothes, she remembered something else. Could it really have been Ramiz who had held her so gently? It seemed so improbable. She must have imagined it. If she had cried out, which she thought she must have, it seemed much more likely that he would have woken her and bade her be quiet. But the arms that had held her had seemed so real, and she had felt so incredibly safe enfolded in them. Was Sheikh Ramiz al-Muhana capable of such tenderness?

Returning properly dressed, complete with the stays whose constraints she was starting to loathe, and a fresh pair of silk stockings she wished fervently to do without, Celia decided simply to pretend that nothing had happened and set about making morning coffee while

Ramiz refilled their canteens. When he asked her how she had slept, she told him very well, and no more was said.

She had expected Balyrma to be a walled city, perhaps built into the mountains which were rising like huge sand dunes in the distance, but as Celia looked down on the capital of A'Qadiz from the vantage point to which Ramiz had led them, her first impression was of lush green, so vibrant and vivid that it looked as if the city had been mistakenly painted into the middle of a desert canvas. It was much larger than she had expected too. A patchwork of fields were laid out, stretching across the plain on either side of the well-formed track they were following, neatly bordered with what looked like cypress trees.

'The mountains on either side protect us from the worst of the sun in the summer, and they provide the water which makes all this possible,' Ramiz explained. 'If you look closely, you can also see that they protect us from invasion. See the little turret there?'

Celia peered in the direction he pointed. 'Are you under threat of invasion?'

'Not for more than five hundred years,' Ramiz said proudly, 'but it is a wise man who is vigilant. There are many who envy us our wealth, and some who would mistake my own desire for ongoing peace as a weakness. As you saw to your cost.'

They made their way with their caravan strung out behind them along the increasingly wide road towards the city. With her veil firmly in place, Celia rode behind

Ramiz, and had ample opportunity to observe how he was received by his people. She knew he was a prince, of course, but over the last two days she had put his status to the back of her mind. It was impossible to do so now, as every one of the multitude of people with their mules, camels, horses and trundling carts who passed them on the approach to the city fell to their knees in front of Ramiz, uttering prayers and good wishes, keeping their heads bowed.

Once again Celia thought of the pharaohs, who had taken their status as gods for granted just as Ramiz seemed to be doing. She realised how much latitude he had bestowed upon her, and wondered how many hundreds of social solecisms she had committed. It appalled her, for she was used to thinking of herself as up to snuff on every occasion, and now here she was, entering a magnificent city in the wake of its prince with absolutely no idea how she should behave when she got there. Nerves fluttered like a shoal of tiny creatures in her stomach, making her feel slightly nauseous. She felt an absurdly childish inclination to turn her camel round and flee.

What would her father think of her? Lily-livered, he would say. Highly unusual as the circumstances were, Lord Armstrong would expect his daughter to think and to act like a statesman. Celia sat up straight in the saddle. Whatever lay ahead, she was ready to face it.

What lay ahead was a startlingly beautiful city. Once they had passed through the fields, groves of lemon, orange and fig trees and terraced olive bushes, they entered the city of Balyrma itself. It was walled after all, she realised as they passed through a majestic portal, their path still bordered with devotedly kneeling citizens, into a city straight out of *One Thousand and One Nights.* Terracotta dwellings with slits for windows and turreted roofs, blank walls with keyhole-shaped doors behind which she imagined cloistered courtyards, fountains tinkling at every corner. Through narrow alleyways she caught a glimpse of a souk selling cloth, colours bright as jewels. From another came the heady scent of spices. As they progressed towards the centre of the city the buildings became more ornate; tiled walls patterned with mosaic, elaborate high shutters on the windows worked with intricate patterns of wrought iron.

The palace stood in the exact centre of the town. A high wall, too high to see over, with two beautiful slender towers marking each of the corners. The wall was pristine white, with a flowing border of blue and gold tiles along the middle, leading to the huge central entranceway protected not just by a set of doors of gothic proportions, but also by a grille plated with silver and gold. It was the sort of fairytale palace that normally stood at the end of a drawbridge, Celia wanted to say to Ramiz, remembering just in time not to blurt out her thoughts. But then, as first the gate and then the doors were flung open to receive them, and she caught her first glimpse of the royal palace of Balyrma, Celia lost the ability to speak anyway—for Ramiz's home looked as if it had been conjured up by Scheherazade herself.

Chapter Four

They left the bedraggled caravan of animals and luggage outside. An army of white-robed servants appeared as if from nowhere, it seemed to Celia, and led them down a short covered passageway dotted with mysterious doors, each with a guard armed with a glittering scimitar. The stark white of their robes was relieved only by a discreet embroidered crest depicting a falcon and a new moon, which she had noticed embossed on the entrance gates too, and by the red and white check of their headdresses.

Following in Ramiz's wake, her head respectfully lowered, Celia felt more overwhelmed with every step she took. The huge courtyard they entered was perfectly symmetrical, the pillars and windows and doors which flanked it all mirroring each other, as did the mosaic design in blue and gold which formed the frieze around the walls, continued on the pillars which bounded the open space, and covered the floor of the courtyard itself.

Two fountains played to each other. Risking a fleeting glance up, Celia saw another floor with a colonnaded balcony, and counted another two above that, all glittering white, trimmed with blue and gold.

Ramiz seemed to have forgotten her presence. Engaged deep in conversation with a man whose robes and bearing clearly proclaimed a higher status from the guards, Ramiz himself seemed to have metamorphosed as they entered his domain. His bearing now was remote and autocratic, that of a man who took his power for granted, as he did the obedience of others. She had no idea what he was saying, but even his voice sounded different—short, staccato sentences, none of the soft vowels and curling consonants she had grown used to.

She felt as if she didn't know him. She forced herself to accept that she didn't. What had happened over the last two days had been an oasis, an exotic interlude in the harsh, unyielding desert of reality. This was his real life. Suddenly she was a little afraid.

She hadn't taken his threat to make her his concubine seriously. She hadn't allowed herself to think about his harem. In fact, she had allowed herself to assume that it simply wouldn't happen, that when they arrived here he would change his mind and—and what?

She was alone. Worse, she was a woman alone, which meant she had neither the right nor the power to choose her own destiny. It wasn't a case of being forced to do Ramiz's bidding. She didn't have any other option.

Powerless. The full meaning of the word hit her like a sack of corn swung into her middle, so that she felt her breath whistling out, her stomach clenching. Celia began to panic, her fevered imagination conjuring up all sorts of hideous fates. It would be weeks—months, maybe—before she was missed. She pictured Cassie waiting anxiously every day for a letter which did not come, trying to reassure Caroline and Cordelia and poor little Cressida, and at the same time attempting to persuade Papa to take some sort of action. But what could he do, so far away in London? Nothing. And in the meantime she, Celia, would probably have been cast out into the desert and left to die.

Fortunately at this point Celia's common sense intervened. If Ramiz had wanted her dead he would not have saved her life. If he'd wanted harm to come to her, he'd have left her on her own at the site of the massacre. She couldn't claim to truly know the autocratic Prince standing a few yards away, oblivious to her presence, but she knew enough about the man to believe in his integrity and honour, and she knew enough of his hard-won and volatile peace to understand that he wouldn't risk upsetting the British government by slaughtering the daughter of one of their foremost statesmen. She was acting like a hysterical female when dignity and calm were what was required. She was in a royal palace, for goodness' sake! She was a citizen of one of the world's great powers. Ramiz wouldn't dare lock her in a harem and expect her to do his bidding.

Nodding to herself with renewed resolve, Celia looked up, but Ramiz was gone. She stood quite alone in the courtyard, with only the tinkling fountains for company. She had no idea which of the doorways he had gone through. Though the doors were all open, each was draped in heavy brocade and gauzy lace to keep out the fierce heat of the day. The keyhole-shaped windows of the salons, with their gold-plated iron grilles, stared out blankly at her.

'Hello?' she called out tentatively, feeling horribly self-conscious as she listened to her voice echo up through the courtyard. There was no answer. This is ridiculous, she thought, deciding simply to select a doorway and walk through it.

She was picking up her skirts and making for the nearest one when a voice halted her. Two men were approaching. Huge men with bellies so large they looked like cushions, dressed not in robes but in wide black pleated breeches and shiny black boots. Each had a vicious curved dagger held in the sash which marked where the waistband had once been. Under their black turbans each had a black beard and long black moustaches.

Like two of Ali Baba's forty thieves, Celia thought a little hysterically as the men stopped in front of her. Then they bowed, indicating that she follow them, and with her heart in her mouth she did, through a myriad of doors and cool dark passageways, until they came to another large wooden door set in another white-tiled wall. One of the men produced a large key and pulled the door wide. Celia stepped through into a courtyard almost a mirror image of the one she had left. She thought at first she was back where she had started. Then the door behind her closed, leaving the guards on the other side, and she realised where she was.

Just as Ramiz had told her she would be, she was in his harem.

* * *

It was everything she had expected, and yet nothing like it. For a start she was quite alone aside from the two maidservants who tended to her, bringing delicious foods, exotic fruits she had never seen before, fragrant meats cooked in delicious spices, cooling sherbets and tea served sweet and flavoured with mint.

Adila and Fatima were shy at first, giggling over Celia's clothes, astonished at the layers of undergarments she wore, and utterly confounded by her stays. In turn Celia, who allowed her dresser to look after her hair for grand occasions, but otherwise was used to managing for herself, found their care for her embarrassing—waving them away when they first attempted to bathe her, submitting only when she saw that she had offended them.

By nature modest, Celia had never shared such intimacies as bathing, even with her sisters, but within the seclusion of the harem it seemed less shocking, and she very quickly began to enjoy the pampering of baths strewn with rose petals and orange blossom, having oils scented with musk and amber gently massaged into her skin and preparations for her hair and for her face, which left her whole body glowing and more relaxed than she had ever known.

The harem itself covered three floors, its upper terraces reached by tiled staircases which zigzagged up through the towers, marking the four corners of the courtyards. These upper rooms were empty, echoing, as if they had not been used for some time. The lower rooms, which led one into another in a square around the terrace, were opulently decorated, with rich carpets on the floors and low divans draped with lace, velvet and silk, the jewel colours of blue and gold and emerald and crimson reflected in the long mirrors which hung on the walls. The only windows looked out onto the courtyard, and the only exit was the one through which she had entered, but once Celia had recovered from the shock of her incarceration and accepted there was nothing she could do save wait for Ramiz to return, she found it astonishingly easy to surrender to the magical world of the harem. She had nothing to do save surrender her body to the ministering of Adila and Fatima, and surrender her mind to the healing process.

As the days melded one into another Celia quickly lost all track of time, so strangely did the tranquil seclusion of the harem play on her senses. She had never been so much alone, never had so much peace to simply be. As the eldest, and having lost her mother not long after her youngest sister Cressida was born, it was second nature to Celia to put others first, to be always thinking ahead and taking responsibility for what happened next. Indulgence and inactivity such as had now been forced on her were quite alien. Those who knew her as always busy, always planning, managing at least ten things at once, would say without hesitation that such a life as she was now experiencing would have her beside herself with boredom or screaming for release. Celia would have said so herself. But right now it was the antidote she required to recover not just from the trauma of losing her husband, but from the trauma of realising she wished she had never married him in the first place. If Ramiz had intended this as a punishment, he had been mistaken.

Almost without her noticing a full month passed, marked by the changing of the moon, whose growth from flickering crescent to glowing whole reflected the healing process taking place in Celia herself.

Then, just as she was beginning to wonder if she would be left forgotten here for ever, and her temper was beginning to recover enough to resent Ramiz's extended and unexplained absence, the man himself appeared without warning.

It was evening. Dinner had arrived—a much more elaborate meal than usual, which required an additional servant to bring it. Out of habit Celia was dressed in an evening gown after the daily ritual of her bath and massage. She stared in consternation at the plethora of little dishes in their gold salvers, wondrously appetising but far too much for just one, set out on a low table in the largest of the salons, around which banks of tasselled and embroidered cushions were strewn.

'I can't eat all this,' she said helplessly to Adila, miming that they should take some of it back, but the maid only smiled behind her hand and backed out, shaking her head.

The door to the outside world opened. Not just the usual tiny crack, barely enough to allow the staff to slip in and out, it was flung wide open. Ramiz strode in, resplendent in a robe of opulent red.

She had forgotten how incredibly handsome he was. She had forgotten how tall he was too. He looked a little tired, though, with a tiny fan of lines crinkling around his eyes. He wore no headdress, no belt, and his full robe was more like a caftan with wide sleeves, flowing loosely down to his feet which were clad in slippers of soft leather studded with jewels. The robe was open at the neck, but for all his dress was obviously informal he looked even more regal, more intimidating than she remembered.

She was nervous. Her mouth was dry. Her heart was bumping a fraction too hard against her breast. Celia dropped a curtsy. 'Your Highness.'

'Ramiz,' he said. 'While we are alone, I am Ramiz.'

Alone. She decided not to think about that. Having imagined this moment many times over the last few days, she decided to act as if it were any other social occasion, and to treat Ramiz as if he were an honoured guest and she the hostess. And not, definitely not, worry about being alone with him in his harem.

'Are you hungry? Dinner is here. I wondered why there was so much of it. Now I see you were expected.'

'You would have preferred some warning?' Ramiz asked, picking up immediately on her unspoken criticism.

'It is your palace. It is not for me to dictate where you are, and when,' Celia said tactfully, preceding him into the salon in which the food was laid out, waiting until he had disposed himself gracefully on a large cushion before she sat down opposite him.

'I've been away. I've only just got back,' Ramiz explained unexpectedly. 'I told you I had urgent business to attend to.' He lifted the cover from a dish of partridges stuffed with dates and pine nuts and sniffed appreciatively.

'You mean only just got back as in today?'

'An hour ago.'

Celia was flattered, and then alarmed, and then nervous again. She poured Ramiz a glass of pale green sherbet and pushed a selection of dishes towards him. 'May I ask if your business was successful?' she said. 'I presume it was to do with the other prince—Malik, I think his name was?'

Ramiz looked surprised. 'Yes.'

'Did you—were you—did you have to fight with him?'

'Not this time.'

'What, then?'

'You really want to know?'

Celia nodded. 'I really do.'

It was not the custom to discuss such matters with a woman. It was not in his nature to discuss such matters with anyone. But it had been a difficult few days, and there was something about this woman which encouraged the sharing of confidences. 'My council all urged swift and brutal retribution—as usual, since I inherited most of them from my brother.'

'But you ignored them?'

'Yes. I don't want to follow that path until there are no other options left.'

'So tell me—what did you do? How do you go about negotiating a deal with a man who wields power through fear? Come to that, how do you set about persuading your own people to accept such an alien approach?'

Ramiz smiled. 'You forget I am a prince too. I don't have to persuade my people of anything. They do as I bid.'

'Yes, that's what you say, but I'll wager that you try all the same,' Celia said, with a perception which surprised him. 'You don't really want to rule in splendid isolation, do you?'

'Splendid isolation? That is exactly how it feels sometimes. You can have no idea how wearing it is, trying to break the ingrained prejudice of years,' Ramiz said wearily. 'Sometimes I think— But that is another matter. With Prince Malik…'

He went on to tell her about the events of the last few days, spurred on by her intelligent interest into revealing far more of his innermost thoughts than he had ever done. It was a relief to unburden himself, and refreshing too, for this woman who talked and thought like a man had a knack for encouraging without toadying, and her shocking lack of deference lent her opinions a credibility he would not otherwise have conceded.

By the time the meal was over the weight of responsibility which was beginning to feel like a sack upon his back had eased a little for the first time since he had so unexpectedly come to power. This woman understood the cares of governing. She would have made an excellent diplomatic wife. George Cleveden had chosen well. But George Cleveden was dead, and Ramiz could not regret it, for the woman who was now his widow deserved better. Much better. Not that it was any of his business.

'Are you comfortable here in my harem?' Ramiz

settled himself back against the cushions. The lamps with their coloured glass shades reflected the light in rainbow patterns onto the mirrors and the tiled white of the salon.

Celia thought she recognised that teasing note in his voice, but she could not be sure. 'Extremely,' she said cautiously. 'Your servants have looked after me very well, but I was surprised to find myself the only occupant.'

'I moved my brother's wives and children to their own palace. Those who wished were returned to their families.'

'And you haven't had time to—to stock up on wives for yourself?'

Ramiz burst out laughing. 'That's one way of putting it.'

'You led me to believe you had many wives.'

'No, you made that assumption yourself.'

Celia bit her lip. 'I suppose you get tired of people like me making such assumptions. You wanted to teach me a lesson, didn't you?'

Ramiz held up his hands. 'I confess. Tell me, what did you expect when you came here? A scene from *One Thousand and One Nights*?'

She blushed. 'Something like that.'

'And now?'

'Now I don't know what to think,' she said, opting for honesty. 'In one way, there's something almost liberating in being so cut off from the world and unable to do anything about it. I feel rested. Cured. Better. I've never had so much time to think. It's like I've been able to sort out my mind, make sense of things.'

'You had problems in your marriage, I think?'

After so many days of silence, so many hours spent scrutinising and questioning, it was a huge relief to speak her thoughts. 'I wasn't exactly unhappy, but I think I would have become so, and I know George already was.' A tear trembled on her lashes. Celia brushed it away. 'He was—he did not want—I think he wanted a companion rather than a wife. How did you guess?' She had not meant to ask, but here in the tranquil security of the harem, with the soft light casting ghostly shadows onto the walls, such an intimate topic seemed natural.

He had been conversing with her like a man, admiring her intelligence and strong opinions. Now he saw in that look stripped of its poise, in the vulnerable trembling of her lip, that she was all woman. He remembered her body, glinting pale and alluring in the moonlight by the oasis—an image which had crept unbidden into his dreams these last five nights, so unwanted, so dishonourable that he had banished its memory in the daylight. Now here it was again, and here in the rooms of the palace set aside for sensual pleasure, rooms he had never himself used, his resistance was beginning to falter.

He wanted her. There was every reason for him to deny himself, but he had done so much denying since his brother died he was sick of it. He wanted her. He wanted to teach her. He wanted her to know pleasure. And he wanted her knowing to be his doing.

Ramiz got to his feet. 'I guessed because you have the look of a woman starved of attention. Come with me,' he said, reaching out a hand to pull her to her feet, placing a finger over her mouth to stop her speaking. He led her out of the salon to the courtyard, where the fountains made their sweet music in the jasmine-scented air. 'Look up there.' The deep sapphire of the night sky was framed high above their heads. 'In my culture, we believe that love has wings—wings which can take you all the way up there to the stars, where the heavenly pleasures of the body are worshipped. It is a voluptuous journey. A journey which leaves its mark upon a woman in her eyes, in the way she walks, the way she learns to nourish and to relish her body, knowing that it is a temple of delights. I look at you and I see a woman who has not yet learned to fly. I look at you and I want to help you experience what it feels like to soar in the high clouds.'

His voice shivered seductively in her ear. They were standing by the fountain, his hands on her arms, stroking feathery light up and down her bare skin. She could feel the brush of velvet from his sleeves. He smelt of lemon-scented soap and night-scented man. She pictured herself flying. His presence, the scent of him, the feel of him, the husky sound of him, gave her a fleeting image of what that might be like. Of what he might do to her to make it happen.

She wanted it. Whatever it was, she wanted it, and she knew she would never find a more able tutor. His confidence was intoxicating. His aura of power equally so. His casual mastery, which could intimidate and anger, was here, under the secret stars fascinating, beguiling, and incredibly persuasive.

'Don't you want to know what it's like to fly, Celia?'

Ramiz spoke into her ear. His lips whispered over her skin.

'I don't know if I can,' she said, which was the truth.

His laugh, like a throaty purr, so filled with assurance, made her stomach clench in anticipation. 'Trust me—you can.'

His tongue traced the shell of her ear. His fingers trailed up her arms to the nape of her neck, circling delightful spirals which whirled little pulses into life. Her heart was beating fast. Faster. She was hot and cold all at the same time. His mouth traced the line of her jaw, and she ached, ached for him to kiss her lips, but instead he moved down her throat. His velvet-soft mouth gave kisses that made her arch back in his arms like a bow, so that she could see the sky now, the stars glinting and beckoning and calling to her as his mouth reached the hollow of her neck, and her skin seemed to reach out to greet him, wanting more than the flickering kisses he gave her.

'Ramiz,' Celia whispered, 'Ramiz, please…I want to.'

He scooped her up into his arms, heading for the nearest salon, which happened to be the one in which she slept. The low divan, with its scattering of pillows and silk covers, took up centre place in the room. It was the strangest bed she had ever encountered, for it was round, with neither head nor footboard. Ramiz set her to her feet before it, gazing deep into her eyes, his own glowing amber in the shadowed light with something fierce she didn't recognise and wasn't sure she liked.

She lowered her lids, but he tilted her chin up, forcing her to look at him again. 'You must not be ashamed of your body; you must learn to enjoy it. That is the first lesson you must learn or you will never leave the ground.'

Then his lips covered hers, fitting so perfectly that she stopped breathing. How could mouths fit like that? But they did. Warmth flooded through her. She stood pliant, unsure what to do, confused by the urgent need to kiss him back, so at odds with what she had been told. Ramiz snaked his arms around her back to pull her close. She could feel the solid hardness of his body pressed into her own softness. She had not thought of herself as soft before. Or curved. She had never encountered such blatant masculinity so close at hand. She was melting, and in the melting she succumbed to temptation and kissed him back.

Her lips were petal-soft against his, beguilingly untutored. Ramiz pressed his mouth against hers, tasting her delicately. He felt rather than heard her sigh. If he had not known better he would have said she had never been kissed. Certainly she had not been taught to kiss back. Her inexperience inflamed him. A primal instinct which surprised him to possess, to own, sent the blood surging to his shaft. His kiss hardened too, his mouth easing hers open, his tongue finding hers, coaxing at first, then forgetting to coax and instead demanding. She tasted of heat and promised ecstasy. An ecstasy he could not wholly indulge.

To give is to receive. Tonight he would give, and the giving would have to suffice. Ramiz tore his mouth away. 'Wait,' he said, breathing heavily. 'Tonight you must allow me to wait upon you.' Then slowly, tantalisingly slowly, he began his controlled onslaught on Celia's senses.

His hands tangled in her hair, pulling out the constraining pins, his fingers combing through the rich copper mass of curls until it was spread over her shoulders, trailing down her back, curling over the pearly white of her bosom. He turned her around to unfasten her dress, his fingers trailing over her skin as he slipped it down over her shoulders to pool at her feet. She could feel his mouth on her neck again, on the knot of her spine. His breath was warm on her skin, but she shivered all the same. He unlaced her stays, pulling her close against him, her back to his chest, her skin against the velvet of his robe. She could feel the hard length of him nestling into the curve of her bottom. So other. So male.

She shivered again, but now she was hot, with fingers of heat creeping surreptitiously over her skin like the fingers of dawn through the mists of morning. Ramiz wrapped his arms around her, pulling her hard against him, nudging his erection into the soft mound of her buttocks. His hands stroked up from her waist to the curves of her breasts, through the soft fabric of her chemise, stroking so that her skin prickled. Her nipples hardened. He weighed her breasts in his hands, his thumbs scraping the tips, making them pucker, making her stomach clench, and between her legs something that felt like another unfurling bud seemed to clench too.

He turned her round, kissing her swiftly on the lips

before he pulled her chemise over her head, leaving her clad only in her lace-trimmed pantaloons, for she had given up on wearing stockings. Instinctively Celia tried to cover herself, but Ramiz pulled her hands away from her breasts. 'How can you expect others to enjoy what you cannot admire yourself?' he said. 'You are beautiful.'

Celia blushed. 'I'm not. I know I'm not. My sister Cassie is beautiful. I'm too thin. I don't—men don't—I'm just not.'

'Look at me.'

She obeyed reluctantly.

Ramiz wound a thick tress of hair around his hands. 'The colour of desire. A reflection of the flames which can burn inside you if only you'll let them.' He cupped her head to look deep into her eyes. 'You have a mouth made to frame kisses. The way your lids hide your eyes, they speak of secrets if only a man knows where to look.' His palms grazed down her shoulders, shaping her breasts. 'Your skin is like alabaster, like cream, to be touched and tasted.' He bent his head and took her nipple between his lips, his tongue flicking over the tip, his mouth sucking slowly, then hard, tugging until she moaned, for it felt as if he had set up a path of flames, like a fuse, burning its way from the painful ache of it down through the pooling heat in her belly towards the curling, tensing heat between her legs.

She fell back onto the divan. Ramiz knelt between her legs, his hands spanning her waist as he kissed her breasts, tugging sensations she had never imagined from her, so that she writhed with them, clutching at the silk of the sheets, then at the velvet of his robe, then at the satin of his hair, wanting more and more of what he gave, at the same time vaguely conscious that this must be wrong—for surely she should not be feeling these things? Surely she should not be wanting in this way, even if she didn't know what it was she wanted? Except to fly, as Ramiz had promised.

He was licking his way down her stomach now, tugging her pantaloons over her legs, gently removing her hands when she would have covered herself, whispering to her in a mixture of his own language and hers that she was beautiful, beautiful, beautiful, until almost she believed him. 'Legs made to wrap themselves around a man,' he said to her as he kissed the crook of her knees, carefully pushing them apart to taste the skin on the inside of her thigh.

She was shocked. She was unbearably tense. She shouldn't be letting him do what he was doing, whatever it was he was doing, but she couldn't bear to stop him because she wanted him to do more of it. And when he did, his mouth just feather-touching the place between her legs where the aching was becoming a pulse, she jerked with both shock and pleasure, relieved that he held her down, released from fighting it when his hands stroked her thighs into position and his tongue eased its way onto her, into her, licking, causing such a fluttering sensation within her that she cried out, because it wasn't too much, it wasn't enough.

She felt them then, her wings budding, like the rippling on a pond when a feather lands. She stilled and shut her eyes tight and then she saw them too, pink-tipped wings, pushing their way out as Ramiz circled his tongue to help them on their way, circling so they could push up more, licking to encourage them, soft so as not to frighten, then harder as her wings grew, and pushed, and trembled with their unfurling, lifting her up so that she gasped with the sudden swoop of them, lifting her up again as they bunched tight, readying themselves. And then with one final burst she toppled, thinking to fall, and her wings opened and she flew, soaring and bucking and diving and swooping and soaring again, crying out with the sheer unexpected delight of it, crying out again until she glided and floated slowly, slowly, sleepily back down to earth, exhausted and sated and filled with the glitter of the stars she had touched.

Past experience had taught him the satisfaction of giving pleasure, but always it had been a prelude to receiving. Now, Ramiz gazed at Celia spread out on the divan before him, her perfect skin flushed with satisfaction, her lips, her nipples, her sex all swollen with his attentions, and felt a new kind of satisfaction. He had done this. He had given her this. Blood surged into his groin, swelling his already hard shaft, though he knew he would do nothing about it. He wanted to, but he did not need to. This was enough—this knowing that he had made his mark, that he had been the first if not to have her, then to pleasure her. He had given her something no one else had. She would not forget him.

As he would not forget this picture she made. Unwilling to tempt his self-control, Ramiz got to his feet and pulled the silk sheet over her. 'Sleep now,' he whispered.

Celia's eyes fluttered open. 'Ramiz, I…'

'Tomorrow we must talk of the future. For the moment, rest,' he said.

Then he was gone. Were it not for the cushions scattered across the floor, the rumpled state of the sheets, the faint tingling she felt all over her body, she could almost have persuaded herself it was a dream.

Chapter Five

Celia awoke the next morning restless and confused, and rather appalled by herself. What she had felt last night had been shocking in many more ways than one. She'd had no idea that women such as herself could experience such raw emotion. Surely it was rather base to have done so? Was not such stuff the domain of courtesans? So she had always believed. Aunt Sophia had said so herself—women endured while men enjoyed. But last night—last night… Celia's face burned at the memory of her own abandonment. Then the heat focused lower as she remembered more.

Stop! She sat up in bed, burying her face in her hands, screwing her eyes tight shut in an effort to obliterate the image of Ramiz like some erotic god in his scarlet robe. It would be scarlet, of course. The colour of sin and shame. What he had done—no! *She had encouraged him. She had to admit it.* Her toes curled into the soft silk of her sheets. She had wanted him. And when he had gone she had wanted him again.

It must be the influence of this place. This harem, these rooms, built as a monument to the pleasures of the flesh. All that bathing and oiling of her body which went on—how could she help it if her mind was filled with indecent thoughts? This was a profane place. What she had experienced was temporal, bounded by the locked door to the rest of the palace, swathed in this secret sanctum by the velvets and silks and lace which screened the doorways, fuelled by her own fevered imaginings from that dratted book, *One Thousand and One Nights*. She was inhabiting a fantasy, that was all. A fantasy in which she might have acted as shamefully as a concubine, but that didn't mean she *was* one. She was still Celia.

Except, she thought, gazing distractedly at herself in the mirror once she had dressed in a white muslin gown trimmed with primrose yellow ribbons, she didn't actually know who Celia was any more. She tried to see herself with fresh eyes. She tried to see the Celia Ramiz saw. Did she look different? She wasn't sure. She felt different—more conscious of her body under the layers of her clothes, of the way the different textures felt against her newly sensitised skin when she walked, sat, stretched. Did she believe herself beautiful? Celia stared. No. Cassie was beautiful.

What, then, did Ramiz see? The beautifying effect of the harem? Perhaps some of its sensuality had rubbed off on her last night, but she could detect no trace of it now. 'What he saw last night, Celia Armstrong, was an available woman,' she said, sticking her tongue out at her reflection, failing to notice that she had reverted to her maiden name, because something else had just occurred to her. If last night had just been about her being available, why had Ramiz not simply taken his own pleasure?

At that precise moment Ramiz was busily engaged in sensitive matters of state, not pleasure. He sighed as he read over the terms of the draft treaty his trusted man of business, Akil, had prepared. Though A'Qadiz was the largest of the principalities involved, and the most powerful, it was a complex and delicate matter, with the disparate customs and rights of so many tribes to take into account.

'Sometimes I can understand my brother's preference for war,' he said, rubbing his tired eyes with the back of his hand. 'At least it is simple.'

Akil, who had known Ramiz since they were childhood friends, smiled thinly. Even in those days Ramiz had been a peacemaker, intervening with their father when his elder brother Asad went too far for their tutor or the families of his bullied victims to turn a blind eye, even if Asad was the royal heir. 'Simple, yes, but not necessarily effective. Don't give up, Ramiz. Your pact with Prince Malik has brought us a huge step forward.'

'If it holds,' Ramiz said wearily. 'What updates do you have regarding the new mines?'

Gold was the main source of A'Qadiz's riches, second only to the plentiful supplies of water which allowed the population not only to live well, but to trade key crops such as dates, figs and lemons. 'Good news,' Akil replied brightly. 'The richest seam yet, and it looks as if your hunch to test for silver to the south has paid off too.'

'Excellent. Let us hope that word of the find does not spread too quickly. For the moment the British and the French are content to bide their time in Egypt, scavenging whatever precious remnants of the past they can lay their hands on. They think us a paltry little country to whom they will throw a few stray crumbs by agreeing to use our port to open up a trade route to the riches of India, but if they find out the extent of the gold and silver we have buried in our land, especially in the mines so near to the coast, they will not be able to resist trying to get their hands on it.'

'The Englishman who was killed—did you find his papers?'

'His name was Cleveden. Yes, I did, but there was nothing in them I didn't already know.'

'What of the woman?' Akil asked diffidently. All of Balyrma had heard of the woman's arrival, but like everyone else he was in the dark as to Ramiz's intentions. Despite their long-standing friendship, Ramiz did not confide in him, nor did he take kindly to having his decisions questioned.

'What of her?' Ramiz asked tersely.

'She is still here, I presume?'

'Of course she is.'

'What do you intend to do with her, may I ask?'

A vision of Celia spread naked on the divan last night flashed into Ramiz's head. He had been unable to sleep for thinking of her, unable to prevent himself from imagining what it would have been like if he had taken her as he had wanted to—plunged his shaft into the soft, sweet depths he had prepared with such delightful relish. What he wanted to do with her was just that.

But, as so often, what he wanted and what he could have were very divergent paths. This time the honourable path was the least palatable. Fortunately he had committed to it before the events of last night. If he had not— But he would not think of that. It was decided.

'I wrote to the British Consul General in Cairo, informing him of what happened,' Ramiz explained. 'I did it as soon as we got here, for I couldn't risk the likes of Malik using it against me by trying to implicate me. I expect they'll send someone to collect her—in fact I'm surprised they haven't done so already. Until then she is safe enough here.'

'In your harem?'

'Of course.'

'Your—until now—empty harem, Ramiz?'

'What is that supposed to mean?'

Akil shook his head. 'You know very well what it means. The Council of Elders have asked me to urge you again to consider their list of suitable wives. It is a year since you came out of mourning for Asad, and they are anxious for your rule to be cemented. Also, the people would welcome a royal wedding. It has been a difficult and unsettling time.'

'Thanks largely to my brother,' Ramiz said sharply. 'It was Asad, not I, who embroiled us in shedding blood. If it were not for me—'

Akil held up his hand. 'Ramiz, no one knows better than I the pain and hardship of the journey which has brought us to peace, but you must understand the people, the council, they do not have your vision. To them, to fight is to prosper. They have not yet seen the benefits your hard-won peace will bring them.'

Ramiz got to his feet and began to prowl restlessly around the room. Aside from the large mahogany desk at which he had been seated opposite Akil, it was lined with bookcases, all of them full, an eclectic selection of works, from the ancient scriptures of his country to Greek and Latin classics and a wide range of modern French and English literature. Much as he respected his heritage, his travels had taught him to respect the culture of all the great civilisations. If only his people were so open-minded.

'So my taking a wife would make everyone happy, would it, Akil?' Ramiz said, resuming his seat.

'If you were to marry one of the princesses the council have suggested, maybe Prince Malik's daughter, it would cement the peace, make us stronger, and make our people more secure. Even if you chose a princess from one of our own tribes—Sheikh Farid's daughter, for example—it would buy you much support. A royal wedding would go a long way to making your people feel—feel…'

'Spit it out, for the love of the gods,' Ramiz said impatiently.

'It would make them feel more secure, Highness. When you have sons, the dynasty will be settled. Without them there is only your cousin, and he is…'

'Weak.'

'Yes,' Akil agreed with relief.

Ramiz frowned. 'Why just one wife, then? If my marriage would cement the pact with Malik, why not do the same with our other neighbours? Why not two wives, or four, or ten?'

'You jest, I think, Highness.' Akil eyed his friend nervously. He looked calm, but Akil was not fooled. Ramiz drummed his fingers on the blotting pad, his mouth held in much too firm a line. Ramiz preferred to wield words rather than a sword, but when roused he had a temper which put his brother's into the shade as a lion's roar would drown out a kitten.

'You can leave off this "Highness" nonsense, old friend. I know you only use it when you want something.'

Akil smiled. 'Ramiz, listen, the council has compiled a list of ten princesses. I have verified it myself. Each one would make an excellent match. You must marry—you know that—for the sake of A'Qadiz.'

'Everything I do is for the sake of A'Qadiz, it has been so all my life, Akil, *you* know that. I never fail to do my duty.'

Akil nodded. 'But this is a pleasant duty, Ramiz. You are a man. All men need a wife to tend to their needs. The women on the council's list, they are not just princesses, daughters of our neighbouring princes and most influential tribes, they are beautiful virgins. Not such an onerous duty as duties go, is it now?'

Ramiz opened his mouth to speak, then closed it again. What was the point in trying to explain what he didn't really understand himself? Akil spoke good sense, he always did, and he spoke it without all the shilly-shallying and obeisance that the council used. He knew he should marry. He knew his marriage would be first and foremost for the good of his country and his dynasty. It was the way of things, had been the way of things for centuries, but the very idea of entering into such a cold bargain repelled him.

Perhaps Akil was right. Perhaps he had spent too long in the West. But he didn't like the idea of himself as some sort of stud stallion, any more than he liked the idea of his wives as brood mares, vying in his harem for his attentions. He didn't want that. He didn't know what he wanted, but it wasn't that.

Ramiz got to his feet again. 'Put these amendments to the treaty before the council. Tell them I'll consider their list of princesses when it is all signed, and the agreement with the British is settled too.'

Akil smiled and bowed. 'A very wise decision, Highness. Your wisdom is only matched by the magnificence of your…'

'Enough,' Ramiz said wryly. 'Go now, before I change my mind. And have the Englishwoman brought to me.'

Celia followed the servant through a maze of corridors guarded by countless sentries, each wearing a white robe with the new moon and falcon crest. She wore no veil, but kept her eyes on the ground, wondering what on earth Ramiz was going to say to her, wondering how on earth she was going to face him after last night without turning the same colour as the guards' checked *keffiyey* headdresses.

The room she was shown into was a library—the first salon she had seen furnished in a Western manner. Ramiz was sitting behind a large desk made of mahogany inlaid with pearl and teak. He was wearing a robe of dark blue, but no headdress, and rose to greet her when she entered the room.

'Sabah el kheer,' Celia pronounced carefully, using one of the phrases she had managed to learn from Fatima.

'Good morning, Lady Celia,' Ramiz said, 'I trust you are well?'

What did he mean by that? 'Yes,' she managed faintly. 'And you, Your Highness?' *Your Highness! After last night!* Celia bit her lip and stared fixedly at the carpet. Silk, it was woven with an intricate pattern of vibrant and beautiful colours. It must have cost a fortune.

'It is Ramiz, and I am very well.'

Celia jumped at the proximity of his voice. He took her hand. How had he moved so quietly? Slippers, she saw, for her eyes were still fixed firmly on the floor.

'I wanted to talk to you. Perhaps you should sit down?'

'Yes.' She allowed herself to be ushered into a chair facing the desk. To her relief Ramiz resumed his seat opposite, putting a solid expanse of inlaid wood between them. 'You have a lot of books,' she said, raising her eyes to cast them around the room.

'I do. You may read any that you wish. I have regular packages sent from London and Paris.'

'Thank you. Although I don't expect I will be here long enough to read many of them.'

Silence ensued. Ramiz drummed his fingers on the blotting pad. Celia risked a glance at him from under her lashes. He was leaning back in his chair, looking quite relaxed, as if last night had not happened. Or perhaps it was because it meant nothing to him. She wondered what the etiquette was for such occasions, but, having no experience of them whatsoever, found herself at a complete loss. She thought of some of the women of the *ton* who were reputed to have *affaires*. She'd always been surprised, for the couples betrayed no sign of affection—except poor Caro Lamb over Lord Byron, of course, but one didn't want to take any leaves out of *her* book!

Perhaps the best thing to do was pretend it hadn't happened after all. Celia sneaked another look at Ramiz, caught his eye unexpectedly and blushed furiously.

'You will be wondering what I intend to do with you,' Ramiz said.

'I beg your pardon?' Now Celia did look up, her eyes flashing outrage.

'I've written to your Consul General,' Ramiz continued blandly, 'to let him know that you're safe.'

'Lord Wincester. Papa was at school with him,' Celia said irreleventl y.

Ramiz raised an eyebrow. 'You are well connected indeed.'

'So I'll be going back soon?'

'In a few days, I expect. As soon as they send someone.'

'Oh.' She should be relieved. 'They'll send me back to England.'

'Don't you want to go back? To see your family? I think you mentioned sisters.'

'Yes, naturally I miss them—Cassie in particular. But—oh, it's nothing. Just that I was expecting to be here in the East for a couple of years, that's all. I was looking forward to seeing it, to learning something new, and now I shall have to go home to do—well, I don't actually know what I'll do, to be honest.'

'What did you do before?'

'Playing hostess for Papa took up much of my time. I looked after the London house, of course, and then there were my sisters. But Cassie, the next in age to me, is coming out next Season, under my Aunt Sophia's chaperonage, and now that he has me off his hands Papa intends to marry again, he told me so himself.'

'So you are worried there will be no place for you when you return?'

'A little.' Celia shrugged. 'I'm being selfish, thinking of myself. I like to be busy, you see, and I'm used to taking charge, having done so since our mother died. It would be too awkward to stay at home if Papa has a new wife, I'd be forever treading on her toes without meaning to, and anyway I'll be expected to go into mourning.'

'But you will marry again, surely?' The moment he said it, Ramiz realised he disliked the idea intensely.

Celia pursed her lips. 'I don't think so. I don't think I'm very good at being a wife.'

'Now you are feeling sorry for yourself,' Ramiz said

with a twisted smile. 'You hardly had the chance to find out one way or another.'

'True, but— Oh, never mind my worries. I am very sure they are extremely trivial compared to yours. The main thing is I shall no longer be your problem.'

'No.' Strange as it was, he had not thought of her simply quitting his life. Their paths would be unlikely ever to cross again.

'And in the mean time,' Celia said bracingly, 'if there is anything I can do to help you, or—' She broke off, seeing his sceptical expression. 'You're going to tell me that business is men's work, aren't you?'

'I don't have to now that you've said it for me.'

'Papa said I had a brain worthy of a man. He often talked things over with me—not so much to get my opinion as to clear his own mind. He said it helped.'

'You're suggesting I confide the business of my kingdom in you?'

Celia could not help laughing at the shocked expression on Ramiz's face. 'The very idea of it—a mere woman giving her opinions. Too much time spent in the West, your people would say. It has infected him. We must lock him up until he is cured.'

Her eyes twinkled with merriment. Her smile was infectious. 'I think Akil would agree with you,' Ramiz said.

'Who is Akil?'

'He is what your father would call my under-secretary, I suppose, but Akil is much more than that. We have known one another since childhood. He is my other hand.'

'And what did you say to shock him?'

Ramiz steepled his fingers under his chin, gazing thoughtfully at the woman across the desk. In the bright light of day her hair was a deep copper, burnished with darker shades of chestnut. When she laughed, it accentuated the upward slant of her lids, making it look as if her eyes were smiling. She had dared to tease him and to question him, and now she wanted to advise him, and she seemed completely unaware of all the rules she was breaking by doing so. She talked like a man, with the assurance of one accustomed to being attended to, but she had a way of listening, of making him feel she really heard what he said, that made him want to know what she thought, that took away any element of condescension or patronage.

'Akil wants me to marry.'

'And has he a list of worthy brides lined up?'

'How did you know that?'

Celia shrugged. 'Papa told me they did the same for our Prince of Wales. Not that I'm advocating Prinny's marriage as a good example,' she said hurriedly, thinking of the lengths to which the Regent had gone to have his wife exiled, and the string of high-profile mistresses whom he courted blatantly in her absence.

'Your Prince George is a man who—you will forgive me for saying so—indulges in all the benefits of power while carrying none of its responsibilities,' Ramiz said thoughtfully.

'You are quite right. I would not dream of comparing you to such a man. In fact I think you are rather the opposite, for it seems to me that you put duty before all else. Many people envy princes and kings for having the world at their command, but I've never been one of them. It seems to me that it is rather the opposite.'

'You mean A'Qadiz has me at its command?'

'Yes, that's exactly what I mean. Ruling can be a very lonely business, I imagine. I would think you'd be pleased to have a wife to share it with you.'

'If—when—I take a wife, it will not be to reign by my side. That is not the way here.'

'But surely…' Celia bit her lip, realising she had been on the verge of overstepping the mark. Her previous exposure to royalty had led her to surmise that they were a selfish, conceited and not particularly intelligent race, decorative rather than useful, who relied upon others to actually get things done. Ramiz was different in every way. His authority was so ingrained that he thought nothing of it until it was challenged, but though the power he held was absolute, he wielded it for the general good, rather than for his own. Which did not mean that he took criticism, even well meant criticism, easily. 'I beg your pardon. It is not my business. I have no right to express an opinion.'

'What were you going to say? Go on. I promise I won't call the *siaf*.'

'Siaf?'

Ramiz grinned. 'The executioner.'

'Good God, I sincerely hope not. I'm very attached to my head.'

'It's a very clever head—for a woman.'

'From you, Your Highness, that is a great compliment indeed. If you must know, I was thinking that, since you are a prince and can do no wrong, there is no reason for you to stick to something just because that's how it's always been.'

'Tradition plays a very important part here. It is what binds many of the tribes together.'

'I understand that, and I'm not suggesting you turn A'Qadiz into a miniature England, but there are some things you could do which surely everyone would see were for the greater good. Like having your wife play more than the role of a brood mare.'

The fact that he agreed with her, that her words were almost an exact repetition of his own thoughts, was disconcerting. He wasn't sure that he liked it. 'A woman's first duty is to her children.'

'A wife's first duty is to her husband,' Celia said tartly. 'I fail to see how she can perform that fully when you lock her away from the world in a harem.'

'I've told you before, it is to protect her.' She was right, he knew that, but he didn't like being forced into defending something he had himself criticised. It put him in the wrong. Ramiz was not used to being in the wrong. 'Not all women are as—as *capable* as you, Lady Celia,' he threw at her exasperatedly. 'You forget that a wife's role is also to be a woman. Women, in case you have forgotten, are supposed to be the gentle sex. We have a saying here: a good woman is one who listens with stitched lips.'

'And we have a saying in England. The road to success is more easily travelled with a woman to mark the route!'

Ramiz threw his head back and laughed. 'Admit it—you made that up.'

He looked so much younger when he smiled. 'Yes,' Celia conceded, 'but that doesn't mean it isn't true.'

'I'm afraid it is a road I will have to travel alone, albeit with a few beautiful princesses in tow.' He did not quite manage to keep the bitterness from his voice.

'Why shouldn't you choose a wife you can like—grow to love, even? You're the Prince. You can do as you wish.'

'What I wish just now is to end this topic of discussion.'

'Ramiz, when you said I was a *capable* woman, what did you mean?'

A faint flush, just the tiniest trace of colour, kissed her cheeks. Her heavy lids veiled her eyes. 'You are not submissive. You speak your mind.'

'I thought—at least I used to think—that was a good thing. It's how I've been brought up—to think for myself, but not to…to trample on the opinion of others. I hope I don't do that.'

'That's not what I meant, and you don't. You listen. You're a very good listener.'

'But what did you mean, then? Did you mean that I'm intimidating?'

'Not to me!'

'But I could be to other men?'

He saw it then. She didn't mean other men. She meant one in particular. Her dead husband. 'A man who is threatened by a woman is not worthy of being called a man, Celia,' Ramiz said gently. 'Below the capable veneer you present to the world, you are every inch a woman. Did I not tell you last night? You are beautiful.'

She shivered as Ramiz lifted her hand to his mouth and kissed her palm. It felt shockingly more intimate than being kissed on the back of her hand. His lips were warm. Instinctively her fingers curled, forming a little hollow for him. She felt his tongue licking over the pad of her thumb and closed her eyes as the muscles in her belly clenched in response. 'Am I? Do you really think so?' she said, her voice sounding as if she were parched.

Ramiz laughed huskily, his breath caressing her fingers. 'Did I not prove that to you last night too? The point is not what I think, but what you think. Until you believe in your own beauty you will never be able to enjoy it. And if you can't enjoy it…'

Celia tugged her hand away, blushing furiously. 'That sort of enjoyment is what your women learn in the harem.'

'As you did.'

'We are not in the harem now.'

Ramiz pushed himself back in his chair, running his hand through his close-cropped hair. 'No, we're not. You're right. You may select some books to take back with you. I have more business to attend to.'

'Ramiz?'

'Well?'

'I meant it when I offered to help. If there is anything I can do—I'm used to being busy. Being waited on hand and foot, having nothing more to do than decide which scent to pour into my bath, is all very well for a few days, but—is there nothing?'

'You're bored?'

She nodded.

'Would you like to see the city?'

Celia's eyes lit up. 'I'd love that.'

'I can't spare the time today, and I would not trust you with another escort, but I will take you tomorrow. I could arrange for you to pay a visit to Akil's wife instead, if you wish. Yasmina speaks good English. You will still be spending the day in another harem, of course, but at least it won't be this one.'

Celia smiled with pleasure. 'That would be lovely. Thank you.'

'One last thing. Delightful as it was, last night was a mistake. It won't happen again. Ever.'

He was gone through the heavily draped doorway before she could answer him. Which is just as well, Celia thought, inspecting the shelves of the library, because I have no idea whether that is a good thing or not!

Deciding it was best not to even attempt to make sense of that, she instead busied herself in preparation for her outing to visit Akil's wife. It would be good to spend time with another woman. It would also be good to spend time away from the deeply unsettling presence of one particular man.

Chapter Six

Yasmina, a rather beautiful woman with eyes the colour of bitter chocolate and skin like toasted almonds, welcomed Celia warmly, pouring tea from a silver samovar into delicate crystal glasses in silver holders, speaking in careful English with a slight French accent.

The harem itself was a smaller version of the one occupied by Celia in the royal palace, a series of salons built around a courtyard with a fountain and lemon trees, but there the resemblance ended. The entrance was a gilded gate, not a door, and though it was guarded it was not locked. The rooms themselves were populated with Yasmina and Akil's four children, Yasmina's mother, Akil's widowed sister and her two children.

'I expect you think all harems are full of sultry slave girls,' Yasmina said, offering Celia a selection of delicately sugared pastries stuffed with sultanas and apricots. 'The fact is that most are like this. We all have our own salons, so we can be private when we wish to, but we eat and work together, we read and sew together, and as you can see we don't have to worry about being veiled.'

'But don't you mind being confined to one place like this?'

Yasmina laughed. 'We're not. The gate isn't locked. It's just symbolic. It marks a border that we can cross only if we are covered. You will find it is the same in all households in the city. In the desert it is different. Women can wander more freely with their tribes.'

'The door to the harem at the palace is locked.'

Yasmina nodded. 'That was Ramiz's brother Asad's doing. Are there still eunuchs?'

'Two of them.'

'Akil says that Ramiz doesn't know what to do with them. There used to be about ten, but the rest of them were happy to return to Turkey, where they came from, when Asad died. Akil says that Asad kept slaves there too.' Yasmina pulled her cushion closer to Celia's and lowered her voice conspiratorially. 'Concubines, from the East. They say they knew things which would make a man faint with delight.'

'What sort of things?' Celia asked, as much fascinated as shocked.

Yasmina pouted. 'I don't know. I asked Akil, but he wouldn't tell me. I don't think he knew either, though he wouldn't admit it. You know how men are—they like to think they know everything. Anyway, when Asad died Ramiz sent all the women home with dowries, and the wives went back to their families. We all assumed it was because Ramiz was going to take a wife, but he shows no sign of doing so. You should be honoured. You are the first woman to be permitted to enter Ramiz's harem. You will be the envy of every woman in the region.'

'But it's not like that. There is no question of me becoming…'

'His wife? Goodness, no,' Yasmina said with a shocked gasp. 'Of course not. A woman like you would not be permitted to marry Ramiz.' She placed the large tray with the glasses and samovar out of reach and beckoned to her two youngest children, a boy of three and a girl of two. 'This is my son, Samir, and my daughter, Farida.'

The little girl clung shyly to her mother's arm, but Samir was bolder, and reached out to touch Celia's hair. Smiling, she took him onto her lap and allowed him to play with her pearls, at which point Farida overcame her fear of the strange woman in the funny dress and demanded a turn. Laughing, Celia balanced the two children on her lap and taught them to play a clapping game which she'd used to play with her sisters, after which Samir insisted she accompany them on a grand tour of the courtyard to meet the other children. Rejoining Yasmina half an hour later, Celia was rather tousled, and extremely grateful for the cool drink of sherbet which her hostess handed her.

'You are very good with children,' Yasmina said, taking a sip of her own drink. 'I hope you have the opportunity to have some of your own one day.'

'That's unlikely now. I doubt I will marry again.' Celia bit her lip. 'Yasmina, when you said a woman like me could never marry Ramiz, did you mean because I am from the West?'

'Well, that is certainly an issue—it is expected he will marry a princess of Arabic blood—but it is not the main problem. It is because you were married.'

'But my husband is dead.'

Yasmina looked at her in surprise. 'That is not the point. You are not a virgin. Ramiz is a prince of royal blood. His first wife must be his and only his. His seed must be the only seed planted in her garden.' Celia blushed, but Yasmina continued, seemingly oblivious of having said anything untoward. 'His second wife now, or his third, if *she* were widowed it would not matter so much, but a first wife like me is the most important,' she said proudly. 'It is she who bears the heir. Not that I expect Akil to take another wife. Unless he tires of me—but that would be unlikely, for I am most skilled.'

Celia was fascinated and appalled. 'You mean there are—there are things that women can do to…?'

'Keep her man?' Yasmina nodded, smiling coyly. 'Naturally. One of the advantages of sharing a harem with other women is the sharing of such secrets. Wait here.'

Left alone, Celia cooled her wrists and temples in the fountain. What had possessed her to ask such a thing? To have such an intimate conversation with a woman who was a complete stranger? It was this place—the heat, the exotic strangeness of it all. The way the walls of the harem seemed to tempt curiosity about such sensuous matters out into the open. It was because she wanted to know. Not to experience, just to know. And if she didn't find out here, then she never would.

Yasmina returned with a small parcel wrapped in silk. 'Take these. They are charm pamphlets. You won't be able to read the spells of course, but the pictures explain themselves.'

Celia took the package with some trepidation. She should not even be contemplating looking at such material, but it would be rude to refuse. 'Thank you,' she said. 'Shukran.'

'It is nothing. You must come and say goodbye to the children now. Akil is waiting to escort you back to the palace. I hope you will come again before you go back to England.'

'I would love to. I've had a lovely time here; you are blessed in your family.'

Yasmina smiled. 'I hope you too will be blessed one day.' She pressed her visitor's hand. 'You must not grow too fond of Ramiz, Lady Celia. He is a very attractive man, and he has an air about him, no? Potent, I think that is the word. But he is not for you—and you, I think, are a type who loves only once. Forgive me for speaking so, but I have the gift. I don't think you loved your husband, but I think you could easily love Ramiz if you let yourself. He is well named. Ramiz means honoured and respected. He may indulge himself with you—he is a man and you are a woman—but he would never do anything which goes against the traditions of A'Qadiz. You will be hurt if you expect too much of him. Don't let that happen.'

'You're wrong, Yasmina, I promise you.'

Yasmina shook her head. 'I have the gift. I am never wrong in these matters.'

Celia returned to the palace in a thoughtful mood, having thoroughly enjoyed the time spent with Yasmina and her family. She had been surprised to discover that Yasmina's eldest daughter attended school every day. A different school from her brother, but she was, contrary to what Celia had been told by the Consul in Cairo, receiving an education.

Seeing a harem as a family enclosure rather than a bordello had been a revelation which made her look at Ramiz and his kingdom in a completely new light. Not that she agreed with everything Yasmina had said, mind you. Offering a home to her mother and her sister-in-law was one thing—indeed, it was in many ways exactly as things were done in larger families at home, right down to the disgraced, divorced aunt Celia had discovered lived in seclusion on the second floor of the harem. Every family had its skeletons. But as to Yasmina's acceptance of the possibility of sharing her husband with another woman simply because Akil had grown tired of her—no! Absolutely not. All Celia's instincts rebelled at the very thought. She knew, as everyone did, that the Prince Regent had married twice, though poor Maria Fitzherbert's wedding was not legal. She knew that many couples, Prinny included, tacitly consented to each other's *affaires* once an heir had been secured. She did not approve, though she knew she would be deemed prudish to say so. But the idea of living in apparent harmony with what must surely be one's rivals—no!

'That,' Celia said decisively, 'I could never do. As well put a notice in the *Morning Post* that my husband finds me lacking.'

'*Afwan*, Lady Celia?'

'Nothing, Adila,' Celia said, smiling at the maidservant and shaking her head, realising she had spoken out loud. 'It's nothing.'

They had run her a bath. Wishing to be alone with her thoughts, Celia dismissed Adila and Fatima, insisting that she could undress herself. She had come to enjoy their gentle ministrations, the daily oiling, massage and bathing ritual, and would miss it when she went home.

Home. The word sat like a stone on her chest. She didn't want to go home yet. 'So much more to learn,' she told herself as she stripped off her stockings and unlaced her stays. 'I've hardly seen any of the city.'

She'd never used to talk to herself. It was a habit she'd acquired here from being so much alone, and now it felt quite natural. Draped in a loose silk robe, she padded barefoot through to the bathing room. White-tiled, it was decorated as all the salons, with a blue and gold mosaic frieze, the bath sunk into the floor, surrounded by four pillars, with a small fountain bubbling icy cold water at one end. The walls above the waist-height frieze were covered in tiles like mirrors, and above the bath the ceiling arched dark blue, painted with a galaxy of silver stars.

Celia climbed up the shallow step and sank down into the soothing water. Tonight it was scented with cinnamon and orange blossom. The bath was deep, unlike the copper tub they used at home, and she did not need to hunch up, but lay stretched full-length, her head resting on the tiles, gazing up at the stars twinkling in the ceiling, her mind floating, randomly sifting through images of A'Qadiz like a colourful collage. The sunrise over the mountains of the desert. The way the sand changed colour during the day, from toffee to the creamy yellow of fresh-churned butter, to white-gold. Her first glimpse of Balyrma, the astonishing green of the fields, the jumble of fortress-like houses, the tiled walls with their keyhole-shaped doors, the minarets and the sparkling fountains, like a child's drawing of a fairytale land.

And Ramiz. She could not think of A'Qadiz without Ramiz. Her first glimpse of him at his most god-like, watching her from the hilltop above the port. Ramiz the warrior, his scimitar glinting like a vicious halo above his head. Ramiz the man, naked in the moonlit water of the oasis.

She had never met anyone like him, and was not likely to again. Every time she saw him she learned something new. He was intelligent. Amusing. Sophisticated. Intimidating. Arrogant. Above all fascinating. Last night when he had confided in her she had glimpsed a vulnerability in him, though it had been quickly cloaked. There were layers to him that no one was allowed to see. He kept himself apart, wearing his princely personality like a costume. No doubt about it—he was the very epitome of a magnificent and omnipotent ruler, but she liked the man beneath even more.

Celia smiled softly. His eyes—the way they changed

colour with his moods as the desert sand did with the heat. The way that little lick of hair stood up like a question mark when he'd been running his hands through it. His lids were heavy, the same shape as her own, and, like her, he used them when he didn't want anyone to know what he was thinking. She liked that she knew he was doing it because she did it too.

And his mouth. Celia touched her fingers to her own mouth, remembering. Kisses like honey. Darker kisses—exotic, crimsoning kisses, filled with promise. She closed her eyes. The way his mouth fitted so exactly to hers. The way his tongue and his lips spoke to her without words, telling her what to do now, and next, and next. Her fingers fluttered down her throat to the soft flesh of her breasts. She traced their shape, made liquid by the lapping water of the bath, trying to recapture the magic of Ramiz's touch as he'd cupped them, grazing her nipples as he had with his palm, his thumb—like this. Like this…

Her breath came shallow and quick. Her heart fluttered like a bird against the bars of a cage. Warmth seeped through her, as if her blood was heating, trickling to the place just below her belly, where it built so slowly she barely noticed it. Last night Ramiz had said she was beautiful. He'd made her feel beautiful. The way he'd traced the lines of her body, as if he would sculpt her, or draw her a picture of herself. Below the water line her nipples puckered and hardened, needles of feeling, bursts of intensity, feeding the pooling beat of arousal lower down, as tributaries would feed a river.

Celia moaned softly. She traced the path of feeling

down, cupping the point where it gathered like a delta. Beneath her palm she could feel herself—a tiny flutter like a whispered cry of need. Tentatively she touched it with her fingertip. Her stomach clenched. The thing inside her, like last night, bunched. The river was dammed, readying itself for the wall to burst. She touched herself again and moaned, imagining it was Ramiz, wishing it was Ramiz, aching for it to be Ramiz.

She moaned again, turning her head restlessly on the hard-tiled edge of the bath. Something moved on the periphery of her vision. She snapped her eyes open, and it was as if she had conjured him. He was standing in the doorway of the bathing chamber, frozen to the spot, dressed in a robe of pale blue, his face set into rigid planes.

'I came to find you to talk about tomorrow. I thought you would be having dinner.'

His voice was harsh, as if he were angry. Celia swallowed. She shook her head, licked her lips. Her mouth was dry. She tried to sit up, remembered her nakedness, and slumped back under the water.

She looked like Venus rising from the waves, her glorious hair tumbling down the side of the bath, damp curls clinging lovingly to her face. The flush of arousal coloured her cheeks and darkened her eyes. He had never seen anything so lovely. Never witnessed anything so intimate as the way she touched herself. Never been so aroused.

He should have left, he knew that, but he hadn't been able to tear himself away, and now he was here he could think of nothing, nothing, nothing but finishing her journey, of travelling with her, just this once. His hands stroking her flesh. Her hands, with their long delicate fingers, touching his skin. His mouth on hers. Her breathy moans of pleasure saying *his* name, wanting *his* caress.

Ramiz was beyond resistance. Beyond anything save the need to hold her, to taste her, to take her to the heights of pleasure and this time soar with her. He strode over to the bath, kneeling down on the top step, careless of his silk robe trailing in the puddles of scented water. For a long moment he simply gazed at her, damp and pink and creamy white, the fire of her hair reflected in the fire of her eyes, the sweetness of her breath like a whisper on his cheek.

'Celia.' He pulled her towards him, his hands slipping on her shoulders, feeling the delicate blades sharp beneath her flesh as he wrapped his arm more firmly around her, the long sleeve of his caftan trailing in the water.

'Ramiz.' Sleepy with arousal, the word wrapped itself around him as Celia's arms twined around his neck, and he was lost.

Water slopped wildly over the sides of the bath onto the shallow step, forming pools on the tiled floor as he pulled her up, kissing her wildly. No slow build, no delicate preliminaries, passion burst like a ripe fig as they kissed, hands slipping and gripping and sliding, the silk of his robe clinging to their skin, their lips, their tongues, kissing as if they would meld.

She had no thought of resisting, was too far gone in

her own imagined lovemaking to refuse her dream made flesh and blood in the magnificent form of Ramiz. They were standing together on the tiled floor by the bath, wet skin, fevered lips, kissing and licking, licking and kissing.

'Celia, Celia, Celia.' Ramiz said her name like an incantation, punctuating it with kisses to her lids, her ears, her throat, his hands urgent upon her, raising torrents of feeling where before there had been only feeble tributaries. His mouth found her breast, his lips fastening greedily round her nipple. The delicious tugging produced such a rush of heat that she moaned, slumping in his embrace, arching her back so that her breasts implored him for more. His attentions moved to the other nipple. She moaned again, saying *his* name now, over and over, a plea for completion, of wanting and desperate need.

Her hands plucked at the silk of his robe, wanting to touch flesh. She struggled ineffectually with the buttons at his neck, eager now, desperate for the feel of his flesh upon hers for the first time. She wanted to touch him. To see him. To savour him. She wanted to give him what he was giving her. She wrenched at a button and it flew through the air to land with a click on the tiles.

Ramiz laughed—a low, husky noise which gave her goosebumps. She watched, fascinated, as he yanked the other buttons free and then, taking the neck of his caftan between his hands, simply tore it apart, casting it aside onto the floor to stand naked before her for the first time.

The word *magnificent* did not do his body justice.

Celia gazed at him in awe—the golden skin stretched taut over the muscles of his shoulders and chest, the rippling ridges of his abdomen, like the contours of the desert sands of which he was prince. The sheen of water like a glaze cast each dip and rise into relief. Where she was curved he was sharper lines. Where she was soft he was…

She reached out her hand tentatively. Ramiz took her by the wrist, encouraging her. Where her skin was soft, like cashmere, his was smoother, like silk stretched on a tambour frame. She could feel the hardness of his muscles underneath. Ramiz pulled her closer. He guided her wrist lower. The concave stomach. Down. Her eyes followed the same path. Down. To the curving length of him, solid, intimidatingly large. She could not imagine how—where—surely it would hurt?

'Ramiz, I…'

'Touch me. There is nothing to be frightened of.'

'I'm not frightened.' But she was, just a bit, and her voice gave her away. She was afraid of her ignorance. Afraid of failing. Afraid that Ramiz would find her lacking.

He scooped her up, holding her high against his chest, pushing his way impatiently out of the bathing chamber to the next salon, where he kicked a heap of cushions together onto the carpet and sank down onto them. Satin and silk and velvet—she could feel them all on her back, her bottom, her thighs. Satin and silk and velvet on her mouth as Ramiz kissed her.

'To touch is to learn,' Ramiz whispered, trailing his fingers over her hip.

He leaned over her, his mouth following where his fingers had led, feathering kisses like whispers, speaking softly of the pleasure to come. She felt her skin tighten as her flesh seemed to swell under his caress. He kissed the crease at the top of her thigh, pulling her onto her side, positioning himself opposite her so that they lay like two crescents curved into each other.

Ramiz dipped his hand between her legs, lightly stroking his way through the moist folds of her flesh. 'Touch me, Celia. Do as I do. Make me feel as you do. Like this.' With his other hand he placed hers onto his shaft, wrapping her fingers round its length and gently guiding her. Satin and silk and velvet.

Her touch was entirely inexperienced and entirely delightful. He thought fleetingly of the man who had been her husband, a man who had obviously taken no interest at all in his wife's pleasure, and then he banished the thought, for he did not want to think of Celia as a wife, or having belonged to anyone else. He did not want to think at all, for to do so would be to stop, and he could not stop. Not now.

He slipped his fingers gently inside her, easing into the swelling heat of her, enjoying the way she clenched around him, the little gasp of pleasure emanating from her. 'This is what you are doing to me,' he said. 'When I do this, and you touch me like that, this is what it feels like.' Slowly he pulled out of her clinging moistness, only to ease back in again.

What he was doing was a prelude. Finally she understood. Her own fingers clasped around the part of him which was designed to meld them together. She stroked him, wondering at the slight curve on the satiny skin, at the astonishing hardness of him, tracing a line up to the tip of him, softer, rounded, velvety. He was watching her. She gasped as he pushed his fingers inside her again, closing her eyes at the peculiar smarting of this pleasure, more insistent, the edges rougher than last night. Then he did it again, and she stroked him in the same rhythm, and saw the pleasure she was giving him etched on his face, in the way his eyes darkened, the way he bit his lip to stop himself from crying out.

It was the same for him. It was really the same. What she was feeling—this mounting tension, this jagged excitement, this feeling of wanting it done, over, of wanting it to last for ever, this wanting to soar and wanting to cling—he was feeling it too as she stroked him and he stroked her. Then he slid upwards, touching her where he had touched her yesterday, and she felt herself began to slip, but forced herself to cling on. Her thumb caressed the tip of his shaft, and Ramiz gasped. Inside her, he worked magic of his own. It was like being pushed inexorably towards something deep and dark, and as she stroked him and circled him she could see he felt the same. His eyes were closed. A dark flush stained his cheeks. He gripped his lower lip with his teeth. His breathing was fast, uneven. Like her own. Her heart was thumping. Her body was cold, cold—freezing except for where Ramiz touched her and she touched Ramiz. She felt him thicken in her hand, felt herself swelling under his hand, heard him say her name, like a plea, for the first time asking something of her, but before she had time to wonder what he wanted the jagged swelling pressure in her burst through, like water coursing through a dam, and she cried out. Ramiz cried out too, spilling his pleasure over her hand as she melted into his.

He was right. To give was to receive. More than last night. More than she had thought possible. Enough to make her wonder what *more* would feel like. Enough to make her realise that she should heed Yasmina's warning. This was a fantasy formed in a harem and being played out free from the disapproval of the outside world. Nothing more. It could never—must never—be anything more.

Celia sat up, pulling a tasselled cushion onto her lap to cover herself.

Ramiz opened his eyes, reluctantly pulling himself back down from the heights to which her touch had sent him. He had not meant this to happen. *It should not have happened! What was he thinking?* He got quickly to his feet, pulling his torn robe around him. 'This was a mistake.'

'A mistake?' she repeated stupidly.

'It was wrong,' Ramiz said tersely. At least he had not risked any consequences! At least his sense of honour had not wholly deserted him.

His robe was soaking wet from the bathwater, but he didn't seem to notice. It clung to him, making him look like one of those naked statues, strategically draped for modesty's sake. Feeling at a distinct disadvantage, Celia hugged her cushion defensively. With his clothing, Ramiz had donned his mask. She hardly recognised the man who had moaned his pleasure at her touch only moments before.

'What do you mean, it was a mistake?'

'You are here under my protection. I should not have allowed myself—this should not have happened. No matter how much the provocation,' he added.

'Provocation!' Celia's face burned with a mixture of shame and anger. 'I thought I was alone.'

'This is my harem.' He was being unfair, but it was true in a way. If she had not been—if he had not seen her in the bath like that… 'My harem,' Ramiz repeated firmly. 'I am free to walk in here any time I wish.'

'That's preposterous. It may be your harem, but as you've just pointed out I am a guest here. I am entitled to some privacy.'

'And I am entitled to expect my guests to behave more decorously.'

'You're being quite ridiculous.'

'You call *me* ridiculous? You forget yourself, Lady Celia. You forget who you are talking to.'

She knew he had a temper, but she had not before experienced it. His face was pale with anger, his mouth set in a thin line, his hands clenched at his sides. She had overstepped the mark as far as he was concerned, but as far as she was concerned so had he. Her own formidable temper was normally kept firmly under wraps, but his heady change of mood from euphoria to accusation sent it spinning out of her control before she could rein it in.

Regardless of her naked state, she flung the cushion away and got to her feet, her hair flying out like battle colours behind her. 'I don't care who you are—you are being ridiculous. I was taking a bath in the privacy of a bathing chamber. The fact that it happens to be in your harem is completely irrelevant. It is not my fault that you fell victim to your own base desires. I won't be branded some sort of siren just to satisfy your honour, be you prince, sheikh, or simply a man.'

He flinched as if she had struck him. As she had—with the truth of the matter. He had been unable to control himself. No matter that he had not taken her, he had wanted to. 'You are right.'

Celia's temper fled as quickly as it had arrived. There was an embroidered cover on one of the divans under the window. She snatched it up, wrapping it around her shoulders. 'Ramiz, you were not the only one to lose control,' she said painfully. 'I did not provoke you deliberately, but I didn't stop you either.' She reached out to touch his arm. 'You are not the only one to blame.'

He shrugged himself free of her hand. 'You are a woman. I should not have allowed you to submit.'

'Submit?' Celia stared at him in confusion. 'Why must you persist in the belief that I don't have a mind of my own just because I'm a woman? I make my own choices, even if they do turn out to be foolish ones.'

Ramiz sighed heavily. 'I am pleased you think this way, even if it is misguided. I hope this—this event—will not colour the view of my country that you take back to England.'

Realisation dawned, cold and savage. 'You're worried that I'll make things difficult for you through my father?'

'We are at a delicate stage of negotiations with your people.'

'I won't be crying ravishment, if that's what you're worried about.' She glared at him, determined not to allow the hurt she felt to show.

It was the last thing he'd been thinking of, but it *should* have been the first. He could not forgive himself. He could not allow himself to think about why he had done what he did. Or how Celia felt. And definitely not how he felt. It was a relief at least that his actions had not offended her. He must ensure he gave her no further cause.

'Tomorrow, if you still wish, I will take you out to see something of Balyrma.'

'Is that my compensation for keeping my mouth shut? If so, I'd rather stay here.'

'I thought you wished to see the city. If you have changed your mind…'

'I'm sorry, Ramiz, I shouldn't have said that.' Celia attempted a weak smile. 'All this—everything here—it's all so strange to me. I feel like I'm in a dream half the time. I'd love to see Balyrma, and if you have the time to escort me I'd be honoured. I'm sure I couldn't have a more knowledgeable guide. Akil told me you've written a history of Balyrma's origins.'

Ramiz shrugged. 'It is nothing. The work of an enthusiastic amateur rather than a scholar. I will have you brought to me in the morning.' He turned to leave.

'Ramiz.' Difficult as it was to speak of such things, she could not square it with her conscience to allow him to think he had forced her, any more than she had been able to accept that she had enticed him. 'Ramiz, I meant what I said. It was as much my fault as yours. You are not responsible for my actions, no matter how accustomed you may be to thinking you are.'

'It does you credit that you say so.'

'I say so because it's the truth.'

Ramiz smiled like a god descending from the heavens to join the mere mortals. It transformed him. 'It is not just me who is accustomed to shouldering the blame, is it? I think you must be a very protective sister.' He kissed her cheek. 'You are certainly a most unusual woman.'

Leaving her to ponder the meaning of this rather enigmatic statement, Ramiz left.

Chapter Seven

Next morning Celia dressed for the promised sightseeing trip in a lemon-figured muslin walking dress with a double flounce along the hem, trimmed with knots of gold ribbon. Gold ribbon was also threaded through the high neckline and the edges of the tight-fitting sleeves, which were fastened with a row of tiny pearl buttons. Adila had found a way for her to attach the gauzy veil of blond lace to the back of her head, rather as Spanish ladies wore their mantilla, obviating the need for a hat, much to Celia's relief. She wore the veil back over her hair while still inside the palace, and carried her gloves as she followed in the wake of the guard. Despite giving herself a severe talking to, playing over last night's conversation several times in her head, she was extremely nervous about meeting Ramiz again, and quite unable to decide how she felt about anything that had happened. In fact, in the bright light of day, released from the harem's sultry ambience, she found it difficult to believe it had happened at all!

Ramiz was in his library, dressed all in white as she had first seen him, complete with headdress and cloak. 'In desert prince mode,' Celia muttered to herself as he nodded a distant good morning from behind his desk and turned back to complete his conversation with Akil, leaving her standing like an unwanted caller at the doorway.

Though she herself had come to think of the harem as a separate place, ruled by the senses rather than the mind, and though she herself had made every effort to put last night's events firmly to the back of her mind, Celia couldn't help resenting the fact that Ramiz seemed so successfully to have done the same. She eyed him from beneath her lids as she wandered over to browse the bookshelves. How she envied him his detachment. How she wished she shared it. She wasn't used to this feeling of constantly being on the back foot. The Lady Celia Armstrong she knew was used to feeling in charge. In control. Calm. Cool. Sophisticated. Not like some country miss in her first Season, having constantly to consult a book of etiquette and even then always on the verge of a fatal *faux pas*.

But she was not that Lady Celia Armstrong, and she knew she never would be again. She could not forget what she had experienced in Ramiz's arms, under Ramiz's tutelage, and she was very much afraid that what he had taught her had spoiled her for ever for any other man—as this place, this whole experience of the exotic world of A'Qadiz, would spoil her even for her beloved England, if she let it.

It was a paradox, she thought, picking up a volume bound in soft blue leather which was on the table with a stack of books recently come from England. A paradox, because here in this kingdom, where women were veiled and segregated, where she spent much of her time behind the locked door of a harem guarded by two eunuchs, she had never been so free.

Celia opened the book. *Emma, a Novel in Three Volumes by the Author of Pride and Prejudice.* She'd really enjoyed *Pride and Prejudice.* They had read it together, she and her sisters, assigning themselves roles from the sisters in the story. She had been Elizabeth, of course, and Cassie had been Jane, the beauty of the family. Smiling to herself at the memory of Caroline and Cordelia squabbling over who was to be the flighty Lydia, Celia felt a pang of homesickness. She wondered what they were all doing now. She didn't even know what time it was back home—later or earlier? Was it sunny or raining? It was strawberry season. Cressida loved strawberries, though they brought Caroline out in a rash when she ate too many, as she always did, no matter how many times she was reminded. Cordelia preferred the strawberry jam they all made together from Mama's treasured receipt book. It had become an annual rite, taking over the kitchen for the day, filling the big country house with the sweetly cloying scent of jam as it bubbled in the vast copper pot. Cassie had charge of the receipt book now. It would be up to her to order the extra sugar, to take Celia's role as Jam-Maker-in-Chief, no doubt ceding her own role of Measurer-in-Chief to Caroline. Celia could already imagine the argument that would induce between the youngest two of her sisters. Poor Cassie, whose gentle temperament made her loath to intervene in any dispute, would wring her hands and implore them to share and tell them that one role was just as good as another, and they would ignore her completely, and Caroline would get involved, and without Celia to knock sense into all of them the whole jam-making would turn into a complete fiasco…

'Of course it will not,' she chastised herself. 'I just want to think so because it makes me feel indispensable.'

'What does?'

Celia jumped, dropping volume one of *Emma* on to the thickly carpeted floor—so thickly carpeted she had not heard Ramiz approach. Now he was standing uncomfortably close. Why did she always forget how tall he was, and how very good-looking? She took a step back. 'I beg your pardon?'

'You said, *"I just want to think so because it makes me feel indispensable."*'

'Oh. I must have been talking out loud. I hadn't realised. I was thinking of my sisters. It's nothing.'

'You miss them?'

'Yes, of course I do. Though I'm sure they're all fine without me,' Celia said, surprised to find her voice a bit shaky.

'But there's a part of you which hopes they are not, hmm?'

She smiled, trying surreptitiously to blink away the

tears which had gathered in her eyes. 'I know it's a dreadful thing to think. I'm afraid I must be a very controlling female.'

'It's not surprising. You took on the role of mother to your sisters at a very early age, yes? It is perfectly natural that you should worry about how they are coping without you. It is something mothers do, even when their children have families of their own. A very feminine trait.'

Celia sniffed. 'Thank you. I think that might even qualify as a compliment.'

'If you wish to write to them, I will see your letter is safely delivered.'

'You're very kind.'

'I should have thought of it earlier. Your people will wish to be reassured that you are safe and well. They will not want to take my word for it. You must write tonight.'

'I see.' He wasn't thinking of her, but of his own reputation. Of his country's interests. 'If you are too busy for our outing today, perhaps we should postpone it.'

'There is no need. I have taken care of business for today, and Akil has it all in hand. Besides, I wish you to see something of Balyrma while you are here.'

'So that I can report back on how wonderful it is?'

Ramiz's eyes narrowed. 'Because I think it will interest you. If I was mistaken…'

'No, you're not,' Celia said hastily. 'I do want to see it. I was a bit disconcerted, that was all—seeing this book, if you must know. My sisters and I read another by the same author.'

'*Pride and Prejudice?* I read it myself, and enjoyed it. A very amusing account of your English manners. The author must be a very perceptive man.'

'You think it is written by a man?'

'The wit is acerbic, none of the characters are sympathetic, and there is none of the sentimental romanticism endemic in female writers. Of a certainty it is a man.'

'Of a certainty? If you say it is so, then it must be so, Highness.'

Ramiz looked startled, and then he smiled, showing gleaming white teeth and menacing amber eyes. 'You are learning, Lady Celia. I am granting you the honour of my company without escort and in public. You must treat me with respect and deference in front of my people, for if you do not I will be forced to confine you to the harem for the duration of your stay. I hope I have made myself clear?'

She met his gaze defiantly for all of ten seconds, then surrendered. In truth, when he looked at her like that she had no wish to defy him. And he *was* honouring her with his presence after all, and she *did* want his company, more than she cared to admit to herself. Celia drew her veil over her face, and her gloves over her fingers. 'Yes, Highness,' she said meekly, following in Ramiz's wake as he led the way across the courtyard. Which meant he did not see her pout cheekily at him as they went through the passageway and out of the gate into the city.

The heat was so intense it knocked the breath out of

her—like walking into an oasthouse after the hops had been roasted. In the cool of the palace she had forgotten how fierce the sun could be, even this early in the day.

She had also forgotten the reverence in which Ramiz was held. People dropped to their knees as he passed. They did not look at him, but Celia could feel their eyes on her, curious rather than threatening. She was conscious of how strange she must look in her tight-fitting dress, and acutely aware, as she watched Ramiz nod and smile to his people, of just how big an honour he was actually conferring on her in being her guide for the day.

It was not yet nine o'clock, but Balyrma was a hive of activity. Ramiz led the way through the dusty streets away from the tiled houses and minarets of the more affluent quarter to the more crowded area nearer the city gates. 'I thought you'd like to see the souks,' he said over his shoulder. 'Each sector of the city is named for different artisans, and each has their own market. This alleyway here is populated by leather workers; down here is where the potters are, and the tile-makers. Come closer. I'm getting a sore neck talking to you like this.'

'I thought I was to follow in your wake to show you respect.'

'You can show respect just as well by doing as you are bid.'

Celia caught up with him. 'You have the makings of a frightful tyrant, you know,' she said with a smile. 'Highness,' she added as a deliberate afterthought.

'And *you* have the makings of a most subversive citizen.'

'I'm sorry if I seem flippant sometimes. It's just that you can be rather intimidating, and I'm not used to being intimidated.'

They had stopped momentarily, allowing the small retinue of children they had collected in their wake to swarm around her, reaching out to stroke the fabric of her dress. She smiled at them all abstractedly through her veil.

'They are not used to seeing clothing such as yours.'

'I wish I did not have to wear it. It's completely unsuited to this climate, and I feel as if I'm being baked alive.'

'You should have said so before. We can get you some fabrics at the souk. I will have the maids make up some traditional outfits if you really want to go native.'

'I would *love* to go native.'

'You never look hot. In fact you always look extremely elegant.'

'Thank you.'

'You are welcome. Do not look so sceptical, I mean it,' Ramiz said with a wry smile.

They set off again at a slower pace, stopping off at a stall selling sugared almonds, dried dates, long sticks of some sort of sticky toffee packed with sultanas and raisins, and all sorts of other sweet delights which had the children staring in wide-eyed wonder. Ramiz selected an assortment which he handed out before they moved on, walking companionably side by side, Ramiz having forgotten all about his desire for protocol.

'I don't know what it is about you that makes me speak

my mind,' Celia said thoughtfully as they approached the fabric district. 'I assure you, every time you goad me into saying something outrageous I wish I had bitten my tongue out.'

'Before I have it cut out, you mean,' Ramiz said.

She could tell by the way his eyes gleamed, the way his mouth firmed into an upward curve that wasn't quite a smile, that he was teasing. 'Yasmina told me you rule with a hand of iron in a velvet glove. She also told me one of the first things you did when you came to power was to completely overhaul the legal system. You don't even have an executioner any more, do you?'

'There is no need. When people have enough to eat, somewhere for their family to live, a way to earn a living, they have no need to turn to crime. And when the punishment for transgression is to lose all that—banishment—I find it is incentive enough.'

'That is a very progressive way of thinking. Far more humane than we are in England, where a starving man who steals a sheep to feed his family can be hanged.'

'If you read Scheherazade's stories more closely you would see she shares my views.'

'And your people?' Celia asked.

'Some of the tribes prefer the old ways. For them, violence—wars, punishment, whatever—is a way of life. I spend a lot of my time trying to prevent them overturning my treaties. I am due to visit the head of one of the tribes later this week, as a matter of fact. They occupy land on the border of A'Qadiz, where the oasis is disputed territory. It is supposed to be shared. I will spend two days reminding him of this, and he will spend two days trying to extract as much gold as he can from me as compensation for what he claims to be his exclusive rights.'

'You bribe him not to fight?'

'Don't look so shocked. It's a tactic your government uses all the time. And for me it's cheaper in the long run than allowing him to start a full-scale war.'

'Can't you just have him—this head man—replaced with someone who believes in what you're trying to do?'

Ramiz laughed. 'That really would start a war. Enough of this talk. They are my problems, not yours. Come, the fabric district is just here. Take your time. Choose as much as you like.'

'Oh, but I don't have any money with me.'

'I will pay.'

'Absolutely not. I cannot allow you to buy my clothes. It wouldn't be proper.'

'It would not be proper for me to allow you to pay.'

'Then I won't have anything.'

Ramiz stared at her in consternation. 'You honestly think I am concerned about the price of a few yards of material?'

'It's the principle of it,' Celia said firmly. 'In England only a—a courtesan allows a man who is not her husband to buy her clothes.'

'We are not in England,' Ramiz pointed out. 'In A'Qadiz it is for the master of the harem to provide them. You are in my harem, I will pay for these, and that is an end to it.'

Celia was not at all convinced, but looking at Ramiz's

face, at his mouth setting in a firm line, she decided not to antagonise him further. The day was young, and she wanted to make the most of it. She wanted Ramiz to enjoy himself, and if that meant breaking one of her own rules to keep his dignity intact, then so be it. 'Thank you, Highness,' she said with a graceful curtsy. 'In that case I will be most honoured.'

Ramiz grinned. 'You don't fool me with that meek and mild act. And you can stop calling me Highness. No one can understand what you're saying.'

'Thank you, Ramiz, then. I trust the royal coffers are sufficiently full, for I intend to make the most of these wonderful fabrics.'

If anyone had told him that he could enjoy the experience of shopping for silks in a souk, Ramiz would have laughed in his face. Though he enjoyed looking at a well-dressed woman as much as the next man, he had little interest in what that dress comprised of nor in any of the frills and furbelows which accessorised it. But Celia's child-like enthusiasm was enchanting, and for the next hour he watched entranced as she threw herself with unwonted zeal into the business of choosing colours and textures and trimmings.

Celia, who had never before seen such a display of colourful silks, rich velvets and delicate gauzy fabrics she could not even name, went from stall to stall in the souk with a rapt expression on her face. She removed her gloves to plunge her fingers into the thick nap of a crimson velvet, to rub a shawl of the softest cashmere against her cheek, to stroke silks and satins and fine net and coarse damask, turning the purchase of cloth into a wholly sensual experience she could never have imagined. In her excitement she forgot all about deference and reserve. She forgot to put her gloves back on and she forgot to replace her veil, but she was so charming, able to make her wishes clear despite the language barrier, and careful to praise even the plainest of fabrics displayed to her, equally careful to spread her purchases over as many stalls as possible, that rather than cause offence she was treated with real hospitality and warmth. They drank several glasses of tea, and Ramiz found himself playing second fiddle for the first time since he had come to power.

'Thank you for that,' Celia said to him as they left a shop specialising in *passementerie*—elaborate braiding made from gold and silver thread. 'I hope you weren't bored.'

'It was an education. Have you had enough?'

'More than. Do you have to go back to the palace?'

Ramiz shook his head. 'I have arranged a special treat for you.' He led the way through the maze of alleys and terracotta buildings with their stalls opening out from the ground floors, back to a large square where a palace guard was waiting with two snowy white camels. 'A short ride—half an hour, no more. Can you manage it in that dress?' Ramiz asked when Celia looked at him enquiringly.

'Where are we going?'

He smiled and shook his head. 'It's a surprise.'

They left Balyrma by a different gate than the one through which they had entered the city. This one led through an olive grove to the south, to a narrow track, only just discernible, wending its way towards the mountains. Ramiz told her a little more of Balyrma's history as the camels made their stately way along the path. As before, Celia's intelligent questions and thirst for knowledge made him relax his guard, drawing him out, making him laugh, extracting things from deep in the recesses of his mind—childhood memories and ancient legends he had forgotten until now. He liked her. It was a strange thing to say of a woman, but there it was. She was excellent company and he liked her.

The mountains seemed to rear up out of the sand like a child's model or an artist's impression, without foothills or any other preliminaries, more like monuments than natural phenomena. There was no path that Celia could see, and her heart sank at the thought of having to climb, until she realised that Ramiz was leading them to what looked like a large fissure in the rock. A cave?

It was not a cave but a narrow passageway, curving in an 'S' shape only wide enough to allow them to pass through in single file. Enchanted, Celia saw that the rock was carved with strange symbols, and little niches contained carved idols scattered at regular intervals. Craning her neck, she could just see the sky, the brilliant blue colour of approaching noon, though here between the rocks it felt cool. Then they turned the final bend and she gasped with astonishment, for they were standing in a large open square and before her lay a ruined city, built into the rock itself.

'The ancient city of Katra,' Ramiz said. 'We don't know how old it is exactly, but we estimate about two thousand years.'

The city was compact, and despite its great age in a remarkable state of preservation. 'I've never seen anything so wonderful,' Celia said as she wandered through the buildings. 'It's marvelous. I can't believe I've never even heard of it.'

'That is because we have been at pains to keep its existence a secret,' Ramiz explained. 'It is well known that the British and French stripped Egypt of many of its ancient treasures during the wars with Napoleon, and it is well known that your Consul General continues to send artefacts collected by his friends from all over Egypt and the Levant to his own little museum in England, as Lord Elgin did with the Parthenon marbles. I don't want that happening to Katra.'

'No, and I can see why. It's beautiful, and quite eerie too. I feel as if the people have just stepped out this morning and will come back any time. But if you don't want anyone to know about it, why have you brought me?'

Why? Because it was special, and he wanted to share it with her. He realised he couldn't say that. He knew he shouldn't have thought it. He hadn't until this moment. 'Because to understand Balyrma's history one must understand Katra's. I knew it would interest you.'

'You've no idea how much. It's one of the most marvellous things I've ever seen. Thank you.'

Celia had pushed back her veil again. She smiled up at him, her eyes alight with excitement that made them glitter like diamond-chipped jade. Her mouth made the most delightful curve—soft and full. The taste of her, sweet and flowery, came back to him like a punch in the stomach. Her lips like petals on his own. Blossoming as she had blossomed under his touch. Bloomed. Ripened. *What was he thinking?*

'It is past noon,' Ramiz said brusquely, looking up at the sun high overhead. 'I have arranged for shade and food. This way.'

For a fraction of a second she thought he had been going to kiss her. Her heart had begun to beat hard and fast, changing its tempo so suddenly she felt dizzy. Now he was striding ahead of her to where the camels were tethered, leading the way on foot back through the passageway so quickly she had to run to keep up.

As they emerged into the blaze of the sun she saw that a tent had been set up directly under an overhanging ledge. Like the one they had abandoned in the desert it was a square in shape, constructed from wool woven from camel or goat, supported by large wooden props tied with rope, but there the resemblance ended. Thick-piled carpets covered the sand. The walls were hung with tapestries depicting scenes from ancient mythology. Tasselled cushions embroidered with silks, embellished with seed pearls and semi-precious stones, were strewn across the carpet around a low table, upon which a selection of gold dishes were covered. The appetising aroma of spit-roasted goat filled the air, making Celia's mouth water.

Damask hangings created a small room to one side, where a pitcher of rose-scented water stood on a marble washstand. Celia rinsed the dust and sand from her face and hands, tidying her hair in the gilt mirror which had been thoughtfully provided, before she sat down to eat with Ramiz.

The food was delicate, packed with the exotic flavours she had come to relish. A lime and mint sherbet quenched her thirst. Aside from the usual selection of spiced meats and palate-cleansing fruits there was something called a *pastille*—a parcel of flaky pastry stuffed with pigeon, almonds and dates. Unlike at home, where it was the custom to partake only of those dishes within reach—even if one's favourite dish was at the other end of the table—she had discovered that it was expected of her to try a little of everything here. It was a practice she enjoyed, and she said so to Ramiz.

'Every meal is like a picnic, and if I don't like something I can just leave it because I've only taken a little bit. At home, especially at dinner parties, it is expected that you eat whatever is put on your plate. I can't tell you the number of times I've had to chew my way through a perfectly inedible piece of over-cooked meat or, worse, under-cooked fish.'

'It is your habit to drown everything in sauces, which I don't like,' Ramiz said. 'It makes me wonder why. Is the food so awful that it can't be eaten on its own?'

Celia giggled. 'You're probably right. I'm afraid that cooking is not high on the list of British accomplishments.'

She dipped her hands into a little fingerbowl in which jasmine petals floated. He watched her, thinking again what a strange mix she was. He could not understand his attraction to her. No doubt she was thinking the same thing. He could not understand why she had allowed him such liberties. He was the first to stir her, he knew that. Perhaps that was why she stirred him so?

As now.

He wanted to kiss her. He had to kiss her. Taking her by surprise, he reached down and pulled her to her feet, pressing her close, satisfyingly close, so that he could smell her scent and hear her breathing. He smiled at the look in her big green eyes.

'What are you doing?' Celia said breathlessly, though she knew full well what he was doing, and she knew full well that she wanted him to. His mouth was only inches from hers. His eyes were like cast bronze, glazed with heat. Her heart pounded wildly. Her mouth was dry. She was acutely conscious of him, the strength of him, the power in him coiled tight like a stalking tiger beneath the silk of his robe. To her shame, she could feel a wicked excitement rising, making her nipples peak painfully against her chemise.

Ramiz groaned—a grating sound—as if it were rasped out of him. Then he kissed her. A hungry kiss without restraint. The kiss of a man pushed beyond endurance. A kiss of surrender, an admission of need that shamed him even as it incited him to pursue that need to its conclusion. His wanting was so urgent and so immediate he felt he would explode with it. Blood rushed to his groin, making him so hard he ached with a painfully pulsing urge to cast off all restraints and thrust into her, to take her fast and hard and thoroughly, to mark her for ever as his. Her lips were swollen with his kisses. A long strand of copper hair trailed down her cheek.

'Last night,' he said raggedly, 'why did you not stop me?'

'I should have, but I somehow couldn't.' Celia bit her lip. 'It is the harem. There is something beguiling about it. Unreal. Otherworldly.'

'Unreal.' Ramiz nodded. 'Will you stop me now? Here?'

Celia veiled her eyes with her heavy lids. 'I think I won't have to,' she said eventually.

Ramiz sighed heavily. His smile was crooked. 'A very diplomatic answer.' He released her, tucking her hair back behind her ear and kissing the tip of her nose. 'We should get back.'

Chapter Eight

Peregrine Finchley-Burke was the fourth son of an earl. Peregrine's oldest brother, heir to the Earldom, was currently delighting the ladies of the *ton* with his illustrious person, and endowing the gaming tables at White's club with his father's guineas. Peregrine's second brother had chosen the army. Captain Finchley-Burke of the Thirteenth Hussars had been wounded at Waterloo—a bullet which grazed his cheek, leaving him romantically scarred but otherwise unhurt. Since returning to England he had been assisting his elder brother's attempts to gamble away his inheritance at the tables of White's. Peregrine's third brother was made of much sterner stuff, however. So imbued with moral rectitude was the Very Reverend Archdeacon Finchley-Burke that the Earl himself was wont to question his wife's fidelity on the few occasions when his son blessed him with his presence.

Which left Peregrine to serve his country by way of the East India Company. He had, in fact, been on his way to India when the vagaries of the weather had left him stranded in Lisbon long enough for the ambassador there to persuade him that by travelling to Cairo on his behalf to deliver some urgent papers he would be doing his country a great service. In fact, although the diplomatic bag entrusted to Peregrine *did* contain some documents pertaining to matters of the state, the consignment of port which accompanied it was the real matter of urgency. Of this fact, as of so many others, Peregrine remained in blissful ignorance.

It was serendipitous for the Consul General of Egypt, Lord Wincester, that Peregrine's arrival coincided with the need to send a messenger to A'Qadiz with a response to Sheikh al-Muhana's communication, informing him of the death of George Cleveden and the whereabouts of the Lady Celia, his widow. The Consul General had a small, overworked staff—a fact of which he was constantly reminding the Foreign Office—so the naïve and clearly biddable young gentleman who had just delivered his long-anticipated supplies of port was commandeered to act as emissary—a suggestion which much flattered the aforesaid young gentleman, who blessed his luck and began to dream of a glittering career in the diplomatic corps.

Thus was Peregrine's onward journey to India further postponed, and thus did he arrive, dusty, sunburned, saddle-sore and feeling considerably out of his depth, at the royal palace in Balyrma, in the company of the Prince's own guard.

Ramiz was informed of the arrival of this unexpected guest by Akil, immediately upon his return from Katra. It had been a silent ride back, giving him ample time to try to regret kissing Celia and ample time to wish that he had kissed her more. Assuming that the visitor had come to reclaim her, Ramiz found himself extremely reluctant to let her go—though he knew he should be relieved, and continued to tell himself so as he bathed and changed his robes.

Without success.

Ramiz arrived in the throne room, where it was the custom to receive foreign visitors, in a black mood. He wore a formal robe of dark blue silk, fastened with gold buttons embellished with sapphires. At Akil's insistence he wore a *bisht* over this, the jewelled cloak elaborately embroidered with his falcon and crescent insignia. It was a heavy garment, and consequently uncomfortably warm, as was the headdress and its gold-tasselled *igal*, which Akil had insisted upon too. With the famous Balyrman scimitar weighing down the belt at his waist, and the great seal of A'Qadiz weighing down the middle finger of his right hand, Ramiz strode into the throne room with Akil behind him, breathlessly attempting to keep up while avoiding the royal *bisht* which trailed along the tiles, and completing the briefing he had in turn received from Peregrine's escort, all at the same time.

'So this man Finchley-Burke is basically a junior secretary?' Ramiz said, throwing himself onto the throne. A large gilded and scrolled chair, it sat on a carpeted dais at the top of the room, which was some sixty feet long—a vast tiled space, with an ornate mosaic floor bordered on each side by ten pillars, lit by ten stained-glass windows, but otherwise empty of furnishings, forcing visitors to stand in exposed isolation in front of the seated monarch. 'What do you think, Akil? Are we to be insulted at this minion's lack of status, or impressed by the speed with which they have sent him to us?'

Akil took his place by Ramiz's side. 'I doubt they intend to insult you, Highness.'

'They certainly don't mean to flatter me either,' Ramiz replied acerbically. 'Nor Lady Celia, for that matter. Do they expect me to provide an escort across the desert for her? They take too much for granted!'

'Maybe they don't want her back.'

'What do you mean by that?' Ramiz asked sharply.

'Nothing, Highness. A jest, that's all,' Akil said hurriedly, wondering at his friend's mood.

'If you can't find anything sensible to say you will do better to hold your tongue. Go and fetch the Englishman. I've better things to do than sit and stew in this outfit.'

'Ramiz, is there something wrong?'

'Only that I seem unable to make myself clear today.'

Akil opened his mouth to remonstrate, caught the glitter in Ramiz's eye, and changed his mind.

Ushering the Englishman in from the ante-room where he had been pacing anxiously, Akil could not but feel sorry for him.

'How do I address him?' Peregrine asked, tugging at his sweat-soaked neckcloth.

'Highness. Leave your hat here, and your gloves. You

must not shake hands, only bow like this.' Akil demonstrated gracefully. 'And do not meet his eyes.'

'What about this?' Peregrine said, pulling a sealed letter from the pocket of his cutaway coat. 'It's from the Consul General.'

'You may kneel at the foot of the dais and hold it out to him. Are you ready? Follow me. He is looking forward to meeting you,' Akil said, making a quick apology to the gods for the lie. 'Try not to look so terrified.'

Peregrine swallowed hard. 'Righty-ho.'

Akil rolled his eyes, nodded to the guard, who threw open the double doors to the chamber, and stood back to watch as the Englishman made his scuttling way across the vast tiled expanse of floor towards the throne, with all the enthusiasm of a thief approaching an executioner.

Ramiz stood to receive his visitor. Though his manner was brusque, it was regally so, showing no sign of ill-temper nor any discourtesy. He took the letter, breaking the seal immediately, and quickly skimmed the contents, relaxing visibly as he did so. To Akil's surprise Ramiz then signalled for tea to be brought, and when it came, accompanied by cushions to sit on, he sat beside Peregrine—an honour of which the young man, awkwardly crouching, seemed unaware.

'So, you are not here to escort the Lady Celia back to Cairo?'

Peregrine eyed the sweet tea in its delicate glass with caution. 'No, Your Highness. That is—no. The Consul General extends his most profuse apologies, but he felt it better, in the circumstances, to summon Lady Celia's father to fetch her.'

'It is to my great sorrow that Mr Cleveden died so tragically while on the soil of A'Qadiz. Do you wish to take his body back with you?'

Peregrine looked appalled. 'Good Lord, no. That is—like a soldier, you know—buried where he fell kind of thing.' He took a cautious sip of tea. It was surprisingly refreshing. He took another, and allowed his ample derrière, aching from the wooden camel saddle, to sink a little more comfortably down onto the cushion. 'Didn't know the chap, of course, but gather he was destined for great things.'

A picture of George Cleveden fleeing the attack flashed into Ramiz's mind. 'Indeed,' he said non-committally.

'Despatch to Lord Armstrong went off in the old urgent bag just as soon as your own letter arrived,' Peregrine said, relaxing further. This prince was turning out to be a very nice chap—not at all the dragon he'd been led to expect. 'Frigate waiting off Alexandria, as a matter of fact. With a fair wind and a bit of luck her family will know she's all right and tight very soon.'

'You are acquainted with Lord Armstrong?'

'Good heavens, no. A bit above my touch. As is Lady Celia, if I'm honest. One of these frightfully clever females—type who has all the inside gen on who's doing what to whom—in a political way, if you know what I mean.' Peregrine tittered, caught Ramiz's stern glare, and lowered his eyes. 'Highness. Your Highness. Beg pardon. Didn't mean to—bit new to all this. Awfully sorry.'

Ramiz got swiftly to his feet. 'You will wish to see her?'

Peregrine, who had been hoping for the offer of some more substantial refreshment than tea before facing the Lady Celia, blinked, tried to get to his feet, slipped, and decided that remaining in obeisance on his knees, while lacking in dignity, was preferable to losing his head.

'Well?' Ramiz demanded impatiently.

'Yes—yes, of course. Highness. Your Highness.'

'Tomorrow, I think,' Ramiz said, much to Peregrine's relief. 'You must be tired after your journey. Akil will show you to the men's quarters now. There is a *hammam* there you can use.'

'Hammam?' Peregrine's eyes boggled. He could not decide whether to be honoured or revolted, for in his mind the word conjured up a fat exotic odalisque, rather like his nanny but in scantier clothing. Younger, of course, and he hoped not really too much like old Lalla Hughes who, now he came to think of it, had a bit of a moustache going.

'Steam bath,' Ramiz explained, trying not to smile, for Peregrine's thoughts were written plainly on his blistered countenance.

'Oh. Quite. Excellent…I suppose.'

'We dine late here, when the sun goes down. You will join me, I hope?'

'It will be an honour,' Peregrine said with a brave smile.

'If there's anything else you require, Akil will attend to your needs.' With a dismissive nod, Ramiz made for the doors, leaving Peregrine stranded on his knees on the floor of the vault-like chamber.

Back in the harem, Celia was unaware of the presence of her country's emissary. She lay on her stomach while Fatima rubbed scented oil into her skin. The girl's touch was gentle, but firm, easing the tension from her back and shoulders. Celia allowed her mind to drift, wholly accustomed now to the intimacy of her own nakedness, and to Fatima's capable fingers kneading her muscles. Strange how this could feel so pleasant, yet so impersonal. Strange how her body could react so differently to touch. Not just because of how it was done, but because of who was doing it. If Ramiz and not Fatima was delivering the massage, she would not be feeling so relaxed as to be upon the verge of falling asleep.

And of course as soon as his name popped into her mind, so too did his face, and his scent, and the feel of him, and she was wide awake. What was it about him that so obsessed her? Why Ramiz? Why now, at the age of four-and-twenty, was she being assaulted by these feelings? Such acute awareness of everything? Not just of Ramiz, but of colours and textures and taste. It was such a sensuous world, A'Qadiz, and Ramiz was at its epicentre, the very epitome of sensuality.

She was attracted to him—of that there was no doubt. She liked the way he looked. And the way he walked. And the way he talked. And the way he could be so arrogant one minute and so understanding the next. And the way he looked at her as if he saw something no one else saw. He made her feel beautiful. He said she *was* beautiful, and she believed him.

She was attracted to him, and he was attracted to her—a little. Probably because she was different. Infatuation, that was what it was. She was in thrall to him simply because he had been the first to kiss her. The first to touch her. The first to make her feel—*that!* The thing she couldn't put into words. Ecstasy. Carnal pleasure. *That!* She was beguiled.

But it felt like more than that. Ramiz made her laugh. They liked the same things. He knew things about her that she hadn't even known herself. And she knew him too, in a way others didn't. He'd let her see, even if briefly, how lonely, how isolated he felt.

Unreal. It was all unreal and meant nothing. Could never mean anything. She knew that. *She did.*

She was not an Arabian princess. In the eyes of his people her breeding meant nothing, for the blood which ran in her veins was English. No matter how many things she and Ramiz shared, no matter how similar their outlook on life might be, no matter even that they wanted the same things, she was not of his world and never could be.

Celia allowed herself to be helped from the divan into a warm bath. Sinking down into the fragrant water, she closed her eyes. Enchanted, beguiled, in thrall, under his spell. Whatever she was, it would not last.

In fact, according to Ramiz it was already over. Whatever it was. She wished it was not. She wished he would come to her again. Take her to the secret places he could conjure one more time. Continue with the fantasy for just a little longer, while she was here in his harem, locked away from the real world and the reality of the rather tedious life which awaited her as George's widow back in England.

She wished, though she mocked herself for doing so, that for one night she could live out her Arabian fantasy. Lying alone in the bath, she knew it was a dream. She thought of Ramiz—his kisses, his touch. She thought of him and the wanting came, and in the dark of the night she allowed herself to dream.

When Adila opened the harem door to one of the guards the next morning, Celia assumed Ramiz wished to see her, but the man who awaited her in a formal salon in the main body of the palace was a complete stranger. Dressed in a bottle-green cutaway coat, teamed with a rather alarming waistcoat embroidered with pink roses, he was about her own height, but considerably wider of girth. When he bowed, which he did with surprising grace given his apple shape, his fawn knit pantaloons stretched in a rather distressing manner, so that Celia dropped her own curtsy very rapidly, anxious to have him return to the upright in the hope of preventing what seemed to her an inevitable unravelling.

'Peregrine Finchley-Burke,' the young man said. 'At your service on behalf of His Majesty's government, Lady Celia.'

Realisation dawned. 'You have been sent to escort me home?'

Peregrine frowned. For a moment he could have sworn the lady was disappointed. 'No doubt you're eager to return to the bosom of your family,' he said cautiously.

'Indeed—though I have been very well treated here, I assure you. The palace is most luxurious.'

'Just so...just so.' Peregrine rubbed his hands together. 'Pleased to hear that, because the thing is I'm not actually here to take you back,' he said, flinching away instinctively as he delivered his ill tidings. To his relief, however, the tall, elegant woman in front of him did not break down into immediate hysterics, grab his hand, plea for mercy or even cry out in dismay. Instead her sleepy eyes widened and a smile trembled on her rather full mouth before she lowered her lids again and looked away into the distance, clasping her hands together.

'Not here to take me back?' Celia repeated faintly. 'You mean I am to stay here?'

'For the present. Thing is—dashed awkward all this. Forgot—should have said straight away have to pass on condolences. Terrible thing to happen. Consul General seemed to think very highly of your husband.'

'Thank you. You are very kind.' Celia rummaged for her handkerchief in her reticule and dabbed her eyes.

'And you, Lady Celia, it must have been a bit of an ordeal.'

'I was very fortunate that Sheikh al-Muhana was there,' Celia said with a watery smile. 'He saved my life, you know. Forgive my rudeness, Mr Finchley-Burke, please do sit down. Have you spoken with the Sheikh? How did he react when you informed him that I was to stay here?'

Peregrine waited for Celia to take a seat before he

eased himself onto a divan opposite her. Having spent the previous evening balancing his bulk on a cushion, feeling like a seal stranded by the tide on a rock which was too small, he was relieved to find that he was not expected to conduct this particular interview on the floor. 'The Prince left this morning—visiting some outlying tribes or something. Won't be back for quite a few days, apparently. Said to pass on his *adieu* and hoped you would be comfortable until his return.'

What was that supposed to mean? Celia thought indignantly.

'Seems a decent enough chap,' Peregrine continued with a touch of condescension. 'Bit on his high horse at first, but suppose that was to be expected.'

Celia raised her brows delicately. 'He is Prince of A'Qadiz, and it is likely that he holds the balance of power in at least four of the neighbouring six principalities. He is also extremely intelligent, and wealthy beyond anything you can imagine. You underestimate him at your peril.'

'Oh, I don't, I assure you—not now I've seen the place for myself.'

'Why exactly are you here, Mr Finchley-Burke, if you are not to take me back? It seems very strange that you have come all this way simply to pass on a message.' *And, now she thought about it, if Ramiz was as indifferent to her presence as he wished her to believe, why had he not insisted that she leave with this rotund young man?*

'Thing is, Lord Wincester sent an urgent despatch back to Blighty—to your father. Thought Lord

Armstrong should be the one to come and get you—best person to make the arrangements and what not, and also best person to complete the negotiations with the Prince, you know? Kill two birds with one stone, so to speak.'

'So I am to wait here until my father arrives?'

'Shouldn't be too long,' Peregrine said bracingly. 'Matter of a few weeks at most. Said yourself you're very comfortable here.' Peregrine opened his watch, wound it up, then closed it again. 'London time,' he said, à propos of nothing.

Celia raised her brows. 'Is there something else you wish to say to me, Mr Finchley-Burke?'

'Well.' Peregrine plucked a large kerchief from his pocket and mopped his brow. 'Well… You said it yourself, Lady Celia, this Sheikh al-Muhana could turn out to be quite an important man. A'Qadiz has the only decent port on the Red Sea. If we can do an exclusive deal with him and Mehmet Ali in Egypt it opens up a whole new trade route to India. Takes the journey time down from two years to only three months. Imagine that!' Peregrine eased forward confidentially. 'Thing is, don't want anyone else to steal our thunder, so to speak. Would be nice to know Sheikh al-Muhana isn't talking to the competition. That's where you come in.'

'Me? But Sheikh al-Muhana won't do business with a woman. And besides, I have not been briefed.'

'No, no. Of course not. Already said—your father coming out here provides a perfect opportunity. Obviously an opportunity borne out of tragedy, I hasten to add. Lord Armstrong is a skilled negotiator. If anyone can strike a deal with the Sheikh then he can.'

'So what exactly do you want *me* to do?'

'Ah. The Consul General said you'd understand because you're Lord Armstrong's daughter and you know what's what.'

Celia shook her head in bewilderment. 'Understand *what* is what?'

Peregrine swallowed nervously. 'He expects you to—to use your position to England's advantage.'

'My position!' Celia jumped up from her divan, forcing Peregrine to rise precipitately to his feet—an act which left him breathless and sweating. 'And precisely what position do you and the Consul General assume I occupy?'

'Well, I didn't mean to imply—' Peregrine broke off, blushing to the roots of his hair. 'I'm just supposed to tell you that your father would expect you to keep your eyes and ears open. You know—find out as much as you can of the situation here. Anything—no matter how trivial. We know so little of the man and his country, and you are in a unique position to…' he faltered under Celia's basilisk stare '…to—you know—glean what you can. Lord Wincester said to tell you that at least this way the whole damned mission won't have been a complete waste of time and money. Except,' Peregrine added contritely, 'wasn't supposed to say it in quite that way. Beg pardon.'

Celia dropped back onto the divan. The idea of trying to extract information by subterfuge from Ramiz was repugnant, and she was pretty certain it would also be completely unsuccessful. She doubted very much that he would give away anything he did not want her to know.

On the other hand, he *did* trust her. He had trusted her with the secret of Katra. He had confided in her some of his troubles with regard to his neighbours too—had seemed glad of the opportunity to talk, in fact, within the cloistered confines of the harem.

No, she should not even be giving the idea thought. Even to pass on the little she already knew would be seen by Ramiz as a betrayal.

But if she refused, what would everyone think of her? What harm would it do poor George's memory that his widow had no loyalty to her country? Bad enough that his widow was relieved she was no longer his wife—surely she owed him this much in reparation? And, after all, Ramiz might never know. By the time he found out, if he ever did, she would be safe back in Cairo. In England, even.

'And if I do not agree with Lord Wincester's proposal, what then?' Celia enquired.

Judging by the startled look on Peregrine's face, this was not a possibility which had been considered. 'Why on earth wouldn't you? England, you know—empire and all that,' he said vaguely. He scratched his head. 'I suppose you could come back with me, but I'm not sure Sheikh al-Muhana would be too keen on the idea of you leaving without his say-so. Then there's the guards. You'd be kicking your heels in Cairo until your father arrived, and there's the issue of the treaty—because if you left against the Sheikh's wishes I don't doubt he'd be insulted, and your father would have come all this way for nothing and—well, you see how it is.' Peregrine spread his hands in a fatalistic way.

If she left it would ruin things, in other words, Celia thought. And, actually, the one thing she was sure of was that she didn't want to leave. She wasn't ready to say goodbye to A'Qadiz—not yet. Nor to Ramiz.

If she stayed she could agree to what Mr Finchley-Burke asked of her without actually acting upon it. In fact, Celia thought brightly, there was no need to make any decision right now, except to agree in principle to try and do as she was bid.

'Very well. I will stay until Papa arrives,' Celia said.

Peregrine executed as dignified a bow as he could manage. 'Excellent. That is excellent news,' he said with a relieved smile. 'Have to say didn't at all fancy having to run the gauntlet of those guards.'

Celia held out her hand. 'Goodbye Mr Finchley-Burke. And good luck with your posting in India.'

'What shall I tell Lord Wincester?'

'You may tell him that he can rely on me to do the right thing,' Celia replied. Which she would—whatever that meant.

Ramiz sent no word to Celia for the duration of his absence, though she learned from Yasmina that he was in regular contact with Akil. She spent another enjoyable day at Yasmina's house, eager to discover for herself what 'ordinary' life in Balyrma was like. Surprisingly like life at home was what she found, with much of the day given over to caring for the children—readying the bigger ones for school, teaching the smaller ones their letters, managing their meals, sewing their clothes, wiping their tears and telling them stories.

'Before Ramiz came to power, only my oldest son went to school,' Yasmina told Celia as the two women sat companionably embroidering a section each of a large forest scene stretched on a frame, while the younger children took their afternoon nap in a separate salon. 'There were no schools for girls. Most of them could not even read, for their mothers couldn't read so there was no one to teach them.'

'Because of course none of the men would,' Celia said sarcastically.

'Of course not,' Yasmina agreed. 'It is the way of things here, Celia. Things are changing, some things are changing very fast, but we must not let the wind carry us to places we do not want to go. Ramiz knows that.'

'I'm sorry, I didn't mean to sound rude. It is just that things are so different.'

'Just because it is different doesn't make it wrong,' Yasmina reminded her gently. 'There are many ways to skin a rabbit.'

Celia smiled. 'We say that too, only it is a cat, I don't know why. Tell me about the schools. What did Ramiz do?'

'Well, he was very clever. He knew unless they trusted the teachers the women would not allow their girls to attend school, so he brought in a teacher to teach the teachers, not the girls. The men didn't like it at first, and even now there are only three teachers and about a hundred girls, so my older daughter is very lucky to have a place, but it is a start, and Akil said Ramiz has big plans. One day everyone in A'Qadiz will be able to read and write. Of course many of our people think this is madness—they say it will change the old order for ever, because people will lose sight of their place and no one will want to do real work, which is why it is all going so slowly. That and the fact that Ramiz is stretched as thin as the finest lace, which is why Akil says he should take a wife.' Yasmina snipped the vermilion thread she had been using and selected a length of burgundy. 'Talking of Ramiz, did you look at those charm books I gave you?' she asked with a slanting smile.

Celia nodded, concentrating on her stitching. The books were filled with extremely explicit pictures showing men and women engaging in an astonishing variety of acts. 'Some of the things,' she whispered, 'I didn't think were physically possible.'

Yasmina giggled. 'I don't think they are. You are not supposed to take them literally. They are meant to inspire, not to instruct. Have they?'

'Have they what?'

'Inspired you?' Yasmina asked with a sly look. 'Don't pretend you haven't thought about it.'

Celia blushed. 'It just seems wrong to plan such things. Shouldn't they just happen—you know, naturally?'

'Of course—at first,' Yasmina agreed. 'And it certainly does not do for a woman to lead the way. Men like to think they do that. But later, when you know each other well, there is much to be said for something different.'

'Oh, well, then, I don't need to worry about it,' Celia said with relief.

'You and Ramiz have not…?'

'No. And we will not. I can't think why we're talking about this, I was just curious.'

'Curiosity killed the goat.'

'We say that too. Only it's a cat again.'

'Be careful, Celia. Remember what I said.'

'I know. He is not meant for me. As if I could forget it,' Celia muttered. Everyone seemed to have an opinion on the true nature of her relationship with Ramiz except her. And Ramiz, of course, who didn't have an opinion because as far as he was concerned there was no relationship. With a sigh, Celia resumed her sewing.

Chapter Nine

The negotiations had stretched Ramiz's patience to the limit. Twice he had threatened to walk away, relenting only because of his determination not to let one of his own people destroy his hard work through ignorance and greed. An agreement had finally been reached and, following the twelve-hour feast ordered by the tribe's elders to celebrate their concord, Ramiz returned to Balyrma exhausted but well satisfied.

It had been a long few days in more than one way. He had found himself missing Celia. It was always a tedious business dealing with the tribes. They favoured a convoluted, highly formal bargaining process with which he was all too familiar, but he hadn't realised how alone it made him feel until now. It was not just the fact that he was one against many; it was also that, being the Prince, he had to appear inviolable and imperious. It was expected of him. Nothing must touch him, which meant there was no one to take his part except himself.

At night, alone in his tent in the middle of the desert, he'd found himself thinking of Celia. The scent of her, the feel of her petal-soft skin against his own. The taste of her mouth, succulent and honey-sweet. He'd wondered what she was doing. He'd wondered if she thought of him. He had cursed himself for wondering, for wasting precious time on such pointless and frustrating thoughts, though still he had indulged them. He had missed her.

He had not intended to seek her out immediately, but upon his return to the palace on the evening of his sixth day away, dusty and tense from the long ride back, that was what he did—without even stopping to change. She was sitting in the courtyard on a cushion, leaning against the fountain. She had been staring up at the stars framed by the square of the top floor of the building, her head thrown back, her long hair rippling loose down her back. When the door opened she turned, startled. Upon seeing him standing there a hand went to her breast.

For a few seconds she stared at him wordlessly. Her skin was ghostly pale in the twilight, her eyes glittering dark. As she got fluidly to her feet, he saw that she was dressed in clothes made from the materials they had bought at the market. Only a week ago, yet it seemed like months. She wore a long caftan slit to the thigh in mint-green silk. The sleeves and hem were weighted down with silver *passementerie* braiding. Loose *sarwal* pantaloons of a darker green, made of some gauzy material transparent enough for him to see the shape of her legs beneath, fluttered out around her. She was barefooted. She seemed to float rather than walk. Her hair rippled like silk ruffled by a breeze. She looked so different. Exotic. An English rose in an Eastern garden.

Ramiz stood rooted to the spot. He hadn't expected this. Hadn't anticipated the unsettling effect seeing her like this would have on him.

'You're back,' she said, stopping uncertainly before him.

'Only just now. I came to see how you were, since I did not have a chance to see you after the visit from your countryman. I half expected to hear from Akil that you had asked to return to Cairo with Mr Finchley-Burke.'

'Since my father has been summoned to complete the negotiations which brought my husband here in the first place, I thought it best to wait. Would you have allowed me to leave if I had asked it?'

Ramiz raised a brow. 'Is that what you would have preferred?'

Celia laughed. 'I should have known better than to expect a straight answer from such an accomplished statesman as yourself.'

'Or from such an accomplished diplomat's daughter as yourself,' Ramiz rejoined with a smile.

'Did your trip go well? You were away longer than you anticipated.'

Ramiz shrugged. 'It's done.'

'At a cost, I take it?'

Ramiz nodded. 'A cost worth paying, though.'

'Have you eaten?'

'I'm not hungry.'

He looked weary. There were little grooves of tiredness at the corners of his mouth. A frown furrowed his brow. Celia's heart contracted. Now he was back, now her heart was beating out its excitement at his presence, she could admit to herself how much she had missed him. Without thinking she reached out to smooth away the lines on his forehead. His skin was warm, gritty with sand under his headdress.

'You're all dusty,' she said inanely, for suddenly she could think of nothing to say, so overwhelmed was she by his presence.

'I should go and change.'

'Stay a while,' Celia said impulsively. 'Talk to me. I've—it's been lonely here without you.'

'You've missed me?'

There was the tiniest trace of a smile at the corner of his mouth. Celia managed a shrug. 'What do you think of my clothes?' she asked, executing a little twirl.

The soft material clung lovingly to her slender frame, hugging the curve of her breasts, the slope of her bottom. He saw the nakedness of her feet on the tiles, the soft flutter of her hair drifting out behind her as she twirled, heard the swish of her caftan as it floated out from her body then settled back down to caress her thighs. The scent of amber and musk drifted towards him, mingling with the warmer, fragrant smell that was Celia, and the whole combination went intoxicatingly to his head. Ramiz reached out to catch a long tress of hair, wrapping it like a bond of copper silk around his hand, pulling her towards him.

Under the caftan she wore only a wisp of silk. She might as well be naked. They were as close as they could be without touching. Heat rose between them. *Could he feel it too?* There was a smudge of dust on his right cheek. His left hand was wrapped in her hair, tugging her head back. The need to touch him was unbearable. Could he see her heart beating? Could he hear how shallow and fast was her breathing? Why was he here? Did she care as long as he was?

'Did you miss me?' Ramiz asked again.

'Yes,' Celia whispered, for it was the truth. She had missed him enormously. She had spent hours and hours wrestling with her conscience over the Consul General's proposal, concluding time and again only that she must do nothing she would later regret, nothing which would compromise her integrity, nothing she could not undo. Which meant avoiding exactly the sort of situation she was now confronting.

But it was all very well to think such thoughts and to hold such high-minded opinions when alone. In Ramiz's disconcerting presence she had no such control. Her mind—that disciplined, logical part of her which had ruled her life until now—was in real danger of surrendering control to her body. And her body was not slow to take advantage, so that without meaning to, without realising she was doing it, Celia closed the tiny gap between them and tilted her head up and put her arms around him. And that was it. She kissed him. She had to. There was nothing, nothing at all she could do about it, for if she did not kiss him she was afraid she would stop breathing.

And when his lips met hers she stopped breathing anyway, just for a moment, so literally breathtaking was the feel of his mouth and the scent of his skin and the complex magic of his just being there. She murmured his name, she pressed herself into the hard lines of his body, and he groaned. And then he kissed her back—a surprisingly gentle kiss, feathering its way along the line of her lower lip, licking into the corners, then the softness inside. His free hand was stroking the nape of her neck, the hollow of her collarbone, the column of her throat.

Then it was over. Ramiz stepped back. He unwound her hair from his hand. He rubbed his forehead, pushing back his headdress so that it fell to the floor. 'I must go and change,' he said reluctantly. 'I must see Akil.'

'Don't go. Not yet. Stay and talk to me. Please.' Celia held out her hand. His hair was rumpled. Without the frame of his *gutra* his face looked younger, almost vulnerable. Her own needs vanished, superseded by the desire to erase Ramiz's lines of fatigue, to ease the tension she could see in his shoulders, just to have him to herself for a little while.

He hesitated, then allowed her to lead him into one of the salons. She made him tea on the little spirit stove there, taking care with the ritual of measuring the leaves from the enamelled chest into the silver samovar, serving it just as he liked it, with no sugar but lemon and mint. And as Celia busied herself with the tea she talked—of her visit to Yasmina, of the books she had read, of her letter to Cassie. Ramiz listened at first with detachment, simply enjoying the graceful way she went about the small domestic task, the sound of her voice and her gentle wit, and then he was smiling over her description of the play Yasmina's children had put on for her, and making her laugh with his description of the English emissary's falling asleep on the cushions over dinner, relaxed enough to tell her about his trip into the desert.

As before, she listened with understanding—sympathetic without being fawning, contributing her own opinions without being asked, contradicting him without offending. Tea was taken, the lamps were lit, and still they sat on, talking and laughing in unperceived intimacy until Ramiz yawned and stretched and said he should go. They both realised that was the last thing they wanted.

'Five nights on a carpet in someone else's tent,' he said, rolling his shoulders. 'I'd forgotten how uncomfortable it can be.'

'Would you like me to give you a massage?'

Ramiz looked as startled as she herself was, for she hadn't meant to offer—only she hadn't wanted him to go, and she wanted to do something that would preserve this unaccustomed intimacy. 'Do you know how?' he asked.

Celia nodded. 'Fatima has shown me what to do, though I've not really had a chance to practise. I find it helps me sleep. Perhaps it would help you too?'

He doubted Celia's touch would make him sleepy. He knew it was one of the things which breached the boundaries he'd told himself to establish, but then so too was talking to her alone like this. And he *was* tired. And sore. And in no mood for anything other than sleep. Not really.

Ramiz got to his feet. 'Where?' he asked, and when

she indicated they use the large circular divan on which she slept he allowed himself to be led into that salon, watched as she spread a fresh silk sheet over the velvet cover while he pulled off his robe, wrapping his lower half in a linen towel, lying down on his stomach and closing his eyes. A swish of material told him Celia had discarded her caftan. He could smell the orange and amber in the oil as she rubbed it onto her hands. When she leaned over him a long strand of her hair brushed his cheek. She tutted and swept it back. Then she leaned over him again. He could feel the heat emanating from her skin, the feathering of her breath on his. Then he surrendered to the supple kneading of her fingers.

She started at his shoulders, where the tension knotted his muscles together like rope. Carefully at first, her touch experimental, she leaned over, trying to keep the contact to her hands, though the temptation to brush her breasts against him, to prostrate herself on top of him, skin to skin, was strong. His eyes were closed tight. His lashes, sooty and soft, fanned onto his cheeks. His hair grew in a shape like a question mark on the back of his head, tapering down like an arrow to his nape. The veins on his neck stood out, so bunched tight were his shoulders. Celia pressed into them with her spread fingers as Fatima had shown her, rolling her thumbs up his spine, circling back down and round again in a soothing motion, pressing harder as she felt Ramiz relax, kneading him with her palms, concentrating on levelling out the twisting stress, smoothing and kneading, pressing and soothing in a smooth rhythm so that she forgot everything except the feel of her hands on his body.

Breathing a little harder with the effort, she leaned a little closer, and a little closer yet, to get just the right angle—until she was kneeling on the divan beside him, then kneeling between his legs as she worked her way down his back, then over him, so that her breasts brushed his heated skin, slick with the delicately scented oil, and her nipples budded through the thin layer of silk which contained them. Below her, Ramiz kept his eyes tight shut. She could feel the steady rise and fall of his chest. Sleeping? The scent of him, a subtle something, male and other, rose like a whisper of smoke from his skin.

She worked her way down to the base of his spine, pulling away the towel which covered him, waiting for a sign that she should stop which did not come. His buttocks were firm and slightly rounded, his flanks were firm too, with a feathery smattering of black hair, surprisingly soft. The softer flesh at the inside of his thighs was hot. Tender from the time spent in the saddle. Heat. It was not just coming from Ramiz.

A trickle of sweat shivered down between Celia's breasts. Wiping it away, she trailed oil over her own skin. She picked up the bottle to trickle more oil onto her hands. A drop escaped onto Ramiz's shoulders. She leaned over to rub it in. Her breasts pressed into his back, her stomach onto his buttocks. Skin slick with oil. A sensual sliding. She lay motionless, relishing the melding of skin on skin, of heat on heat. Below her, Ramiz lay still as a statue.

She had convinced herself he was asleep. Then, as she

sat up, he turned underneath her, so quickly she would have fallen had he not grasped her by the arms, rolled her with him, so that somehow she was under him and he was on top of her, and he did not look at all as if he had been asleep.

His eyes blazed like molten bronze sparked with gold. A slash of colour highlighted his cheekbones. His chest rose and fell, rose and fell almost as rapidly as her own. She could feel the pounding of his heart. Then he kissed her, wildly and passionately, yanking away the strip of silk which covered her breasts. And then he devoured them.

His mouth was on her nipples, hot on their aching hardness. His hands moulded her breasts, shaping them and stroking them, and his mouth was sucking and nipping, making her writhe and moan, strange little gasping pleas she didn't recognise as she bucked under him. Her own hands were grasping and pulling at him. The hardness of his erection was pressing solid and insistent against her thigh. In minutes, seconds, it would be too late. She knew that absolutely—as she knew absolutely that she would not stop him. She wanted this with an urgency she had not dreamed possible. Something as fundamental as the stars urged her on, made her push against him, arch into him, pluck at him as if she would spread him over her, all the time gasping and moaning his name. His mouth on her nipples forged a burning path of sensation, stirred up a cauldron of heat in her belly, and their oiled skin slid and glided and clung.

Her gauzy pantaloons were pleated into a sash at her waist. Ramiz pulled it open. She struggled free of their constraints with neither shame nor modesty, wanting only to feel him against her, beside her, inside her. They lay facing each other, kissing. Mouths fervent with need, eyes burning with desire, fingers seeking out secret creases, stroking into them, until she felt his hand between her legs, cupping her, stroking her, and the hot surge of wet pulsing need made her clench and clench again as he touched her exactly where she needed him to touch her. No teasing this time, no drawing out, just there, and there, and *there*, reading her wants as she moaned and dug her fingers into his shoulders, and jangled like a puppet on strings which Ramiz pulled, until she felt that plundering, plunging sensation build. She jolted as her climax took over, barely noticing that he had rolled her onto her back, that he was between her legs, pushing them up, angling himself over her until he thrust hard and powerfully into her and she screamed out—not with pleasure but with pain.

Ramiz froze. The expression on his face was ludicrous in its intensity. Sheer disbelief, swiftly followed by horror. As the sharpness of the pain receded, and she realised he was going to pull away, Celia clutched at him. 'No.'

But she could not hold him. He cursed long and viciously in his own language, pushing her hands away and pulling himself from her in one move. He grabbed his robe from the floor and pulled it over his head. There was no mistaking the anger which froze his face into rigid lines. His eyes were cold too, glinting chips of amber. Celia sat up, clutching the sheet around her. Bright beads of blood showed crimson on its pristine white, like berries in snow. Hastily she twisted the sheet, but Ramiz had already seen them. He wrenched it from her grasp, forcing her to scrabble for her caftan to cover her nakedness.

'A sheet any bride would be proud of,' Ramiz said through gritted teeth, holding it up so that the traitorous blood spots could not be avoided. 'But you are not a bride. Why in the name of all the gods did you not tell me? Do you think I would have? Do you think I would have let you—allowed myself—? You don't know what you have done.'

'What I have done?' Celia stood up, glaring at him.

'What *I* have done, then. Something your husband evidently did not!' Ramiz ran his hand through his hair. 'Why didn't you tell me?'

'You didn't ask!' But even as she threw the words at him she knew how unfair they were. The reality of the situation came crashing down like a sudden cloudburst. *What had she done?* 'George didn't want—we didn't—he said it would be easier if we waited until we knew each other better,' she said quietly. 'But we never did.'

'Evidently,' Ramiz said bitterly.

'No.' Celia blinked, determined not to allow the tears which burned her eyes to fall. 'I doubt we ever would have, to be honest. I'm sorry. I'm sorry I didn't tell you. I didn't mean this to happen. I should have stopped you. I'm sorry.'

She brushed the back of her hand across her eyes. The defiant little gesture touched him as tears would not have. 'Celia, did I hurt you?'

She shook her head.

'Are you sure?'

She managed a weak smile. 'Just a little.'

'Next time it won't be so—' Ramiz stopped. There would never be a next time for them. There should not have been a first. He should be thanking the fates that he had managed to stop—that shock had allowed him to stop. Only he didn't feel like thanking the fates. Horrified by his own base desires, by the persistence of his erection, which nudged insistently against his belly, he realized that what he wanted to do was to finish what they had started. To sheath himself in the luscious delight of her, to thrust deeper and deeper, until he spent himself inside her, to claim her as his. As his own. As her first.

No! He could not. He would not. Not even if it meant another would take what rightfully should be his.

No! No! No! He would not think of Celia with another. Looking at her trying so hard not to cry, the flush of passion fading from her cheeks, her mouth bruised with his kisses, the delicate creamy white of her breast showing the imprint of his touch, Ramiz fought the urge to take her in his arms and soothe away the hurt he had caused. The stain on his honour, the tangible evidence of that stain on the sheet he gripped, held him back. 'What have I done?'

'It wasn't just you. It was my fault as much as yours,' Celia said resolutely.

'I have deflowered you. The dishonour!'

'Ramiz, as you have already pointed out, I was married. In the eyes of the world I was already deflowered. There is no dishonour because no one will know.'

'*I* will know!'

'Well, I'm sure you'll learn to live with it.'

'Is that all you can say?'

She bit her lip. What she wanted was to know how it felt to really make love. How it felt to have him move inside her. What she wanted was to complete and to be completed—because that, she realised, was what it was really about. Two people as one. That was what she wanted to say, but she couldn't, because for Ramiz it had clearly been nothing more than the easing of tension. The natural conclusion to her massage.

'I think you should go now,' she said instead, wresting the horrible evidence of her virginity from his hands. 'I think we should agree to forget all about this.'

'Forget?'

'Yes. It's for the best.'

'Is this your famous British stiff upper lip? It doesn't suit you.'

'It's what we British call being practical. You're tired. Exhausted, in fact. Go to bed.'

'But you...'

'I will be fine.'

She was right, but it felt wrong. He didn't want to leave her—which was exactly the reason why he should. Nothing about this was right. Staying would only heap more wrong on wrong.

He didn't like the way she was so determined to take her share of the blame. And he definitely didn't like it that it was she and not he who insisted he go. It was all the wrong way round. Where was the clinging vine? Why must she be so stoically independent? He didn't like it, but there wasn't a thing he could do about it either.

Ramiz shrugged. 'Goodnight,' he said coldly. Then he left without another word.

Alone, Celia picked up his headdress from where he had dropped it carelessly on the floor. The square of white silk smelled of him. She clutched it to her chest. Then she curled up on the divan and gave way to racking sobs and blinding tears.

Peregrine Finchley-Burke's confidence in the efficiency of the Royal Navy was not displaced. Lord Wincester's despatch reached England less than three weeks after it had been written. The special courier arrived mud-spattered, his horse's flanks speckled with foam, at the country estate of Lord Henry Armstrong just as its owner was preparing for a long overdue meeting with his bailiff. The contents of the missive, perused in the seclusion of his study, were shocking enough to require sustenance in the form of brandy, despite the early hour. Throwing back the large snifter, Lord Henry read the letter for a third time. A frown marred his normally serene countenance, for the consequences of the matter were potentially far-reaching. A delicate situation. Very delicate indeed, he thought, scratching his bald pate. It was a good thing his sister Sophia was here. He could trust her to manage the girls. But what to do about it all was another matter.

'Damn the man,' Lord Henry muttered, staring at Lord Wincester's signature. 'Bloody fool. Only reason he's out there is because of that fracas in Lisbon. He thought it was all hushed up, but *I* know the real story.' He poured himself a second snifter. 'Damn the man,' he said again, more loudly this time. 'And damn George Cleveden too! You'd have thought he'd have more wit than to get himself killed in such a manner.' Lord Henry leaned over to ruffle the fur of his favourite pointer bitch, sitting obediently at his feet. 'Bloody stupid thing to do, if you ask me.' The dog whined. 'You're quite right. Time they were all told,' Lord Henry said, bestowing another affectionate pat upon the animal before he got to his feet and left the library in search of his family.

He entered the blue drawing room to find the collective eyes of his four daughters and sister Sophia upon him. Not for the first time he wondered at his own inability to father a son. Girls were all very well, but he couldn't help thinking five girls excessive. And expensive. 'Well, well, here you all are,' he said, with an air of false bonhomie which he mistakenly imagined would reassure them.

Cassandra, the beauty of the family, had been rather too aptly named, for she had a propensity for prophesying tragedy. She clutched dramatically at her father's coat sleeve, her lovely eyes, the colour of cornflowers, already drowning in tears. 'Papa! It is Celia, isn't it? She is—oh, Papa—tell me she is not—'

'Celia is absolutely fine,' Lord Henry said, detaching her fingers from his coat sleeve. 'It is George, I'm afraid. Dead.'

Cassandra collapsed back into a convenient chair, clutching her breast, her countenance touchingly pale. Caroline gave a little gasp of horror. Cordelia and

Cressida simply stared with mouths wide open at their father. It was left to Lady Sophia to seek clarification. 'May one ask what happened to result in such an unfortunate outcome?' she asked, rummaging in her reticule for the vial of *sal volatile* she kept there for such occasions.

'He was murdered,' Lord Henry replied flatly.

This shocking news gave even the normally redoubtable Lady Sophia pause. Casting a baleful look at the two youngest of her nieces, who had squealed in a most unrefined manner, she thrust the *sal volatile* under Cassie's nose.

'May I?' asked Sophia, holding her hand out imperiously for the despatch which Lord Henry was only too happy to hand over. She read it with close attention, her eyebrows rising fractionally as she digested the content. 'You may leave this to me, Henry,' she said to her brother.

Only too happy to obey, Lord Henry left the room.

'I am sorry to inform you that George has indeed been murdered,' Lady Sophia informed her nieces. 'Brigands. It seems he and Celia were on their way to a place called A'Qadiz, which is somewhere in Arabia, on a special assignment which entailed a journey across the desert. That is where poor George met his fate. He died bravely, serving his country,' she said with an air of assurance and a complete disregard for the truth. 'That fact will, I do most sincerely trust, mitigate the rather vulgar manner in which he was slain.'

'And Celia?' Faced with a genuine crisis, Cassie had abandoned her vapours and, though prettily pale, was composed enough to join her sisters on the sofa, putting a comforting arm around the two youngest. 'What does the despatch say of Celia? I take it she is now under the care of the Consul General? Or perhaps she is already on her way home?' she said hopefully.

'Hmm.' Lady Sophia inspected the lace of her sleeve.

'Aunt?'

'Hmm,' Lady Sophia said again. 'Celia is still in A'Qadiz, I am afraid.'

'What? In the desert?'

'She is apparently resident in the royal palace there. As a guest of a Sheikh al-Muhana. Prince al-Muhana, I should say.'

This information was met with stunned silence. Lady Sophia twitched at her lace.

'Cassie, is Celia being held prisoner?' Cressida's chin wobbled.

'Cassie, will she be locked away and have to tell the Sheikh a story every night to stop her getting her head cut off?' Cordelia, aged twelve, asked. Too late she remembered that Aunt Sophia had forbidden them to read *that* book. Cordelia blushed. Cressida pinched her. Caroline drew her a look.

The ensuing reprimand distracted Cassie temporarily from the question nagging away at her. 'Why has Celia been left alone with Sheikh al-Muhana?' she asked, when order had finally been restored.

'A very pertinent question,' Lady Sophia answered dryly.

'A very pertinent question indeed,' Lord Henry said

as he re-entered the room. 'Wincester is a buffoon and a liability, which is why I'm going out there personally to sort this mess out. Don't worry about your sister's safety in the meantime. No foreign power would dare harm the daughter of a senior British diplomat.'

'Papa, Celia has witnessed the murder of her husband. She has been kidnapped by a man who for all we know could have her under lock and key in his harem,' Cassie said, her voice rising as the full horror of her sister's plight began to sink in.

'Now, now,' Lord Henry said, eyeing his daughter warily, 'no point in letting our imagination run away with us. Celia is a sensible gal, and I'm sure the Prince is an honourable man. I'm sure there's no need to worry on that score.'

'No need to…' Cassie stared at her father in disbelief. 'I take it you *are* going to Egypt at once?'

'Well, of course I am.'

'Then I am coming with you,' Cassie said resolutely.

'Don't be ridiculous, girl.'

'I am coming with you, Father, and nothing you can say will dissuade me. Celia is my beloved sister. Heaven knows what she has gone through—is going through even now,' Cassie said with a shudder. 'She will need me to support her. I am coming with you and that's that.'

'Sophia, can't you talk some sense into the girl? The desert is no place for a young lady of breeding.'

'You might have thought of that before you despatched your other daughter, then,' Lady Sophia said witheringly. 'Cassandra is quite right. Celia will need her sister. And what's more she will need her aunt too. I am also coming with you.'

'Eh?'

'You heard, Henry,' Lady Sophia said, fixing her younger brother with one of her glacial glares. 'Now, since time is of the essence, I will go immediately to attend to my packing. You will summon Bella Frobisher to look after the girls. Since it is your intention that the woman is to be their new stepmother, she might as well make a start in getting to know them. Come, Cassandra. We will leave in an hour, Henry.'

Lord Henry Armstrong was renowned as a tough and unyielding negotiator, who had faced down the most cunning and powerful courtiers in all of Europe, but he was no match for his sister and he knew it. 'As you wish, Sophia,' he said resignedly, before leaving to go in search of the brandy bottle for the second time that morning.

Chapter Ten

Ramiz wandered alone in the gardens of the royal palace. The relatively compact area was divided by a series of covered walkways and winding paths, linked with fountains and small pavilions to give it a sense of space. Watered by an ingenious system of sprinklers fed by underground pipes, it combined the traditional plants of the East, such as fig, oleander and jasmine, with a number of species brought back by Ramiz from his travels. Amongst these were several roses. One of his favourites, the lightly scented pink rose which climbed round the gilded trellis by the fountain where he sat now, had been given to him by the Empress Josephine herself, from her treasured garden at Malmaison. The petals appeared almost white when furled, the pink revealing itself like a blush only when the flowers opened fully.

They made him think of Celia. Three nights had passed since his last visit to the harem, and the only conclusion he had reached was that it was best to keep away from her. He had taken something precious, and there was nothing he could do to recompense her for the loss. What he had done was wrong, without a doubt, and Ramiz was unused to being in the wrong. He had never before been in a position where he could not put a wrong right, and he was wholly unused to the position in which he now found himself—torn between the desire to make amends and the equally strong desire to make proper love to Celia.

That was the most shocking thing of all. He had done wrong, commited a sin of honour, but he was struggling to regret it.

The fact that Celia herself refused to accept his crime didn't help. Why had she not stopped him? Why had she not confessed? Why was she determined to brush it off as something trivial? Didn't it matter to her? What did she want of him? Could it be that she was a pawn in some diplomatic game, ready to cry ravishment in order to gain advantage for her country? But she had already insisted she would *not* cry ravishment, and one of the few things he was certain of was that she did not lie.

So why? The last time he'd asked her, after the visit to Katra, she had blamed it on the harem. *Unreal*, she'd said. As in a fantasy? From the start she'd shown a fascination with the harem, or with her perception of the harem drawn from that set of fairytales *One Thousand and One Nights.* Like her compatriots on the Grand Tour, perhaps she was indulging in a fantasy safe from the prying eyes of her peers. It made sense. It made a lot of sense.

The only way to eliminate temptation is to yield to it. An old saying of his brother's. As the eldest son and his father's heir, Asad had been much indulged. Asad had preferred action to words. 'Women talk, men act,' he'd used to say. 'The sword is the instrument of the Prince. To his subjects falls the task of writing down his words.' Too quick to the flame, their father had always said of Asad, but he'd said it in such a way as to make his pride in his eldest son clear.

If truth be told Ramiz and Asad had rarely seen eye to eye. If truth be told, Ramiz thought wryly, nor had he and his father, but that didn't stop him missing them both. Nearly two years now since Asad was killed, and in that time Ramiz's life had been turned upside down. While he had always felt strongly about what he would do differently were he to become ruler of A'Qadiz, he had never seriously considered it happening. Putting his long-considered policies into action had gone some way to help him through the loss of his last remaining close relative, for his mother had died when Ramiz was a teenager, but it had also prevented him from thinking too much about the loss itself. He missed Asad. Why not admit it? He was lonely. He was a rich prince, with thousands of loyal subjects, and he had everything except someone to confide in.

He hadn't noticed until Celia came along. He'd been too immersed in state policy and state negotiations and state legislation. No time to think about anything other than A'Qadiz. No time to think that maybe he needed something for himself. Someone for himself. Perhaps Akil was right. What he needed was a wife.

But the idea of marrying one of the princesses from Akil's list was even less appealing than ever. Such a wife would be taken for the sake of A'Qadiz. Such a wife would not give him anything other than more responsibility, one more thing to worry about. Such a wife would not be like Celia—would not *be* Celia.

Ramiz growled with exasperation. A whole hour wasted thinking, and he was right back where he started. *The only way to eliminate temptation is to yield to it.* One thing Asad had always been good at was getting to the nub of a problem. Lady Celia, with her copper hair and her creamy skin and her forthright opinions, was in danger of becoming an obsession. If she did not think herself dishonoured, why should he worry about it? Why not indulge her in her Arabian fantasy and at the same time rid himself of his unwelcome obsession?

The problem was he didn't like being thought of as *unreal*. He didn't like the idea of her thinking of him only within the confines of his harem. If he was to be her first lover, he wanted her memory of him to be very real and lasting.

Ramiz looked up at the sky, where the sun was just coming into view on its slow arc over the northern wall of the garden. A slow smile crept over his face. He would bring her into the light of day, away from the shady confines of the harem. Seeing her more clearly would surely speed the cure along.

'You wanted to see me?'

Celia stood before Ramiz, his desk serving as a barrier between them. She wore a caftan of cerulean blue, with slashed sleeves pulled tight at the wrist, over a pair of pleated *sarwal* pantaloons the colour of the night sky. It was the traditional costume of a woman at home, but with her mass of copper hair uncovered and dressed in its usual fashion, piled in a knot on top of her head with wispy strands curling over her cheeks, the simple outfit seemed exotic. A lady dressed in the garb of an odalisque. Though she was draped with propriety from head to foot, the fluttery fabrics drew attention to the softness of her body underneath. He caught a glimpse of her forearm through the slashed sleeves of her tunic. Creamy skin. Ramiz dragged his eyes away. It was only her arm! But already he could feel himself hardening.

'Sit down,' he said, annoyed to find that his voice sounded harsh, while Celia looked composed as she took the chair opposite. 'You are well?' he asked.

'Certainly I am well cared for,' she said carefully.

'What does that mean?'

She raised an eyebrow at the tone of his voice. 'Is there something wrong, Ramiz?'

'That is what I have just asked you.'

Celia clasped her hands in her lap. 'I told you, I am well. In fact I'm so well looked after that I'm in danger of forgetting how to do anything for myself. Adila and Fatima anticipate my every need.'

'You mean to tell me you are bored?'

'I was trying to be tactful about it, but yes. I am not used to having nothing to do save embroider and read.'

'But you have been visiting Yasmina?'

'Yes, where I embroider and play with the children—which is lovely, but…' Celia bit her lip. The last few days, without so much as a glimpse of Ramiz, had given her ample opportunity to try and put her feelings for him into perspective, but it was almost impossible to do that within the confines of the harem, redolent as it was with sensuous overtones, not to mention the scalding memory of their previous fevered couplings. There, she was in thrall to him, obsessed by the feelings he could arouse in her. If only she could see him in more mundane surroundings—or what passed for mundane surroundings, given he was a prince. Then she would be rid of this continuous need to be with him, able to acknowledge that she was lonely, and she was bored, and that her body, having discovered something new and enjoyable, was quite naturally wanting to experience it again. That was all it was. Absolutely nothing else!

'I've been thinking,' Ramiz said, interrupting her musing. 'It would be a good idea for you to see more of A'Qadiz, to learn more of the problems we face—I face—in trying to bring our country into the modern world of the nineteenth century.'

Celia stared at him in astonishment. *Was he a mind-reader?* 'But what about—? You said because I am a woman that…'

Ramiz shrugged. 'If I choose to bend a few traditions, that is up to me. You said so yourself, did you not?'

He smiled. Perfect white teeth. Eyes cold glinting metal. Had he guessed what Lord Wincester had asked her to do? Her stomach clenched at the very idea. But if he knew he would surely not be offering her such an opportunity to observe. Was he testing her? She knew with sudden blinding clarity that it was a test she would not fail. She could not possibly betray this man who had saved her life, made her feel alive for the first time in her life and who clearly trusted her. 'I would love to see more of A'Qadiz,' Celia said excitedly. 'What did you have in mind?'

'A significant number of my people belong to Bedouin tribes. They live in the desert, moving from place to place with their livestock according to the season and their own inclinations. We have a tradition here of allowing them to petition the crown for alms. Three times a year they can come to me and ask for assistance.'

'You give them money?'

'Sometimes. Although more often it is food or animals. Money doesn't mean much to the Bedouins. It's not just that, however. I act as arbitrator in their disputes between families and between tribes. It is an opportunity for me, too, to see how things really are and to assess where I can best help them. You must not be thinking these are simply poor nomads. Some of them are very powerful men. It would not do to offend them.'

'So you go to them rather than ask them to come to you?'

'Exactly. We will be away about a week or so. You will come?'

'I would love to.'

'Good. You may go now. I will see you first thing tomorrow morning. We will start before dawn.'

The caravan which snaked out behind them put the one with which Celia had arrived in Balyrma firmly into the shade. She counted at least twenty guards on camels, and it looked like double that number of servants with mules. Akil took on the role as leader of the train. To Celia's surprise Ramiz insisted she ride ahead with him, mounted on a camel as snowy white as his own, its saddle draped with a bejewelled cloth of crimson damask, silver bells jangling on its reins, which were adorned with golden tassels. Covered by an *abeyah* of gold silk—a long robe with side slits to make riding astride easier—and with her hair and face protected from the sun and prying eyes by a headdress of the same colour, Celia felt like an Arabian princess.

She said so to Ramiz, who laughed and said no one looking at her could ever mistake her for what she was: an English rose disguised as a desert flower. He was in a strange mood. She would almost call it relaxed. They would dispense with the formalities and deference while they were in the desert, he told her. She was to remain by his side at all times. She was to address him as Ramiz. She was free to ask whatever she wished to know. He valued her opinion.

At first she thought he was teasing her, but as they rode through the day she discovered he meant it—telling her unprompted all about the meetings to come, the ritual and the forms, even sketching out the main personalities for her. He was altogether charming, showing a side of himself she had not seen before. As the miles of the desert stretched out behind them he became almost carefree. The tension in his shoulders eased. The lines around his eyes relaxed. The formidable air departed, leaving a stunningly attractive man who was frankly beguiling.

And Celia *was* completely beguiled. Perhaps even mesmerised, for she noticed no one but Ramiz. The caravan might as well not have existed. As far as she was concerned they were alone in the desert, riding forever onwards across the sands under the blazing sun, to a destination which would remain elusive, for to arrive would be to break the spell, and she didn't want that to happen.

But when they arrived at the oasis where they would rest for the night the magical atmosphere continued. Instructing Akil to see to things, Ramiz led Celia away from the braying mules and bleating camels and muttering guards to a secluded part of the oasis, where a small pool lapped around a group of palms. The stars above them were like saucers of beaten silver.

'It's a full moon,' Celia said, sitting down by the edge of the pool and removing her sandals to trail her bare feet in the water.

'Qamar,' Ramiz told her, sitting beside her. 'A time for wishes to be granted.'

His thigh was pressing against hers. Her shoulder brushed the top of his arm. Celia circled her ankles in the cool of the water. 'What would you wish for, Ramiz?'

'A starry night. A tent to cover me. A beautiful woman to share it with.'

She tried to laugh, but it sounded more like a choke. 'Well, you've got the first two, at least.'

'No, I have it all.' Ramiz cupped the back of her head, gently turning her towards him. 'See—above us the starry sky. Over there the tent. Beside me a beautiful woman. And I intend you to share it with me, Celia. All of it.'

Before she could ask him what he meant, he kissed her. His kiss made his intentions clear, and as she kissed him back she signified her agreement with no thought of refusal. It was why she was here. In his desert. In his arms. It was why he had brought her, and it was why she had come. It was what she wanted more than anything. She saw that now with a brilliance and clarity to match the very moon suspended above their entwined bodies.

Celia put her arms around Ramiz. She nestled into the familiar stirring scent of him. She parted her lips at his bidding, and kissed him in such a way as he could be under no misapprehensions. She would share the night with him. All of it.

They kissed for long, languorous seconds, their arms entwined, their tongues tangling, their toes touching in the cool of the water. Then Ramiz broke away and got to his feet, pulling her with him. 'You understand?' he said. 'There is no going back from this moment.'

Celia nodded.

'It is what you want?'

'Yes.'

'Though ultimately it can mean nothing?'

She knew that! Why did he have to say it? But she knew that too. Ramiz was a man who liked the rules of any pact clear cut and neatly drawn. 'Yes,' she said again. 'I understand, I assure you.'

He nodded. For one ridiculous moment she thought

he would shake her hand, so formal had he become in that moment, but then she realised he was almost as tense as she was. She followed him back to the camp, where a small village of tents had appeared and fires were burning. The smell of goat and rabbit roasting should have been appetising, but though she was hungry it was not for food.

Two larger tents sat at a distance from the others. Ramiz led her towards one, pulling back the damask cloth which covered the entrance to usher her inside. Celia gave a gasp of amazement. Like the tent in which they'd had lunch the day Ramiz took her to the lost city of Katra, the walls were covered in tapestries and the floor in rich carpets. But this tent was much bigger, the coverings in the soft lamplight richer and more colourful.

'Do you like it?' Ramiz asked, smiling at the look of wonderment on her face.

'It's amazing. Like a mobile palace.'

'I must go and speak to Akil. Make yourself at home. I won't be long.'

Alone, Celia wandered around the tent, running her fingers over the tapestries, curling her toes into the luxurious carpets, stroking silken cushions and rubbing her cheek against velvet throws. A second room was obviously intended as a sleeping area. Here her luggage sat and her dressing case had been placed on a low table, beside which stood a full-length mirror. A smaller room led off from this one, where she was astonished to find a copper bath, already filled with water and scented with petals. Without further ado she stripped her dusty clothes off and sank into the water.

Clean, scented, and dressed in a loose caftan of organdie the colour of the setting sun, Celia returned to the main room. In her absence someone had set out dinner—an array of covered dishes from which delicious smells wafted towards her. She was investigating their contents when Ramiz entered the tent.

Like her, he had bathed and changed. His cropped black hair sat sleek on his head. He wore a robe of his favourite dark blue velvet. Though the tent was large, it seemed suddenly very small. His very presence seemed to fill it. It felt incredibly intimate, much more so than the harem. Against the soft drapes and jewelled colours of the hangings Ramiz looked very male. Very intimidating. Celia was assaulted by a jangle of nerves, taking up residence in her stomach like a cloud of little birds.

'Dinner's arrived,' she said. 'Are you hungry?'

'No,' Ramiz replied baldly.

'Would you like something to drink, then?' She reached for a jug of sherbet.

'No.'

'How is Akil?' Celia asked, realising even as she spoke just how ridiculous was the question.

'Celia, come here.'

She put down the jug, but made no move towards him.

'If you're having second thoughts, now would be a good time to tell me.'

'I'm not.' She adjusted the sleeve of her caftan. 'I'm

just a bit—well, as you know, I've never done this before.'

She tried to smile, but her mouth trembled. Her eyes were mossy green, fixed on him with a combination of appeal and defiance that he found irresistible. Ramiz strode over to her and swept her into his arms. 'There's no need to be nervous. I'll show you.'

He nuzzled the tender skin in the crease behind her earlobe. The scent there was pure Celia. He tasted her with the tip of his tongue. Such a vulnerable spot—the softness of her lobe, the delicate bone of her ear behind it, the endearing little crease they formed together which he licked into. Something clutched at him, piercing its way into his heart like the lethal tip of a dagger. He would remember this always.

'Ramiz?'

'Come.' He took her by the hand and led her through to the sleeping chamber. He dispensed efficiently with Celia's robe, tugging it over her head before she could protest. She stood before him naked, blushing, fighting the urge to cover herself with her hands.

Her eyes betrayed her confusion at his lack of tenderness. His instincts were to be tender. It was what she needed. What she wanted too. But it was not what this was about. It was about finishing what they had started. It was about taking what he needed from her in order to cure himself of her too-tempting presence.

'Lie down.'

She did so without a word. He glanced down at her and caught his breath. She looked like the moon goddess, all creamy flesh and blushing curves, with the dark shadow of curls between her legs, the rosy tips of her nipples, the lush pink of her mouth, the deep copper of her hair spread out behind and over her. 'Beautiful.' The word was drawn from him, harsh and grating. He was hard. More than ready.

Ramiz hauled his robe over his head and stood before her, hugely aroused. Celia stared up at him. Wanting hurtled through her, fierce and hot, made urgent by the undertone of fear she was trying desperately not to acknowledge. He looked so remote. Like a conqueror standing over the vanquished—which was exactly how she felt. Except that the blade which would claim her as his was no scimitar. Her eyes were riveted on the curving length of his erection. It seemed impossible that she could contain such a size.

'Ramiz,' she said, sitting up. She wanted him to kiss her. 'Ramiz…' She held out her hand to him.

He stared at her for a long moment, an expression like pain slanting across his face. Then he was beside her. On top of her. Kissing her. Pressing her down under him, his mouth hard, his hands rough, his manhood insistent between her thighs. She was overwhelmed by the intensity of his passion, but excited by it too, and as he kissed her and touched her she became infected by a carnal need of her own, feverishly stroking and nipping and licking, until she was aware of nothing but skin on skin, heat on heat, the scent of him, the sound of his breathing, harsh, rapid, shallow, the thrumming of her blood raging like a torrent through her veins, the clenching pulse of her muscles hurtling her forward, upwards, mercilessly on to some destination of which she was only vaguely aware.

Ramiz grazed her nipples with his teeth. She dug her nails into his back. He moulded her breasts in his hands. She stroked the taut sloping muscles of his buttocks. His fingers found her entrance and slipped carefully inside. She moaned. He slid over the swollen centre of her, around and over, around and over, so that she could scarcely bear the tightening, clenching, sharpness of her response, resisting it, holding tight to it like a swimmer to a rock. But his fingers stroked and circled remorselessly, and she let go with a cry, arching under his touch, barely aware of him readying her, tugging her to him, until she felt the nudging of his shaft.

She closed her eyes and waited for the thrust and the pain, determined not to cry out, but he entered her so slowly, so carefully, she felt only a sort of unfolding as the aftermath of her climax drew him in. She opened her eyes. Ramiz was watching her, the strain of the care he was taking etched on his face. He pushed further into her and she moaned. He stopped. She reached for him, pulled his face towards her and kissed him deeply, tilting her hips encouragingly, moaning again, with pleasure this time, as he sheathed himself in her slowly, slowly, until she thought he could go no further, pausing, pushing again, waiting until she could not bear the waiting. He withdrew from her slowly, and thrust back into her again, slowly and deliberately, watching her, and she knew that she was going to lose herself again. This time she clung to him, felt the frisson of her muscles on his shaft from base to tip, then tip to base as he pushed back into her. She tilted instinctively, wrapping her legs around his waist, and he pushed higher, harder, making her moan and clutch at his back as the ripple of her climax started to build again, or started to finish, and still he continued to thrust, each plunge more deliberate, higher, until she could feel the tip of him touching some tender spot high inside her and she lost control instantly, crying out. Her surrender acted like a trigger. Ramiz lost control almost as she had, thrusting fast and hard with abandon, until she actually felt him swell before he pulled abruptly from her, spilling hot over her belly before collapsing on top of her, wrapping his arms so tightly round her, kissing her so hard that there was no space at all between them as their skin and mouths clung to each other, because to let go would be to die.

She lay exhausted, saturated with a bone-deep heaviness that pinned her to the bed, feeling weightless, as if she was gliding. As Ramiz's breathing steadied he unwrapped himself from her. As he rolled away from her, Celia felt as if her wings had been clipped, so suddenly did she plunge back down to earth.

'Did I hurt you?'

'No.' She wanted him to hold her again, wanted reassurance, words of endearment, but she knew she could have none of those things, so she lay still, holding herself instead.

'Are you hungry now?'

She was, surprisingly, but it seemed rude to say so.

'I'm starving,' Ramiz said with a grin. 'Come on.'

Before she could move, he scooped her up in his

arms, striding with her held high against his chest to the other room. 'We can't eat like this,' Celia said, for they were both still naked.

Ramiz grinned again. 'Trust me—we can.' He kicked a heap of cushions together on the floor, and picked up the huge silver tray upon which the dishes were held, placing it on the carpet in front of the cushions before sitting down. 'Come here.' He patted a cushion invitingly. When Celia didn't move, hugging her arms around her breasts, he caught her hand and pulled her down beside him, so that she sprawled, half lying, half sitting, on a huge tasselled velvet cushion.

Ramiz lifted the cover from a dish and took out a *pastilla*, breaking it open so that some of the pastry flaked onto Celia's arm. He leaned over her to lick it off. Then he offered her a bite of pastry, licking the crumbs from her lips when she bit, before popping the rest into his own mouth.

A pomegranate salad was flavoured with lime juice and finely chopped onion. He fed her from a silver spoon. The lime gave their kisses a tangy taste which sparkled on their tongues.

Roasted aubergines and sweet peppers drizzled with olive oil were next. The oil dripped over her fingers and Ramiz sucked at them, drawing each one into his mouth and licking it clean before moving to the next.

The juice of a pineapple which had been roasted with sugar and ginger he deliberately allowed to trickle down the valley between her breasts. By this time they had given up all pretence of eating. It was a game of call and response. Where Ramiz led Celia followed, so that what had started as his teasing was in danger of turning into his own undoing.

He feasted on her breasts, tasting pineapple juice and salt and sugar, and underneath the delicious tang of what he had already come to think of as essence of Celia. She lay beneath him, aroused, flushed, her hair tangled, her eyes alight with the passion he knew she could see reflected in his. He had never known this feeling before. He couldn't put a name to it. It was as if she was drawing something out of him, mixing it with something of her own, so that she mingled in his blood, so that he felt mingled in hers. As if he knew her. Was inside her. As if she was inside him somehow.

He fastened his mouth around her nipple and sucked, then tugged, then sucked again, delighting in the way she cleaved to him, the way he could make her arch or jolt or writhe, depending on how soft or hard he licked or sucked or nipped. He sucked again, and cupped his palm over the mound of her curls between her legs. Damp. Hot. He pressed the heel of his hand against her in a little circling motion, felt the responding clenching at the base of his shaft. He wanted her again. Now. Urgently.

He nudged her legs to part them, but Celia resisted. Before he could stop her she had pushed him over onto his back. Before he could resist her she'd dipped her hand into a dish of something and trailed it neatly in a line from the middle of his ribcage. Down. It was cold. Creamy. Yoghurt of some sort, he thought vaguely. Then he stopped thinking as Celia began to lick it, daintily flicking her tongue along the path across his abdomen, dipping into his navel, down to where the path ended, at the point where his hair began to thicken. Ramiz closed his eyes and held his breath. There was a pause, during which he thought he would cry out with frustration, and then her tongue flicked over the tip of his shaft. Stopped. Another flick—a little longer. Another. Down. Down. Down the length of him and then back up, in one fluid movement that made him jolt with pleasure. Blood surged. He felt the tightening in his groin that presaged his climax. Dear heavens, he thought he would die with the pleasure of it. If only she would—now—like—just exactly like that! And like that. And—oh—like that!

'Celia.' She stopped. He didn't want her to stop. Ramiz reached down to grip her by the shoulders. The look of surprise on her face would have been funny if he had been in the mood to be amused. He wasn't. He pulled her down over him. Her knees brushed his shoulders. Her breasts were crushed into his stomach. Her mouth was back where he wanted it. And his was exactly where he wanted it to be too. He put his palms on the delightful swell of her bottom, he put his mouth over the delightful mound of wet curls and tender folds between her legs, and moaned as he tasted her and breathed her and sought out the nub of her. He moaned again as she followed him, reflecting and echoing every lick and stroke, resisting, but only just, the urgent clamouring of his climax until he felt hers, and then he let himself go as she came, and he had never, ever felt anything quite so heady as that feeling of her sweetness in his mouth as he surged and pulsed into hers.

It felt right. Which was absolutely wrong. But for now Ramiz cared for nothing, nothing—at all.

Chapter Eleven

Ramiz did not sleep in her tent but returned to his own. For a long time Celia gazed at her reflection by the light of the lamps. She barely recognised the woman staring back at her from the mirror. Her hair was a tangled mess. Her eyes were huge—a darker green than she had ever seen them. Her bottom lip seemed swollen. Her skin was flushed all over, with the faint marks of Ramiz's fingers on her breasts, a slight bruise on her bottom. Between her thighs she was tender. Under one of her nails was a trace of blood where she had dug her fingers too deep into his back. Something else she couldn't put a name to shone from her face too. A different kind of glow she hadn't experienced before. Sensual, that was what it was, she finally decided. Wanton, even. For the first time since she had arrived in the East she saw the point of the veil. She would certainly not like anyone else to see her like this. They'd know straight away.

Sliding between the silk sheets of the divan, she wondered if Ramiz looked the same. Somehow she doubted it. None of this was new to him. They had done nothing he had not done before, and no doubt he would do it again. The idea of him with another woman made her feel sick.

She must be careful. Though she had pleased him, though he had seemed most reluctant to leave, she must remember it meant nothing to him. And he was just a passing fascination for her. She would do well to remember that, too. It meant nothing. No matter how right it felt, or how amazingly he had made her feel. Ramiz was an oasis of sensuality in the desert of her life.

Celia chuckled at that, for it was the sort of thing Cassie would have said. She wondered if he was sleeping. She wondered if he was thinking about her. Celia drifted into a deep sleep, most certainly thinking about him.

When she awoke, the sun was rising and the caravan was already being prepared to depart. She ate a hurried breakfast alone in her tent, conscious that the men were waiting to take it down. Ramiz was waiting with her camel, anxious to make a start, leaving Akil to lead the caravan which would again follow in their wake.

She expected Ramiz to ignore her. She expected him to be brusque, to have returned to his princely remoteness now he had what he wanted from her, but he surprised her, helping her onto the camel with a smile so warm it might as well have been a kiss. They set out as yesterday, in companionable closeness. If this were not Ramiz she would feel she was being courted. But it *was* Ramiz, and he could never court her.

They made camp that night in the same manner as before, but this time they were not alone. 'Sheikh Farid and his tribe,' Ramiz told Celia, nodding over at the cluster of tents about five hundred yards distant. 'We must pay our respects tonight. Dress up. It is expected.'

'You want me to come with you?'

'If you don't he will be insulted. You think they haven't heard of the mysterious English lady travelling with me?'

She hadn't given it much thought, though she realised now that she should have. 'What will they think of me?'

'I have asked Akil to put out the word that you are here as an emissary of the British Government.'

'A woman! They'll hardly believe that.'

Ramiz shrugged. 'Just another Western quirk—treating a woman as a man. It is why we have separate tents. You would not want them to think you my concubine.'

'No, of course not. I—thank you, Ramiz.'

'It is my own honour as much as yours I must protect. Besides,' he added, acknowledging Akil's summons, 'Sheikh Farid's daughter is one of the princesses on my council's list of brides.'

She had been touched by his care for her reputation. Now she saw it was care for his own, and was angry—not at Ramiz, but at herself for reading something into nothing. Celia made her way to her tent, mortified and fighting a wholly unaccustomed feeling which she realised, as she stepped into her waiting bath, was jealousy. 'Of a woman I have never met,' she muttered in disgust, 'and whom he may not marry in any event.'

The bath calmed her, and the oil she rubbed into her arms and legs afterwards soothed her. She must find out the receipt for it from Fatima. Cassie would like to try it, and she knew they would not be able to buy such a thing at home.

Home! The word startled her. Soon she would be going back to England. Far away from the heat and the smells of this beautiful land, from the contrasts of barren deserts and green oases, from A'Qadiz and its exotic foods and vibrant colours. And far away from Ramiz. She wasn't ready to go, not yet, but, counting up the days, she knew it could not be long before her father arrived in Cairo. 'Home.' She said it out loud, experimentally, but it still didn't work.

She couldn't bear the thought of leaving Ramiz. She couldn't imagine her life without him. 'Because I might as well admit it,' she said to her reflection. 'I'm not just beguiled. I'm not just in thrall to him. I'm in love with him.'

Her reflection smiled. A soft, tender smile, which crept warily across her lips. 'I'm in love with Ramiz.' Her smile spread. Her skin tingled. 'I'm in love with Ramiz. Oh, God, I'm in love with Ramiz.' Celia tottered backwards onto the divan. 'I'm in love with Ramiz, and I'm just about to meet the woman he may well marry.' A hysterical little bubble of laughter escaped her, followed by a large solitary tear which trickled like acid down her cheek.

She was in love! Who'd have thought it? Certainly she'd never considered herself capable of such a thing. Not this kind of love, at any rate. She'd always thought of love as something comfortable, something that grew slowly over time, something stolid, dependable, rather than essential. But this, this thing she called love, was nothing at all like that. It glowed inside her like a living thing, pulsing and throbbing with life, the source of her being rather than a pleasant appendage. The reason for her being. Ramiz completed her. He was the heart which beat in her, the sun around which she revolved.

Celia laughed. Such fancies were the stuff on which Cassie thrived, and she had always mocked them, but now she found they were true. It was all true. She had been waiting to be woken. The way he made her feel, the way only *he* could make her feel, was nothing to do with the harem and everything to do with Ramiz. Her body was in thrall because she was in love. Her body responded to him at some elemental level because it had recognised, long before her mind did, what he meant to her. She loved him.

And Yasmina was right too. She would always love him. She was not the type to love twice. There would never be anyone else. She loved Ramiz. He was the beginning of her story and the end.

Except there could never be a happy ever after.

Fortunately Celia had never allowed herself to hope for one. There would be an end to this, and she would have to cope with it. Cope with it and never allow

Ramiz to know. For if he thought she cared he would feel responsible, and that responsibility would touch his honour and—no, she could not allow that.

Celia dressed with care in a pair of lemon pleated pantaloons bound at the ankles with silver and pearl beading. The same design was embroidered onto the long loose sleeves of her caftan, which was velvet, in her favourite jade green, and on the matching velvet slippers too. Around her neck and wrists she roped her mother's pearls, and there were pearls in her hair too, which she wore up, but with a loose knot over one shoulder.

Passable, she thought, looking at herself again in the mirror. The caftan, which was slashed to the thigh, drew attention to her height, and the length of her legs. The pearls lent their lustre to her skin. Her hair was glossy from the care lavished on it by Adila and Fatima. She looked exotic, she realised. Although the outfit covered more of her than a ballgown, the diaphanous material of the pantaloons, visible through the caftan's vents, made her legs clearly visible. The soft folds of the caftan itself hinted at her uncorseted shape beneath. Celia laughed, wondering what Aunt Sophia would think of her going to pay a visit without her stays!

Ramiz might not love her, but he desired her, and in this outfit even Celia could see that she had a certain allure. Which was consolation enough, she told herself firmly as she left the tent.

Ramiz was conferring with Akil. Dressed in his formal robes, white silk edged with gold, the state scimitar glinting at his waist, he looked every inch the regal prince. He was preoccupied, giving her a cursory glance only as he rapped out instructions to the guards, inspected the gifts which were to be given to Sheikh Farid, and listened impatiently as Akil read through his seemingly endless notes.

The procession they formed to walk the short distance to the Bedouin tents was impressive. Ramiz took the lead, preceded by his Head of Guards, a great hulk of a man whose robes, Celia thought, were large enough to form a tent of their own. She herself followed Ramiz, with Akil behind her, flanked by the remainder of the guards carrying blazing torches to light the way.

Sheikh Farid was a small man of about the same age as Celia's father. He was simply dressed, in a black robe and red-checked headdress, but his womenfolk more than made up for his lack of ostentation. Celia counted six wives, bedecked in so many gold anklets, bracelets, necklaces and earrings that they jangled when they moved. Bedouin women covered their skin with complex ink and henna tattoos—swirling designs encompassing leaves and flowers, mixed in with ancient symbols. Their nails were stained red with henna, and their eyelids stained black at the corners, much in the way the eyes of the pharaohs were painted. They did not wear the veil, and stared with blatant curiosity at Celia, though when she smiled in their direction they giggled and lowered their eyes.

She kept discreetly in the background, under Akil's watchful eye. Though he had said nothing, she was aware that Akil did not approve of her presence here. No doubt he fretted over the propriety of it, and she could not blame him—especially since his suspicions had all too recently been proved correct. He would think her a loose woman. No doubt he would be glad when she was gone, for he could not approve of her relationship with Yasmina. It saddened Celia, and she determined to do all she could to ensure she intruded on official business no more than necessary.

As it turned out, she enjoyed her role as onlooker immensely, for it gave her the opportunity to observe Ramiz the Prince. It was a role he performed with the assurance and dignity she had come to expect of him, but as the ritual of the alms-giving got underway what impressed her most was his complete lack of arrogance. Throughout the long process of receiving each person who wished to make a plea, Ramiz showed only patience and concern. He had that rare ability to talk without talking down, taking time to calm the most nervous of the supplicants or the most aggressive of the litigants, treating the ancients with touching deference, joking with the younger men as a contemporary. Despite the long line of supplicants, there was no sense of hurry. Every case was given due consideration, every decision proclaimed formally to the audience before the next commenced. Not everyone received the outcome they'd hoped for, but all seemed to be treated fairly, and Celia realised that this, and not the sums of money given out in alms, was the point. Prince Ramiz was seen to be fair and just, as well as accessible.

She was impressed and touched—not just by Ramiz's humanity, but by his vision, for he was obviously intent on demonstrating to his people the principles by which he ruled. The principles to which too many other rulers, in Celia's experience, paid merely lip-service. He truly was a remarkable man. She loved him so much.

Humbled, and slightly overcome by the strength of emotion which enveloped her, Celia crept unnoticed from the ceremony. Away from the blaze of the torches which lit Sheikh Farid's tent, the full moon cast a ghostly light across the Bedouin encampment. She wandered a little distance from the tents, absorbed in her thoughts, enjoying the cool of the evening and the scents of the desert which came to life after dark. The vast stretches of sand which surrounded her began to have their usual effect, imbuing her with a strange combination—a sense of her own insignificance and at the same time a feeling of endless possibilities. Desert euphoria, she called it, for it was both exhilarating and chastening, like flying in Signor Lunardi's balloon, which Papa had been fortunate enough to witness on its inaugural flight from Moorfields.

A shuffling sound alerted her to the presence of another person. A glint of steel showed the shadowy figure to be one of Ramiz's guards, no doubt instructed to keep an eye on her. Strange to think that when first they'd met she would have been insulted by this apparent lack of trust. She knew better now, and recognised it for a combination of deeply embedded chivalry and an equally strong duty of care which was an essential part of him. She had come to like it.

Nodding to the guard as she passed, Celia made her way back to the Bedouin camp. The line of people was coming to an end. Fires had sprouted up outside many of the tents, and the smell of cooking filled the air. Women were gathering around the glowing embers, chatting and laughing. A group of semi-naked children were playing a ball game. As Celia stopped to watch, the ball landed at her feet, and before she knew it she was embroiled in the game, whose complex rules were explained with many gestures and much hilarity.

Her regular visits to Yasmina's extended family had given her a smattering of the language, and when the ball game petered out Celia recognised the word for story as the children gathered around her and tugged pleadingly at her caftan. Sitting cross-legged on the sand, surrounded by a circle of expectant faces, she prayed that her enthusiasm and the children's participation would make up for her lack of vocabulary, and launched into one of Samir's favourite stories, which happened to be one of her youngest sister Cressida's too. *Ali Baba and the Forty Thieves.*

'As-salamu alaykum,' Ramiz said to the last of the supplicants, a man seeking arbitration over the return of his divorced daughter's dowry. 'Peace be with you.'

'*Wa-alaykum as-salam*, Highness,' the man replied, bowing backwards out of the tent.

Ramiz rubbed his temples and looked around. 'Where is Lady Celia?' he asked Akil sharply.

'She left some time ago.'

Ramiz glared at him. 'I told you to keep watch over her.'

'I did, Highness. A guard is with her.'

Ramiz made to leave.

'Majesty?'

Ramiz eyed the restraining hand on his arm with a cold hauteur which made Akil step hurriedly back. 'Well?'

'I have arranged with Sheikh Farid to have his daughter formally presented to you tomorrow. I apologise if I speak out of turn, but you would do well to leave the Lady Celia to her own devices,' Akil said, blanching at his friend's glacial expression but remaining firm. 'No-one believes this story you have had me put about,' he hissed, ushering Ramiz to one side, away from listening ears and prying glances. 'Anyone with eyes can see what you are to her. She turns to you as a flower does to the sun. And you, Highness, if you are not careful you will fall under the spell she casts. Her father is an influential man. Do you think he will take kindly to having his daughter used as a concubine?'

'How dare you speak to me on such a subject? Just because you are my friend, Akil, do not think I will tolerate interference in my personal life.'

'Ramiz, you are a prince. Unfortunately you do not have a personal life. It is because I am your closest friend that I dare to speak. You think I don't know how tirelessly you have worked in the last two years? You think I don't know how much you have done for A'Qadiz? How much more there is still for you to do? It would be foolish to offer insult to the English over such a trivial matter as a woman, and equally foolish to insult Sheikh Farid, whom you know holds sway over almost all of our Bedouins. Trust me on this matter. Leave that woman alone, or if you must go to her bed at least have the discretion to do so away from the eyes of those who hold power.'

There was a long silence. Furious as he was to be spoken to in such a way, Ramiz was even more furious at himself. He rubbed his eyes. 'If I have been indiscreet it shall be remedied, but you are making a camel out of a flea. Lady Celia is under no illusions about our—our relationship. She is perfectly well aware of its temporary nature and will make no trouble.'

'Ramiz, I tell you she is in love with you.'

Ramiz shook his head. 'You are quite wrong. Like all foreigners she is obsessed with the sensual elements of our culture, and who can change her, coming as she does from a people who make a virtue of indifference, who equate virtue with frigidity and passion with vice? Lady Celia is indulging her passions safe from the prying eyes of her compatriots. She is simply taking advantage of the situation.'

'Is that what you're doing?'

Ramiz clenched his fists. 'You overstep the mark, Akil. What I am doing is enjoying the company of one who wants nothing from me except myself. A rare enough thing since I came to power, you will agree.'

'Ramiz, if it is just a woman you need, you could—'

'Enough! That is quite enough!' Ignoring the sudden hush around them, ignoring the guards who had rushed towards him at the sound of his raised voice, even ignoring Sheikh Farid, who was making his way towards the commotion, Ramiz gripped Akil by the shoulders. 'She is not *just a woman*! If I *ever* hear you speak so

discourteously of Lady Celia in my presence again, I will have you banished—do you understand?' he said through gritted teeth.

Akil nodded.

'And if I ever hear from Lady Celia that you have treated her in any way disrespectfully, or if I hear from her that you have allowed your wife to see your own prejudices, I will have you banished. Yasmina is Celia's only friend here. It would be a great shame if she were to lose her. Do I make myself understood, Akil?'

White as his master's headdress, Akil nodded again.

Ramiz released him. 'Then let us put this behind us. We go too far back to allow it to come between us.'

Akil straightened the *igal* which held his own headdress in place. 'I hope that is true,' he murmured, but he did so very quietly.

Ramiz's anger had shocked him to the core. For once Akil was certain he knew better than his friend. The sooner Lady Celia was on her way back to Egypt the better, so Ramiz could get on with the serious business of taking a suitable wife.

In search of a little quiet before the feasting began, for it would last much of the night, Ramiz encountered Celia in the centre of a circle of ragged children with rapt expressions on their faces. Taking care to remain out of sight, he watched, fascinated, as she recounted a tale, amused by the clever way she encouraged the children to join in with words and gestures when her own surprisingly large stock of vocabulary failed her.

He hadn't known she could say anything other than good morning and thank you, but she'd picked up a lot more than that in the time she'd been here. From the maids, he presumed. And Yasmina, of course.

Akil's words had angered him, but he knew his friend well enough to understand how strong his feelings must be for him to have spoken in such a way. He was wrong about Celia, though; it was a ridiculous notion to think her in love. Almost as ridiculous as the idea that he, Prince Ramiz al-Muhana of A'Qadiz, could feel such a thing. Princes did not fall in love except in fairytales. English roses did not fall in love with Arabic princes except in fairytales—which was almost certainly how Celia saw it, and exactly what he'd just said to Akil.

He looked at her now, absent-mindedly stroking the hair of the little girl who sat by her side while balancing another on her knee. He'd noticed it the day she'd arrived at the port, and again the day they went to the market in Balyrma—how children were drawn to her, how naturally she talked to them, stooping down to their height, never using that patronising tone with them which so many childless women used. Affinity—that was the word. It must come from looking after her sisters.

Akil worried too much. He was so focused on his great plan to tie up their hard-won peace with a good marriage that he couldn't see clearly. No matter how comfortable Celia might look here, A'Qadiz was not her home. No matter how incredible last night had been, it was just a temporary passion. Like all passions, it would take flight sooner rather than later. Sooner, if he continued to indulge it. She would be gone soon enough. He would do his duty to A'Qadiz, as he had always done his duty. After thirty-five years of doing so he deserved these few days.

The privilege of sitting in Celia's lap was now being disputed by a little boy. Without pausing in her narrative Celia managed to accommodate both children, but it left her no hands free. 'Open sesame!' she declared, but without being able to throw her arms wide the English version of the words fell flat. The children looked puzzled.

'Iftah ya simsim,' Ramiz said, unable to resist joining her, much to the children's awed delight. 'Open sesame,' he said carefully, lifting up a small boy to clear a space by her side.

'Open sesame,' the children repeated gleefully.

'Thank you,' Celia whispered. She smiled at him—a smile he hadn't seen before. Tender. It must be the children. She was thinking of her sisters. Akil was wrong.

Akil was definitely wrong, Ramiz thought again later, much later, as they made their weary procession back to the tents after a long drawn-out dinner. He nodded goodnight to his friend. Akil bowed stiffly and retreated to his own tent without a backwards glance, still piqued by the dressing-down Ramiz had administered.

Celia would be asleep by now. She had eaten separately, with the women, and been escorted back at least an hour ago. Ramiz had intended going straight to his own divan, but Akil's unspoken disapproval and the need to prove him wrong sent him to Celia's tent. If she was asleep he would not wake her.

But she was not asleep. When he pulled back the curtain the lamps were lit in the main room. She was reclining, still dressed in her velvet caftan, on a heap of cushions, reading a book which she put immediately to one side as soon as he appeared in the doorway, holding out her hand invitingly.

Ramiz hesitated. She didn't look any different to him. Beautiful. With more awareness, maybe, in the way she smiled at him—but that was because she was more aware of her body. Of how it could feel. Of what he could do to it. Of what she could do to him. His manhood stirred.

'Celia, you do not—you know this cannot last?'

She lowered her eyes. 'Of course not. Are you come to tell me our fairytale is over already, Ramiz?'

'Fairytale?' he repeated, taken aback by her repetition of the very word he himself had used.

'That is how I think of it. Don't you?'

He took her outstretched hand, allowing himself to be pulled down to join her on the cushions. 'A fairytale? Am I your prince?'

'Yes.'

'Then you must do my bidding,' Ramiz said, pulling the pearl pins from her hair and running his hands through it.

'Your wish is my command, master.'

'Excellent,' Ramiz said, pulling her caftan over her head. He ran his palms down her shoulders, across her breasts, skimming the indent of her waist to rest on the curve of her hips before tugging his own robe over his head. 'Though tonight I think it should be your wish which is my command. What would you like me to do with this?'

Sheikh Farid presented his daughter Juman the next morning. The visit was obviously expected. Watching from the shade of her tent, Celia saw Akil fussing over the positioning of the furnishings in the tent in which Ramiz slept. The whole front of the main room had been lifted up to reveal an interior bigger and much richer than the one she enjoyed. Akil was supervising the placing of a tea service, watching carefully as one of the servants polished the gold samovar to his satisfaction, while Ramiz sat in a corner reading.

Sheikh Farid arrived on horseback—a magnificent and extremely rare black thoroughbred which contrasted perfectly with the grey on which his daughter was mounted. A third horse, another grey, pranced delicately on a leading rein behind them. Even from a distance Celia could see that father and daughter rode well—hardly surprising since she had learned last night that the thoroughbreds, with their distinctively arched necks and high, swishing tails, formed a significant part of Sheikh Farid's livelihood.

The Sheikh's daughter was younger than she had expected—nearer Caroline's age than Cassie's, perhaps only sixteen or seventeen. Though Yasmina had told her that girls married young here in A'Qadiz, Celia could not help thinking that sixteen was far too young for Ramiz. The girl would bore him to death. What on earth were Akil and the council thinking about, suggesting such a baby for a man like Ramiz?

But, watching her spring lithely from the horse, she began to see exactly why this girl had been recommended, and when she was invited to join them for tea in Ramiz's tent her understanding was completed. Juman Farid was extraordinarily beautiful, with ebony hair that shone with health, almond eyes which managed to be both mysterious and seductive, and vermilion lips which no matter how hard Celia stared at them showed not a trace of artifice. She had a figure which was a perfect hourglass too, and not only that she was quite obviously as blue-blooded as the horse which had carried her here. No doubt, Celia thought bitterly to herself, she had a pedigree just as long and impressive, for she was the firstborn of Sheikh Farid's first wife, and even Celia knew how important such precedence was.

Though she was dressed in the traditional *sarwal* trousers and tunic under the *abayah* which had cloaked her upon the horse, Juman's charms were nonetheless subtly on display, for the gauzy gold and crimson chiffon left little to the imagination.

So Celia thought—until she realised what she was thinking and castigated herself for it. She was jealous! It was hardly Juman's fault that she was so attractive and so eminently suitable a princess for Prince Ramiz. It was not as if she was behaving with anything other than perfect propriety either. Juman spoke only when spoken to, insisted that Celia pour the tea, and kept her eyes discreetly lowered. Only when Sheikh Farid suggested she show Ramiz the horse they had brought for him to try out did she leap up excitedly and clap her hands, her enthusiasm shining through in a way so entirely genuine that Celia was mortified.

It was Akil who suggested to Ramiz that he try out the horse's paces, and Akil who suggested to Sheikh Farid that he allow Juman to accompany Ramiz. Sheikh Farid agreed, but only on the proviso that he go along as chaperone. Celia was ashamed to find herself relieved by this, but it was still with a heavy heart that she waved them off.

She retired to her tent, occupying herself with the embroidery of a caftan which she intended to leave as a present for Ramiz when she left. As the sun rose to its apex she fell asleep, waking in the afternoon to discover that the trio had gone straight to the Bedouin camp, where a new tribe of supplicants had arrived.

'You may join them if you wish,' Akil told her, in a voice which suggested she should not. She took heed of it, eating a lonely supper and retiring early to her divan with her book.

But Ramiz arrived as he had the night before. And, as he had the night before, he made love to her with a fervency and a passion which took them both by surprise all over again.

So it continued the next day and the next, as each new tribe arrived, with Celia spending some time alone, some time at the camp with the children, but avoiding Ramiz in public. Ramiz's spare time was monopolised either by Akil or Juman, but his nights were reserved for Celia.

They made love. They talked. She read to him. He told her of the more interesting cases he had adjudicated that day. She shared with him her ideas for a school camp which could be set up like the alms camp, where Bedouin children could come for at least a smattering of education, even if they did not stay long.

'If you chose one of the bigger oases, where they are likely to stay longer, and made sure the teacher did not mind that one day her class might be five strong, another fifty, then I think it would work,' she said eagerly. 'They are such a huge part of A'Qadiz's population, yet they have virtually no schooling. Yasmina told me one of your sayings: not having the opportunity to test your talents does not mean you do not have them. It's not as if they don't want to learn; it's just that they don't get much opportunity. Their parents have no education either, and cannot teach them.'

With Ramiz's encouragement, she went on to outline in more detail the practicalities of how her 'tent school', as she thought of it, would work.

'You've thought this all through very thoroughly. I'm impressed,' Ramiz said, looking at her with new respect.

'Will it work, do you think?'

'With the right teachers, I don't see why not. But where am to find people willing to take on such a challenge?'

'I would do it,' she said, without thinking.

'Live in a tent teaching Bedouin children? I don't think so. Your father would never permit it.'

'Probably not.'

'What will you do when you go back to England?'

'I don't know.' Celia looked away, biting her lip. 'I don't know. Perhaps I will teach at a charity school there. There is no shortage of children in England needing education, and I seem to have a gift for it.'

'You should have children of your own,' he said, then wished he had not, for the idea of Celia bearing anyone's child but his was unexpectedly painful.

'Ramiz, let us stop this conversation,' she said gently.

'You mean it is none of my business.'

'Ramiz, don't! I do not ask you whether you will marry Juman, but it does not mean I don't think about it. It does not mean I don't feel horribly guilty thinking about it, and what we do here in this tent every night. I don't feel guilty enough to stop, but that is because I know it will end anyway—and soon. I do not ask you because I don't want to know, and because, as you say, it is none of my business—as my life will be none of yours when I leave here.'

His expression darkened, his anger arriving without warning and whipping him into a stormy rage. 'I won't be marrying Juman. She is a child, and she bores me rigid with her endless talk of horses, horses, horses and nothing else. I cannot contemplate taking her or any other woman into my bed when I have you waiting for me. You obsess me! Do you not understand? I cannot get enough of you—yet I must, for you must return to your homeland.'

'Ramiz, it is the same for me.' She gripped his arms, shaking him so that he looked at her. 'Can you not see it is the same for me? I want you. All the time I want you.'

'Celia, I…'

'For heaven's sake, Your Highness, just shut up and kiss me.'

And, for once in his life, Ramiz did exactly as he was commanded.

Chapter Twelve

Lord Henry Armstrong, who had hitherto considered himself in robust health, had been much worn down by the journey across the Mediterranean in the cramped and infested quarters of His Majesty's frigate *Hyperion*, suffering grievously from *mal de mer* exacerbated by some rather vicious fleabites. While the redoubtable Lady Sophia flourished under the conditions, her brother and niece were laid low, forced to remain below decks upon their bunks for much of the voyage. Lady Sophia it was who saw to it that the invalids were provided with what little nourishment their delicate stomachs could tolerate, and it was she who obtained a salve from Captain Mowbray himself, which rid Lord Henry of his unpleasant infestation.

And upon their arrival in Alexandria it was Lady Sophia again who rose to the occasion, conjuring up the transportation which hurtled the travellers onwards so quickly that Lord Henry had no time at all to recover from the pitching of the ground beneath them before being besieged by the bone-jolting experience of an unsprung carriage travelling an unmetalled road with his daughter rather vulgarly urging the driver to 'spring 'em' every time they stopped for a change.

They had arrived at Lord Wincester's residence in Cairo at some God-forsaken hour last night, and now here was Cassie, having made a remarkable recovery, demanding that they resume their journey not twenty-four hours later.

'Absolutely not!' Lord Henry exclaimed. 'I cannot journey another inch without a day's rest.'

'But, Papa, you cannot have considered—'

Lord Henry looked at his daughter with an eye which was considerably jaundiced. He had the tic. He had a splitting headache. In fact there wasn't a bit of him that didn't ache in one way or another. 'You worry too much. What is another day, after all this time?'

Cassie who, after seven hours' rest and a bath had made a remarkable recovery, was back in full Cassandra mode. She wrung her hands. 'Another day of suffering, Papa. Another day of Celia wondering when we will come to rescue her. Another day of gazing through the bars of her prison and *praying* for her release.'

'For God's sake, daughter, you should be on stage! You know, I can't understand how someone who looks as if a puff of wind will blow her away can survive such a journey as we have made with so little visible effect. I congratulate you on your constitution but—*but*, I say—I do not share it. I need another day before I go traipsing off across the desert. Apart from anything else, I must consult with old Wincester. The negotiations that George Cleveden was sent to conclude are extremely important—far too important to make a mull of because I didn't have time to receive a proper briefing. Damned inconvenient of George to get himself killed in the middle of it all, I must say.'

'But, Papa, surely my sister is the more important issue at stake? Aunt Sophia!' Cassandra turned large blue eyes, wide with appeal, upon her aunt. 'I beg you, let us make haste today. Apparently it is only a very short trip to the Red Sea, where we can take a boat to this A'Qadiz. A gentle sail, Lord Wincester says it is.'

'What the devil does old Wincester know about it? He's never been,' Lord Henry exclaimed exasperatedly. 'Instead of treating me to histrionics, you'll make far better use of your time talking to that fellow—whatshisname—Finchley-Burke. He saw Celia only a week or so ago. Now, go away and allow me the dignity of recovering my health in private.'

Recognising the note of finality in his voice, Cassandra was forced to retreat, stopping only to press upon her father some most efficacious powders, before returning to the drawing room with her aunt.

There, Peregrine awaited her nervously, torn between a desire to pay homage at the temple of her beauty and an equally strong desire to avoid her terrifying aunt, whose baleful eye reminded him rather too much of his mother.

'You will accompany us, naturally. We need someone who knows the ropes,' Cassie informed Peregrine, putting her new-found seaman's slang into use. 'You've done the journey before, and you know all about camels and such. In fact compared to everyone else here, including even Lord Wincester, you are quite the expert,' she said, conferring upon the young man one of her most beguiling smiles.

Peregrine blushed. Now that Lord Henry Armstrong, with his reputation for honesty and integrity, was actually here in Cairo, the Consul General was regretting the liberties he had taken in suggesting that the Lady Celia's incarceration in A'Qadiz could be of service to her country. In fact Lord Wincester had forbidden Peregrine from mentioning it, putting Peregrine in a very awkward position indeed. Not even Lady Cassandra's charming countenance and nymph-like figure could tempt him into spending any more time in her presence than necessary, lest he betray himself.

'Thing—thing is, Lady Cassandra,' he stammered, appalled at the very notion of having to keep her, her esteemed papa and formidable aunt company on a trek across the desert, 'thing is, I have to go to India.'

'Mr Finchley-Burke!' Cassandra exclaimed. 'Surely you would not let us down?'

'Eh! No, no, didn't quite—that is—you don't need me. You'll need a guide for the desert, but you'll be able pick one up at the port—don't want me along, keeping you back.' But Peregrine knew he was clutching at straws.

'India will wait, Mr Finchley-Burke. My sister cannot. You, I am sure, will not wish to think of her incarcerated in that place a moment longer than necessary.'

Peregrine's memory of Lady Celia was of a female perfectly content to stay where she was, but he did not quite know how to put that to her sister.

'How did you find my niece, Mr Finchley-Burke?'

Peregrine jumped, for he had quite forgotten Lady Sophia's presence. Now, faced with her gimlet gaze, he quailed. 'Well, it was quite simple, really, once I got to the palace.'

Lady Sophia rolled her eyes. 'No, you nincompoop, I'm referring to her health, her mental state.'

'Oh! Yes! Quite! She actually seemed remarkably well. Very composed young woman, Lady Celia. Seemed to be handling it with real aplomb,' Peregrine said bracingly.

'Ah, that does sound like Celia,' Lady Sophia said placidly.

'Of course it does, Aunt Sophia. Celia is not the type to have hysterics, you know that, but just because she does not show her feelings it does not mean she has none.' Cassandra clasped her hands to her bosom, unwittingly drawing Peregrine's attention to her curves. 'Remember, this man—this Sheikh al-Muhana—has her in his harem. I picture him rather old, with a black beard and a sort of grasping look.'

'As to that,' Sophia said with pursed lips, 'I have been making enquiries, and believe harems are not all decadent places. It may be that he has placed Celia in his harem simply to keep her safe. Do not let your imagination run away with you, Cassandra. I have every confidence in Celia's sense of propriety and her good sense.

You must rid yourself of the notion of her as some sort of concubine.'

'But, Aunt, what if Celia's choice is to submit or surrender her life?' Cassandra asked tragically, once more allowing *One Thousand and One Nights* the upper hand.

'There is no point in wasting our time on idle speculation,' Lady Sophia said acerbically. Realising her niece was genuinely upset, and upon the brink of tears, she softened her expression marginally. 'Really, Cassie, you know your sister well enough. Celia is hardly the type to appeal to a sheikh, for she is not in the least exotic—and even if she did, which I strongly doubt, she is not the type to simply submit. Celia,' Lady Sophia said with authority, 'is not a tactile woman.' She got to her feet. 'We will leave you to your arrangements now,' she said to Peregrine. 'Come, Cassandra, what you need is some rest. Fortunately I have some laudanum in my reticule.'

'Sheikh Farid has requested an audience with you.'

The servants were packing up the camp in preparation for the journey back to Balyrma. 'With me?' Celia closed the lid of her dressing case, and turned towards Ramiz, who was standing in the doorway. 'What can Sheikh Farid wish to say to me?'

'I've been telling him about your idea for a Bedouin school. In amongst that gaggle of little admirers who follow you about wide-eyed, begging for stories, are three of Sheikh Farid's youngest children, and their mothers have been singing your praises.' Ramiz grinned. 'You've made quite an impression on them.'

'But what can I say? You said yourself the problem is finding teachers.'

'"*To him that will, ways are not wanting.*" If Sheikh Farid wants a school for his people, teachers can be found. He has not until now believed it is what his people want. It looks as if you may have changed his mind.'

'You will be coming with me, won't you, Ramiz?'

'Yes, but you don't need me to tell you how to behave any more than I need to remind you of the honour Sheikh Farid is conferring upon you. You have a very charming way of making whoever you speak to feel as if they are the most important person in the world. Even me.'

'In your case it is because it is true.' The words were out before she could stop them.

Ramiz stilled.

'I mean,' Celia said lightly, 'in the eyes of your people, of course.'

'Of course,' Ramiz said thoughtfully.

'Does Sheikh Farid wish to see me now?'

'Yes, now. Akil can go ahead with the caravan. Tonight will be our last night in the desert. Tomorrow we will be back in Balyrma.'

'It will be strange, being back in the harem.'

'Celia, you don't regret what has happened? Between us, I mean?'

He looked troubled. *Was it he who had regrets?* She could not bear that. Though she rarely took the initiative, even in the most commonplace of touches, Celia took Ramiz's hand and pressed a kiss onto his palm.

His skin was warm, his taste tantalisingly familiar. 'I will remember it always,' she said, rubbing his hand against her cheek. 'This last week has been magical. I will never regret it. Never.'

'Celia…'

She had a horrible suspicion he was going to apologise. Or, worse, offer her some sort of reparation. 'Please, Ramiz, don't.'

'Don't what?'

'Don't spoil it. As an interlude from reality it has been perfect.'

He pulled his hand away. 'That is still how you see it?'

She looked at him in bewilderment. 'Do not you?'

Ramiz shrugged. 'We will take the camels to Sheikh Farid's camp. That way we will waste less time.'

'Ramiz…'

But he was gone. She stared at the spot in the tent where he had stood. In the last week she'd thought she had come to understand him completely, but today she had no idea what he was thinking—what it was she had said to him to make him look so…what? Angry? A little, but not just that. She pulled an *abeyah* the colour of cinnamon, embroidered with russet and gold, over her caftan, and checked her appearance in the mirror. He had seemed almost disappointed. But why?

Tonight would be their last night in the desert. Their last night together in her tent. When they returned to the palace would it all be at an end? Was that what he meant? That he would not visit her in the harem? Had he had enough of her? Was he letting her down gently?

A horrible sick feeling made her slump down onto the divan. When he'd said it was their last night in the desert, he'd meant it was to be their last night. Ever. There could be no other meaning. Celia blinked rapidly to prevent the hot tears which welled up in her eyes from spilling. She'd known it would end, but she'd hoped it would last until she had to leave. Now she saw he was right. To drag it out, waking each morning wondering if it would be this day or the next when her papa would arrive, would be unendurable.

Her papa would take her home. But home was here, with Ramiz. Without him she might as well be condemned to a nomadic life, just like the Bedouins. Celia sniffed and blew her nose, and chastised herself for the fanciful turn her imagination had taken. She had tonight. She had the memories. Things could be worse, she told herself bracingly, though she wasn't exactly sure how.

The meeting with Sheikh Farid went well. Celia was nervous beforehand, worried she would let Ramiz down. 'It's not possible,' Ramiz had said reassuringly, surprised to find that he meant it. 'I trust you.'

He had meant that too, which was more of a surprise, for the truth was he didn't normally trust anyone completely to act on his behalf, to act without his explicit instructions, to think for themselves—not even Akil. Yet he trusted Celia. He trusted her judgement and he trusted her ability. Sitting by her side, translating only when consulted, he watched with admiration as she set about charming Sheikh Farid as she seemed to charm everyone she spoke to, from the market traders in the souk, to Yasmina, his servants, every child who came within a hundred yards of her, and now this wily old Bedouin, who was already smiling and making jokes after just fifteen minutes in her company—something it had taken *him* many visits to achieve.

Sheikh Farid summoned his wives and younger children. Ramiz recognised the little girl who made a beeline for Celia's lap as the one he'd seen her with the day before. They had been counting out numbers using pieces of straw. Now Celia encouraged the child to show her father what she had learned.

The meeting concluded with a promise on Sheikh Farid's part to give thought to the problem of finding teachers—a giant leap forward as far as Ramiz was concerned.

'You are blessed in your visitor from the West,' Sheikh Farid told Ramiz. 'She has the brains of a man in the body of a beautiful woman. If only you could be persuaded to stay,' he continued, turning towards Celia, 'I would be happy to take you as my next wife. Though I fear that Prince Ramiz here would have something to say to that.' Sheikh Farid smiled sadly. 'I should not grudge him, for I already have six fine wives and this poor man has none, but you must understand I speak as a father. I had hoped my Juman would please the Prince, but I can see she is not to his taste.' The Bedouin touched his hands together and bowed. 'Safe journey, my friends. Peace be with you.'

Celia returned the gesture. '*Wa-alaykum as-salam*, Sheikh Farid. May our paths cross again one day.'

'I will pray for it.'

Celia's farewells to the many Bedouin children who crowded round her, tugging at her *abeyah* for attention, were less formal and more protracted. Ramiz watched almost unnoticed, content to remain in the background, a strange emotion tugging at his heart. It was pride, he thought. He was proud of her, and proud to be in her company. It felt good, this sharing. A taste of what it could be like to have a consort. A partnership.

'She has the brains of a man in the body of a beautiful woman.' Sheikh Farid's words were a high compliment indeed, and Celia deserved it. She was exceptional. She deserved to be recognised in such a way—as herself, on her own terms. It was only in seeing someone else do so that he realised he had long since stopped trying to slot her into any preconceived role himself. She was Celia. Unique. He would never meet anyone like her again.

She finally escaped the clambering embraces of the children and allowed Ramiz to help her up onto the high saddle of her camel. Smiling and waving, the children followed them for about a hundred yards, Sheikh Farid's little daughter being among the last to give up the chase. Celia, touched immeasurably by the affection she had been shown, was dabbing at her eyes with a scrap of lace. Beside her, Ramiz kept his camel to a slow trot to allow her to regain her composure. The reality of her leaving was beginning to dawn on him with cold clarity.

This 'interlude', as she called it, he had intended as his cure. *The only way to eliminate temptation is to yield to it.* Asad's words, which only a few days ago had seemed to be the answer to his prayers. Now they mocked him. He had yielded to temptation, he had abandoned his principles to do so, but far from being sated, he was now addicted. Addicted to Celia's body. Addicted to her company. Addicted to her mind.

He needed her. He craved her. He could not imagine how it would be without her. Loneliness loomed like the vast desert plain stretched out before them in the rising heat of late morning, scorched of life, bleached of colour, dusty and arid.

A messenger had come in the night. The English had arrived at the port. The escort Ramiz had organised to attend them was even now leading the caravan across the desert to Balyrma. By the time they returned to the city tomorrow Celia's father could be waiting to take her home. They had only tonight. Just one more night.

Ramiz could hardly bear to look at the bleakness which was his future. Almost he resented Celia for doing this to him. Until she'd arrived he hadn't even known he was lonely. Until she'd arrived he hadn't needed anyone or anything. Only A'Qadiz mattered. A'Qadiz was his life and his reason for being. Now A'Qadiz without Celia seemed as drained of colour as an English morning in November.

Tonight would be their last together. Tomorrow he would cut her from his life. Why did it feel as if he would be severing a part of himself? He didn't even know what she felt about it all, not really. He hated the way she looked so cool and collected, when he ached with something horribly akin to love. But he could not love her and he would not—any more than she could or would love him.

Tonight was all they had left to them. Tonight must be enough, for there was no more to be had.

When Ramiz joined her in the tent he seemed different. Celia couldn't say how, just that he was. He had been in a strange mood since the morning's visit to Sheikh Farid. Distant, but watchful. Every time she looked at him he was looking at her, his eyes slits of amber, the tiny lines at their edges more pronounced than usual, as if he were frowning, but he did not seem angry. He seemed tense. And now, prowling around her tent in a dark blue caftan, restless as a caged tiger.

Neither of them had eaten much over dinner. They had not spoken much either. Celia was aware—too aware—of the fact that this was the last time. She could feel her heart beating, marking time like a pendulum, swinging inexorably back and forth, back and forth, counting out the seconds and the minutes and the hours.

She was apprehensive, waiting for him to make the first move as he always did when they came together. Excitement lay like a sub-strata beneath the layer of tension. Tonight she wanted it all. She did not care about the risk. She did not care about the possible consequences. She did not care about anything other than knowing, experiencing the completion of their union inside her—something Ramiz had been extremely careful never to allow. She loved him for it, and knew she should be grateful for his self-control. She was, but it left her feeling as if something was missing, something lacking. It left her feeling empty. She wanted him to make complete love to her. Just once.

But she was nervous. And if she hadn't known him better she'd have said Ramiz was nervous too. Something was bothering him, though he denied it when she asked him.

'I've made you a present,' she said, pulling the caftan she had so carefully embroidered out from under a cushion and handing it to him.

Ramiz shook it out and examined it. Dark blue silk, she had copied its pattern from one of his others. The long sleeves were embroidered in shades of blue in the traditional pattern which Yasmina had shown her. The same pattern was repeated around the hem and at the neckline, delicate but unobtrusive, designed to give weight to the garment rather than adornment. The most intricate work was on the motif she had sewn on the left breast. A crescent moon and a falcon—Ramiz's own insignia—but the bird was in full flight, and in its beak it carried a rosebud.

Ramiz gazed at it in silence, tracing the image with his finger.

'Do you like it?'

He laid the caftan down carefully on a divan. 'It is a very evocative image.'

'It's how I think of you. Me. This.'

'Us,' Ramiz said softly, stroking her hair behind her ear so that he could lick into the little crease behind her lobe, inhale the scent of her that lingered there, feel the strength and the fragility of her that seemed to be encapsulated at that precise point, in that combination of soft flesh and delicate bone.

'Us,' she said breathlessly, allowing herself to feel

the word, to think the word, to believe that it could be true just for tonight.

Ramiz pushed back the heavy fall of her hair to flutter kisses onto the nape of her neck, his fingers kneading her shoulders, stroking the wings of her shoulderblades. He pulled her against him, slipping his hands down to her waist, wrapping his arms around her, folding her into him.

She could feel his erection pressing against the base of her spine. She could feel the wall of his chest, his heart beating slow and sure against her back. Her head nestled into his shoulder. She closed her eyes and drank in the scent, the feel, the soft sound of his breath—drank it all in so that she would remember it for ever.

Ramiz turned her round in his arms and kissed her. So tenderly. So softly. Holding her as if she were something precious, his hands on the side of her face, his thumbs caressing her jaw, his eyes warm and golden, with such a look that she felt as if she were melting. She closed her own eyes and surrendered to the moment, which was like no other moment that had passed between them. A long, languorous moment, as if they had all the time in the world just to kiss and kiss and kiss. Gentle kisses, gentle caresses, as if they would soothe rather than arouse, as if they would coax and cajole, a slow burn—so slow that they barely noticed the flames rising.

Her clothes disappeared as if they had melted. His hands were on her breasts, touching her as if he had never touched her there before, his fingers marvelling at the roundness, the smoothness, the creaminess of her skin, the pink puckering of her nipple. His mouth landed like the whisper of a butterfly, sipping and sipping and sipping until she was nectar, trickling hot and sweet in a path downwards from her nipples to her belly to the darker, more sumptuous heat between her thighs.

He was naked. She was naked. Liquid with desire, molten with it, she lay touching and being touched, kissing and being kissed, stroking and being stroked. His shaft throbbed under her caress, but he seemed in no hurry, intent on tending to every curve and dip and swell, every crease and pucker, rolling her onto her stomach to kiss down her spine, the curve of her bottom, the back of her knee, the hollow of her ankle bone, then on to her back, to work his way up again, reaching the softness of her thighs, the damp heat between them, jolting her from floating bliss to jagged desire in an instant.

Celia moaned and clenched back on her climax, catching Ramiz unawares when she wriggled out from under him, rolled him onto his back, placing herself on top of him, leaning over him so that her breasts were crushed into his chest, her nipples taut and hard on his skin, his shaft taut and hard between her legs. She kissed him urgently. She saw the urgency reflected in his face, his eyes dark with it, his skin flushed with it, and then as she kissed him she felt herself lifted, his hands gripping her waist, and he thrust up and was inside her, deep inside her, as he let her fall on top of him at the same time.

She gasped her pleasure, lying still over him. He pushed her gently upright, steadying her by the waist, and the action allowed his shaft to forge deeper. His thrust forged it deeper again, touching something, a spot high inside her, that triggered an instant clenching and pulsing climax, sending her over in a headlong rush so that she was barely conscious of him thrusting inside her still, of the tension of his control etched on his cheekbones, on the rigid muscles of his shoulders, the corded sinews of his arms as he gripped her and thrust, and she lifted and fell in the same rhythm, lifting and falling, feeling him building and thickening as with every thrust he hit that same spot again and she trembled and shuddered.

She could determine the moment when he would push her from him by the way his eyes lost focus. She could see the resolution in him in the way his grip changed. She could feel his climax tightening in the base of his shaft. She could feel him swell, her own muscles gripping and holding, furling and unfurling against him. Ramiz groaned. She fell on top of him, pushing him down as he thrust up, pushing him hard down so that he couldn't move, and with a harsh cry he came, pouring hot and endlessly, high and deep inside her, and it was more, more than she had ever imagined it would be—for it was as if their essences mingled, and for now, in this instant, they truly were one.

They lay melded together for long moments, breathing fast, hearts thumping in wild unison, limbs entangled. Celia's hair trailed over Ramiz's shoulders, over his arms, which were wrapped tight around her waist in an iron grip, pressing her against him as if he would never let her go. She floated on a cloud of ecstasy, glided on a current of the sweetest, warmest air, heavy yet weightless, finally understanding the word *sated.*

Gradually their breathing slowed. Ramiz's hold on her relaxed. She waited, but the anticipated rejection did not come. He smoothed her hair back from her head. He kissed her gently on the mouth. He turned her onto her side and cradled her into him—two crescents fitting perfectly together. He ran his hand possessively down her flank and held her thus until she slept. And when she awoke in the dark of the night, when the lamps had burned out, he was still there. Still holding her.

'Celia.' Ramiz kissed her neck.

She tensed. Now he would leave. Now he would say something. But he didn't. Except her name. 'Celia…' in that husky voice, raw with passion, brushing over her skin like velvet, and he turned her to face him and then he kissed her, and it started over again—except this time Ramiz took control, Ramiz lay on top of her. It came harder and faster, their joint climax, as he thrust with her legs wrapped around him, and he poured himself into her with no need for her urging, his cry one of abandon she had never thought to hear and would never forget.

In the morning when she awoke he was dressed, sitting on the edge of the divan, with his formidable look back in place. She stretched out her hand. 'Don't hate me.'

Ramiz shook her away. 'If I hate it must be myself. A man must take responsibility, since a woman must bear the consequences. It should not have happened.' *It should not, but he could not regret it.* His own intransigence confused him.

'It was my fault.'

'No. The fault was mine. We must trust to the fates that you are not punished for it.'

Celia bit her lip. Punished! He was talking about the possibility of a child, their child, as punishment. She sat up. 'I should get dressed. You wanted to make an early start.'

His mind seethed with words. His heart seethed with emotions. He couldn't understand it—any of it. He couldn't think straight. He wanted to shake her until she told him what she really felt. He wanted to make love to her again, to experience that sweet perfection of their union, a perfection he hadn't known possible until last night.

Ramiz got to his feet, running his hand through his hair. 'A messenger arrived yesterday. Your father is here in A'Qadiz. He arrived at the port two days ago. He will be at Balyrma shortly—perhaps even before us.'

'You knew last night?'

Ramiz nodded curtly. 'This is the end.'

'You knew last night?' Celia repeated stupidly.

Her eyes were like moss damp with dew. Her hair curled like fire over the creaminess of her skin, over the soft mounds of her breasts. She looked like Botticelli's *Venus*. He had never seen anyone so beautiful or so irresistible. Having her, taking her so completely, possessing her, had made it worse, much worse. Knowing did not satisfy. It only made the wanting more painful, for he knew now what he would be missing.

'Why didn't you tell me, Ramiz?'

He had no answer—none he could give which would not force him to confront—what he did not want to confront—so Ramiz shrugged. 'You know now. There are two women with him also. One young, one old.'

'My aunt? The other is probably a maid.'

Another shrug. 'Get dressed. You will find out soon enough.' He turned to go.

'Ramiz?'

'Well?'

'You were saying goodbye, weren't you? I understand. It was perfect while it lasted—our fairytale. I want you to know that.'

He blanched. The words were almost his undoing. A fairytale. That was all it was. Ramiz left the room.

In the main part of the tent he saw the caftan she had embroidered for him. He picked it up. The motif dug like thorns into his heart. He could never wear it. Never. But he folded it carefully and took it with him all the same.

It came to him then, as he strode across the sand to his own tent. He loved her. That was what it was—this craving, this need to be with her. It was because she was part of him.

She was his. He felt it more fiercely than the burning heat of the sun. She was his. He loved her. And soon she would be gone.

Chapter Thirteen

Contrary to Ramiz's expectations, when they arrived at Balyrma there was no sigh of Celia's relatives. In fact dusk was falling and Celia was beginning to think they would not arrive at all that day when the doors of the harem were flung open and, to her astonishment, not just Aunt Sophia but Cassie stood before her, looking extremely dusty, exhausted and bewildered.

'Celia? Is that you?' Cassie was the first to speak, standing transfixed before the exotic-looking creature who bore a distant resemblance to the sister she had come so far to rescue. She hesitated, unaccountably nervous.

'Cassie!' Celia flew across the courtyard to embrace her sister. 'Cassie, I can't believe it's really you. Are you well? I can't tell for all the dust. Cassie, it really is me, I promise.' Celia kissed her sister's cheek. 'And Aunt Sophia. You've come all this way, and so quickly. You must be exhausted. Please come in. Fatima, Adila—here are my aunt and my sister. They will want food.' Celia broke off to issue instructions in Arabic, before ushering Cassie ahead of her to her favourite salon.

'You have learned the language?' Cassie said in amazement.

Celia laughed. 'A little only.'

Cassandra paused at the fountain, trailing her fingers in the water and looking around her at the lemon trees, the tiled pillars, the symmetry of the salons running round the square, one leading into another. So strange, yet Celia looked so at home here. Even the way she walked in her jewelled slippers was different. She seemed to float and ripple.

'You look like Scheherazade in these clothes,' she said, regarding her sister with a mixture of envy and awe. 'So very glamorous. I hardly recognise you.'

Celia made a little twirl. 'Do you like them? They are so much more suited to the heat here, and such lovely colours.'

'Celia, are you—can it be that you have *abandoned* your corsets?' demanded Lady Sophia, looking at her niece's all too obvious curves, revealed by the clinging fabrics. 'I do trust you do not leave your rooms in such a toilette?'

Celia laughed. 'No one wears corsets here, Aunt, it is far too hot.'

'And your hair—is it the custom to wear it down like that?'

'Not outside. Then it is covered by a veil.'

'And you have no stockings. What are these things

under your robe? They look remarkably like pantaloons. Do you tell me it is also common to have one's *undergarments* on display?'

'Dearest Aunt, they are called *sarwal* pantaloons, and, yes, I am afraid it is quite acceptable. Oh, Cassie, Aunt Sophia—I can't tell you how wonderful it is to see you. Please do sit down. Adila will bring you some sherbet. You will like it; it is most refreshing.'

'Where do we sit?'

'On the cushions. Like so.'

Celia floated gracefully onto the carpeted floor. Cassie followed suit, but Lady Sophia took a seat with extreme reluctance. 'Only heathens sit on the floor.'

'Where is Papa, Aunt?'

'He has an audience with the Sheikh.'

'How are the girls? Are they well? Did you get my letters?'

'Yes, they are all very well and send their love. But, Celia—' Cassie looked anxiously at her sister '—are *you* well?'

'Do I not look it?'

'Yes. Very. In fact I don't think I've ever seen you look better. You look—older, but more beautiful,' Cassie said, sounding as confused as she felt. 'Not in the least like our Celia. I have to confess I am a little intimidated by you.' Her laugh tinkled like the cold water of the fountain. 'What do you think, Aunt?'

Lady Sophia pursed her lips. 'Hmm.' She took a cautious sip of the sherbet which Adila had handed to her on a silver tray. 'Do they speak English?' she asked, nodding at the maidservants.

Celia shook her head.

'And this place we are in—is this what is known as the harem?'

Again Celia nodded.

'Where are the other women?' Cassie asked, looking around her as if she expected a flock of scantily clad females to suddenly appear.

'Sheikh al-Muhana is not married. He has no wives,' Celia said with a smile.

Lady Sophia cleared her throat. 'Celia, I must ask you. Has that man committed any—any improprieties with you? You must know that your sister has been most concerned for your—your… I told her not to worry, of course. I told her you would not—but you must put her mind at rest. Tell us plainly, child, have you—have you been forced to—? In short, Celia, this man has not laid a hand upon you, has he?'

Though she tried desperately to stop it, when she was faced with the frank blue eyes of her sister and the worried grey of her aunt, Celia felt a blush steal over her cheeks. 'Sheikh al-Muhana has treated me with the utmost respect,' she replied falteringly. 'He was conscious from the first that I—that my family—that Papa… He has done nothing to compromise the relationship between our two countries,' she finished with a tilt of her chin. 'In fact it was Ramiz—Sheikh al-Muhana—who saved my life when we were attacked by the brigands who killed George.'

Needless to say this statement produced a welter of questions from Cassie. Though Celia tried to gloss over George's role in events, Aunt Sophia's sharp nose scented scandal. 'George Cleveden was reputed to be an excellent shot,' she said. 'I cannot understand how he came not to defend himself.'

'He did not have the opportunity to fire his gun. It was all so sudden.'

'And it was early morning, you say? How came it that you were not in the tent with him?'

'I found the tent claustrophobic and chose to sleep outside.'

'Had you and George quarrelled?'

'No, Aunt Sophia, nothing of that nature. We had not long been married. We were still…well, getting used to each other.'

'Hmm.' Lady Sophia treated Celia to her Sphinx look. 'You should know that your sister and I came all this way in anticipation of having to support you through the trial of your husband's death and your subsequent incarceration here. Cassie in particular has been most upset by the idea of your suffering inopportune advances from this Sheikh al-Muhana.'

Celia pressed her sister's hand. 'Have you been worried about me, Cassie? Poor thing. There was no need as I have been very well looked after, I promise. I am so sorry to have caused you to fret.'

Cassandra examined the intricate silver *passementerie* braiding on the sleeve of Celia's caftan. 'What is it you're not telling us?' She lifted her eyes, meeting her sister's with a puzzled look. 'It's true I've been worried sick about you, and I can't tell you what a relief it is to see you in one piece, looking so well, but—but that's just it, Celia, I don't understand it. What has happened to you?'

Celia pulled her sister into a tight hug. 'Cassie, nothing bad, I promise.'

Cassandra sniffed. 'You've always told me everything.'

'Hmm,' said Lady Sophia once more. 'Celia, I believe Cassandra would be the better for a wash and change of clothes.'

'Of course she would.' Celia clapped her hands to summon the maids. 'Cassie, go with Fatima and Adila. You will be amazed by the bathing chamber, and they will give you some of my clothes to try if you wish. Then you will see that they are just clothes, and I really am your sister. Go on—you will feel much better.'

Cassandra left. 'Well,' Lady Sophia said when they were alone, 'since it is obviously not George Cleveden who is responsible for that glow you have about you, young woman, I presume it is this sheikh. You will tell me, please, now that your sister's blushes have been spared, what exactly is going on here.'

Lord Henry Armstrong's meeting with Ramiz was conducted on much more formal terms, in the splendid surroundings of the throne room. Ramiz, clad in his royal robes of state, sat on the dais, with Akil standing in attendance. To Peregrine's relief two low stools had been placed in front of the throne, and to these Ramiz graciously waved his visitors.

'I think we have met before, Your Highness,' Lord

Henry said, sitting cautiously down, having made his bow, 'though I can't recall where.'

'Lisbon, about four years ago,' Ramiz replied. 'Until my brother was tragically killed in battle I spent much of my time abroad as my father's emissary, and my brother's too.'

'Thought I recognised you,' Lord Henry said with satisfaction. 'Don't often forget a face, though I'm not quite so good with names. Well, now, tragic business this, but no point in dwelling on it, so we might as well get straight to the point. George Cleveden came here with the objective of agreeing rights of passage through A'Qadiz's port. I've been authorised to conclude those negotiations.'

'I am sure we can reach terms agreeable to us both, Lord Armstrong,' Ramiz said smoothly. 'I know how very important the route is to your East India Company.'

A lesser diplomat would have expressed surprise, but Lord Henry's experience stood him in excellent stead. Like a good gambler, he knew when he had been trumped. 'Quite so,' he said. 'Three months is a considerable advantage over two years. What is it you seek from us in return?'

'We will discuss the details tomorrow, but let me just say it pleases me to be able to conclude a pact which I believe will be to the long-term advantage of both our countries. Tonight I am sure you wish to rest after your journey. The desert can be unkind to those unfamiliar with it. And you will obviously wish to see your daughter.'

'No rush on that. Celia and Cassie will have their heads together, happy to wait until our business is concluded.'

Peregrine frowned. His instructions from the Consul General were clear. The Lady Celia was to be questioned prior to the treaty for any pertinent information. Acutely uncomfortable as he was with the damnable position in which Lord Wincester had placed him, he was even more terrified of disobeying the explicit orders of such an influential man. He tugged on Lord Henry's sleeve. 'My Lord, would it not be wise for us to speak to Lady Celia now?' Peregrine said with a significant look. 'Find out how she is, what she has been up to, et cetera. She'll be anxious to tell you all about her adventure, if you get my drift.'

'Dammit, man, I said it can wait,' Lord Henry said, frowning.

'But, My Lord—' Peregrine persisted awkwardly.

'I said not now,' Lord Henry said furiously. He turned towards Ramiz. 'You will forgive my assistant. He is rather tired,' he said, drawing Peregrine a censorious look.

Ramiz clapped his hands together and the doors at the far end of the throne room were flung open. 'Indeed—as I am sure you are too, Lord Armstrong. My servants will escort you to your quarters, and to the men's *hammam* baths. I will join you later for dinner.' He nodded his dismissal. 'Akil, a word, if you please.' Waiting until Lord Henry and Peregrine were safely out of earshot, Ramiz got to his feet and cast his jewelled headdress onto the throne. 'Get that idiot assistant on his own.

There is something going on and I want to know what it is.'

'And the treaty?'

'As we agreed. Lord Armstrong knows his position is not strong. Give a little to massage his ego, and he will not argue with the main points. Are Lady Celia's sister and aunt with her in the harem?'

Akil nodded. 'If things go well, Lady Celia can leave tomorrow.'

'Why do you dislike her so much?'

Akil hesitated. 'It's not that I don't like her. Under different circumstances I would like her very well. But she does not belong here, Ramiz.'

'You saw how Sheikh Farid took to her. And his wives.'

'And many other people—my own wife included. The Lady Celia is undoubtedly charming.'

'But?'

Akil shrugged. 'You know what I think. Do not let us quarrel over it. It is not just that she doesn't belong here, Ramiz, her family would no more accept it than your own people. In the eyes of the likes of Lord Armstrong we are heathens. It wouldn't surprise me to find that he suspects his daughter has been kept in your harem as a concubine,' he said with a smile.

'If he thought that he would hardly have been so polite just now,' Ramiz snapped.

'He is a statesman first, a father second. He will get the treaty signed to advance the British cause, and then he will worry about his daughter. Mark my words, Ramiz, he says nothing for the moment, but that does not mean he will remain silent. We must hope the Lady Celia has nothing to complain of.'

Ramiz cursed. '*You* must rather hope for your own sake that *I* have nothing to complain of. Find out what Finchley-Burke was so cagey about and report back to me before dinner. And bring Yasmina to the palace tomorrow, Celia will wish to say her farewells.'

'She *is* going, then?'

Ramiz ran his hand through his hair. 'Would it be so impossible to imagine her staying?'

Akil shook his head and made for the door. 'You don't really want me to answer that,' he said, and left.

For a long time afterwards Ramiz stared absently into space. The problem was not that it was impossible to imagine Celia staying; it was that it was impossible to imagine her leaving. He did not know how it had come about, but she had become indispensable to him. He, Ramiz al-Muhana, Prince of A'Qadiz, did not want to contemplate the rest of his life without her. Now he wondered if he had to. If Sheikh Farid accepted her, why not others? As his consort, with the fulfilment she would bring to his life, would she not more than make up for any potential backlash which failure to marry to one of his neighbours' daughters would inevitably bring?

After last night he was as certain as a man could be without hearing the words that she loved him. Last night she had made love to him, as he had made love to her. Last night had not been about the pleasures of the flesh—it had been something more fundamental, almost religious. The worship of a lover by a lover. The desire to create one being from two separate halves. The need to celebrate that union with the planting of a seed. How much he had derided that idea until now. He wanted Celia by his side. He wanted her to be his and only his. He wanted children—not as the means of cementing the succession, but as the fruit of their love.

It would be asking much of her. To stay here in A'Qadiz, to surrender her family, to exchange her loyalties from one country to another, to commit herself not just to him but to his kingdom, a place steeped in custom and traditions alien to her. It was not something she could do half-heartedly either, if she was to be accepted. There would be changes, and with Celia by his side some of those changes would come more quickly than he had planned, but some things would never change. As his princess she must not just pay lip-service to their traditions, she must embrace them. It was much to ask. Perhaps too much.

Ramiz forced himself to imagine life without her. His mind refused to co-operate. She was his—had always been destined to be his. Tomorrow, in the clear light of day and before her family, he would claim her.

Filled with determination, and a lightness of heart which it took him some time to realise was a foretaste of happiness, Ramiz retired to his chambers to change. He wondered how Celia's reunion with her sister was going. He wondered what she was saying of him, if she was confiding anything about him. No, she would not. His Celia—for already he was thinking of her thus—was fiercely loyal. She would tell nothing which might compromise his relationship with her father. Nothing which would put his treatment of her in anything other than a favourable light. She loved him. He was almost sure of it.

The urge to seek her out and declare himself was strong, but duty forbade it. As Ramiz finished bathing and donned a clean robe in preparation for dinner, Akil arrived, looking sombre.

Dismissing the servants, Ramiz turned to his friend. 'Well?'

'I spoke to Finchley-Burke as you suggested, Highness.'

'You call me Highness. It must be bad news,' Ramiz said with an ironic smile. 'Spit it out.'

'Ramiz, you must understand if I was not absolutely sure of this…'

Ramiz's smile faded. 'What is it?'

'The Lady Celia.'

'What of her?'

'She has been spying on you.'

'Don't be foolish.'

'Perhaps spying is the wrong word. She has been collecting information about our country.'

'A natural curiosity, Akil.'

'No, Ramiz. I'm sorry, but it's more than that. They left her here deliberately, with instructions to make use of your attraction for her.'

'You are being ridiculous.'

'I'm not, I assure you. Oh, nothing improper was asked of her. According to Finchley-Burke it was all neatly veiled—her duty to her country, the memory of her dead husband…you know the kind of thing.'

'You are saying that Celia was instructed to extract

information from me that might prove useful to the British government by—? No, I can't believe it.'

'Ramiz, I'm sorry.' Akil put a hand on his friend's shoulder but it was shaken off. He took a step back, but met Ramiz's eyes unflinchingly. 'I *am* sorry, but you must ask yourself why else would a woman of her birth have allowed you such liberties? Come on, Ramiz, it's not as if she put up much resistance, is it?'

Ramiz moved so quickly that his fist made sharp contact with Akil's jaw before he had a chance to defend himself. Akil staggered back against the wall, frightened by the blaze of anger he was faced with.

Ramiz took a hasty step towards him, his fists clenched, but stopped short inches away. 'My hands are shamed by contact with you. You deserve to be whipped.'

'Whip me, then, but it won't change the truth.' Akil spoke with difficulty, for his jaw was swelling fast. There was blood on his tongue. 'She has used you. It is as well we found out before tomorrow, for you can be sure her father would have found an opportunity to allow her to brief him. She has used you, Ramiz, we are well rid of her.'

'Get out! *Get out of here!*'

'Ramiz…'

'Now!'

Akil bowed, still clutching his jaw, and fled. Alone, Ramiz slumped down on his divan, his head in his hands. There must be an explanation. But Akil would never lie to him. He knew that for a certainty. There was no reason either for Finchley-Burke to concoct such a story if it was not true. He would not demean himself by asking the junior diplomat to repeat it. Celia would answer to him personally.

Lady Sophia, having much food for thought, graciously agreed to permit Fatima to help her bathe, after much encouragement from Celia. 'Please, Aunt, I promise you will find it a most amenable experience.' Celia had also been fulsome in her descriptions of A'Qadiz, and her recent trip to the desert in Sheikh al-Muhana's caravan, but despite being pressed had said little of the Sheikh himself—even less of her relationship with him.

Cautiously lowering herself into the scented water of the tiled bath, Lady Sophia realised that it was Celia's very reticence which gave her most grounds for concern. The girl was smitten, it was obvious. She would consult Henry in the morning, for the sooner Celia was removed from this sheikh's beguiling presence the better.

Left alone together with Cassie, Celia gave in to her sister's plea to be allowed to try on her exotic outfits. She was sitting on her favourite cushion, watching Cassandra parade before her, laughing and telling her she looked rather like the Queen of Sheba, when the crash of a wooden door slamming with force onto tiled walls made the smile die on her face and had her leaping to her feet.

Celia reached the doorway in time to see Ramiz stride across the courtyard. His face was set and white with fury. 'What's wrong? Is it my father?'

'Traitor!' He stood before her wild-eyed, his chest heaving.

'Ramiz! What on earth is the matter?'

'I trusted you! Dear heavens, I trusted you. I who trust no one. And you betrayed me.'

Anger glittered from his eyes, mere slits of gold under heavy lids. His mouth was drawn into a thin line. Celia clutched a hand to her breast. 'Ramiz, I have not betrayed you. I would never—what has happened? Please tell me.'

'You lied to me,' he snarled.

'I did not lie to you,' Celia responded indignantly. 'I would never lie to you. You're frightening me, Ramiz.'

'I doubt it,' he flashed. 'I doubt anything frightens *you*, Lady Celia, consummate actress as you are. I should have known. Akil was right. I should have guessed from the start that such a delicate English rose would not subject herself to the brutal caresses of a heathen like myself without reason. Do they *know*, my lovely Celia?' he hissed, nodding contemptuously at Lady Sophia and Cassie, paused on the brink of intervention in the doorway of the main salon. 'Have you told them the price you paid for whatever pathetic little snippets of information you have garnered for them?'

As realisation dawned Celia began to feel faint. 'Mr Finchley-Burke,' she said, her voice no more than a whisper.

'Precisely. He is here with your father. You didn't expect that, did you?'

Horribly conscious of the presence of her aunt and

her sister, Celia shook her head miserably and moved a little further down the courtyard. 'Ramiz, it's true. Mr Finchley-Burke asked me to—to keep my eyes and ears open. Those were his words. It is also true that I thought about it—but only for a few moments. I was just relieved to have an excuse to stay here, Ramiz. I never intended—I would never use—especially not now, after…'

'I don't believe you.'

'Ramiz, please.' Celia took a step towards him, her hands held out in supplication, but he shrank away from her as if she were poison. She swallowed hard. Tears would be humiliating. 'It's the truth. Even if I did consider it at first…'

'So you admit that much?'

Celia hung her head. 'I thought if I could salvage something from George's death… But it was a thought only—a fleeting one. I never really intended—I know I never would have. And that was before you and I…'

'There *is* no you and I. Not now.'

'*Ramiz!* Ramiz, you can't seriously believe that I would have made love with you for any other reason than—' She broke off, realising that what she had been about to say was exactly what she had sworn never to say. That she loved him. Looking at him in anguish, she could think of nothing *except* that she loved him.

Now he did touch her, pulling her into his arms, pushing her hair back from her face, forcing her to meet his hard gaze. 'So why did you, Celia? Why did you allow me such liberties? Why did you give *me* what you gave no other man?'

'You know why,' she whispered. 'I couldn't stop myself.'

'How can I believe that when you obviously had no such difficulty in denying your husband?'

'George has nothing to do with this.'

'But he has everything to do with it. Was it not for the sake of his memory that you did all this?'

'Ramiz, have I ever asked you anything remotely sensitive when it comes to A'Qadiz? Have I prodded you for information? Have I ever attempted to cajole secrets from you? You know I have not!'

But he was beyond reasoning. 'You have done worse than that. You have forced me to betray my honour. You gave yourself to me. You threw yourself at me in the hope that I would succumb and I did. I do not doubt for a moment that your intention is to cry ravishment now, thus allowing your father the moral upper hand, which he will have no hesitation in using to his advantage.'

Celia stared at him in absolute astonishment. 'I truly thought you knew me. I thought you understood me. I thought I understood you too. But I don't. I would die rather than do such a thing.'

'I didn't expect you to admit it. I just wanted you to know that I'd found out. It is I who would die rather than allow you to take further advantage of me. There will be no treaty. Never. Now get out of my sight.'

He threw her from him contemptuously. Celia staggered. 'Ramiz, please don't do this. Please.'

'I am done with you. All of you. You will leave Balyrma tomorrow. I will have an escort to see you out of my kingdom. I don't want to see or hear from you ever again.'

The harem door clanged shut behind him and he was gone. As Celia crumpled to the floor, covering her face with her hands, Lady Sophia and Cassandra rushed towards her, helping her to her feet and back to her salon, seating her on her divan and wrapping her in a velvet throw.

'It's all right, Celia,' Cassie said, holding her tight and casting a bewildered look at her aunt.

Almost oblivious of their presence, Celia huddled under the soft caress of the velvet. It would never be all right. Nothing she could say would make any difference. Ramiz despised her. It was over.

Chapter Fourteen

'Let me in! Open up at once, I say.'

Celia raised a weary head from her pillow and listened.

'Open up! Dammit, my daughters are in there. Will you open the door?'

'Papa?' Celia stumbled from her divan to the courtyard, to find Cassie and Aunt Sophia staring in consternation at the closed door of the harem. 'Is that Father I can hear?'

'We can't get the door open,' Cassie said. 'There's no handle on this side.'

'Open up,' Celia called to the guards in Arabic. 'It is my father.'

The door swung open, revealing an irate Lord Henry with a red-faced Peregrine beside him. The eunuch guards had drawn their scimitars and were barring the way. 'For goodness' sake, Celia, tell these men to let us through,' Lord Henry said testily.

'This is a harem, Papa. Sheikh al-Muhana is the only man who is permitted to come here. Why did you not just send for me?'

'Couldn't get anyone to understand a damned word I was saying.'

'But where is Ramiz?'

'If you mean the Prince, I have no idea. Didn't turn up for dinner with us last night—haven't seen him this morning. Took us the best part of the last hour to track you down here. I've never seen so many corridors and courtyards in my life. This place is like a maze.'

Celia spoke softly to the turbaned guards, gesturing to her father. Reluctantly, they sheathed their scimitars. 'I've told them to leave the doors open and promised we will remain in full view in the courtyard,' she said, gesturing her father in. Peregrine, who looked as if he would prefer to stay on the other side of the door, entered with some reluctance.

Lord Henry looked about with interest. 'Well, so this is the harem. Where are all the other women?'

'There aren't any. Prince Ramiz is not married. What has happened, Papa? You look upset.'

'Well, and so I bloody well should be,' Lord Henry said, casting a contemptuous look at Peregrine. 'Come here, Celia, let me look at you.'

Lord Henry inspected his daughter, who was dressed in a green caftan of lawn cotton, with her copper tresses flowing down her back, in some state of disorder from sleep. Perfectly well aware that the trauma of the scene with Ramiz and her consequent disturbed night showed in the dark shadows under her eyes, Celia put her arms round her father's neck, avoiding his scrutiny. 'It is lovely to see you, Papa. I'm sorry you've had to come all this way.'

'Aye, well, providential as it turns out. Or at least,' he said, glowering once more in Peregrine's direction, 'I thought it was until this damned fool told me what he and that idiot Wincester had cooked up.'

'Lord Armstrong, I assure you I was just the messenger,' said Peregrine. 'Wouldn't dream of— Would never—' He broke off to look beseechingly at Celia. 'I beg of you, Lady Celia, to inform your father of what passed between us.'

'Let us sit down,' Celia said wearily, clapping her hands to summon Adila and Fatima, and asking them to arrange divans in the courtyard for her guests, much to Peregrine, Lady Sophia and Lord Henry's relief. Celia and Cassie, who was dressed in one of Celia's outfits, though she retained her corsets, sat on cushions, leaning against the fountain.

Once coffee was served, and the maidservants had retired, Celia took a deep breath and recounted her original interview with Peregrine. 'I assure you, Papa, he was most circumspect in his request, and most painfully embarrassed by it too. I admit, I did consider the possibility of disclosing any information which I obtained here—not by subterfuge but simply because I *was* here—but after Peregrine left I decided I could not. Lord Wincester may consider my first loyalty is to my country, but while I am a guest of Sheikh al-Muhana, my country is A'Qadiz, and I would not insult him by betraying him. If I did, would I not be betraying my country rather than serving it?'

'Quite right, quite right,' Lord Henry said. 'Well said, daughter—exactly as I would have told old Wincester myself, if I had been consulted. Call me old-fashioned but diplomacy is an honourable vocation. I'll have no truck with stooping to nefarious methods. Britain can fight her corner without resorting to that.'

'Yes, Papa. I only wish I had said as much to Mr Finchley-Burke at the time,' Celia admitted, shame-faced.

'And why did you not, may I ask?'

She coloured, but met her father's gaze. 'I wanted to stay here. I was glad of the excuse not to leave. I didn't say as much to Mr Finchley-Burke, but I think he guessed.' She turned to Peregrine. 'Did you not?'

He shrugged in agreement.

'But why?' Lord Henry looked at his daughter afresh, seeming to notice for the first time her loose hair and traditional dress. His eyes narrowed. 'Why are you dressed like that?' He cast a worried glance at his sister. 'Sophia?'

Lady Sophia, looking unusually disconcerted, in turn cast a warning glance at Peregrine. 'Perhaps if you are finished with Mr Finchley-Burke, Henry…?'

Immensely relieved, Peregrine rose from his seat, but Lord Henry detained him. 'He made this mess—damned fool confessed all to that Akil chap last night—so he can stay where he is until we've agreed how to patch things up. Which I won't be able to do until I know all the facts.' Lord Henry got to his feet, dipping his hand into the fountain as if to test the temperature, and sat back down again. 'Out with it,' he said, looking at Sophia. 'What is going on?'

'Papa, there is nothing going on,' Celia said hurriedly. 'Only that I—that Ramiz and I—that Sheikh al-Muhana and I...'

'Celia thinks herself in love with the man,' Sophia said testily. 'That is why she stayed.'

'In love! With a sheikh! Are you out of your mind, Celia?' Lord Henry leapt to his feet once more, looming over his eldest daughter. 'I hope—I do most sincerely hope—that you have not lost all sense of propriety as to have been spending time alone with this man.' He eyed his daughter's guilty countenance with astonishment.

'I am afraid, Henry, that after the scene Cassandra and I witnessed last night there can be no doubt at all that she has,' Lady Sophia said grimly.

'Eh? What scene?' Lord Henry demanded, now looking thoroughly bewildered.

'Sheikh al-Muhana came here last night, presumably as soon as he had discovered the Consul General's little subterfuge,' Lady Sophia explained, with one of her gimlet stares which made poor Peregrine quake. 'While Celia chose to keep the detail of what passed between them private, it was obvious from the—the manner in which they spoke that Prince Ramiz and your daughter are no strangers to one another's company.'

'Dear heavens.' Lord Henry staggered back into his chair. 'What on earth are we to do? The treaty,' he said, staring at Celia in horror. 'That treaty—you have no idea how important it is. A long-term commitment like the one we're aiming for is crucial. Fun-da-mental,' he said, banging his fist on his knee, 'is that we trust one another. Now I find that the Prince thinks my daughter has been spying at our government's instigation, and not only that she has been behaving like some sort of—of…'

'Papa!'

'Father!'

'Henry!'

'I say, sir…'

Lord Henry glared at the four shocked faces surrounding him. 'Well, how the hell do you think it looks?' he demanded furiously. 'Must I spell it out for you?'

'No, Henry,' Lady Sophia said hastily. 'I don't think that is necessary.'

Lord Henry mopped his brow with a large kerchief and sighed heavily. His Lordship was not a man prone to fits of ill temper. Indeed, his success as a diplomat was in large part due to his ability to remain level-headed in the most trying of circumstances, but an arduous trip by sea and sand, the incompetence displayed by everyone involved in this sorry matter, and now the scandalous and highly uncharacteristic behaviour of his eldest daughter had sent him over the edge. 'What were you thinking, Celia?' he said, his voice heavy with disappointment.

Celia, who by now was feeling about one inch tall, bit her lip. 'I wasn't thinking, Papa, that is the problem,' she said stiffly. She got to her feet with as much dignity as she could muster, shaking out her caftan and pushing her hair back from her face. 'Ramiz is an honourable man, and one who values the welfare of A'Qadiz over everything else. I am sure, with a few concessions on your part to compensate him for the misunderstanding, he will still be prepared to come to an agreement over the use of the Red Sea port. It will do your cause no harm to inform him that the matter has been a cause of estrangement between you and I, for upon that subject I think you will find you and he are in complete accord.'

'On the contrary, Lady Celia, I would be most upset to discover that I was the cause of your estrangement from your family. I know how much they mean to you.'

All eyes turned to where Ramiz stood, framed by the doorway. A night alone under the stars in the desert had done much to cool his temper, and with an element of calm had also come rationality. It was true Celia had never made any attempt to extract information of any sort from him, but more fundamentally he felt in his bones that she would not lie to him.

In his determination to be rid of her, Akil had exaggerated. With the discovery of his love still young, and Celia's feelings for him as yet undeclared, the situation had punctured Ramiz in his most vulnerable spot, but with the dawn had come renewed certainty. He loved her. He was sure of it, though he had never loved before—and never would again. He loved her. She was his other half, and as his other half could no more do anything untrue than he could.

Ramiz had returned to the palace filled with hope. Making immediately for the harem, he had come upon the open door, through which he had witnessed most of the courtyard scene. He had not stopped to wash or change. His cloak and headdress were dusty, his face showed a blue-black stubble, and there were shadows under his eyes. Ignoring all but Celia, he now strode into the room.

'I must speak with you,' he said urgently, taking her by the arm.

'You will unhand my niece at once, sir,' Lady Sophia said brusquely. 'You have done quite enough damage already.'

Confronted with a sharp-eyed woman bearing a remarkable resemblance to a camel dressed in grey silk, sweeping down upon him like a galleon in full sail, Ramiz stood his ground and kept his hold on Celia. 'Lady Sophia, I presume?' he said haughtily.

'And you, I take it, are Sheikh al-Muhana. I do not offer my hand, sir, nor do I make my bow, for you do not merit such courtesy. Unhand my niece, sir. She has suffered quite enough of your attentions.'

Ramiz's eyes narrowed. He took a step towards Lady Sophia, who flinched but did not give ground, then halted abruptly, snapping out a command in his own language. The two eunuchs came immediately into the courtyard, their swords drawn. Before they could protest, everyone except Ramiz and Celia had been ushered with varying degrees of force from the room. The harem door banged shut.

'Ramiz, what…?'

'I'm sorry.'

'What?'

'I'm sorry.'

'I've never heard you say that before,' Celia said, with a fragile half-smile.

Ramiz took her hand between his, holding it in a warm clasp. His face was stripped of its mask, leaving him exposed, raw, and there was something more there—something she recognised but had never dreamed to see, had never even allowed herself to hope for. It looked like love.

Celia caught her breath. 'Ramiz?'

'Celia, listen to me. I heard what you said to your father just now, but you have to believe I came here to ask you to forgive me for doubting you before I heard the words. What I heard just confirmed what I knew. What I should have realised last night—' He broke off and ran his hand through his hair, pushing his headdress to the floor. 'I wasn't thinking straight. I'd only just realized—only just begun to wonder if it was possible—then when Akil told me—I simply lost control. But there's one thing I'm sure of—will always be sure of. I love you. Without you my life would be a wilderness. I love you so much, Celia, say you love me and I will be the happiest man on earth. If you will just—'

'Ramiz, I love you. I love you. I love you.' Celia threw herself into his arms.

'Celia, say it again!'

'I love you, Ramiz.' She beamed at him. 'I love you.'

Finally he kissed her, his mouth devouring hers, the day's growth of stubble on his chin rasping against her tender skin, his hands pressing her so close she could scarcely breathe. She kissed him back with equal fervour, whispering his name over and over in between kisses, relishing the feel of him hard against her, the familiar scent of him, the wildly exhilarating excitement of him, and underpinning it all the simple rightness of it.

They kissed and murmured love, and kissed and repeated each other's name in wonder, and kissed again until, breathless and transformed, they sat together entwined in one another's arms on the floor of the courtyard, becoming dimly aware of an altercation on the other side of the door which seemed to have been going on for some time.

'My father,' Celia said. 'He probably thinks you're ravishing me.'

'If he would go away and leave us alone I would,' Ramiz replied with a grin. 'I did not like the way he spoke to you, or of me,' he said, his tone becoming serious. 'And your aunt too. They do not relish your choice of husband.'

'Husband?'

Ramiz laughed, a loud, deep and very masculine laugh of sheer joy. 'My love, light of my eyes, you cannot be imagining I mean anything else. You are the wings of my heart. I must tether you to me somehow.'

'But, Ramiz, what about tradition? I'm not a princess, and in the eyes of your people I'm not pure. Yasmina said…'

'Celia, what *I* know and what *I* think is all that matters. You *are* a princess—you are my princess. I will be a far better ruler with you by my side than alone. It is you who has taught me that, you who has made me realise that in order to be the man I ought to be I must have you with me.' Ramiz took her hand and bent down on his knee before her. 'Marry me, my lovely Celia, marry me. Because I love you, and because you love me, bestow upon me the honour of calling yourself my wife, and I will do you the honour of being your husband for ever, for even death will not part us. Marry me, and make me the happiest man on this earth and beyond.'

'Ramiz, that is the most beautiful thing I have ever heard.'

'Yes, darling Celia, but it was a question.'

'Yes.' Celia smiled and laughed and cried all at once. 'Yes.' She threw herself into his arms, toppling them both back onto the cushions. 'Yes, yes, yes,' she said, punctuating each affirmative with a kiss.

A loud thump outside the door startled them both. 'I think we'd better face your father before my guards are forced to use their scimitars on him,' Ramiz said.

It was not to be expected that either Celia's parent or her aunt would accept her marriage without protest. Ramiz listened with remarkable patience while first Lord Henry and then Lady Sophia asserted that such an alliance would end in disaster, would make Celia miserable, and would be the downfall of her sisters, who would be quite lost without her.

Celia countered by pointing out that her marriage to the ruler of a kingdom rich in natural resources with a port of immense strategic importance could hardly be deemed a misalliance. 'In fact,' she asserted, 'you should be honoured to have Prince Ramiz as a son-in-law, Papa, for association with him can only enhance your own career prospects—provided you can persuade him to forgive your rudeness.'

Lord Henry was much struck by his daughter's good sense. From that moment forward his affability towards Ramiz was marked. Indeed, in a lesser man such extreme cordiality might well have been branded obsequiousness.

Lady Sophia, whose objections were, to be fair, based upon her real affection for her niece, took rather more persuading. At Celia's behest Ramiz left the matter most reluctantly in her hands, concentrating his own efforts on discussions with Lord Henry on settlements, dowries and the all-important treaty.

'You talk as if I will be living here in isolation from the world,' Celia said to Lady Sophia as they walked in the palace gardens later that momentous day, 'but I hope you don't mean to deprive me of the company of either yourself or my sisters. I will be expecting all of you to stay here with us for extended visits—starting with Cassie, if she wishes,' she said, smiling at her sister. 'Though she may not wish to postpone her Season.'

Cassie clapped her hands together in excitement. 'What is a Season compared to this? Say I may stay, Aunt. I can come out next year, and anyway,' she said mischievously, knowing perfectly well what her aunt thought of Lord Henry's intended, 'I don't want to steal Bella Frobisher's thunder by having my come-out ball in the same season as her wedding.'

As the day progressed, and Lady Sophia graciously permitted Ramiz to take her on a tour of the royal palace and its famed stables, her stance visibly mellowed. The following morning, a visit to Yasmina cemented the seal of approval. Yasmina's mother was visiting—a formidable woman of Lady Sophia's stamp. The two ladies spent a most amenable few hours together, with Yasmina translating, at the end of which Lady Sophia was able to declare herself happy with her niece's proposed marriage, and even prepared to remain in A'Qadiz in order to attend the nuptials.

'Ramiz came to call this morning,' Yasmina said to Celia over a glass of tea. 'Such an honour—our neighbours will be talking about it for ever.'

'He and Akil are reconciled, then?'

Yasmina nodded happily. 'He knows Akil only acted for the best. He loves Ramiz like a brother.' She pressed Celia's hand. 'I have never seen Ramiz so happy. You will forgive me if I spoke out of turn when we first met?'

'Yasmina, I trust you will always say what you think. Your friendship means a lot to me, I would hate it if you started treating me differently when I am Ramiz's wife.'

'Not just a wife, you will be a princess.'

'I will still be Celia, and it is as Celia that I ask you to be frank with me, Yasmina. What will the people really think about our marriage? Ramiz says that what makes him happy will make his people happy, but I know it's not that simple.'

Yasmina took a sip of tea. 'I will not lie to you. There will be some who will find it difficult to accept simply because it is a break with tradition. But Ramiz has come to symbolise change for A'Qadiz, and a Western bride will not be such a huge surprise as it would have been two years ago when Asad ruled.'

'You said that because I was married before—'

'"A prince's seed must be the only seed planted in your garden,"' Yasmina quoted. 'I remember. But it has been, hasn't it? The man you were married to was a husband in name only. You need not be embarrassed. I told you, I have the gift.'

Celia shook her head, blushing. 'No. Ramiz was the first—has been the only…'

'Then, with your permission, that is what I will say. People will listen to me as Akil's only wife,' Yasmina said proudly, 'and it is natural to talk of such things. You need not worry. I will drop the word in a few ears, and you will see. Now, we must go and talk to your aunt and my mother, and Akil's mother too. We have a wedding to plan.'

It took four long weeks to orchestrate. Four long weeks during which it seemed to Celia that she hardly saw Ramiz, what with the need for him to personally invite all the ruling families of all his neighbours, and the need for her to receive endless visits from the wives of Ramiz's most esteemed subjects, to say nothing of the terrifying amount of clothes which Yasmina declared necessary for a princess, and the equally terrifying regime of buffing and plucking and pampering and beautifying to which Celia was subjected.

At Ramiz's insistence, Celia and Cassie rode out every day, with only a discreet escort, signifying to the people of A'Qadiz the start of a new regime of freedom, and signifying to his beloved Celia and her sister the trust he had in their ability to treat such freedom with discretion.

Aunt Sophia left with Lord Henry for Cairo, promising to return in time for the week-long celebrations. Having heard her confess that her one remaining reservation was that the wedding would not be a 'real' one, Ramiz suggested that he would be happy for an English priest to participate if she wished. Suitably reassured, she informed him that she would not insult him by demanding any such thing.

Abstention from intimacy of any sort was part of the tradition surrounding the celebrations. This Ramiz and Celia managed with extreme difficulty, but were assisted by Ramiz's frequent absences, Cassie and Yasmina's perpetual attendance upon Celia, and the fact that the palace harem was suddenly overrun with female visitors.

By the time the week of her nuptials finally arrived Celia was beginning to think it never would, so slowly had the days passed despite the frenzied activity.

The formal betrothal, which took place in a packed throne room, was the first ceremony. Celia, dressed in richly embroidered silks and heavily veiled, was presented to Ramiz by her father. The ring, a fantastic emerald set in a star-shaped cluster of diamonds, was placed on her right hand.

Next came a round of pre-wedding visits and feasts, with the women and men strictly segregated. Lord Henry accompanied Ramiz on the most important of these, returning after each one more exuberant as the extent of his future son-in-law's wealth and influence was revealed.

The night before the wedding was spent by Celia in the harem, where her hands and feet were painted with intricate designs of henna like the ones she had seen on Sheikh Farid's wives. Ramiz's formal wedding gift was delivered—a casket of jewels which it took two men to carry, including an emerald necklace, bracelets and anklets to complement her ring, each beautifully cut stone set in a star of diamonds.

Finally it was the wedding day. Dressed in gold, veiled and jewelled, and almost sick with anticipation, Celia stood before her sister and her aunt.

Cassie, in a traditional Arabic dress of cornflower-blue silk the colour of her eyes, hugged Celia tight. 'I'm so happy for you.'

'And I too.' Lady Sophia, splendid in purple, her grey curls covered by a matching turban in which feathers waved majestically, gave her a peck on the cheek. 'Good luck, child.'

Ramiz was waiting for Celia at the doorway of the harem, which she crossed for the last time, for they would share rooms in a newly decorated part of the palace—another tradition he had broken, having insisted that they would not spend another night apart. He was dressed in white trimmed with gold, the pristine simplicity of the tunic and cloak showing to perfection his lean muscled body, the headdress with its gold *igal* highlighting the clean lines of his face, the glow in his copper eyes which focused entirely on his bride.

They progressed under a scarlet canopy through the city, a band of musicians preceding them, family and close friends taking up the rear. Crowds sang and prayed, strewing their path with orange flowers and rose petals. Children clapped their hands and screamed with delight, jostling with each other for the silver coins which were thrown for them to gather. And through it all Celia was conscious only of the man by her side, of the nearness of him, of the scent of him, of the perfection of him.

Ramiz. Her Ramiz. Soon to be her husband.

The wedding ceremony itself took place in an open tent in the desert on the edge of the city, strategically placed on a hillside to accommodate the massive crowd. The bride and groom sat side by side on two low stools on a velvet-covered dais, while first Lord Henry spoke, in the hesitant Arabic in which Akil had coached him, before formally handing over his daughter. The *zaffa*, Sheikh Farid himself, declared the couple man and wife. Ramiz removed Celia's ring from her right hand and placed it on her left. Then he helped her to her feet and removed her veil. She was dimly aware of applause. Dimly aware of Cassie crying and of Aunt Sophia sniffing loudly. What she was most aware of was Ramiz. Her husband.

'I love you,' he whispered, for her ears alone, his voice sending a shiver of awareness through her. 'My wife.'

'I love you,' she said, looking up at him with that love writ large across her face. 'My husband.'

The applause became a roar as Ramiz kissed her. The music started, and she and Ramiz performed their first dance together—she nervously, he with aplomb. They sat together as the feast got underway, receiving congratulations, but as dusk fell and the first of the stars appeared Celia thought only of the night to come. They left, covered in rose petals, on horseback—a perfect black stallion for Ramiz, a grey mare for Celia, the wedding gift of Sheikh Farid. Their journey through the desert was magical and brief, silent with promise as the horses picked their way through the sand until the dark shadow of palm trees marked their arrival at an oasis.

A single tent. A fire already burning outside it. An ellipse of water lapping gently at the shelving sand. The stars like silver saucers. The new moon suspended in the velvet sky.

'Hilal,' Celia whispered to her husband, as they stood hand in hand looking up at it. 'New beginnings.'

Ramiz smiled tenderly. 'New beginnings. Come with me. I have a surprise for you—a gift.'

'Darling husband, you have done nothing but shower me with gifts since our marriage.'

'And I will continue to shower you with gifts for the rest of your life, since you are the greatest gift of all. Come with me.'

Ramiz led her over to the tent. As they grew nearer Celia could make out a strange contraption. It had a round base from which a wooden pole rose to support an irregular shape. It looked a bit like a very odd sundial. As they got closer Celia realised that the bulky shape was made of cloth. It was some sort of covering. She looked at Ramiz in puzzlement. He put a finger to his lips before carefully removing the cloth. There, on a perch, sat a hooded bird of prey, white and silver with black wing-tips. 'A falcon!'

'*Your* falcon, my beloved.'

'Oh, Ramiz, he's beautiful.'

Ramiz removed the hood from the bird and, taking Celia's hand, pulled a leather gauntlet over it. 'Keep very still.' She hardly dared breathe as he placed the bird carefully on her arm. 'The wings of my heart,' he said to her, 'my gift to you.' He jerked her arm and the bird flew high, its magnificent wingspan outlined against the crescent moon. 'Now, hold out your arm again, and whistle like this,' Ramiz told her, and Celia watched breathlessly as the bird glided back, landing delicately on her gauntlet. 'Like the falcon I fly, and like the falcon I will always return to you,' Ramiz said, putting the hood back on the bird.

He led her into the tent. 'I hope these are happy tears,' he whispered, gently kissing Celia's eyelids.

'I didn't know I could be so happy,' Celia replied, twining her arms around his neck. 'I didn't think it was possible. Love me, Ramiz. Make love to me.'

'I intend to, my darling. Tonight. Tomorrow. And tomorrow. And tomorrow, and...'

But he had to stop talking to kiss her. And to kiss her. And to kiss her. Until their kisses burned and the abstinence of the last few weeks fuelled the flame of their passion, and their love made that passion burn brighter than ever—brighter even than the stars in the desert sky which glittered above their tent. They made love frantically, tenderly, joyously, with an abandon new to them both, whispering and murmuring their love, shouting it out to the silent desert in a climax which shook them to the core, and which Celia knew, with unshakeable certainty, truly was the new beginning heralded by the crescent moon.

A new life together beckoning her.

And a new life growing inside her.

* * * * *

Historical Note

While I've tried very hard for historical accuracy, I've taken a few liberties with timings and some events referred to in the story which I hope you'll forgive me for.

In 1818, Mehmet Ali had already wrested control of Egypt from the Ottoman Sultan, and the major powers, primarily the British and the French, were maintaining a local presence in the hope of rich pickings when the Ottoman Empire collapsed. The British Consul General was Henry Salt, a renowned Egyptologist who did, like my fictional Consul General, regard the relics of ancient Egypt as there for the taking, but there the similarity between my bumbling diplomat and the real one ends.

Obviously, A'Qadiz is an invented kingdom. In my imagination it sits in what is now Saudi Arabia with a coastline a couple of days' sail away from Sharm-el-

Sheikh, which would be an ideal port for the "fast" route to India via the Red Sea. This route did play a significant role in reducing the overall journey from two years to three months, but it was about fifteen years after the story is set that this came into use, and not until 1880s that the Suez Canal made it commercially viable.

In real life, it could take up to three months to get from England to Arabia, depending upon the weather, the type of ship and the number of stopovers, though at a push it could perhaps have been done in about three weeks. Since I needed Celia's family to come to her rescue, this proved to be a bit of an issue. I speeded up the process by giving them access to the Royal Navy, but there is no doubt that I've stretched credibility a bit by expecting a letter to get from Cairo to London, and Celia's family to get to Arabia when they receive it all in the space of about six to seven weeks.

Richard Burton's (bowdlerized) translation of *One Thousand and One Nights* is the most well-known, but it was not published until 1885. The French edition was published in 1717 however, and this is the one Celia has read.